ORDER OF THE CHIMERA

Estrea
Basilia
Viridis
Hesperus
Acrya
Tebru
Mare
Vates
Anderida
Imber
Salix
Malphas University
Ferox
Verona
Travesura
Aesernia

Vagary
Hirane
Loughney
Northry
Lisrary
Brigid
Wexlone
Soliel
Oscen
Longmeath
Alneyn
Ilatin
Flirie
Hirie
Acron
Frey

ORDER OF THE CHIMERA

ORDER OF THE CHIMERA
BOOK 1

LAYLA KING

Cover art and maps by Layla King

ISBN: 979-8-9985712-0-6 (Hardback)

ISBN: 979-8-9985712-1-3 (Paperback)

ISBN: 979-8-9985712-2-0 (Ebook)

For Sleep Token

For the emotions, the darkness, and the beauty in between.
Your music has been a constant inspiration in bringing this story
to life.

CONTENTS

1

GHOSTS

DHANIRDAY, TWENTY-THIRD OF THE
REAPING MOON, YEAR 449 OF THE GODDESS

Seere jolted awake, thrashing wildly as shallow gasps tore from her lips, ripping the silk sheets from her body as if they were ropes that bound her. Her heart hammered against her chest, the last fragments of the nightmare still clinging to her mind like cobwebs. Her hands fumbled across the bed for a weapon. Every flickering shadow twisted into the shape of hooded figures lurking just beyond the edge of her bleary vision.

But as her hand finally found the cool hilt of her dagger, she stilled. Reality sank in. She was not bound. There were no cold, stone walls, no ropes or iron shackles biting into her wrists. Slowly, the familiar details of her surroundings anchored her. The soft silk sheets tangled around her legs, the delicate scent of rosewater drifting through the air, the high ceiling draped in darkness that she knew was painted with an array of flowers. She was in her bedroom—safe, at least for that moment—in her heavily guarded citadel.

With a sigh, she pushed herself upright and ran her free hand through her hair, untangling the wild lavender waves.

Her skin felt clammy, and her pulse still thudded painfully in her ears. Then she threw her legs over the edge of the bed and crossed over to one of the arched windows, the floor cold beneath her bare feet. The waning moon glowed faintly in the night sky. Judging by its position, it was likely around four in the morning. It was too late to go back to sleep, yet it was too early to start her day.

Her gaze dropped from the sky to the sprawling city surrounding the citadel. The city of Acron. It was the very capital of the kingdom she had built from the ground up at the age of seventeen. As she observed the stillness of her city, a smile lifted the corners of her lips. Even after being sentenced to death for a crime she didn't commit and going on the run, she had still managed to create something beautiful. She didn't care that the outside world looked upon it with disdain.

With a heavy sigh, she turned from the window, surrendering to the fact that she was awake and there was no chance of returning to sleep. Especially not when those nightmares threatened to return—threatened to torment her. Nightmares... Memories... they all bled together.

As she slipped into the adjoining bathroom, the enchanted sconces on the walls slowly flared to life. They framed her reflection in the wide mirror above her wash basin, casting delicate light across her features. She glanced at herself as she pulled her chemise over her head. Lavender hair tumbled over her shoulders in tangled strands, and her pale green eyes—so bright they bordered on unnatural—stared back at her, sharp and unyielding.

Her gaze dropped to the tattoo that snaked along her body. Green vines with soft lavender blossoms wound from her left hand, spiraling up her arm, trailing around her torso, and wrapping down her left leg to her ankle. The whole tattoo looked delicate, almost fragile.

She turned on the faucet over her bath and waited for it to fill with hot water. When she finally stepped into the bath, the water was soothing against her skin. For a brief moment, she let herself relax, leaning back against the porcelain as steam curled into the air. However, her mind refused to be still. The nightmare always left her thoughts spinning. There were too many ghosts circling her thoughts like vultures.

Hooded figures, shrouded in darkness, their identities hidden behind gleaming metal. She could still hear the low murmur of their voices, whispering words she could no longer recall as they freed her from the cell her sister locked her in. She had spent years chasing answers, desperate to know who they were—and what they wanted. But the truth remained maddeningly out of her reach.

She exhaled sharply, scrubbing her skin with vanilla-scented soap as if she could wash the memories away along with the grime. But no amount of soap would erase the past. The memories were too deeply engraved into her soul alongside every regret.

Eventually, she drained the water and stepped from the bath. She absently toweled herself dry before wrapping herself in a robe and slipping from the bathroom. She crossed to her wardrobe and flung it open, her gaze wandering over the ample amount of clothing. She settled on black leather clothing that clung to her like a second skin, offering her both protection and flexibility. She stepped into her leggings, pulled on her blouse, and fastened her corset on with the ease of someone who had done it a thousand times before. Each sheath was set in its place, every secret throwing knife stashed carefully, turning her into something more—something sharper, something dangerous.

She found one of her many masks and set it over the lower half of her face, concealing only her mouth and nose. The hooded cloak came last, the heavy fabric settling over her shoulders like a shadow that refused to lift. It wasn't just armor—it was the identity she had built from the ashes of her old life.

She crossed back to where she had left her dagger on the nightstand. She picked it up, examining the silver blade, down to the sapphire encrusted in the crossguard, to the hilt that she had wrapped in black leather to conceal the phrase etched beneath it. Without another thought, she slid the dagger into the sheath at her thigh and headed for the door.

Six guards stood at attention outside her bedroom, their armor glinting in the dim light of the hallway. They straightened as she stepped into the corridor, falling into formation behind her without a word.

The citadel halls were quiet, the only sound being the soft click of her heeled boots against the stone floors and the clanking of armor behind her. A few servants crossed her path, their eyes widening when they saw her. They bowed deeply, their heads low in deference.

Seere lifted a gloved hand in dismissal, waving them off without a word. She had no desire to inspire fear, though she knew it followed her like a shadow. The world, and especially the people within her citadel, called her the Queen of Assassins, a title whispered with both reverence and dread. While Seere was grateful for the title and the power it granted her, it wasn't all in the name.

She made her way into the training grounds, her gaze briefly shifting to the horizon, where the first traces of dawn stretched across the sky. The air was cool, almost biting, and she felt its sharpness seeping through her cloak. In this pre-dawn stillness, the world seemed to hold its breath—a quiet she found both comforting and unnerving.

She shrugged off her cloak and selected a practice sword from the rack. The weight was unfamiliar—heavier than her usual dagger—but it would serve her purpose for now. She twirled the weapon in her hand, testing its balance, then turned to face the straw dummy standing before her—a crude, silent opponent, but a worthy one when paired with her imagination.

Without hesitation, she launched into her drills, her body moving with a fluidity born of countless hours of prac-tice. She swung the blade in tight, precise arcs, each strike controlled yet powerful, slicing through the air with a low hum. Her muscles burned, heat spreading through her limbs, but she pushed herself harder, her mind latching on to the burn as proof of her vitality.

Each thrust and strike brought faces to mind: the silver-masked figures who haunted her dreams, her sister Selina, even the memory of herself as a child, fragile and terrified. She fought against the phantoms, her movements sharp and strategic, determined to purge them from her mind one blow at a time.

She moved into a spinning kick, her boot slamming into the straw dummy with a force that sent bits of hay scattering across the stone courtyard. She didn't stop. With a quick pivot, she brought her sword down in a sweeping arc, striking the dummy's side and reversing the blow, imagining the resistance of flesh and bone which she'd only driven a blade into a limited number of times. Her body sang with the effort, her pulse matching the rhythm of each strike, each twist, and dodge.

Her footwork was deliberate—each step calculated to maintain her balance, to keep her centered. In battle, any loss of footing was deadly—a vulnerability she had learned to eliminate through rigorous practice. She worked herself into a rhythm, the pattern of strikes and parries becoming almost meditative, the ache in her muscles blending with the memories she was trying to exorcise.

The dummy was just a stand-in—a blank canvas for her anger, her fear, and her frustration. The dream she'd had, the memories that haunted her—it all fueled her now, driving each blow harder and faster. Her heart raced, but it wasn't from fear; it was from the thrill of control, from knowing that she could channel her pain into something tangible, something real.

With a final, brutal strike, she drove her sword deep into the straw figure, watching as the blade sank in and held firm. She paused, breathing hard, her chest heaving as the last of the tension drained from her body. For a few moments, she simply stood there, her hand resting on the hilt of the practice sword, her gaze fixed on the dummy as if it could somehow absorb all the turmoil within her.

In the quiet moment that followed, she could hear the faint chirping of birds in the distance, the first sign of life stirring as dawn began to break. She straightened, pulled the sword free, and wiped a bead of sweat from her brow with the back of her gloved hand. Her muscles were tight, her body worn, but there was a deep sense of satisfaction that came from knowing she had left her fears, if only for a moment, there in the training ground.

The peace, however, was short-lived. She felt a presence

—a shift in the air—and turned to find Belial watching her from the doorway to the citadel, his expression unreadable but his topaz gaze intense.

"Couldn't sleep again?" he asked, his voice gentle but carrying the weight of knowing.

Seere gathered up her cloak, her breathing steady despite the workout. "What's on the agenda?" she asked, brushing past his question.

Belial pushed off the wall as she walked past him, drawing her cloak and hood back over her. "Correspondences and reports first," he said, his tone professional. "Ingram has new intelligence on Empress Selina's movements. We'll go over it during the council meeting."

He gave her a sidelong glance. "There were also a few nobles requesting audiences. They're eager for your attention."

Seere let out a quiet, frustrated sigh. "It's going to be a long day," she muttered.

Belial offered her a small, knowing smile. "When isn't it?" he asked, brushing an onyx hand through his curly black hair.

She scoffed softly but said nothing more. The two of them walked in silence, the rising sun casting long shadows across the citadel walls—shadows that, no matter how far she ran, always seemed to follow.

2

FOUND

DHANIRDAY, TWENTY-THIRD OF THE
REAPING MOON, YEAR 449 OF THE GODDESS

The throne room was bright, yet shadows clung to the stone walls like a blanket of frost. The burning sconces on the walls and the chandelier hanging above the council's heads were ineffective at chasing them all away.

Seere was seated in her throne, concealed beneath her dark hood and mask. Her piercing green eyes studied the figures gathered before her—assassins, spies, and rogues from her inner circle, each posed as nobles throughout the Domain. Each was a powerful ally, skilled in their own right. Yet, trust was a luxury she could not afford, even among these select few. She'd learned long ago that loyalty could be fleeting, and alliances were only as strong as mutual benefits allowed.

Discussions flowed around the room as her council brought up a range of pressing issues: rising crime, smuggling in the northern villages, disturbances in the capital, recent trades with the Noctivagus Kingdom, and occasionally, even the Envie Empire. They spoke of riots in the northern villages, where discontent simmered, and she listened in silence, her gaze intense as she weighed each word. She could sense the growing unrest, the uncertainty threatening to erupt if left unchecked. Coldly, she made a decision.

"Increase the guard presence in the north," she said, her voice smooth but commanding. "Send spies as well—quiet ones. I want to know who is causing trouble for everyone. Now, to shift the conversation to other matters, I read in a correspondence that the Empire is being difficult. Will someone elaborate on this?"

Argus, a man of about fifty, stepped forward. He had dark, graying hair and pale blue eyes. His face was etched with frown lines far deeper than his smile lines. "Your Majesty, our *friends* from the Empire are refusing to deliver the goods they promised in exchange for ours. They claim that our trade offer wasn't worth their resources," he said bitterly. "They are demanding that we send them Eulla Blossoms."

A rare white flower known as Eulla Blossoms grew only on the Domain. It was named for the Goddess of Light due to its great healing properties. It was immensely valuable and could only be found either on the island or very rarely on the mainland. No one but the Domain had managed to successfully grow it in nurseries.

Seere sighed heavily, leaning back into her throne. "Of course they want our flowers, but the Empire will never offer enough in exchange," she muttered. "Perhaps I need to hold a meeting with them in person. Letters don't travel nearly fast enough across the ocean."

"That seems dangerous, Your Majesty," Ingram said as he briskly walked over to the base of Seere's dais. His hair, which was a shade of silver even at the age of thirty, was slicked back neatly. His pale brown eyes were stormy, and frustration was evident in the furrow of his brows. "The Demon Empress is too cold and cruel. She would attempt to kill you, and war would ignite between our nations. I have good reason to believe she is planning to send her spies here directly."

"That's why we'd invite her here. She's been trying to pay a 'visit' for years now. I believe we are established enough to hold our own—"

Seere paused as the sound of shouting and clanking armor from outside the throne room reached her ears. She frowned, her sharp gaze flicking to the double doors, her senses instantly alert.

"What's going on?" one of the council members whispered, their voice edged with unease.

Before anyone could answer, a resounding boom shattered the air. The throne room's great doors quaked under the force of something immense before they burst inward with a deafening crash, the wood splintering like dry twigs. A wave of magic rippled through the room, blowing out the torches. The sudden onslaught sent the council scattering against the walls, where they tried to hide in the shadows.

"Guards!" Ingram barked, his voice sharp and calm even as he darted to stand before Seere like a shield.

Seere stood slowly, her movements deliberate, calm in the face of chaos. Her dagger was in her hand before she even registered drawing it, the sapphire in its pommel catching the light. The guards stationed on either side of the dais surged forward, forming a protective ring around her as the dust began to settle.

From the broken remnants of the doorway, a figure

emerged, stepping confidently into the room as if he owned it. He was young—no older than twenty-five—but carried himself with a commanding presence that belied his age. His raven-black hair was neatly combed, not a strand out of place, and his dark evergreen eyes gleamed with cold amusement. His pale, porcelain skin seemed almost ethereal in the flickering light of the room as torches reignited of their own accord. He moved with an unsettling grace, his footsteps echoing sharply in the hushed chamber.

Seere's pale green eyes narrowed as she studied him, noting every detail—the precision of his movements, the faint smirk tugging at the corner of his lips, the calculated way his gaze swept the room. But what struck her most was the look in his eyes when they finally locked onto hers. A wicked gleam flickered there, a flash of malice so sharp it made her grip tighten on her blade. Beneath the surface, she saw something else—hatred, seething and barely concealed. It was not the blind, impersonal kind she was used to, but something pointed, intimate.

Her breath caught, just for a moment. There was something familiar about him. The way he looked at her, as though he could see straight through her carefully constructed facade, unsettled her more than she cared to admit.

"Stop where you are," one of the guards barked, their swords gleaming in the low light as they stepped forward. "Identify yourself."

The man paid them no mind, his gaze solely fixed on Seere. He tilted his head slightly as though appraising her. His lips curved into a slow, mocking smile that made her stomach churn. He looked at her not as an equal, but as if she were a specimen laid bare for his scrutiny.

"Enough," Seere said sharply, waving her hand at the guards so that they would part around her. Her voice carried through the room, authoritative and cold. The guards hesitated but obeyed, their weapons still at the ready. She stepped down from the dais.

The man stopped a few paces from her, clasping his hands behind his back in a gesture of feigned civility. She realized then just how tall he was—even with her heeled boots bringing her to nearly five-foot-seven, he still towered over her. He looked utterly unbothered by the tension in the room or the dozen blades pointed at him. If she'd had his power to blast things apart, Seere probably would have been just as carefree.

"Well?" she demanded, her voice slicing through the silence. "Who are you, and why have you barged into my throne room unannounced?"

The man's smile widened slightly, his voice calm and almost pleasant. "I come on behalf of King Hubert and Queen Frieda of Noctivagus."

His words hung in the air, the name of the powerful kingdom causing murmurs to ripple through the council. Seere's eyes narrowed, her suspicions growing. "That hardly answered my question. And I was under the impression that we had a good relationship."

The man's smirk only brightened as he inclined his head in a small, mocking bow. "Please forgive me, Your Majesty," he said, his tone laced with amusement. "I am Orias Roderick, Headmaster of Malphas University for Nobles."

The name hit Seere like a blade to the chest. Malphas. A name that still haunted her—the man she'd once killed. The headmaster of the assassin's academy she had been shipped off to at eleven and graduated from at fourteen. Back then, all of her peers had been adults, and all of them had either wanted to kill her or become her ally. She'd heard the school had been repurposed as a symbol of something far removed from its bloody origins, but she had yet to investigate further into those rumors.

"You're a long way from Malphas, Headmaster. State your purpose."

Orias' gaze sharpened, his smirk growing almost imperceptibly. "I am here to deliver an urgent request from His Majesty himself. There have been numerous attempts to assassinate Crown Prince Felix, and troubling rumors are circulating about a larger plot against him. King Hubert requests that you send your very best to protect the prince, for who better to defend him from assassins than the Domain of Assassins?"

The room was silent as his words settled over them like a storm cloud. Seere's jaw clenched. "And you've come to my citadel, uninvited and unannounced, to deliver this... request?"

"Indeed," Orias replied smoothly, as if her anger didn't faze him. "And just to be completely clear, the 'very best' refers to none other than yourself, Your Majesty."

The way he said it, with that infuriating smirk, sent a ripple of irritation through her. Seere studied him for a long moment, her mind racing. He knew too much—his words, his confidence, his very presence all pointed to someone who held more cards than he was showing.

"You are requesting that I, the queen of the Domain of Assassins, abandon my people for months at a time to protect another kingdom's prince?"

"I wouldn't have expected you to turn down such an opportunity," Orias replied thoughtfully. Then, leaning in slightly, he delivered his next words with deliberate weight. "In return, you gain freedom from the Empire. Recognition as a legitimate kingdom for your assassins. Even a marriage alliance with the prince himself. Name your price, Your majesty."

"And what if I don't go along with your request?" she questioned, though she had a feeling she knew what his answer would be. She wasn't surprised when it did come.

"The Demon Empress of Envie will release her full wrath upon your little domain for *harboring* the assassin of her parents," he said.

Her blood turned to ice, though her mask betrayed nothing. The arrogance. The confidence. The insufferable smirk. He had caught her. She didn't know how, but he knew her true identity.

Everyone turned their gaze on Seere in complete disbelief. Belial looked horrified, and Ingram looked immensely curious. Seere was glad she couldn't be seen under her hood and mask. She wanted to stab the man before her, but she didn't doubt his cleverness. He likely had plans set for the instance in which he didn't get out alive. He likely had someone waiting to deliver evidence of her identity to Empress Selina. Her sister.

"Then I will see to the safety of Prince Felix as requested of me. You ask that I send my best, so I shall. I leave my Viceroy and my council in charge until my return. I trust that they will make wise choices in my stead," she announced, her gaze turning to Belial, who still stared at her with a look of complete horror. "I will retrieve my belongings and we will depart immediately."

"Good," Orias said.

"Wait, what?" Belial exclaimed as Seere turned on her

heel and left the dais. "Your Majesty! You can't just leave! There is still a council meeting to conclude!"

With her decision made, Seere left the chamber to make arrangements. She felt Orias' gaze following her as they walked away. Belial quickly followed, his expression a storm of worry as he walked beside her, hands clenched tightly.

She paused and turned to a maid just outside the throne room who had been eavesdropping on the meeting. "Call my best carriage to the front," she ordered before she hurried to her room.

To his credit, Belial waited until they'd stormed into her bedroom to begin his speech. A speech Seere had little capacity for. "There are riots to be discussed in Ilatin, the crime rate is at an all-time high in Vanta, and we find ourselves with a lack of provisions made evident by Ingram!" Belial exclaimed, waving his hands in the air. "And what is this about harboring the assassin of the former emperor and empress? I thought we all agreed that if she appeared, we would turn her in. Last I checked, that agreement still stood. What about your throne! Without you here, it's in danger."

Seere glared at Belial, though she knew he couldn't see it. "In this instance, it is in danger regardless," she argued. "You, as my viceroy, have been entrusted with taking care of events when I am unable. If there is something truly troubling you, send a message in code and I will respond accordingly. I want monthly letters."

"I don't work under pressure half as well as you do, my Queen," Belial said softly, turning away sheepishly.

Seere rolled her eyes and turned away. "You will have Ingram at your side. I trust him most out of anyone else in that throne room."

She dragged a large trunk into the center of her room,

then crossed to her wardrobe. She shoved half of her clothes into the trunk, hardly taking care to fold them properly—she would do that on the ship.

She froze when her fingers brushed over a cloak that had been gifted to her by a little girl. It was made from a thick velvet and trimmed with fur. She carefully packed it and moved on. She had made a point not to have many sentimental items or items that were particularly fancy like the cloak. Not like back when she was a princess of the Envie Empire, constantly decorated in extravagant gowns. After being sent off to the assassins academy, dresses seemed frivolous.

Seere shook the thoughts from her mind before she turned her attention from her folded clothes to her stash of weapons that she carefully sneaked into the trunk. She even stashed away her crown. Its stones were of onyx, the band and ornate swooping arches were silver.

"Are you certain that you must go, my Queen?" Belial questioned.

"Yes, I am," she said.

"You won't take him up on his offer to marry the prince, will you?" he questioned, then quickly added, "Your Majesty."

She sighed indignantly. "Prince Felix would never agree to wed me," she said, though her words came out as something of a whisper. She regretted the way the firmness of her voice faltered and died. She cleared her throat as her hand fell to the dagger strapped at her thigh. "Though if it's being offered, it would be of great value to the Domain."

"I suppose this is true..." Belial murmured. "But they would keep a tight leash on you."

Seere closed her trunk and looked around her large

room. She'd managed to fit all of her most important pieces in the one. The remainder of her belongings were unnecessary.

"They would try," she agreed, turning her attention to Belial finally. "Again, I trust that you can take care of things while I am away. If I am killed, the throne is yours by right, Viceroy Belial. Command with authority, pride, and wisdom."

"Seere," he breathed, shaking his head and taking a step towards her. "You're not going to die. You have a kingdom to return to."

"If my death protects this kingdom, then so be it," she said coolly before nodding to the guards behind him.

Two marched in, one of them taking either end of her trunk before they followed her from the room. She had no interest in waiting there any longer. She hated the puppy eyes Belial gave her and suspected he would do something brash if she allowed him the opportunity.

"We will take a carriage to Flirie," Seere said the moment she entered the room that had emptied of everyone but Orias, Ingram, and a handful of her guards. "The ship that brought you—is it still docked to return me as well?"

Orias smirked at the sight of her packed up. "Indeed, it does, Your Majesty," he said.

"Good."

Together, flanked by guards, they walked out to the carriage that already awaited them. It was one of her finest— pristine ivory walls, ebony trim, crimson velvet cushions, and gold leaf scrolling along the frame. While she lacked power in her situation, she wanted to make it appear to everyone else that the opposite was true.

"For being called the Domain of Assassins, you have a

surprisingly lovely kingdom, *Amaris*," Orias said, his gaze trained on the window.

Wordlessly, Seere removed the mask from her face and pushed her hood back. For the first time in seven years, she allowed someone else to see her face. Orias' gaze turned to her, his eyes widening. She had shed her mask—and in doing so, surrendered the illusion of control. It was a silent admission of defeat.

"Lavender?" was all he said in response, his eyes wandering over her features curiously. He was taking every detail of her in.

"You know my identity. So tell me what yours is," she said, leaning towards him.

He frowned and stiffened. "I am Orias Roderick—"

"The Rodericks were slaughtered over a decade ago—every last one—for crossing the late emperor. And they never had a son." She leaned in, voice sharp. "So, who are you?"

"Believe it or not, *Queen Seere*, I am who I say I am. Not all of us conceal our identity behind a cowl because we were framed for a ghastly crime," he said darkly.

Seere opened her mouth to argue before she froze and stared at him. Suddenly, her view of a cruel and cunning man shifted. "You know that I was framed?" she asked, her words small and shocked.

"I do, and I have the man who killed your parents in custody. If you complete this job, he is yours to do with as you please," he said, a smirk tugging at the corners of his lips.

Suddenly, the deal he offered was so much sweeter. If she kept Prince Felix alive, she could clear her name, she could take off her mask, she could avenge her parents, set Empress

Selina right, and fix everything. Her heart fluttered wildly at the prospect, a foolish fantasy finally within her grasp.

"What is his name?" she questioned.

"Verrine Sallos."

A name she remembered well. Verrine had graduated a year before her at Malphas. He'd been seventeen and had held the record for the youngest graduate until she took it when she graduated at fourteen. She remembered watching him from afar as he trained, deadly calm and precise. He'd killed many of their fellow students during his attendance, and many others had attempted to persuade him to kill her, something she remembered vividly. Yet he had never so much as looked her way.

"I see," she breathed. "Then I want him."

"Very well, Your Majesty. Complete this job and he is yours," he said.

3

STORMS

ESLADAY, TWENTY-FIFTH OF THE REAPING
MOON, YEAR 449 OF THE GODDESS

Seere was quickly reminded why she loathed sailing. The days at sea always felt extra long and far from interesting. The ceaseless rocking of the vessel and the vast, empty horizon were a constant reminder of how far she already was from her domain. Despite the monotony, she remained an object of fascination and unease for the crew. Cloaked and masked, she moved like a shadow among them, her presence a whisper of danger. Their wary glances and muttered speculations followed her everywhere, but she paid them no mind.

When Orias invited her to dinner, Seere debated declining but ultimately relented, curiosity outweighing her reluctance. Which was how she found herself making her way through the narrow corridors of the ship; she could feel the stares of the crew even through the bulkheads, their fear clinging to her like a second skin.

When she reached Orias' cabin, she hesitated for the briefest of moments before knocking. Her knock echoed softly against the worn wood. The door swung open at once as if he had been waiting for her.

Orias stood in the doorway, his posture casual, but his evergreen eyes keen as he glanced over her fitted black dress and the makeup that decorated her eyes. "Right on time," he said, stepping aside to let her enter. "But you can't eat with a mask on."

"I can't reveal my face to the entire crew of this ship," she said coolly.

The cabin was surprisingly spacious for a ship, its modest furnishings arranged with care. A single lantern cast warm light over a small table set for two, the polished wood gleaming faintly. Two plates sat neatly on the polished wood, piled with roasted meats, root vegetables, and warm bread—far too luxurious for a sea voyage. She guessed that someone had purchased them back in the Domain. There was also a decanter of wine set between the plates, two glasses already poured.

Seere removed her mask and pushed back her hood, shaking out her lavender hair as the door closed behind her. The tension in her shoulders did not ease, even in this more intimate setting. She hardly trusted Orias, especially not after the hate she'd seen in his eyes when he stood before her in the throne room.

"Is this supposed to impress me?" she asked, her tone edged with sarcasm as she took her seat.

Orias smirked, closing the door behind her. "I wasn't aiming to impress you, but if it works, I won't complain."

She rolled her eyes and speared a grape with a fork from her plate. "And if you're trying to poison me, you should know that it's a waste of effort," she said.

"I know poison won't work on you, darling," he teased, though his gaze was meaningful.

Seere raised a brow, curious about how he knew poison couldn't harm her. No matter how strong the dosage was, it always failed. She had never told anyone before. However, she said nothing and popped the grape into her mouth.

Her eyes scanned the room once more, lingering on the subtle details—books stacked neatly on a shelf, maps pinned to the wall, the faint scent of parchment and ink mixing with the aroma of their meal. It was an organized space, carefully curated, much like the man who occupied it.

Orias took his seat, leaning back slightly as he studied her. "You look lovely this evening. Did you doll up just for me?" he remarked, a playful note in his voice.

Seere's lips twitched in irritation. "I assure you, I didn't," she retorted, adjusting her cloak that still clung to her shoulders. "This is typical of what I wear to dinners with my nobles. Only they don't see my face. Now, let's get to the point, Roderick. Tell me everything I need to know about this mission I've been recruited for."

His expression shifted then, the teasing edge giving way to something more serious. He sipped his glass of wine, his gaze steady on her. "Have you heard of the Order of the Chimera?"

"I have. Rumor has it they are a cult with delusions of grandeur. They think they can 'liberate the continent of sinners.' Each member bears a tattoo of a goat, a lion, or a serpent behind their right ear," she answered.

Orias hummed thoughtfully. "You're well-informed," he noted.

"Information is currency, Roderick," Seere replied curtly.

Orias nodded, conceding the point. "And what do you know about Rosyn?"

"That she was the goddess of life and death. Labris, the God of Balance and Wisdom, cleaved her soul into two halves. This subsequently created Eulla and Eslia, the Goddess of Life and the Goddess of Death, respectively."

"Correct. Just as I thought." He leaned in. "Then this next part may not surprise you: the Order's true goal is uniting Aevrath under a single ruler. They believe doing so will make Rosyn whole once again. They believe that, because it split at the same time she did. To them, that means they can reconnect the souls of Eslia and Eulla once again."

Seere leaned back, startled despite herself. "They do this for Rosyn? But the devout of Eulla preach that reuniting Eslia and Eulla would spell the end of the realm as we know it."

"That is precisely why we cannot let it happen," Orias agreed. "And yet the Order is convinced otherwise. They're the ones threatening your betrothed's life—"

"He is not my betrothed," Seere hissed.

Orias smirked faintly. "The Order happens to be the one threatening Prince Felix's life. His death would leave Noctivagus vulnerable, and their plan to conquer the continent would be one step closer to succeeding. So you can either keep him alive or have his heir."

Seere glared at him. "I'm surprised he isn't already married with a child on the way," she said coolly.

"He's been holding out for Princess Amaris, convinced she will one day return to him," he said. There was a hint of amusement and disgust in his words, even so, that didn't stop them from making her heart flutter as her fingers instinctively shifted to her dagger.

"Where did you get all of this information from? I have spies all over the continent trying to glean everything we can about the Order. Yet we find little."

"Verrine Sallos is very talkative when you apply the right methods," Orias said smoothly. "You might also find it interesting to learn that your father was once a member of the Order."

Seere froze, her expression hardening. "Of course he was," she said bitterly. Memories of her father, the late Emperor of Envie, surfaced unbidden. His ambitions had been as ruthless as they were grand. "My Father meant for me to marry Felix, kill him once I wore the crown, and let the Empire sink its claws deep into Noctivagus. It was never going to succeed, but it's the very reason I was sent to the assassin's academy."

Orias studied her silently, as if weighing her words. "Why wouldn't it have succeeded?" he questioned.

"Because I once had every intention to kill my father myself, only I never would have been caught," she answered. "But it seems Sir Sallos had other plans for me. Where is this assassin? I would like to properly—"

The ship lurched suddenly, throwing them both off balance as a deafening crack of thunder rolled through the cabin. Rain lashed against the porthole, and the room tilted violently as the ocean churned outside.

"Ah, it seems there is a storm about us," Orias remarked, steadying himself as the ship swayed violently.

"Damn it," Seere muttered, pushing herself to her feet. She slipped her mask back over the lower half of her face, sparing a glance at her plate that she'd barely touched. Then she pulled her hood over her head. "This is hardly just a storm."

Orias arched an eyebrow, leaning casually back in his seat even as the ship threatened to tip. "Oh, what makes you say that? Because it came out of nowhere or do you feel the divine energy of Aldros in the air?"

"Both."

She could feel the crackle of power that arced through the air around them. She could feel the cold hatred of the God of Storms and Discord. She was not safe on this ship.

"It seems there's a god that does not like you," he said thoughtfully.

"No, most of them don't," she agreed sharply.

Her sharp gaze snapped to the door as another wave slammed into the hull. She hurried towards it. The wood creaked and shuddered under the strain, the sound like a living creature groaning in protest.

"Running off already?" Orias asked, his tone light despite the circumstances. "We were just getting to the good part of the evening."

Before she could respond, the ship rocked harder than before, throwing her off balance. Her hand shot to steady herself against the wall, but she had been unprepared. Orias moved in an instant, his arms sliding around her in a firm grip that kept her on her feet.

The contact was electric, not with warmth or butterflies, but raw tension. Seere's reaction was immediate. Her dagger flashed from its sheath, the blade pressing against the hollow of his throat before either of them had time to think.

"Don't touch me," she hissed, her voice sharp and edged with venom.

Orias froze, his evergreen eyes flickering down to the blade at his neck. Slowly, deliberately, he raised his hands in a gesture of surrender. "Noted," he said evenly, though his smirk was unmistakable. "Next time, darling, I will just let you fall."

Seere withdrew her dagger but didn't sheath it, keeping it in her grip before she stepped back. "There won't be a next time."

Orias shrugged, the motion was casual as if they weren't teetering in a storm's chaos. "If you say so."

Seere turned away, pulling her cloak tighter around herself. The door to Orias' cabin banged open with the force of the wind, slamming against the wall. The storm's feral roar filled the room, drowning out even the ship's groaning protests.

Seere swore as she raced through the doorway and to the stairs that would lead her above deck. She heard Orias shout after her, realizing what she intended to do.

"You're going out there in that?" he asked as he caught up, pulling his cloak over his shoulders. She glanced back and watched as he gestured to the dress she wore. Elegant as it was, the garment was far from practical, especially as the wind whipped her cloak open and sent the hem fluttering like a tattered banner.

"I don't have time to change," she snapped, her feet skidding slightly as the ship tilted again. She adjusted her footing and pushed forward.

"Well, this should be entertaining," Orias muttered, slipping into the hallway behind her.

They emerged onto the deck, and it was as if the world itself had turned against them. Rain lashed down in icy sheets, carried by winds so fierce they stole the breath from her lungs. Waves towered over the ship, their peaks glowing silver in the lightning flashes before crashing against the hull with enough force to shake the planks beneath her feet.

The crew was a whirlwind of motion, sailors shouting orders and securing ropes as best as they could. Some wrestled with sails that had been torn free, others tried to clear the deck of loose barrels and crates that skidded dangerously with each tilt of the ship.

Seere moved toward the nearest group of struggling sailors, her dagger still in hand. The crew paused for a split second when they saw her, their eyes widening in a mixture of awe and terror at the sight of the Assassin Queen walking into the storm.

"Move!" she barked, cutting through their hesitation.

The sailors obeyed without question, even as they exchanged uneasy glances. Seere grabbed a flailing rope and began pulling it into place with surprising strength.

Orias joined her side, tugging another rope free from a tangled mess with ease. He glanced at her, rain streaming down his face as a grin tugged at the corners of his mouth. He secured the rope and gestured for her to follow him toward the mast, where a group of sailors were struggling to tie down a shredded sail.

Together, they worked side by side, their movements surprisingly synchronized as they braved the storm. Seere's dress was a hindrance to her, its soaked fabric dragging at her legs, but she ignored the discomfort and focused on the task at hand.

When a massive wave crashed over the deck, sending a wall of water surging toward them, Orias grabbed her arm and pulled her toward the mast. The wave hit like a hammer, nearly knocking them both off their feet, but they managed to hold on, the saltwater drenching them from head to toe.

Seere coughed, shoved her wet hair out of her face, and

glared at Orias. "If I die because of this storm, I'm haunting you."

"I'd expect nothing less," he replied, his grin widening.

They moved with urgency, tying down equipment and gripping wet ropes as the ship pitched and groaned beneath them. Despite the chaos, Seere noticed how at ease Orias was, his movements fluid and sure as if he had faced storms like this countless times before.

When another bolt of lightning split the sky, illuminating the deck in stark white light, Orias turned to her, his smirk undimmed. "You were right. The gods really do seem to hate you," he said, his voice barely audible over the howling wind.

Seere let out a derisive snort, her dagger flashing as she cut away a tangled rope. "Did you really expect anything less?"

Orias laughed—carefree, bold—like the eye of the storm itself.

4

MALPHAS

DHANIRDAY, SEVENTH OF THE DRAGON MOON, YEAR 449 OF THE GODDESS

The carriage rocked gently as it ascended the winding mountain road. Seere sat with her arms crossed, her dark cloak wrapped tightly around her. Across from her, Orias lounged casually, one arm draped over the back of his seat, his evergreen eyes glinting with amusement. The silence between them was heavy but not oppressive.

Seere found herself watching the world below them shrink as they climbed higher and higher. She saw a village not so far away, and beyond that was the sprawling city of Soleil, Envie's capital. A place she hadn't set foot in for years.

They hadn't stopped anywhere near the capital, luckily enough. Rather, they stopped in the village of Cegwin and boarded a carriage. She hadn't ascended the mountain in several years. Back then, it had been a cruel hike meant to weed out the weak. So many had died trying to scale its loose rocks and avoid the beasts that once made the path their home. She was relieved to find it had been turned into a road, no matter how unforgivingly rough it was. She preferred a carriage ride over a harrowing hike.

"You seem to be staring an awful lot at the Empire," Orias finally said, his voice cutting through the stillness.

"And?" Her gaze didn't waver from the horizon.

Orias tilted his head, the faintest smile tugging at his lips. "It seems to me that you still long to be part of it. The prodigal princess gazing wistfully at her homeland."

Seere's jaw tightened, and she turned her glare on him, her pale green eyes frosty like a forest in winter's harsh embrace. "It doesn't concern you."

He chuckled, unfazed by her sharp tone. "Ah, but it does. You were meant to live among them, weren't you? A pampered princess, dancing at court, flirting with simpering nobles. Perhaps even—" He leaned forward slightly, his smile growing wicked—"marrying the dashing Prince of Noctivagus."

Her hand drifted toward the dagger at her side, a warning motion. "I suggest you drop the subject, Orias."

His laughter was a soft rumble, full of confidence. "I'm merely remarking on how fate has a sense of humor. Instead of the pretty, obedient princess they wanted, you became the Assassin Queen of a new nation entirely. The very thing they fear most."

"Say one more word, and I'll slit your throat."

Orias didn't flinch. Instead, he reclined back into his seat, a smirk playing on his lips. "Darling, I'd like to see you try. You might even succeed." He gestured lazily. "But then you'd have to explain to King Hubert why his headmaster never returned, and I don't imagine that he'd be thrilled."

The threat passed between them like a blade, sharp and

unspoken. Seere finally tore her gaze away from him and stared out the window once more, willing herself to ignore his presence.

"You know," Orias said, his voice casual but probing. "I find it curious how your eyes are so drastically different from your sisters'. Their brown eyes are cold and cruel, while yours..." His voice trailed off, and he grinned as she turned her glare back on him. "Yours strike fear into the hearts of most men."

"They inherited their mother's eyes," Seere replied flatly. "I inherited mine from my mother."

Mock surprise lit his face. "Ah, so you don't share the same mother?"

"No," she said curtly. "I'm a bastard."

Orias raised an eyebrow, intrigued. "The infamous Assassin Queen, the court of Envie's dirty little secret. How scandalous."

"I wasn't just a secret," Seere said bitterly. "I was their shame."

He studied her for a moment, his usual teasing smile tempered by curiosity. "And your mother? Who was she?"

Seere's expression hardened. "That's none of your concern."

Orias held up his hands in mock surrender. "Fine, fine. I'll be a gentleman and wait for you to tell me."

Seere didn't bother to respond, and for a while, silence filled the carriage.

Finally, she broke it. "Why was Malphas turned into a university for nobles? It seems like a waste of perfectly good shadows."

Orias' grin returned, though it was softer this time. "Ah,

yes. The Assassin Academy of legend. It was discovered about six years ago after falling into disrepair due to the death of the headmaster, emptied of its killers, and repurposed to suit the kingdom's needs. A little ironic, don't you think? The very place that trained the world's deadliest assassins now shapes its noblest warriors."

"It is ironic," Seere agreed mildly.

"Well," Orias said, his tone brightening, "you'll get to see it for yourself soon enough."

The carriage slowed, and the sound of hooves grew louder as they approached the fortress, echoing off the stone. Seere pulled her hood lower and secured her mask.

Orias watched her carefully, his gaze lingering on her hidden face. "You know, for someone who claims not to care, you're awfully concerned about what others might see."

Her eyes cut to him like daggers. "I don't need to explain myself to you."

He chuckled again, shaking his head. "Of course not, Your Majesty. But do try not to kill anyone important on your first day, won't you?"

Seere said nothing, but the icy silence that followed made her thoughts abundantly clear.

As the carriage rounded a final bend, the fortress came into view. Perched atop the mountain like a sentinel, Malphas University loomed grand and imposing. Its ancient stone walls, polished and fortified, were adorned with blue and white banners bearing the emblem of a humanoid raven wielding a spear, its wings outstretched. The same emblem that the school carried when it was used to train assassins.

The fortress itself seemed to pierce the clouds, its spires reaching skyward as though defying the heavens.

The courtyard was bustling with activity. Professors,

students, and guards moved with purpose, their eyes turning toward the arriving carriage. A welcoming party had already assembled at the base of the fortress steps, their faces a mixture of curiosity and apprehension.

Seere pulled her hood lower as the carriage came to a halt. Orias exited first, his commanding presence drawing the attention of the gathered crowd. He turned and extended a hand to Seere, his eyes glinting with amusement. "Shall we, Your Majesty?"

Ignoring the offered hand, she descended gracefully on her own, her dark cloak billowing around her. The murmurs began immediately, the gathered individuals whispering in awe and fear. The Assassin Queen was a title that carried weight even here, and she could see it in their wide eyes and stiffened postures.

At the forefront of the group stood Prince Felix, his cobalt blue eyes narrowing as they fell on her. His auburn hair glinted in the sunlight, his posture regal yet tense. He was far taller than she remembered. Under his right eye was a small birthmark—a mark she had once thought charming.

Beside Felix were his closest companions, Foras Andromal and Rowan Naberius. Foras was rather short, though still a few inches taller than Seere herself. He had sandy blond hair, amber eyes, and a fair complexion. Rowan was in every way his opposite, with his inky black hair, deep bronzed skin, and hazel eyes.

Seere's heart had lurched at the sight of Felix, though she hid her reaction behind her mask. He wouldn't recognize her, she reminded herself. That was the entire point.

"Welcome to Malphas University," one of the professors said, stepping forward with an exaggerated bow. "We are honored by your presence, Your Majesty."

Seere recognized him immediately. Professor Vidal hadn't changed much since she'd last seen him, even though it had been six or seven years. However, he now had gray hair peppering his ginger head and his face, once smooth, had aged and become lined with wrinkles. He had pale blue eyes and rough ivory skin. He was dressed in the typical woolspun garb of a fighter, and a broadsword hung at his side.

Seere inclined her head slightly, the gesture was regal yet distant. She wasn't ready to offer them her voice. It felt like giving up something that would make her just a little more vulnerable. She would withhold as many pieces of her as possible for as long as she could.

"See to it that Her Majesty's belongings are brought to her quarters immediately," Orias said to a group of servants who scurried over to unload the carriage, then he led Seere by the hand up the steps like a gentleman. It startled her. "Prince Felix, Professor Vidal, if you would come along with us to discuss arrangements that would be most appreciated."

"Yes, Sir," Felix said, and the sound of his voice sent a jolt down Seere's spine. It was smooth, low, and something she had missed terribly.

Orias nodded and offered his elbow to Seere. Begrudgingly, she allowed her gloved hand to slide into his arm. She would play his game for the time being, but once she discovered the rules, it would be her game he played.

The inside of the fortress was both familiar and foreign. The dark, somber tones of her past had been replaced by bright banners and polished marble. Gone were the crests of assassins long dead, replaced instead by plaques commemorating knights and scholars.

Students crowded the cozy entrance hall as they fought

to get a good look at Seere. She assessed as many as she could as they walked by, finding most leaning over and whispering to their neighbors. In their black uniforms with baby blue trim, none of them looked particularly threatening. Only one stood out as dangerous to her.

She caught the cold gaze of her younger sister, Princess Cotoria of the Envie Empire. She stood off to the side with a small group of other students. Her chestnut eyes, which had once belonged to Seere's stepmother and should have been warm and inviting, were instead filled with ice and hatred. Cotoria had the same platinum blond hair as their father and their older sister, a trait Seere also carried but hid under lavender magic.

Seere's sharp gaze left Cotoria and flitted over every corner, cataloging exits, vantage points, and potential hiding places. The weight of her past pressed against her like a physical force. This had once been her home—a place where she'd honed her craft, forged alliances, and betrayed them in turn before they could betray her.

"Your Majesty, are you alright? You are squeezing my arm quite firmly," Orias said in a hushed voice that was laced with amusement.

"I'm fine," she answered simply and loosened her grip on his arm.

"You know that we will protect you from your sisters while you are in our service, right?" he asked, and his words were surprisingly gentle.

"I don't need your protection."

Orias only chuckled before he led her and everyone else following into a vacant hall. They made their way into the stairwell that she quickly recognized as the old tower that had once belonged to the former headmaster. She supposed it made sense that Orias would have claimed the same tower.

Eventually, they stopped at an arched door that was tightly shut and painted a dusty shade of blue. Engraved into the wood was the emblem of the school. She watched as Orias produced a key from the pocket of his jacket before inserting it into the door. When it clicked, he pushed it open and gestured for Seere to enter first.

She walked inside and gazed around the room. It was far larger than she remembered and was decorated much differently from what the previous headmaster kept. Rather than displays of weapons and grotesque trophies from his old kills, there were trinkets and tools that an astronomer might use to study the sky. Everything was a shade of royal blue and gleaming gold. The furniture was dark oak, and it smelled of parchment and ink, a signature scent of Orias, it seemed.

Orias slipped past Seere to stand behind his desk, which was littered with papers and books. "As you know, Your Highness, your father and I have decided that your best source of protection from an organization like the one we face comes from the Assassin Queen. She knows the shadows like no one else," he said, beginning the conversation that no one else wanted to start.

"Yes, I am quite aware," Felix said, glancing at Seere warily. His cobalt gaze was almost debilitating to be trapped beneath. "But why should I entrust my life to someone who could very well be *the* assassin out to kill me?"

"If I were to kill you, you would already be dead," Seere said flatly, her voice cutting through the room like a blade. She didn't bother to look at him, instead inspecting the layout of the room with sharp, calculating eyes.

Foras stepped forward, his amber gaze burning into her. "And what guarantees do we have of your loyalty? You don't exactly seem the type to do charity work."

"I'm here because it benefits me," Seere replied bluntly, finally turning to meet his gaze. "Your life means nothing to me, but I was... persuaded to assist. Rest assured, I'll keep you breathing. Not out of loyalty, but because failure isn't in my repertoire."

Rowan chuckled softly, cutting through the tension in the room with unexpected ease. "She's got quite the way with words, doesn't she?" His hazel eyes sparkled with amusement as he leaned back in his chair. "But I think you're missing the point, my lady. Why *you*? Surely there are others in your little domain who could handle this."

"Because she is the best," Orias interjected smoothly, cutting off any further argument. "And because she's uniquely qualified for this assignment. Seere's reputation precedes her, and I trust her to handle this with precision."

Felix's jaw tightened. "I don't trust her."

"Good," Seere said simply, crossing her arms. "Trust gets you killed."

The room fell silent for a moment, the weight of her words hanging heavy.

Orias straightened, glancing between them. "Regardless of trust, this arrangement is non-negotiable. Seere will share your schedule, Your Highness, and her quarters will be directly across from yours. She'll be present at nearly all times to ensure your safety."

"Is there anything else I must be made aware of?" Seere asked impatiently.

"Ah, yes. You will attend classes as a student beginning tomorrow morning. Other than those in this room, the staff, and a few guards, no one knows the reason behind your being here. They all believe you to be a student who is attending late," Orias explained. "Felix has already been tasked with showing you the ropes through your first week here."

"Very well."

"Oh, and one other thing," the headmaster said, giving Seere a once-over. "We will have a seamstress brought in to tailor uniforms for you. We can't have you wearing that cloak every day."

"I will not wear a uniform, but I will forgo the cloak. If that is all, I wish to be shown to my quarters," she said.

"I will take you, Your Majesty," Prince Felix said, though his words were filled with apprehension. He turned and led the way out of the study with Foras and Rowan in tow.

Seere sighed quietly before she turned and followed Felix. She spared a glance over her shoulder as she left the study, noting the way Orias turned to Professor Vidal with a cold gaze. She regretted being unable to eavesdrop.

As they passed through the halls, students still stopped to stare. Many broke into whispers and pointed fingers, none of which were as subtle as they seemed to think. She overheard various comments about her being a reaper, the goddess of death incarnate, or that she was a lot shorter than anyone expected. She found their ignorance quite amusing.

They left the fortress through a side door. Seere was surprised to find that the barracks, the place they were headed, had been significantly added onto since she'd last attended. It had to have been triple its previous size. A small smile tugged at the corners of her lips at the thought of the renovators finding the secret stash of weapons she hadn't been able to recover before she left.

Felix guided her inside, and she found that the entrance hall was a cozy lounge of green decor and chestnut furnishings. Oil lamps bathed the room in a comforting yellow light. It was far more pleasant than the yellow of the magic fluorescents that illuminated most homes and streets these days.

The students who milled about the lounge had their noses practically glued to books, or they were too wrapped up in their conversations to notice Seere. A few others, however, did look up to see who entered, curious about the cloaked one.

She turned her gaze away from them, her attention returning to the path they took. Down a hall to the right, up a flight of creaky stairs, before they stopped in front of a door. It was unassuming aside from the brass nameplate. Seere Cross was engraved into it elegantly. The door opposite, in the same font, had Felix Martell etched into its nameplate.

"This is your room," Felix said, holding out a key for her to take. The key was beautiful, its handle ornately etched with vines and blossoms.

She accepted the key and unlocked her door. Stepping inside, she found herself in a well-furnished front room. Seere was surprised to find that her dorm was far nicer than she had expected. To her left, there was a small kitchen with marble counters, white cabinets, and wine already stashed in racks. The center of the room had a white circular dining table. The far right of the room was a lounge with plush sofas in the shade of baby blue. At the back of the room were two doors that she was sure would lead to a bedroom and a bathroom.

"Is it to your liking, Your Majesty?" Felix questioned. He

stood in the doorway, watching her as she explored the space she would be stuck in for the foreseeable future.

"The wine is a nice touch," she answered as she opened the door of her bedroom to investigate.

Her trunk sat at the foot of a large canopied bed, its white drapes matching the school's signature shade of baby blue bedding. There was a white wardrobe, a desk, a vanity, and even a chest where more blankets were likely stored.

"You have an excellent imperial accent," Foras commented.

"Not a single person on that island is native to the Domain," she said in answer, turning her gaze to the man. "You expect their queen to be?"

"It would make sense," he said, his gaze narrowing on her.

"Foras, you're being impolite," Rowan chided under his breath.

Seere rolled her eyes and took to searching every nook and cranny for hidden secrets. The prince and his two friends watched her curiously as she worked. She checked the windows to make certain they were locked and shut the curtains on each of them. She triple checked behind paintings, cabinets, rugs, and even furniture. She wasn't about to risk being caught unaware of any hidden entrances to her room.

"Paranoid much?" Foras questioned when he realized what she was doing.

"You would be 'paranoid' if you ruled over assassins, rogues, and thieves," she said, shooting a glare over her shoulder at him.

"Is that why you wear that hood?" Rowan asked.

"No."

"Are you ever going to take it off?" That question came from Foras again.

"When I am alone."

"Why not now?"

She sighed heavily and turned her glare on them. "Because I have opted not to," she said coolly. "Now, I ask that you leave."

"You are not a very agreeable person," Foras commented.

"I could say the same about you. Now, I know you are not deaf to my words. Leave. It is impolite to remain past your welcome."

"As you wish, Your Majesty," Foras said coolly before he left with his friends in tow.

Felix spared a glance at Seere, but he didn't wait long.

She locked her door behind them. Immediately after, she stripped herself free of her cloak. She slipped back into her bedroom and wasted no time in unpacking her belongings into the white wardrobe. She picked out a chemise and a bottle of wine so that she could find some semblance of comfort in the chaos her life had become.

Once she wrestled the cork free, she slipped into the bathroom for a long soak in hot water.

She had no intention of wandering the fortress. She already knew every stone, every corridor, every secret tucked inside it. And she wasn't ready to risk running into Cotoria. As much as she longed to speak to her little sister, distance was the safer option.

Seere sank into the steaming bath, the wine bottle in one hand and her dagger in the other. She set the bottle down on the cold tiled floor and slowly unraveled the black leather wrapped around the hilt, letting the strip fall to the ground outside the tub. Her fingers traced the words carved into the ebony wood, each letter a fresh wound.

"For my betrothed. May we carve out our futures together."

She swore under her breath and let the dagger clatter to the floor.

Seere was screwed. Utterly and completely screwed.

5

OLD FRIENDS

EULDAY, EIGHTH DAY OF THE DRAGON
MOON, YEAR 449 OF THE GODDESS

Seere pushed herself to her feet when she realized soft gray light filtered through the curtains of her room. The chill of the mountain air seeped through the walls of the dorm, cold and sharp, but she didn't mind it —it grounded her.

Her gaze drifted to the mirror perched on her dresser. Crossing the room, she began her morning routine. Her lavender hair spilled down her back in soft waves, catching the light like frost. She brushed through it with slow, deliberate strokes.

When she finally met her own eyes in the reflection— those eyes she'd trained to betray nothing—she let herself feel it. Just for a moment. The weight of the day before settled over her shoulders like a second cloak.

She didn't belong in a place like this—a university for knights, filled with starry-eyed warriors and noble dreams. Yet here she was, tangled in a mission that felt more like punishment than purpose.

Finally, she slipped her mask on. Then she dressed in

her typical attire: leggings, a blouse, a corset, and boots. Instead of hiding beneath her hood, she took time to make her hair presentable.

There was a knock on her door, and a sigh escaped her. She knew that it could only be Felix, no matter how much she wanted to pretend it wasn't. With a begrudging sigh, she crossed to the door and opened it.

Felix's eyes widened in surprise when he saw her, his gaze catching on her hair. "I didn't know your hair was... purple," he said, his words tinged with shock.

A faint smirk tugged at Seere's lips, amused by his reaction. "Not what you were expecting?" she teased, tilting her head slightly. "Is there something wrong with it?"

He raised a brow. "I don't know what I expected, but it certainly suits you."

"I suppose you expected me to have fiery red hair to match my fierce personality?" she asked, her tone playful. "Or maybe jet black, like the villain I'm so often painted to be?"

Felix chuckled softly, his shoulders relaxing just a bit. "Something like that."

"I prefer to do the unexpected," she said and stepped through her doorway. "Where are we headed first?"

"I am about to join Rowan and Foras for breakfast. You are more than welcome to join us if you wish," he said as he turned and headed through the hall.

"I go where you go, Your Highness."

There was a heavy silence between them as they walked through the busy halls of the barracks. Students raced around in a flurry. It reminded her of the old assassin's academy, though it couldn't have been more different. Back then, it wasn't uncommon for someone to bleed out on the front steps simply because they got in the way. Seere had always been careful to climb through her window and sneak through side entrances to get by unscathed.

"So," Felix began, glancing at her as they stepped outside, "this mission of yours. Protecting me. Why'd you agree to it?"

Seere let out a bitter sigh, her breath visible in the cool air. "I didn't exactly jump at the chance."

"Then why?"

She hesitated, her fingers brushing the edge of her cloak. Finally, she muttered, "Orias blackmailed me."

Felix stopped in his tracks, turning to face her fully. "Blackmailed you? How?"

Her pale eyes, the only part of her face visible, narrowed slightly. "I don't see how that's any of your concern," she said sharply, resuming her pace.

Felix caught up to her, his expression thoughtful. "I'd say it is, considering you're here to keep me alive."

"I agreed to the mission," Seere said, her tone signaling the end of the conversation. "That's all that matters."

They walked in silence for a moment before Felix spoke again, his voice quieter this time. "I just want to understand why someone like you would even care about a place like this—or a person like me."

Seere didn't answer immediately, her gaze fixed on the path ahead. Finally, she said, "Maybe I don't."

But the lie sat heavy in her throat, like ash she couldn't quite swallow. She quickened her pace, leaving Felix to follow behind her, the weight of unspoken truths hanging between them.

The towering doors of the great hall loomed ahead, their intricate carvings of ravens and mountain peaks glinting faintly in the morning light. As Seere and Felix approached, the low hum of conversation seeped through the cracks.

Felix pushed the heavy doors open, and the pair stepped inside. The hall was alive with activity. Long tables stretched across the room, packed with students and staff, their voices blending into a symphony of chatter, clinking utensils, and laughter. The banners of Malphas University—blue and white with the raven emblem—draped from the high, vaulted ceilings, swaying gently in the draft.

As they walked in, all eyes seemed to find Seere.

The hum of conversation faltered as whispers spread like wildfire. Students craned their necks to catch a glimpse of the infamous Queen of Assassins, their gazes flicking between her mask and Felix's calm demeanor beside her.

Seere's sharp eyes scanned the room, her head held high. Despite the whispers and stares, she moved with the quiet confidence of someone who had nothing to fear.

Felix led the way to a small table near the head of the hall, where his friends had already gathered. Rowan Naberius, the ever-charming troublemaker, leaned back in his chair with a mischievous grin, while Foras Andromal sat beside him, his severe gaze fixed intently on Seere.

"Well, well," Rowan drawled, standing as they approached. "The mysterious Assassin Queen. You've certainly caused quite a stir, haven't you?"

Seere arched a brow, her eyes glinting. "Did you expect anything less? And I wasn't aware that I needed your approval for such things."

Rowan laughed, unbothered by her sharpness. "Approval? My Queen, you don't need it. It's fun to watch the chaos. By the way, can I just say that you are exceptionally lovely? The lavender hair adds a most unique and myste-rious quality to you."

Foras elbowed Rowan roughly. "Stop gaping," he hissed. "She's still the Assassin Queen underneath that pretty skin."

"You still think I'm pretty," Seere commented, earning a snicker from Rowan.

Felix gestured for her to sit, and she chose the spot oppo-site Rowan, which allowed her a view of the entire hall. Felix took the spot beside her, his movements easy but deliberate, a subtle show of unity that didn't go unnoticed by others.

Rowan leaned forward, his hazel eyes sparkling with curiosity. "So, mysterious assassin queen, tell us—what's with the mask exactly? Some dramatic flair, or is there a tragic story behind it?"

Seere's lips curved into a faint smirk beneath the mask. "Why not both?" she replied, her voice tinged with sarcasm.

Rowan laughed, clearly entertained, but Foras was less amused. "Tragic or not, it makes you stand out. Isn't that dangerous for someone in your line of work?"

"Only if I let it be," she said, meeting his gaze with an unflinching stare.

"Well, if the mask stays, we'll have to speculate. I'm guessing... horrifically scarred from a duel with a vengeful lover?"

Felix sighed softly. "Rowan, that's enough."

But Seere leaned back, unfazed. "Close, but not quite. A fire. Long ago."

The lie rolled off her tongue effortlessly, and Rowan's playful expression faltered for a moment, replaced by a flicker of sympathy.

"Ah," he said, the levity in his tone fading. "I didn't mean to—"

"It's fine," she interrupted, her voice cool. "We all carry scars. Some are just less visible than others."

"Did you know, Your Majesty, that particular shade of purple is a favorite of Princess Amaris?" Foras questioned, eyeing her hair.

Seere lifted her chin slightly. "You mean the dead princess? I was unaware."

"Dead?" Felix asked, sounding almost startled.

"How many years has it been since anyone last heard from the princess? Six? She must either be dead or far overseas at this point," she explained.

Several emotions flashed across his face in quick succession. She saw rage, sorrow, and regret, and then he was stoic again. He shook his head slightly. "She must still be alive," was his only response.

"Why do you say that?" she questioned.

He examined her curiously, his eyes sweeping up over her as if trying to decide what exactly to say to her. "It hardly matters," he murmured.

Before Seere could dig any deeper, the room seemed to grow colder as a new presence entered. Seere's gaze shifted to her sister as she swept into the hall, her icy blond hair catching the light as her honey-brown eyes scanned the room.

The moment Cotoria spotted Seere, her lips curled into a faint sneer, and she swiftly crossed the room to them. "Ah, the infamous Queen of Assassins," she said, her voice dripping with mockery. "I've heard so much about you. Of course, you're far less imposing than I expected, especially without the ridiculous hood."

"Was there something that you needed, Princess?" Foras questioned irritably.

Cotoria glared down her nose at Foras. "I wanted to get a look for myself at the devil incarnate. I must admit, I'm curious." Her gaze zeroed in on Seere's mask. "What is it you're hiding behind that thing?"

Seere finally looked up, her pale eyes meeting Cotoria's with a calm intensity that belied the tension in the room. "What I hide," she said coolly, "is none of your concern."

Cotoria tilted her head, her smile growing sharper. "Isn't it? You arrive here, cloaked in mystery, and expect us to just trust you? Or perhaps you wear it because you're afraid."

Seere's smirk grew, her voice dropping to a deadly calm. "If you're so curious, Princess, why don't you take it off yourself?"

The challenge struck like a blade. Cotoria's smile faltered for a fraction of a second, a flicker of uncertainty crossing her face. However, her confidence returned with a flash of anger. "What a bold tongue for someone who relies on a disguise to face the world."

"Princess Cotoria, if you have issues with Her Majesty's presence at the school, you may take it up with me in my office."

Seere's gaze shifted to the headmaster, to Orias, with an amused smile. Cotoria whirled around, her expression a mix of horror and irritation. However, it was clear within moments which emotion outweighed the other.

"In the dress code, wearing masks is strictly prohibited," Cotoria snapped, shooting a glare at Seere. "She isn't even wearing the proper uniform."

"Her Majesty and I have made prior arrangements regarding her mask and uniform. She outranks everyone here in her current standing and therefore can do as she pleases," Orias explained. "Now, if you have finished causing a scene, return to your seat near Miss Bolbec before I have you removed from the hall."

Cotoria glared at Orias darkly. "She is no queen *here*," she snarled before turning on her heels and storming back to the other end of the room.

"Thank you, Headmaster," Felix said, bowing his head politely.

"No need to thank me. I came over to request Her Majesty's presence over dinner this evening in my study," he said, his gaze turning to Seere. "There are a few things I would like to discuss with you after your first day is complete."

"Of course," she said simply.

Orias gave her a once over then bowed his head and left them to their breakfast. A breakfast Seere hadn't touched. She watched him, frozen in her place, as he sauntered from the great hall. He was a complete mystery to her, and she wanted to unravel him.

Rowan let out a low whistle, breaking the silence at their table. "Well, that was fun. I give Cotoria a solid eight out of ten. Could have used more creative insults, though."

Felix massaged his temples. "She never knows when to stop."

Foras, who had been silent throughout the exchange, finally spoke, his tone thoughtful. "You handled that well. Though I wonder—do you always provoke people like that, or is it just Cotoria?"

Seere shrugged, her tone light but edged with subtle defiance. "I don't provoke, Foras. I defend. If she felt provoked, that's her problem, not mine."

She gazed around the room, taking in the tension that had come as a result of her interaction with Cotoria. Every guard that lined the walls on her side of the room had their hand over their weapon and their gaze on her. She got the sense that Orias had ordered them to watch her carefully. It seemed that he expected her to kill someone during her stay there.

"Are you alright, Seere?" Felix questioned.

"I'm fine. I just don't appreciate the way the guards eye me so closely."

Foras scoffed, his silverware clattering on his plate as he dropped it harshly. "Can you blame them? Everyone sees you as a harbinger of death and war. Your Majesty, I'm not sure how you've missed it, but you don't exactly cause warm fuzzy feelings in the stomachs of the people you're near."

Seere glared at him, absently picking up a knife at the table and twirling it around her fingers. "I have no intention of ever becoming the type of person that is warm and fuzzy."

"Cotoria is a beast wearing a crown," a new female voice said suddenly. "It's unavoidable to make enemies of her unless you share her ideals. Like Malkyn de Bolbec or Alsariph Farcyne."

Seere turned to find the familiar face of Enora Blackwood standing just behind her. Her blonde hair caught the light that filtered through the windows, shimmering like spun gold. Her emerald green eyes sparkled with enthusiasm as she looked Seere over. She had a sporty yet graceful build, having dreamed of becoming one of the knights of Noctivagus even though that role was reserved almost exclusively for men.

Beside Enora was a young woman Seere didn't recognize. She radiated a quiet grace, her petite frame wrapped in a dark cloak that billowed softly in the breeze. Her raven-black hair framed a pale, heart-shaped face, and her eyes—an unusual shade of violet—seemed to pierce through everything they landed on. She carried herself with an air of mystery, her expression unreadable. Seere had the unsettling sense that this woman might be capable of killing her, if asked.

"Felix, you didn't tell me that we'd be graced with such illustrious company today," Enora said, her tone chiding.

Rowan jumped to his feet with a grin. "Oh, Enora! Introductions must be made! Queen Seere, this is Enora Blackwood of Noctivagus and our beloved friend Achlys Alerie of the Asora kingdom! Enora, Achlys, this is Queen Seere of the Domain of Assassins."

Enora's eyes only brightened, and she stepped forward, extending a hand toward Seere. "It's a pleasure to make your acquaintance, Your Majesty. I've heard many stories about you!"

Seere looked at the offered hand for a moment before giving it a brief shake, her grip firm but not overly so. "Stories have a way of exaggerating," she said, her tone measured.

Meanwhile, Achlys observed silently from her place beside Enora. When the introductions turned to her, she inclined her head slightly, her expression remaining neutral. "Achlys Alerie," she said, her voice soft but tinged with a rich, lilting accent. "It is... intriguing to meet someone of your reputation."

"Likewise," Seere replied evenly, nodding back.

The two women held each other's gaze for a moment longer than necessary, a subtle but silent exchange of mutual respect—or perhaps wariness.

Enora grinned after a moment, then turned to Felix and kicked the underside of the bench where he sat. "I know you guys are still eating breakfast and all, but we really ought to be getting to our first class. Professor Vidal doesn't have any tolerance for tardiness."

Felix huffed a laugh before getting to his feet with a sigh. "Fine," he said.

The whole group exited the great hall together and swiftly made their way out of the fortress. The crisp mountain air chilled Seere as she allowed Felix to guide them down the cobblestone paths leading to the back of the fortress. Her boots clicked softly against the stones as she surveyed the area around them.

Felix cast a glance over his shoulder at Seere, catching her gaze. "The training grounds are through the western gate," he explained, though she didn't ask.

"I remember," she replied simply, her voice cool but not unkind.

"You've been here before?" Enora asked, her curiosity piqued.

Seere's eyes flitted to him, a flicker of something unreadable passing through her expression. "I thought that was common knowledge. I attended this school when it was still an assassin's academy."

"Oh, well, it would seem I missed that detail," Enora said thoughtfully. "Well, what do you think of Malphas so far? I mean, it must be strange, coming back after all these years."

"It's... different," Seere replied, her tone polite but distant.

"Well, I think you'll like it," Enora said, undeterred. "The training grounds are amazing. There's a chapel that's been added—probably for those nobles who fake piousness... Oh, and the Library! Have you seen it yet? It's enormous!"

"I haven't had the chance," Seere said, glancing briefly at

Enora before returning her gaze to the path ahead. She loathed the idea that a chapel had been added. She wanted to be as far from the gods, especially Eulla, as possible.

Achlys, walking a few paces behind, spoke up for the first time since their introduction. "You do not strike me as someone who seeks comfort in books," she said, her tone neutral but probing.

Seere glanced at Achlys, her expression unreadable. "I seek knowledge, not comfort," she replied.

Achlys inclined her head slightly, as though approving the answer. "A wise distinction."

Seere got the sense that she was going to get along well with Achlys.

The training grounds tucked behind the fortress were just as she'd remembered. There were rings to spar in, an entire jungle gym to help train assassins in the art of scaling walls and ceiling rafters. It was there that she learned to wield a blade while hanging from a bar in the torrential rain or biting hail.

The grounds hummed with energy as students gathered, their weapons glinting in the sunlight. Professor Vidal stood at the center of the grounds, his arms crossed over his chest, his sharp eyes scanning the group with the precision of a hawk. The imposing figure exuded authority, his dark hair streaked with silver, his weathered face marked by countless battles won.

"Listen up!" he barked, cracking like a whip across the training ground. "Today's lesson is about one of the most crucial aspects of battle: defense. Any fool can wield a weapon, but only a true warrior knows how to protect themselves. Leave even the smallest gap, and you might as well hand your enemy the victory."

He stepped forward, gesturing to a rack of training weapons. "I want you to spar with each other. Focus on closing off your vulnerabilities. If your opponent lands even one strike, you've failed. But," his gaze swept over the group, landing on Seere, "to make things interesting, we'll have a demonstration."

Seere glared at him. "Damn you," she hissed under her breath, drawing Felix's attention as he stood close beside her.

Professor Vidal's eyes lingered on Seere for a moment before he turned to another figure—a young man of about thirty who was dressed in full brigandine armor. He had dark hair that he kept tied back, a short beard, and blue eyes. Something about him was starkly familiar, but she couldn't place it. At his hip hung a broadsword, ready to strike at a moment's notice. Seere wasn't certain that her dagger would fare well against a blade the size of his, but it wouldn't be the first time she'd had to fight off a sword.

"Captain Fraser," Vidal called, "you'll be sparring with our newest addition, Queen Seere of the Domain. Let's see what the Queen of Assassins can do against someone of your caliber."

A murmur rippled through the students. All eyes turned to Seere, who remained composed, her pale gaze steady. She stepped forward without hesitation, drawing her dagger from where it rested at her hip.

"Are you certain?" the captain of the Malphas guard questioned as he drew his blade and brandished it. His gaze shifted to her dagger warily as if worried he might harm her, seeing that all she carried was a tiny blade.

"I am," she said, raising her dagger.

"Take your positions," Professor Vidal called.

"On your guard, my Lady," the captain said with a wicked grin. "Don't hold back."

It struck Seere then with a start as she recognized the man before her. Memories of her sparring against a dark-haired man in these rings flashed through her with a vengeance. He had been the only person to know her identity, taking her under his wing like an older brother.

"I never do," Seere replied, a faint smirk tugging at the corner of her lips. "*Shax*"

At Vidal's command, the duel began.

Aurelian—Shax—moved first, his strikes precise and calculated. He wielded his sword with the skill of a seasoned fighter, each blow aimed to test her defenses. Seere, however, was faster. She dodged and parried with an almost lazy grace, her movements fluid.

The crowd watched in awe as the two exchanged blows. Shax pressed hard, but Seere's defense was impenetrable. She countered with a sharp feint, forcing him to step back, and followed up with a quick strike that nearly disarmed him.

Her footwork was flawless, her every movement a dance of deadly precision. Within less than a minute, she found an opening. With a swift twist of her wrist, she disarmed Shax, sending his sword clattering to the ground. She followed through with a sweeping kick, knocking him off balance, and pinned him to the ground with her boot pressed lightly against his chest.

Half of the students erupted into cheers. Many of the others gaped in shock, their gazes filled with uncertainty.

Shax looked up at her, surprise and amusement in his eyes. "Well done," he said, grinning. "It seems that I am at your mercy, Your Majesty. As always."

Seere stepped back, offering him a hand. He took it, and she pulled him to his feet.

Only then did the crowd erupt into full-blown cheers. It had been as if they feared for their captain's life. Seere smirked and sheathed her dagger. "You were a worthy opponent, old friend," she said warmly.

"It's good to see you again, *little Flower*. I'm sure you can imagine my shock when I heard you would be coming here," he said with a chuckle.

"Why didn't you ever come to me?" she asked, stepping away from him. "I would have put you on my court."

He chuckled. "Dearest sister, I needed to be here to protect you from afar. You wouldn't believe the number of assassins and bounty hunters I've thwarted thanks to the race for your head," he said, offering her a sad smile. "I am also married and I have two children. I couldn't just uproot them."

Seere's eyes widened in disbelief, and then she smiled brightly. "Really? Then you should have written! I would have visited," she exclaimed, though her voice remained quiet to keep others from overhearing, stepping from the ring with him as the lesson continued.

"I didn't think you would have any free time being the Queen of Assassins," he said with a laugh.

"More than you think," she said.

"Well, to make up for it, why don't you come with me this Dhanirday to visit us? We just live in Cegwin," he said.

Seere winced and her gaze turned towards Felix as he paired up with a man she didn't recognize to spar. "I would love to, but I am here on the orders that I protect the prince," she said dryly.

"I did hear about that. He and his friends are welcome to

join, though my wife might have a heart attack over the state of the house," he said with a chuckle. "Toddlers, especially two little girls, are a whirlwind of chaos."

"I will speak with him. I'm certain the prince will be fine," she said warmly. Though truthfully, she wasn't certain how she felt about the idea of bringing the prince and likely his friends into something as personal as her found family. "Foras and Rowan may request to join him... Will that be a problem?"

"No, Asteria makes enough food for an army. She loves to cook," Shax said, and she realized quickly that that had to be the name of his wife.

"Good," she said with a soft smile.

6

AGGRAVATE

EULDAY, EIGHTH DAY OF THE DRAGON
MOON, YEAR 449 OF THE GODDESS

Seere had barely wiped the sweat from her brow after an intense sparring exercise with Shax when she was ushered off with Felix and the others were ushered into a sprawling gymnasium. High ceilings stretched overhead, and the space was divided into zones for strength, endurance, and agility exercises. Students scrambled across climbing walls, dragged weighted sleds, and sprinted through drills under the watchful eyes of several assistants. At the center of it all stood the obstacle course—a maze of walls, ropes, and narrow beams that Seere remembered all too well.

Her eyes lingered on the familiar setup, a relic of her assassin training, though it had been modernized for the knights. Memories of her youth flared in her mind, and she briefly considered how quickly she could still complete it.

Forneus, the professor in charge, stood like an immovable monolith near the obstacle course. His broad shoulders and tree-trunk arms made him seem more like a warrior than a teacher, and his perpetual scowl gave the impression he was ready to crush anyone who failed to meet his standards. His booming voice cut through the hum of activity.

"New blood," he barked, his icy eyes fixed on Seere. "Step forward."

The entire room fell silent as Seere approached. Felix and the rest of the group exchanged uneasy glances but said nothing.

Forneus folded his massive arms across his chest, his lips curling into a sneer. "You've earned quite a reputation, haven't you? Let's see if it's warranted. Run the course."

Seere tilted her head slightly, her glare fixed on the towering man before her. "Are you asking or commanding?" she replied, her voice dripping with mock politeness.

Forneus' expression darkened. "Run it," he growled. "Or are you afraid you'll embarrass yourself in front of your peers?"

Her jaw tightened, but she let the insult roll off her like water. Without another word, she strode to the start of the course, her boots clicking against the gym floor.

"Good luck," Rowan called out, his tone lighthearted. His smirk suggested he was entirely confident she would complete it.

Seere ignored him still, focusing on the first obstacle: a towering wall with only a thin rope for assistance. She leaped, her hands gripping the rope as she scaled the wall with practiced ease. From there, she transitioned seamlessly into a series of horizontal bars, swinging herself forward with precision and grace.

The course was a blur of movement—vaulting over walls, sprinting across narrow beams, ducking beneath low-hanging beams, and netting. Her body moved on instinct, years of assassin training taking over as she navigated each challenge with startling speed. The room was silent except for the sound of her boots hitting the ground and the occasional gasp from the watching students.

When she landed at the finish line, she straightened, brushing off her gloves as if she'd merely gone for a stroll. She turned to face Forneus, whose jaw was clenched tight.

"Record time," one of the assistants muttered, glancing down at a brass stopwatch.

Felix broke the silence with a low whistle. "Impressive."

Forneus, however, wasn't ready to concede. "Beginner's luck," he muttered, though his gruff tone betrayed his frustration.

Seere's lips curved into a subtle smirk. "Care to test that theory?"

Before Forneus could reply, Foras stepped forward, placing himself between the two and surprising Seere. "I think she's proven her skill," he said, a note of amusement in his voice.

For the rest of the class, the students were divided into smaller groups to complete various drills. Seere stayed close to Felix and Foras, the three working together on a series of strength and endurance exercises. As they jogged around the perimeter of the gym, Felix struck up a conversation.

"Forneus isn't exactly known for his charm," Felix remarked, glancing at Seere. "But I don't think I've ever seen him this annoyed. You've made quite the impression."

A smirk tugged at Seere's lips beneath her mask. "If by impression you mean he now plots my untimely demise, then yes."

Foras, who had been quietly observing, chimed in. "You have a knack for making enemies, don't you?"

"Only when they deserve it," Seere said with cool certainty.

The jog continued in relative silence until they passed Rowan, who had abandoned the drills entirely in favor of showing off for a group of girls. He was flexing his arms and flashing his trademark grin, clearly enjoying the attention.

"Does he always do this?" Seere asked, raising an eyebrow.

"Every chance he gets," Foras muttered, shaking his head.

As the class drew to a close, Forneus called the students back to the center of the gym. His glare was colder than ever as he dismissed them, though Seere caught the faintest flicker of respect in his expression as he looked at her.

The group left the gymnasium in a mix of sweat and lingering adrenaline, their boots echoing on the fortress' stone floors. Felix walked at the head, maintaining a brisk pace that forced everyone to keep up. Foras followed close behind, his sharp eyes occasionally darting toward Seere as if trying to unravel her secrets through sheer observation. Rowan brought up the rear, entertaining Enora and Achlys with exaggerated tales of his 'heroic' antics in the gym.

Seere kept to herself, her expression hidden behind her mask. She was alert, her sharp gaze scanning the fortress's corridors out of habit. The halls were alive with the buzz of students moving to their next classes, the noise bouncing off the stone walls.

"Where are we going now?" she asked coolly, breaking the silence.

"Tactics and Strategy," Felix replied over his shoulder. "One of the more mentally taxing classes, if you're not used to it. Of course, it isn't arithmetic."

"I'm sure she'll manage," Foras said with a sly glance at her. "Assuming she's not all brawn and no brains."

Seere ignored the jab, though her fingers itched to unsheathe a blade—just for show. Instead, she quickened her pace and overtook him, falling in step beside Felix as they climbed the winding stairs to the war room at the top of one of the tallest towers.

As Seere walked into the vast room, she took her surroundings in carefully. She made note of the vaulted ceilings, the sturdy wooden rafters, and the windows that were tucked discreetly out of sight. For an assassin, it was a strategic access point. Most people only looked for danger on the ground level.

Tapestries hung on the walls depicting scenes from famous battles. Below them were display cases of formidable weapons, and on either side were shelves and cabinets with glass doors filled to the brim with books, scrolls, and manuals to be used for study material.

Finally, her gaze returned to the table. There were enough chairs to sit around forty people. Seere froze, her breath catching in her throat as her gaze settled on the man already sitting at the head of the table. Farhan Manfredonia.

Her uncle's presence caught her off guard, and a flood of emotions swept through her. He had aged. He was around fifty, his mousy brown hair graying and lines etched into his face. His brown eyes were still bright, and his commanding presence hadn't diminished as he sat tall in his gray scholar's robes.

He had been the only member of the Envie royal family who had ever treated her with kindness. Warmth flared—unwelcome, unbidden—and she buried it beneath the assassin's stillness she'd perfected long ago. She took a seat beside him at the round table with forced calm.

Farhan began the lesson with a sharp clap of his hands once the seats were all filled. "Today, we'll test your ability to think critically under pressure. War is not won with swords alone—it is won with strategy. You will each be given a scenario and expected to devise a plan of action. Success depends on your creativity and your ability to anticipate your opponent's moves."

The students murmured nervously as Farhan divided them into small groups and assigned each a different battle-field scenario. Seere found herself grouped with Felix, Foras, and Cotoria. The latter had been glaring daggers at her since breakfast and now looked as though she'd been asked to scrub chamber pots with bare hands.

Their scenario involved defending a fortress against an overwhelming force of enemies. Farhan set the miniature figures on the map and gestured for them to begin.

Felix immediately took charge, pointing out defensive positions and potential choke points. Foras offered calculated suggestions, his tone clipped and professional. Cotoria, however, spent most of the discussion shooting barbed comments at Seere.

"Perhaps our mystery guest should contribute," Cotoria sneered. "Unless, of course, she prefers to sit silently while the rest of us think."

Seere leaned back in her chair, feigning indifference. "I was waiting for you to finish bickering. Now, if we're done wasting time..."

She reached for one of the figurines and moved it to a position on the map that disrupted Cotoria's formation. "You've focused too much on the front line. They'll flank us through this pass and collapse our defenses unless we station a small unit here."

Felix studied her adjustment and nodded thoughtfully. "She's right."

Cotoria bristled. "You don't even know who she is! For all we know, she's here to sabotage us."

"Then it would be all the more embarrassing if I bested you, wouldn't it?" Seere replied with a sharp edge in her voice.

The tension between the two was palpable, but Felix quickly redirected their focus to the scenario. With Seere's input, they devised a layered defense that impressed even Farhan, who nodded approvingly as he reviewed their strategy.

"You've made clever use of limited resources," Farhan said, addressing the group but looking directly at Seere. "That's the kind of mind I'd want at my side on the battlefield."

She suppressed a smile, though her heart swelled at his praise. She remembered spending many hours of her past life as Princess Amaris studying his tactics and learning his strategic brilliance. He was her uncle, but he had acted as her father figure where her father had failed until she was sent away to the assassin's academy. She never expected to find him in a school for young nobles.

"As Queen of the Assassins, I imagine your strategy meetings are quite different from ours. Let us take your being here as an opportunity for all of us to learn from one another," he said warmly.

"The last thing we should be doing is teaching the *Assassin Queen* our strategies," Princess Cotoria said coolly from the opposite side of the table.

Seere's gaze shifted to her younger sister, though it momentarily caught on the girl beside her. She was slender, with short brown hair, honey-colored eyes, and rosy, tanned skin. She hadn't seen Malkyn in years, but she'd recognize that sinister glint in her eyes anywhere.

"I already know your tactics, Princess," Seere replied smoothly and then immediately regretted it. The last thing she should have been doing was proving to Cotoria that she knew more about Envie's inner workings than she should. "I have spies everywhere."

Rage darkened Cotoria's expression as she turned her attention to Malkyn.

As the class ended, Felix lingered near Seere, clearly impressed. "You really do have a sharp mind," he said. "I can see why the headmaster wanted you here."

"Flattery won't work on me," Seere replied, though there was a hint of warmth in her tone.

Foras joined them, his gaze still as calculating as ever. "You're full of surprises. I wonder how many more you're hiding."

"Keep wondering," Seere said lightly.

As they descended the tower for their lunch break, the tension between the group began to ease, though Seere and Cotoria's animosity remained sharp.

SEERE SAT QUIETLY in the great hall, her focus split between the food that she stirred absently and the whispered conversations around the room. Across the hall, Cotoria sat with Malkyn and another man—a striking figure with golden blonde hair and aristocratic features. Seere guessed this was Alsariph Farcyne, another noble tied to the

Empire. The trio's glances frequently darted in her direction, only to shift away the moment they noticed her watching.

Her hand toyed idly with her fork as she kept an eye on their movements, analyzing every glance and hushed word. It was almost laughable how unsubtle they were.

"Why do you insist on angering her?" Foras' calm voice broke her focus.

"Angering her isn't my intention," Seere replied, finally tearing her gaze away from Cotoria. "I'd rather not be the object of her attention at all. I just don't trust her."

Foras arched a skeptical brow. "Why would she harm Felix? Doing so wouldn't get her anything but a war."

"She might not," Seere allowed, her tone clipped. "But she could lead me to those who do. And for many, war is reason enough. Orias mentioned that there was a particular group that seemed rather keen on war."

"Since when are you on a first-name basis with the headmaster?"

Seere raised her brow at him. "I'm not. Headmaster Roderick is just too much of a mouthful."

Rowan let out a light laugh from his spot beside her. "Fair point. Both are, actually."

Foras, undeterred, leaned forward slightly. "If you want to avoid drawing attention, you might consider blending in better. A natural hair color, the school uniform, and losing the mask would be a start. People might even trust you."

Seere's lips curved into a sharp, humorless smile. "I'm not one to blend in," she said coolly. Her gaze shifted to Felix. "Your Highness, what is your next class?"

"History," Felix replied, though he frowned slightly. "Foras isn't entirely wrong, though. You should tread carefully around the Empire. The Demon Empress isn't a foe to take lightly."

"I've heard the stories," Seere said dismissively, though her jaw tightened slightly. She knew the Demon Empress better than anyone, considering Selina was her sister.

"They're more than stories," Rowan interjected, his voice dropping to a conspiratorial whisper. "They say she burns anyone she suspects of plotting against her. Whole villages have been wiped out."

"No, that is true," Seere said, her tone tight with bitterness. Her grip tightened on her fork. "I barely escaped one of her infernos with my life. That was also the last time anyone saw Princess Amaris."

Felix's head whipped toward her, his cobalt blue eyes wide. "Is that where you met her?"

"Yes," Seere said, her voice colder now. She refused to meet his gaze, focusing instead on the plate before her.

"How did you escape?" Rowan asked softly, his curiosity tempered by caution. "It's said there were no survivors."

Seere let out a hollow laugh. "Easier than you'd think. I used the screams and chaos of the dying as cover and ran."

"So your claim about the burns wasn't entirely a lie," Foras said, his tone laced with skepticism.

She had almost forgotten about that particular fabrication from earlier that morning. "No, it wasn't," she replied curtly.

"How old are you?" Foras pressed, his gaze narrowing.

"How old do I look?" Seere leaned forward slightly, her tone filled with mischief. "Answer carefully."

Foras paused, studying her face intently. "If I had to guess, I'd say you're around Princess Amaris' age."

"Fair guess," Seere said lightly, leaning away from him. "I'm the youngest person to build a kingdom, though."

"When's your birthday?"

"The first of the Frost Moon," she lied without hesitation, a small, smug smile playing on her lips.

Foras blinked, clearly unimpressed. "Do you think anyone believes that? The first day of the year is the most generic answer a liar could give."

"My kingdom believes it," she shot back smoothly.

"So you lie to your own kingdom?" he challenged, his tone sharpening.

Seere scoffed bitterly, crossing her arms. "Name one ruler who hasn't lied to their kingdom. Withholding information counts, you know. Even the priests of Eulla's church lie about their goddess' story."

Foras opened his mouth to retort but stopped short, his eyes shifting to the high windows at the head of the room. A faint bell rang in the distance, signaling the end of their break.

"I think it's time for the next class," he muttered, standing abruptly.

The group rose in silence, and as they began to file out of the hall, Seere couldn't resist one last glance at Cotoria and her companions. They were still watching.

She smiled under her mask, sharp and full of quiet challenge.

7

FRUSTRATION

EULDAY, EIGHTH DAY OF THE DRAGON
MOON, YEAR 449 OF THE GODDESS

The lecture hall for history was steeped in the ambiance of a timeworn library. Shelves of ancient tomes lined the walls, and artifacts from centuries past rested in glass cases along the edges of the room. Professor Alma Dubois stood at the head of the class, her stout frame silhouetted by the golden light streaming through high-arched windows. Her piercing eyes scanned the room as she began to speak, her tone deliberate and commanding.

"Four hundred years ago, Aevrath was not the patchwork of kingdoms and empires we know today," she declared, her voice echoing off the stone walls. "It was one vast, united empire, a beacon of prosperity and innovation. Under the banner of Emperor Kaelios I, the people of Aevrath shared their wealth, their knowledge, and their devotion to the goddess Rosyn. But as history often teaches us, prosperity is a fragile thing."

The students listened, some more attentively than others. Seere sat near the back, her arms crossed as she leaned against her desk. Though her mind wandered, her sharp gaze never left the professor, assessing every word.

"A faction of the empire's people," Dubois continued, "felt abandoned, neglected by the capital's wealth and influence. These marginalized voices grew louder until they became a roar. The Civil War of Aevrath was born, and it would rage for nearly a century, staining the soil with blood and shattering the bonds that held the empire together."

A dramatic pause followed, and the professor's expression darkened. "It is said that on the hundredth anniversary of the war's beginning, the goddess Rosyn herself descended from the heavens, her heart heavy with sorrow for her people. She raised the jagged mountain spines that now cleave the continent in two, dividing Aevrath into the Empire of Envie and the Kingdom of Noctivagus."

Dubois gestured toward a large tapestry that hung behind her. It depicted a celestial figure, Rosyn, with her arms outstretched, mountains erupting from the continent at her command. The scene was vibrant but imbued with an unmistakable sense of loss.

"But," Dubois said, her tone sharpening, "the act of dividing Aevrath came at a great cost. The goddess Rosyn, overcome by the weight of her decision, split herself into two beings: Eulla, the Bringer of Light and Life, and Eslia, the Mother of Crows and Darkness. The two halves of Rosyn embodied opposing ideals. Eulla represented the hope for harmony, while Eslia embodied the inevitability of strife."

She turned her attention to Foras, who had muttered something under his breath. "Foras," she snapped, "perhaps you'd like to enlighten the class. What did Eulla say when the mountains were raised?"

Foras sighed and answered, "'The barrier will fall when we find peace.'"

"And what of Eslia, her counterpart?" Dubois pressed.

Foras recited with equal precision, "'The people of Aevrath shall never find peace so long as my kin draw breath.'"

Dubois nodded approvingly. "It is because of those words that the Hunt on Eslia began in the Empire of Envie. It was believed that Eslia's children carried within them the seeds of discord. The emperors of Envie decreed that these children must be eradicated to bring about the peace promised by Eulla."

A heavy silence fell over the room as the professor gestured to another tapestry. This one depicted a horrific scene: children and adults alike burned at the stake, their faces twisted in agony. Above them loomed a shadowy figure with outstretched wings, the unmistakable representation of Eslia.

Seere's voice cut through the silence, low but firm. "A fool's errand," she muttered, her words drawing the attention of the entire room.

Dubois froze, her sharp eyes narrowing on Seere. "Your Majesty," she said, her tone dripping with bitterness and authority that had no power over Seere, "how much do you know about the Hunt on Eslia?"

Seere's lips curved into a faint smile, though her expression remained unreadable behind her mask. "More than most," she replied, ignoring the audible groan from Cotoria.

"And what exactly do you mean by that?" Dubois pressed, clearly intrigued despite her irritation.

Seere's gaze flicked to the tapestry of burning children. Her voice was calm, almost detached, as she said, "The Hunt is nothing more than a cruel lie. It's a story perpetuated by Lady Eslia herself, a way to ensure that hatred and fear continue to fester in the hearts of mortals. As long as the gods exist, there will always be war, rebellion, and death. The Hunt is just another tool to keep the cycle turning."

Dubois' expression twisted in surprise. "Why would you believe such a thing?"

Seere shrugged. "Logic. That, and I enjoy being controversial."

Foras scoffed. "At least you're self-aware."

"Painfully," Seere replied, her eyes meeting his with a faint smirk.

Cotoria's glare could have melted steel, but Seere ignored her, turning her attention back to the professor.

Dubois cleared her throat, regaining her composure. "Regardless of your... theories, the Hunt on Eslia is a pivotal part of Aevrath's history. Understanding its origins and its consequences is essential to understanding the conflicts that still plague our world today."

Seere's mind wandered. She thought of the countless lives lost in the name of the Hunt, of the lies woven so deeply into the fabric of history that they had become indistinguishable from truth. She thought of her place in this fractured world and the secrets she carried—secrets that could ignite a war greater than any the continent had ever seen.

When the class finally ended, Seere rose from her seat, her expression unreadable. As the other students filed out, she lingered for a moment, her gaze fixed on the tapestry of Rosyn.

"*Peace*," she murmured to herself, the word tasting bitter on her tongue. "What a lovely myth."

· · ·

THE WARM SCENT of freshly brewed tea filled the room, mingling with the delicate aroma of lavender and rose petals. Sunlight streamed through tall, mullioned windows, casting soft patterns on the polished wooden floors. The classroom was a vision of refinement: small round tables draped in fine linen, each adorned with a delicate porcelain tea set and fresh flowers in crystal vases.

Professor Amy Viné, a slender woman with silver-streaked hair pulled into a flawless chignon, moved gracefully between the tables. Her sharp, discerning gaze caught even the smallest breaches of etiquette as she offered gentle but firm corrections. Her voice was melodic yet commanding, a tone that brooked no nonsense.

"Hospitality," she said, addressing the room as she clasped her hands before her, "is not just a skill, but an art. It is the first impression we offer, the foundation of diplomacy, and a reflection of our character. Today, you will learn to pour tea, arrange refreshments, and conduct conversation with grace."

Seere sat stiffly at a table with Felix, Rowan, and Achlys. Most of the other students had pointedly avoided joining her, their curiosity about the masked woman tempered by unease. Felix, however, seemed determined to make the best of the situation, his demeanor polite but guarded.

Rowan, ever the charmer, leaned toward Achlys, his hazel eyes sparkling with mischief. "Lady Achlys, do you take sugar in your tea? Or is sweetness redundant in your presence?"

Achlys, who had been carefully arranging scones on a plate, didn't even glance up. "If you're trying to flatter me, Naberius, you'll need to work harder," she said coolly, her accent sharpening the edge of her words.

Rowan laughed, unbothered by her rebuff. "Ah, so there is a chance then?"

Felix rolled his eyes but said nothing, instead focusing on pouring tea into a delicate cup with precise movements. Seere watched him closely, noting the steadiness of his hands and the way he measured the perfect amount of tea without spilling a single drop.

"I imagine this isn't your first tea party," Seere remarked, her tone neutral but faintly amused.

Felix glanced at her, a small smile tugging at the corner of his lips. "It's definitely not. And what about you, do you have many in your court?"

She shook her head slightly. "I attended a few years ago. However, they're not exactly in my area of expertise."

He raised an eyebrow, intrigued. "And what *is* your area of expertise, if I might ask?"

"Did I not demonstrate it well enough in physical training this morning?" she asked, her gloved fingers idly tracing the rim of her untouched teacup.

Felix chuckled softly, a sound that carried a hint of warmth. "Oh, you most certainly did."

Across the table, Rowan was still attempting to engage Achlys, who remained steadfastly unimpressed. "You know," Rowan said, adopting a mock-serious tone, "you'd make an excellent diplomat with that icy demeanor. I'm half-tempted to commission a statue in your likeness—call it *The Muse of Rejection*."

Achlys finally looked up, leveling him with a withering stare. "Do you ever stop talking?"

"Rarely," he admitted with a grin.

Seere's gaze flicked between them, her expression

hidden but her amusement evident in the subtle tilt of her head. "Persistent, isn't he?" she said quietly to Felix.

"Annoyingly so," Felix agreed, though there was no malice in his tone.

As the lesson progressed, Professor Viné approached their table, her critical eye scanning each student. "Prince Felix," she said, nodding approvingly, "your presentation is exemplary as always. Achlys, your arrangement of the scones is impeccable."

She turned to Rowan, her sharp gaze softening only slightly. "Mr. Naberius, your manners could use some refinement. Flattery should be genuine, not excessive, and please refrain from insulting."

Rowan placed a hand over his heart, feigning offense. "Professor, you wound me."

"And Lady Seere," Professor Viné continued, her tone turning curious as she regarded the masked woman, "it's rare for someone to leave their tea untouched. Is there a reason?"

Seere met the professor's gaze evenly. "It would be improper for me to drink without removing my mask, and I wouldn't wish to cause a disruption."

Viné studied her for a moment before nodding. "A considerate response. However, one must always find a balance between personal boundaries and social expectations. Keep that in mind."

As the professor moved to the next table, Felix leaned slightly toward Seere. "Ah, so you can deflect gracefully."

"When necessary."

Toward the end of the lesson, as the students began cleaning up their tables, Felix turned to Seere. "I've been meaning to ask... would you consider helping me with some extra training in the evenings? Your skill in combat is... unique."

She tilted her head, studying him for a moment. "You want my help?"

He nodded. "I think I could learn a lot from you."

After a brief pause, she inclined her head. "Very well. We'll start tonight after dinner."

A flicker of surprise crossed his face, quickly replaced by gratitude. "Thank you, Your Majesty."

Seere was relieved when classes were finally dismissed for the day. Achlys seemed quite glad as well, considering how quickly she got up and left the etiquette classroom. Seere remained close to Felix, not wanting to lose sight of him.

"You might be the first person I've heard speak up for the children of Eslia," Felix commented once they were in a less busy corridor.

Seere shook her head in frustration. "It's cruel. No one should be punished for the mistakes of their parents," she said. "Not even the children of the Goddess of Death."

A chill ran down her spine, and she spun around, dagger drawn and poised to strike the fool who dared to sneak up on her. The entire hall froze. Everyone froze, stunned, as she held her blade to Headmaster Orias Roderick's throat. The headmaster only smirked in amusement, his gaze never leaving hers.

"Well, that's one way to greet someone," Orias said with an amused chuckle, his hands raised in a show of mock surrender.

Seere's eyes narrowed. "You should know better than to sneak up on me."

"And you should know better than to be so jumpy," he teased, his tone light but laced with familiarity.

She slid the dagger back into its sheath, her movements precise and controlled. "I don't let my guard down for anyone. Especially not you."

"Wise," Orias said with a smile that was equal parts approval and amusement. "Still, you might consider relaxing just a little. I've come to collect you."

She frowned. "Collect me?"

He gestured for her to follow. "Dinner. My study. I'd like to hear about your first day. Unless you'd rather skulk around in the shadows, keeping everyone at arm's length."

Seere hesitated, her eyes narrowing in suspicion. She spared a glance over her shoulder at Felix, who watched from several paces away, and then lowered her voice. "And if I refuse?"

"Then I suppose I'll have to try harder to charm you next time," he said with a devious grin.

With a faint sigh, she relented. "Fine. Lead the way."

Orias guided her through many corridors before coming to a tower, which she quickly recognized as the old tower that had once belonged to the former headmaster. She supposed it made sense that Orias would have taken up the same tower.

When they entered his office, she was surprised to find a modest feast set atop his desk. There were platters of roasted meats, fresh bread, cheeses, and fruits, along with a bottle of wine and two delicate glasses.

"Please, sit," Orias gestured to a chair across from him. He took his place behind the desk, pouring wine into the glasses with practiced ease.

As Seere settled into her chair, she allowed herself to

relax slightly, though her posture remained alert. She accepted the wine he offered but didn't drink immediately, instead eyeing the contents of the table with cautious curiosity.

"I hear you've frustrated half of your instructors already," Orias began, his tone light but probing.

"It seems I can't help it," Seere replied mildly, her fingers resting on the stem of her glass.

"And then there's the fact that you're not getting along very well with your little sister."

Her eyes flickered to him sharply. "Did you expect us to be best friends? I stand for everything the empire hates."

Orias leaned back, his expression one of practiced nonchalance. "Not exactly, but just so you're aware, she did come to me with the request that we send you back to your island," he said with a shrug. "Apparently, she finds your presence... disruptive."

Seere smirked faintly, removed her mask, and finally took a sip of the wine. It was fruity and sweet, a blend she found surprisingly agreeable. "I'm not surprised. Cotoria doesn't take well to challenges."

"Regardless, it seems you've made fast friends with the captain of our guard," Orias said, his tone shifting to one of curiosity.

"Don't act like you didn't orchestrate our meeting," she muttered, setting the cup down.

Orias chuckled, the sound low and dark. "Seems nothing gets by you."

"I try not to let it. What did you want from me, Orias?"

"I only wanted to see how you were holding up after your first day back in this place," he said simply.

"I'm well enough."

"And Felix? Is he treating you well?"

"He is."

"And Foras?"

She let out a slow breath. "He knows something—or at least suspects something. He's trying very hard to uncover my identity."

Orias' lips curled into a sly smile. "Would that be so terrible? For Felix and the others to know who you truly are?"

Her gaze hardened. "Yes. It would."

As their conversation lapsed into a brief silence, her eyes drifted to a book on one of the shelves behind Orias. The spine caught her attention, and she read the title with a faint sense of disbelief: *Seere and His Bride*.

It was an old story about a former king called Seere. He was the son of Aldros. During a venture into a city, King Seere caught sight of a young maiden and fell madly in love with her. One night, he had her kidnapped and brought to him. Through the story, he cherished her, and little by little, she fell in love and even bore his child. However, the story ends brutally with her death. The very people who had gone to rescue her from the clutches of King Seere killed her when they realized she loved him.

"That's an interesting choice of book," she said softly, her voice tinged with curiosity.

Orias followed her gaze and smiled faintly. "I've been trying to understand why you chose him as your namesake."

Her gaze lingered on the book for a moment longer before turning back to him. "I expect that my life will be as much of a tragedy as his was," she said simply.

Orias studied her for a long moment, his expression unreadable. "Perhaps. Or perhaps not."

She rose from her chair, leaving her food untouched,

slipping her mask back over her face with a practiced motion. "Thank you for dinner," she said, her tone cool but polite.

Orias inclined his head. "Goodnight, darling. And... be careful."

Without another word, she drew her mask back over her face and left the study, her steps measured and deliberate as she descended the winding staircase. The night air that greeted her outside the office was crisp and cool, but it did little to ease the tension that lingered in her chest.

THE TRAINING GROUNDS were alive with the sounds of clashing steel, heavy footsteps on the sand, and the occasional sharp intake of breath as strikes landed. The waning light of the evening cast long shadows across the arena, illuminating the intensity in each fighter's movements.

Seere arrived with measured steps, her keen eyes scanning the scene. Felix and Achlys were deep in their sparring match, their movements precise but markedly different. Felix's strikes were calculated and disciplined, but he was holding himself too rigidly. Achlys, in contrast, fought with fluidity, her agility making her a difficult target as she moved like a shadow around him. Not far off, Rowan and Foras sparred with equal vigor. Their duel was marked by occasional taunts and bursts of laughter that made it clear neither was taking the bout too seriously. Shax observed them, offering taunts of his own.

On the sidelines, a small group observed. Enora stood with her arms crossed, her sharp gaze moving between the fighters. Beside her was Alsariph Farcyne, whose attention lingered a little too long on Achlys, his expression caught between admiration and calculation. Two others stood near them—Raphael, a towering figure whose broadsword gleamed faintly in its sheath, and Emeline, a raven-haired young woman exuding quiet curiosity. Both were unfamiliar to Seere as they were nobles from Noctivagus that she had met briefly when she visited years before, and she noted their presence with mild interest.

As she approached, her appearance drew Felix's attention. His split-second distraction was all Achlys needed. She swept his legs out from under him, sending him sprawling into the sand. The impact earned an audible *oof* from Felix and a smattering of applause from Alsariph, who looked impressed.

"Stop checking out Her Majesty, Your Highness, and focus on the opponent in front of you!" Enora called, her tone half-teasing, half-chiding.

Seere sighed heavily as all eyes turned to her. Raphael and Emeline shot to their feet, bowing deeply.

"Your Majesty!" they exclaimed in unison, their voices reverent.

"Relax, you two. She isn't a god," Alsariph said mockingly, clearly amused by their display.

"But she *is* a queen," Enora countered sharply. "And thus should be treated like one."

Seere ignored the back-and-forth, her attention snapping back to Felix. "Your Highness, relax your shoulders slightly. It'll help you move more fluidly. You're far too tense."

A low, familiar voice at her side broke the silence. "They know I'm not your brother," Shax muttered, stepping closer to her.

Seere glanced at him, her expression unreadable. "I figured they'd realize eventually."

"You don't care?"

"Well, I don't want them knowing my true identity," she replied evenly. Her gaze flicked toward Alsariph and Enora, still locked in a bickering match. "It's safer if they remain unaware for as long as possible. There are too many people here who want me dead, and too many who'd kill anyone associated with me."

Shax nodded slowly. "I see."

A flicker of regret crossed Seere's face, brief but sincere. "I'm sorry," she said softly, her voice almost lost in the sounds of the arena. "I put you and your family in danger."

"I've been in danger since the moment I met you, my Lady," Shax replied, his tone gentle as he nudged her shoulder lightly.

Her lips quirked in a small smile. "Did you ask them about dinner this weekend?" she asked, nodding toward Felix. "I never got the opportunity."

"Yes," Shax replied lightly. "I'll let my beloved know she can make as much as she wants."

"Sounds lovely." Seere winced as Achlys once again swept Felix to the ground, using the same tactic as before. She shook her head and called out, "Your Highness, you need to practice your footwork!"

"I see that," Felix grumbled, allowing Achlys to haul him up once more. "I'll be more careful this time."

From the sidelines, Shax smirked. "I want to see Miss Alerie and Her Majesty pair up together. Who would win?"

"Her Majesty would win," Achlys answered without hesitation.

"Don't doubt your abilities, Lady Alerie," Seere said, her tone firm yet kind.

A rare smile graced Achlys' features. "Oh, I don't," she replied. "But I can tell when someone surpasses me."

"Then perhaps we should train together sometime," Seere suggested, her voice thoughtful. "If only to refine the skills you already possess."

"That would be helpful," Achlys said with a nod. She turned back to Felix, her stance already shifting into readiness. This time, he responded more quickly, their blades clashing as sparks flew.

Seere couldn't help but admire Achlys' style. The girl turned every part of her body into a weapon, her movements precise and unrelenting. Watching her was like seeing a reflection of herself, though Achlys carried a freedom in her stride that Seere could never afford.

"She fights well," Shax murmured, his tone contemplative.

"She does," Seere agreed. Her gaze lingered on Achlys a moment longer before she turned to the rest of the sparring field, a quiet determination settling in her expression. But even as she watched, unease coiled in her chest—something unseen was shifting beneath the surface.

8

———

DINNER

DHANIRDAY, FOURTEENTH OF THE DRAGON MOON, YEAR 449 OF THE GODDESS

The week passed in a rhythm that Seere found both strangely comforting and annoyingly predictable. Classes filled her days, each one a mix of academic challenge and social tension. Evenings brought sparring sessions with Felix, where he worked tirelessly to improve under her tutelage. Foras had grown slightly less combative, though he still eyed her with suspicion. Cotoria, however, remained relentless, seizing every opportunity to challenge Seere, whether in words or deeds.

By the seventh day, the training yard buzzed with anticipation as students lined up along the edge of the sparring ring, murmuring and placing bets on who would dominate the day's challenges. Professor Vidal stood at the center, his voice commanding yet amused as he announced the rules.

"Today, you will test your skill against one another in single combat, putting everything you've learned over the last month on display. This is not about strength—it's about strategy, discipline, and knowing when to press an advantage or concede defeat. Let's see what you've learned so far."

Cotoria climbed over the ring's fencing clumsily, her confidence palpable as she tossed her platinum blonde hair over her shoulder. Seere knew immediately what was coming when her sister leveled her green eyes on Seere and smirked. "I challenge the Assassin Queen. Let's see if she can actually fight, or if she's all talk and theatrics."

The crowd erupted in whispers and excited gasps as everyone looked around eagerly. Seere rolled her eyes and unclasped the cloak she wore before handing it off to Felix, who took it without complaint. Then she gracefully vaulted over the fencing just as she had done days before. Her movements were deliberate, almost feline, as she crossed to the center of the ring and adjusted the gloves on her hands.

The two squared off. Cotoria wielded a rapier with a jeweled hilt, her stance rigid and formal. Seere stood with her hands at her sides, her dagger still sheathed at her hip.

Cotoria sneered at the sight. "No weapon? How cocky. How foolish."

Seere smiled, shrugging lightly. "I am just confident in my abilities."

At Vidal's signal, Cotoria lunged, her blade aiming for Seere's side. Seere moved as though she'd known the attack was coming, stepping aside and twisting her body just enough to let the blade pass harmlessly. Cotoria stumbled slightly but recovered, slashing again and again in quick succession.

Each attack missed its mark. Seere evaded with minimal effort, her movements fluid and almost mocking.

The crowd was riveted. Seere could see Felix standing at the edge of the ring, his fists clenched in anticipation, while Foras watched with a calculating gaze, his lips pressed into a thin line.

"Fight me, you coward!" Cotoria snapped, her face red with exertion and embarrassment.

Seere tilted her head, amusement flashing in her pale eyes. "If you insist."

The moment Cotoria lunged again, Seere's hand shot out, catching the rapier by its blade. Gasps echoed around the ring as Seere yanked it from Cotoria's grasp, spinning her around and locking her in a grapple. Cotoria struggled, but Seere's strength and technique were undeniable.

With a sharp twist, Seere sent Cotoria sprawling onto the ground, pinning her with a boot lightly pressed to her back.

"It's over," Seere said coolly, tossing the rapier to the side.

The crowd erupted into cheers and laughter, with Enora's voice ringing out above the others. "Well done, Cotoria! You lasted a whole ten seconds!"

Cotoria pushed herself up, her face flushed with rage and humiliation. She stormed out of the ring without a word, her fists clenched at her sides.

Seere stepped out of the ring, brushing invisible dust off her gloves as she rejoined Felix and the others.

"You didn't have to be so brutal," Rowan said, though he was grinning.

"She asked for it," Seere replied, shrugging.

Felix clapped her on the back, his grin wide. "You were incredible!"

Seere set her hand over his, where it rested on her shoulder. "I know," she said playfully.

She turned her gaze back to the ring as she recalled a time from when she was fourteen. She had been sent to stay in Noctivagus at the palace to meet Felix, the boy who was meant to one day become her husband. Back then, she had sparred against Foras, and Felix had cheered only for her.

The sparring matches continued, with students facing off in bouts of skill, speed, and endurance. Felix took his turn against another student, his strikes strong but unpolished. Seere watched intently, mentally noting areas where he could improve.

When it was Foras' turn, he dominated his opponent with a mix of calculated moves and brutal strength. He stepped out of the ring, barely winded, and met Seere's gaze.

"Care to challenge me next?" Foras asked, a hint of a smirk on his lips.

"Not today," Seere replied evenly. Though her eyes held a glint of amusement, she felt anything but excited for the day when she was paired against Foras. She knew he, of all people, would remember her fighting style better than anyone. "I wouldn't want to bruise your ego."

Foras chuckled. "That's assuming you could, Your Majesty. Perhaps it is you who fears an ego bruising."

"You could never bruise my ego," she said lightly.

Seere boarded a carriage with Felix, Rowan, and Foras bound for Cegwin. She pulled her cloak tight and raised her hood, obscuring her face entirely. She leaned back in her corner, sharing her bench with Felix, who sat back comfortably.

"You haven't worn your hood all week. Why such a mysterious getup now when we're just visiting your old friend?" Rowan questioned, quirking a brow up at her.

"Perhaps she plans to murder us," Foras muttered.

"A precaution," Seere said, glaring at Foras. "We'll be stopping in a village full of guards that are quick to draw their weapons, and I'd rather not bring unnecessary atten-tion to us."

Foras studied her intently. Odd, isn't it? That you're so cautious?"

Seere crossed one leg over the other as she eyed Foras curiously. "No, I don't think it is."

"No one else hides their face and lies about having burn scars," Foras argued, coolly.

"You were lying about those?" Rowan questioned.

Felix watched Seere now, his gaze full of curiosity. She made no sudden moves, she refused to shift and give away her discomfort. She hated how intently all of them stared at her.

"Assume everything I say and do is a lie. As the queen of assassins, rogues, and cutthroats, it's safe to assume nothing about me is true. Perhaps even my very existence is false," she said, leaning her head back against the carriage wall. "In any case, my country has its share of disputes with Envie over trade. I'd rather not deal with any of it tonight."

Felix nodded in understanding then. "Envie has always been difficult to deal with. They've been very stubborn about opening their borders ever since Ris vanished..." he trailed off slowly, his gaze filling with sorrow.

A chill ran up Seere's spine, and she glanced away from Felix, not wanting to see the hurt she caused him. "Envie discovered that I have been sending Noctivagus *far* more Eulla blossoms than what they receive, and they are angry about it, but they refuse to give a trade equal in value to those blossoms."

"I can't imagine how they discovered that... We keep that information tightly locked away," Felix said softly, frowning at the carriage floor.

"I assume one of my spies let it slip at some point over the last year," she said, tracing the sapphire in the hilt of her dagger that was strapped at her thigh. "However, I have no evidence, and therefore I can't do anything to stop the traitor."

The remainder of the carriage ride was filled with silence. Hours passed before the village came into view, a beacon of light in the darkness left by the sun's disappearance. Seere's eyes were on the forest around them, watching for any shifting shadows, any sign that someone might be waiting to ambush them.

Finally, they rolled through the gates, passing by heavily armored guards who eyed their carriage warily. Seere's hand had tightened around the hilt of her dagger. Then her gaze met Foras as he watched her with a raised brow.

"You seem rather tense, Seere. Anything you'd like to share with the class?" Foras questioned.

"No, there isn't," she said coolly, removing her hand from her dagger.

Eventually, the carriage rolled to a stop in front of a small cottage on the outskirts of the village. Seere was out first, scouting the immediate area for any threats. When she found none, she gestured for the other three to join her.

"I will wait out here, Your Majesty," the driver said, settling back against his bench.

"Very well," Seere said before she turned and headed for the front door.

Before she could even lay her knuckles on the door to knock, the door was being opened. A little girl of about six stood on the other side, a brilliant smile on her face, though it faltered slightly when she saw the hood over Seere's face.

"Ah, you made it!" Shax said brightly just as he appeared

in the entryway. "Come on in! Circe, open the door wider so Her Majesty can enter."

The little girl's smile returned as Seere pushed her hood aside and stepped in. "The road was long, but we're finally here. I don't know how you make that trip so frequently."

"The journey really isn't so bad once you get used to it," he said, glancing behind him as a young woman with auburn hair and gentle hazel eyes stepped into the room. "Speaking of my wife, Seere, this is Asteria. Asteria, this is my old friend, Seere. Then we have Prince Felix, Foras, and Rowan."

"Your Majesty, Your Highness," Asteria said, curtsying low.

"Please, just call me Seere. You needn't be so polite," Seere said warmly, offering her hand to Asteria, who took it hesitantly. "I am human too."

"I doubt that," Foras muttered behind her.

Felix stepped up beside Seere, a warm smile on his face. "And you may just call me Felix," he said warmly. "Titles hardly befit me these days."

It was then that Seere noticed the other little girl hiding behind her mother. A small smile lifted the corners of her mouth as she sank to her knees and held out a hand to the girl who looked to be around four. She looked so much like her father with dark hair and blue eyes.

"Why do you wear a mask?" the little girl asked.

Seere smiled and dropped to her knees so that she looked far less menacing. "Sometimes it's better to stay a bit hidden," she replied, her tone light. "It adds a little mystery, too, don't you think? What's your name?"

"Lilith," the little girl answered, a smile turning the corners of her lips up.

"Well, Lilith, I think your name means 'Belonging to the night,' which is even more mysterious than Seere."

"Really?" the little girl asked, her eyes lighting up excitedly.

"Definitely."

"Why doesn't he think you're human?" Circe piped up, pointing to Foras.

"I'm fairly certain she's a demon," Foras said, earning a sharp glare from Seere when the girls took a quick step back.

"I am no demon. He just doesn't like me much," Seere said, standing again.

"Well, regardless of whether you are a demon or not, you are welcome to eat at our table," Asteria said. "Come, I have made a lot of food that needs to be eaten."

Asteria hadn't been lying. As everyone sat around the table laden with food, she brought out one last pot of soup. The table was covered in a spread of roasted meats, root vegetables, fresh bread, and a variety of cheeses.

"This smells incredible," Felix said sincerely, which earned a blush from Asteria.

"You're too kind, Your Highness," she said bashfully.

"Not at all," Felix assured her. "I mean it."

Seere sat at Shax's left side, watching everyone as they dug into their food. She noticed the way Foras watched her intently as if waiting for her to remove her mask so she could eat. However, she refused, no matter how enticing the food looked.

"How is life as a queen treating you, Seere?" Shax questioned, breaking through her thoughts.

"Well enough," Seere answered, looking up at her friend. "Nobles are always difficult, but mine are very attentive to the needs of the people, so I don't mind too much. They act as my eyes when I can't see everything for myself."

"Nobles that are genuine? Hard to believe such a thing exists," Shax commented, then he glanced at Foras and Rowan. "Forgive me. I don't mean any offense to your houses."

"When you live in the empire, your distaste for nobles is understandable," Rowan said, glancing away. "I mean, when your ruler is known as the Demon Empress…"

"It's definitely not an easy life out here," Asteria murmured.

"If you ever need to escape, you are always welcome in the Domain. It isn't as awful as it sounds," Seere said softly.

"How does your kingdom work?" Shax questioned. "I've heard many interesting rumors."

Seere glanced at Foras. "What sort of rumors have you heard, and perhaps I can tell you whether they are true or not," she said hesitantly.

"There are whispers that those who enter the kingdom uninvited never return. They say that on nights of a blood moon, the kingdom conducts a mass culling of anyone deemed a traitor…"

"Only the nobility of Envie is uninvited within our borders. Most who sneak into the Domain are refugees from Envie who are seeking solace and cannot find it in Noctivagus, so we allow them in," Seere explained, glancing down at her empty plate. "And no, we do not hold a purging on each blood moon."

"If we're throwing out rumors here, I've heard that the very streets and walls are alive and that shift to trap intruders," Rowan said.

"Oh, that is a favorite one of mine. My streets *are* alive

and my walls *do* have eyes, but not in the sense you might think," she said.

"And I've heard that you're harboring a king slayer," Foras said.

Seere's gaze snapped up to meet his. "Not that I am aware of."

"Then why have I been hearing whispers about the Assassin Queen hiding Princess Amaris within her walls?" Foras questioned. "You're not the only one with eyes and ears everywhere, Seere."

"Foras, please," Felix said, his voice strangled. "Leave it be."

"Perhaps you should seek the willow at dusk then," Seere said coolly, giving Foras a look of barely contained distaste. To seek the willow at dusk was a phrase used by those who knew the shadows by heart, a phrase meant to inform another person to meet later in private. A phrase that could be condemning for Seere.

"Seere," Shax hissed under his breath. It was a sharp warning that Seere already understood.

"Very well," Foras said, leaning back in his seat. He wore a look of triumph that Seere hated and no one else understood.

Dinner passed quietly after that. What was meant to be a pleasant affair had turned tense and dark. The rumors of Princess Amaris being alive unsettled everyone, even Amaris herself. Seere desperately wished she could take her words back. The last thing she wanted was to meet Foras in private. She did not want him to know her identity for certain.

When it came time to leave, Asteria handed Seere a carefully wrapped bundle of leftovers. "You take care of yourself, all right?" she said warmly.

"I will," Seere promised, holding the bundle close. "Thank you."

As the carriage pulled away from the house, Rowan stretched and let out a satisfied sigh. "Asteria's cooking is magic. It's too bad Foras ruined the atmosphere."

Felix nodded in agreement, his expression thoughtful as he watched Seere. She remained silent, her hood drawn low once more as the carriage rolled through the darkened streets. She had no interest in speaking to any of them for the rest of that night.

The carriage turned a corner, nearing the edge of the village, when the sound of boots on stone halted the horses. The coachman cursed softly, and the carriage jerked to a stop.

"What's going on out there?" Rowan asked, sitting up.

Felix pushed aside the curtain, peering outside. "Guards," he said, glancing over at Seere.

The carriage door opened abruptly, and four Envie guards stepped forward. Their polished armor caught the moonlight, and their stern expressions left no room for pleasantries.

"We're conducting inspections," one of the guards announced gruffly. His gaze swept over the group in the carriage, lingering on Seere's hooded figure. "State your business and identities."

Felix leaned forward, his princely demeanor radiating authority. "I am Prince Felix of Noctivagus, and these are my companions. We've just dined with Captain Aurelian Fraser and are returning to the Academy."

His gaze locked on Seere. "Who is she?"

The air in the carriage grew tense. Rowan glanced at

Seere, his brow furrowed, while Foras' sharp expression turned calculating.

Seere remained still for a moment before she sighed softly. "Very well," she said, her voice cool and steady.

She pulled off the glove with deliberate slowness, revealing her pale hand adorned with her tattoo and the gold signet ring bearing the unmistakable crest of the Domain of Assassins: A crow feather through a crown.

The guards stiffened, their faces paling. One of them took a half-step back, his hand falling from the hilt of his sword.

"Does this satisfy your curiosity?" Seere asked, her tone edged with cold authority. She rose slightly from her seat, her hood falling back just enough for the dim light of the street lamps to catch the piercing look in her pale green eyes. "Now, I suggest you decide quickly whether to let us pass or whether you'd like to test your luck tonight."

The lead guard swallowed hard, his grip tightening on his spear. "My apologies, my lady. There's no need for trouble," he said hastily.

"Good." Seere's tone softened slightly, though her gaze remained icy. She sank back into her seat, pulling her hood into place once more. "Close the door."

The guard nodded sharply, and the soldiers stepped back. One of them shut the door with a clang before gesturing for the coachman to move along.

As the carriage started rolling again, Rowan let out a low whistle. "I never want to get on your bad side," he said, his tone half-joking. "I've seen you fight, but I know these guards haven't. Yet they fear you so deeply."

Felix glanced at Seere, his expression thoughtful. "You handled that with remarkable poise," he said carefully.

Seere didn't reply immediately, her attention seemingly fixed on the passing scenery outside. After a moment, she spoke, her voice quiet. "Usually, a sharp tongue and a sharper reputation are more effective than a blade."

Foras leaned back, his arms crossed as he studied her. "That tattoo on your hand," he said, his tone probing. "Is it just decoration, or is there more to it? I see that the flowers are the same color as your hair."

Seere shrugged, tossing her hood off once they passed safely through the gates of Cegwin. "I thought it was lovely," she said.

"How big is it?" Rowan questioned.

"It starts at my left hand and ends at my left foot," she said lightly.

9

CONFRONTATION

DHANIRDAY, FOURTEENTH OF THE DRAGON MOON, YEAR 449 OF THE GODDESS

The carriage pulled into the Academy grounds well past midnight, the moon casting a silver sheen over the immense fortress. The group stepped out in silence, the chill of the night settling into their bones. Felix, clearly exhausted from the day's events, let out a long sigh as he made his way toward the dormitory building.

"I'll walk you to your door," Seere said, her voice low and even.

"Thank you," Felix said warmly, having no interest in objecting to her company. It was drastically different from the apprehension he had shown her when she first arrived at the school.

However, Foras followed Seere like a vengeful ghost. The click of his boots on the stone was loud as he purposefully made his presence obvious to her. She could feel his sharp gaze fixed intently on her cloaked figure. He was angry, and she would have to deal with it.

"Foras, you're going to wake the whole school with your seething," Seere called lightly over her shoulder.

Felix chuckled beside her. "Please, relax. We're all tired," he said, pausing his steps only briefly to look at Foras.

Foras' frustrations only seemed to ignite hotter than before. "Right," he said coolly, glaring at Seere.

When they finally reached Felix's dorm, Seere paused and stepped aside, giving him a slight nod. "Goodnight, Your Highness," she said, glancing over her shoulder at Foras, who had stationed himself a little ways down the hall.

Felix looked at her for a long moment, hesitating. His tired eyes were filled with something unreadable. All she knew was that he wanted to say something more. Ultimately, he just gave her a tired smile, his gaze shifting to where Foras stood. "Goodnight, Seere."

Foras, to his credit, waited until Felix's door clicked shut and the lock turned. The moment it did, the calm facade he'd put up for his prince cracked as he stepped forward. "Alright, Your Majesty, enough games," he hissed, taking another step closer to Seere as she slowly turned to face him. His tone was low but firm, his sharp gaze boring into her soul. "Who are you? Really?"

She swept past him, her glare sharp as she stormed through the dorm halls. She headed back towards the exit. "We will speak in the headmaster's office," she said coolly. She had a horrible feeling that Orias had been concealing things from her and that he had an accomplice in Foras when he had come to find her. She also preferred to have a second person present during the upcoming conversation in case things turned dangerous for her or Foras.

"I've been patient," he continued, his voice rising slightly. "I've played along with this charade, but I'm not an idiot. I've pieced together enough to know you're not who you claim to be. Or I suppose to know that you are who you claim not to be."

"Shut it," Seere hissed over her shoulder.

"I—"

Seere drew her dagger as she whirled on him. She stormed forward, pressing the blade against the soft spot under his chin. He immediately silenced, earning a smirk. She must have looked as murderous as she had intended.

"If you don't stop talking, I will take your tongue," she growled. "Do not speak until we are alone with Orias and in his study."

Foras glared at her, but he said nothing more.

She stormed out of the dorm building and swiftly crossed to the fortress. Gravel crunched beneath her boots as she walked. Foras, obviously undeterred by the threat of Orias' involvement in the conversation, followed close behind her. She could sense the frustration radiating from him and the way it only seemed to grow.

The only sound came from the clicking of their heels as they stormed up the tower to the headmaster's office. The moment they reached his heavy oak doors, she threw them open, storming inside without so much as a knock.

Orias, who had been seated behind his desk with a book in hand, looked up with a start. His brows knitted together as he frowned at Seere charging in. "Your Majesty," he began, but his gaze shifted to Foras, who entered behind her, and his confusion only deepened. With the absent wave of his hand, the door shut quietly behind them. "What is this about? I was enjoying a good novel in peace."

Seere wasted no time as she reached up and tore her mask from her face. Foras inhaled sharply, recognition and triumph flashing across his expression.

Seere ignored him, her attention solely on Orias, her voice like steel. "You've been hiding things from me. Why didn't you tell me that you've been working with *him* this entire time?" she snapped, jabbing her finger in Foras' direction.

"Amaris," Foras breathed, a smirk appearing across his face. "I was right."

Orias leaned back in his chair, his expression unreadable. "And what if I have?"

Seere's eyes narrowed. "Then you've been wasting my time for your amusement," she snarled.

Foras stepped forward then, his anger flaring. However, this time it was not directed at Seere. It was entirely focused on Orias. "She has been here for a while now. When were you going to tell me that we were correct? You clearly knew this entire time that she was Amaris!" Foras snapped.

"I didn't owe you anything, Foras," Orias said coolly as he massaged his temples. "And where is the fun in giving everything away to you freely. I knew you'd figure it out swiftly. You're nothing if not agonizingly persistent. What I want to know is how Seere figured out that we were 'working together.'"

"He mentioned that rumors were swirling around about me harboring Princess Amaris. However, I know my nobles wouldn't give out such information so willingly, and I know Belial would hide it very carefully for me," Seere answered. "I never expected Foras, of all people, to be so sloppy."

"You think highly of your nobles," Foras said.

"Because I picked my nobles very carefully. I had trained with each one of them when I attended the Assassin's Academy," she explained, her words slow and deliberate, meant to sink in. "I told you before that I am not Amaris. I haven't been Amaris since my father shipped me off to be an assassin. I have always been Seere Cross and I will continue to always be Seere Cross."

"Amaris—"

Seere's hand moved faster than Foras could react. In a single motion, she drew her dagger and pressed it beneath his chin, forcing him to tilt his head back. Her grip was steady, her expression was cold.

"My name, to you and Felix and anyone else, is Seere. If you breathe a word of this to anyone, your life is forfeit," she said, her voice deathly quiet as she slowly backed Foras into a wall.

Foras glared at her, looking as though he wished he could shred her. "What about your betrothed?" he questioned. "He still loves you."

"He loves Amaris, not me, and I think it's high time he's moved on," she said, pressing her dagger firmly to his throat when he hit the wall. "We have not been betrothed to one another since the Frost Moon of year four hundred and forty-three. Yes, I was there for the speech his father gave about hunting me down."

Foras swallowed hard. "We know now that you did not commit the crime of killing your parents. It was a result of the Order of the Chimera. Felix has been searching for you, Amaris. I have been searching for you. Not to expose you, or kill you, but to protect you," he said, his tone turning imploring.

Seere let out a dry laugh, the sound dry and humorless. "Protect me?" she repeated, her tone disbelieving. "I have made myself the most feared queen in this realm. What do you think he can do that I haven't already done for myself?"

Foras' eyes softened slightly, but otherwise they

remained just as harsh as her own. "He still considers you as his betrothed."

The words hit her like a blow, but her expression didn't falter. She stared at him for a long moment before she lowered her dagger, before she stepped away and turned her gaze towards Orias as if just remembering he was there. "Then he's a fool," she said coldly. "Whatever bond we shared had died the moment I was accused of murder. I do not need his protection, and I won't risk starting a war for his sake or mine."

Foras rubbed the underside of his chin where the dagger had pressed, his gaze lingering on her. "You can pretend all you want, Amaris, but Felix will not give up on you," Foras said.

"The only person I have ever pretended to be was Amaris. It is you and Felix who are delusional," she whispered. Her gaze then shifted to Orias, who watched her intently. "Nothing from you either. I will slaughter you if I ever find out that you shared my identity with another soul."

"Of course, Your Majesty. I wouldn't have it any other way," Orias said with an amused smirk. His evergreen eyes swirled with amusement and mischief. "Don't try running now. You still have to watch over the prince."

"I'm painfully aware," she said coolly.

"Oh, Seere, this came in for you. I believe it's a letter from your viceroy," Orias said, holding out an envelope to her.

Seere swiftly snatched it out of his hands, investigating the seal to make certain that it hadn't been tampered with.

"Very well," she said bitterly. Her gaze shifted towards Foras, who watched her intently. "Leave."

Foras scowled. "He will figure it out," he said, his tone low in warning. "He's already suspicious, *Seere*. If you want to keep this secret identity, I suggest you change up some tactics. You haven't changed as much as you think you have over the years."

With that, Foras turned and stalked from the office. Seere waited until she could no longer hear his footsteps on the stone stairs before she opened the envelope and read through its contents. It was indeed an update from Belial.

"Did you have a reason for sending Foras out of the room?" Orias questioned, pushing himself to his feet.

"Not particularly. I was just tired of his staring," she said bitterly, her gaze never leaving the parchment.

"Why are you still here? It's well past your curfew, Your Majesty."

"Curfew?" She looked up at the headmaster, who watched her warily, his hands braced on his desk. "Demons like us never sleep, Orias."

"I suppose you have a fair point."

She smiled ruefully, pulled her mask on, and left the room.

10

SHADOWS

LABRISDAY, NINETEENTH OF THE DRAGON MOON, YEAR 449 OF THE GODDESS

Days passed uneventfully, but tension hung heavy in the air. Seere kept to herself, exchanging very few words with anyone during and between classes. The once-lively conversations at meals were strained, punctuated by awkward silences.

Foras watched Seere more closely than ever. Whenever anyone asked what was going on between them, they responded with curt dismissals. Their clipped tones discouraged any attempts at further inquiry.

Evenings during their sparring sessions were extra tense. Rowan, who typically paired off with Foras to practice his skills at swordplay, received quite the beating each night. More than once, Seere had to replace Rowan with Enora or Achlys so that Foras could fight someone at a skill level more equal to his own.

When Labrisday came around, the fifth day of the week, Seere was more than relieved to find that it would only be her working with Felix that evening. Rowan had found himself a date, Achlys and Enora needed to use the library for homework, and Foras had no desire to be around without the rest of the group as a buffer.

This was how she found herself deflecting each of Felix's attacks late into the evening. The moonlight and lanterns cast dark shadows around them. The evening autumn air was cool, and the quiet was only broken by hooting owls and the clash of Felix's sword against Seere's dagger.

"Good," she said, stepping back as Felix lunged forward. "Keep your stance low, and watch your footing. You're too open on your left side."

Felix hummed in acknowledgment, adjusting his position and striking again. Seere parried with ease, her movements fluid and precise. The spar dragged on, neither of them in any rush to call it a night. Seere didn't question why Felix's usual companions weren't present—she preferred the solitude anyway. For her, it was enough to focus on Felix's form and technique, pushing away the lingering frustrations of the week.

Eventually, she called for a break. They lowered their blades. She crossed to the edge of the ring and leaned against the fencing as she watched Felix down his canteen of water. It was the first time she truly allowed herself to look at him—the first time they had been truly alone together.

After so many years, she wasn't sure what to make of him anymore. In so many ways, he was the same person he'd been when he was fifteen and she was fourteen. However, in many more ways, he was completely different.

Back then, he'd been entirely carefree. He walked with high shoulders, and they would banter and tease one another during sparring matches until they were on the ground laughing. He had been her first kiss. He had been her first true promise. He had been the one who broke the rigid wall built up within her by the assassin's academy.

Seven years later, he walked with shoulders that seemed to carry the weight of the world. His eyes carried a pain that she would never be able to share the burden of. He had built his rigid walls, and she would never be the one to tear them down.

"I can't imagine I'm all that interesting to stare at, Your Majesty," Felix said, snapping Seere out of her reverie.

"Your hair is sticking up in odd angles," she said simply.

"Can I ask about what's going on between you and Foras?"

Seere looked up at him, her gaze sharp. "Apparently, you can," she muttered, looking down at the soft dirt of the ring. "He is just convinced that I am harboring a dead princess within the walls of my kingdom."

Felix looked away, the pain in his eyes igniting brighter than ever. "She can't be dead," he whispered, shaking his head.

"If that's what you truly wish to believe," she murmured, pushing off the fencing. "Back to the center. Keep sparring with me."

However, as she spoke those words, she froze. Her gaze darted upward to the rafters of the stables, her sharp eyes catching the faintest flicker of movement.

"Felix, get down!" she shouted.

Felix hesitated for half a second, but it was long enough. A cloaked figure dropped from the shadows above, a blade gleaming in the moonlight as it arced toward him.

Seere surged forward, grabbing the figure mid-air and yanking them away from Felix. The assassin hit the ground hard, and Seere was on them in an instant, her knee pressing into their firm chest as she wrenched the blade from their grip.

The assassin thrashed beneath her, but Seere held firm. With one hand, she ripped back the silver mask with gold detailing they wore to reveal the face of a young man. He was unfamiliar to her, but his expression was one of cold resolve. Behind his right ear, she caught a glimpse of a snake tattoo. A mark that would identify him as a member of the Order of the Chimera.

"Who sent you?" she demanded, her voice low and dangerous.

The assassin glared up at her. He was silent, still fighting against her.

"Answer me!" she hissed, digging her knee into his chest painfully.

The man's lips curled into a defiant smirk. Before Seere even knew what was happening, he bit down hard, his jaw locking around something in his mouth.

"No!" she shouted, but it was too late. The assassin convulsed, gargled up foam, and then fell limp. He was little more than a corpse. A corpse with secrets upon secrets that she wanted to uncover.

She cursed under her breath, shoving herself off the body and turning to Felix. "Are you hurt?" she asked, rushing to search him for any sign of injury.

Felix shook his head quickly, his face pale. "I'm fine."

"His blade didn't nick you at all? It may have been laced. Are you absolutely certain?" she asked, taking his chin in her hand to turn his face side to side.

Gently, his hand cupped hers. "Seere, I am completely unharmed. Thanks to you," he assured her, lowering her hand from his face. "He didn't so much as scratch me."

"Good. We need to alert Orias," she said softly, glancing up towards the tower she knew his study was in. A heavy sigh escaped her as she grabbed Felix's wrist and guided him in that direction.

Mirroring six nights ago, Seere stormed into the Headmaster's study as if she owned the place. She was immediately met by the sight of Orias speaking quietly with Professor Vidal. However, whatever important conversation they were sharing hardly mattered to her at that moment.

"Orias," she called sharply, cutting through their conversation fully.

Orias frowned, setting his quill aside. "Seere, what is the meaning of—"

"There was an assassination attempt on Felix," she interrupted, her tone leaving no room for argument. "I subdued the assassin, but he poisoned himself before I could get answers."

Vidal stiffened, his hand instinctively going to the hilt of his sword. "Where's the body?" he asked.

"In the training yard," Seere answered.

Orias rose from his chair. "Professor, please escort His Highness to Andromal's dorm room and station guards outside of it," he ordered before his gaze fell on Seere. "You will come with me. I need to issue an alert to lock down the school, then we will investigate the body."

"Yes, Sir," Professor Vidal said, and Seere nodded her assent.

Felix looked as though he wanted to argue, but he said nothing. He gave Seere a wary look before he turned and followed Vidal from the room. Seere's gaze turned to Orias as he raced to a coat hanger to retrieve a heavy cloak for warmth.

"There's something you're withholding about the body," he said, sparing a glance at Seere. "What is it?"

She tapped the spot behind her ear. "He had a tattoo," she answered simply. "A snake."

Orias sighed heavily and nodded. "Very well. Let's go investigate properly," he said and headed for the door. "Alert every guard we pass to the threat."

THE TRAINING YARD was eerily quiet, the stillness broken only by the sound of Seere and Orias' boots crunching on the gravel. A cold breeze swept through the open space, making her shiver. Orias followed close behind, his robes rustling faintly as he carried a lantern that cast long, flickering shadows across the ground.

The assassin's body lay exactly where Seere had left it, sprawled awkwardly on the dirt. His eyes were open, glassy and lifeless. The faint smirk he'd worn in death was frozen on his pale lips.

Orias knelt beside the corpse, his expression grim. He set his lantern down and, with a gloved hand, rotated the corpse's head so that he could see the tattoo behind the ear. "He is indeed part of the serpent faction," he said, glancing up.

Seere had paused a few steps away, her arms crossed over her chest as her gaze examined the body. "Do you have any information on that faction? What sets them apart from the rest?" she questioned, wishing her sources had provided her with such information in the past.

"I suppose I forgot to explain that detail to you... The serpent faction is composed of assassins. The lions are soldiers, and the goats... are a bit more complicated. They keep everything operating smoothly within," he explained.

"They are tricky," Seere muttered. "How is it that you know so much about them?"

"That, my darling, is a tale for another day after I am at least four drinks in," Orias said, his attention swiftly returning to his examination of the body.

He carefully pried the man's lips open. The faint residue of poison clung to the assassin's teeth—a subtle but unmistakable sign of the capsule he had bitten down on.

"They train them well," Seere said, finally crossing over. "He used his death as a weapon against us. They cover their tracks fairly well..."

Orias hummed in agreement, pulling the assassin's cloak back to inspect his clothing. He searched with practiced efficiency, checking seams and hidden pockets. "That doesn't mean they don't carry clues," he said, more to himself than to her. "I have found many bodies carrying something from their employer. A token, a cipher..."

Seere tugged off the assassin's left boot with a sharp motion. Inside the hollowed sole was a small compartment, something that would easily go unnoticed by anyone else. With the tip of her dagger, she pried it open, finding a small strip of parchment. She opened it and frowned at the intricate symbols that she did not recognize.

"Do they ever write in a language you've never seen?" she asked, offering the slip to Orias.

Orias looked up at her, brow raised, before he reached out and took the parchment from her. His dark eyes wandered over the symbols before his brow furrowed in a frown, one that told her he was confused.

"Good eye," he said.

Seere shrugged, leaning closer as he put the parchment up to the light of the lantern. Even in the extra light, she couldn't recognize the words scrawled across it. "What is it?" she asked.

"I'm not certain," he said dryly. "Another language, to be sure. It'll take some time to decipher."

"But you can do it, right?" she asked.

"Most definitely," Orias said, his lips quirked into a faint smile. "I've been dealing with these kinds of things far longer than you have, Amaris."

Seere bristled at the use of her given name. "Don't call me that," she snapped.

Orias smirked. "Right, forgive me, *Seere*," he said. "I forget that Amaris is dead, as you claim..."

She shot a glare at him before her gaze shifted down to the body. She searched the corpse carefully. She found nothing more than a few carefully concealed weapons. Part of her wondered if the assassin knew who she was before he attacked or if she was truly a player he had not foreseen.

A chill ran down Seere's spine as she spared a glance up at Orias. She watched him tuck the parchment into one of his pockets, his gaze never leaving her. Even after she looked away from him, she could still feel his gaze on her as if searching her soul.

"Do you always stare so much?" she questioned bitterly.

"I'm merely observing," he said, his tone teasing.

"Observing or scrutinizing?" she quipped, finally pushing herself to her feet and meeting his gaze.

Orias leaned closer, the faintest hint of a smile on his lips. "Perhaps a bit of both."

Her heart skipped a beat. "If you're done 'observing,' I

think we should head inside and see if the guards found anything."

"I suppose that would be the next best thing to do," he said thoughtfully.

"You told me before that the Order wishes to revive Eulla by reuniting the continent under one ruler again. I don't see how killing Felix will do anything to further that goal," she said softly. "They are being obvious in their attacks, which means they aren't trying to incite a war by framing his death on me or Empress Selina."

"I don't understand what they are trying to accomplish by ending the prince's life," Orias admitted, falling into step beside Seere. "But that's why we have you here. To help us get to the bottom of it."

"I've been hired to save the person that I was meant to marry and then kill oh so long ago. The irony is not lost on me," Seere muttered, as they ascended the steps up to the fortress's side door. "What confuses me most is why the Order didn't use me to unify the realm under one ruler." Then Seere froze, her hand on the door as she turned and looked at Orias. "That's exactly what they were doing, wasn't it?"

Orias chuckled, crossing his arms as he eyed her curiously. "I thought you would have put that bit together long before now," he said, giving her a once-over. "You aren't nearly as clever as I had once believed."

"Forgive me if I've been a little distracted. I've had Foras on my back since I arrived," she said bitterly, glaring at the man before her with renewed resentment.

"So touchy. There is much we need to discuss, but tonight is not the night for it. Right now, I need to join the investigation that's underway. I bid you a goodnight, Seere," Orias said, as he slipped past her and into the fortress.

11

SKULKING

ESLADAY, TWENTY-THIRD OF THE DRAGON
MOON, YEAR 449 OF THE GODDESS

The school being stuck under lockdown for the past three days had everyone on edge, but for Seere, it provided extra cover for what she did best—moving unseen as she searched for something, anything, that might tell her more about the people who wanted Felix dead.

The fortress was shrouded in an uneasy stillness as she slipped through its dimly lit halls. She avoided patrols with practiced ease, her footsteps silent on the stone floors. Having walked through the fortress's halls hundreds of times before, she knew them like the back of her hand. This place had been more of a home to her than her palace in Envie, where she had been an unwanted bastard princess.

Seere paused as she reached a corner. Slowly, she peered around it and swiftly darted back when she caught sight of a guard walking her way. She glanced around the hall in a panic. There was no classroom to slip into. There was no potted plant to disappear behind. She found no alcove that would allow her to tuck herself into.

Focusing on herself and the shadows around her, she drew on a power she kept buried deep within her. She tugged on the magic like pulling on a rope that someone yanked back on in a game of tug-of-war. When she grasped it, she draped it over herself like a shroud and watched as her body blended in seamlessly with the walls, turning her entirely invisible.

Seere held her breath as the guard walked past her. She willed her heartbeat to slow, to ease her panic. She had never known a guard to walk along these tucked-away corridors that seemingly led to nothing. When she attended the assassin's academy, this had been a section of the school long forgotten.

It wasn't until the guard slipped away that she dropped her magic. Immediately, the whispers flooded into her mind, crashing against her skull viciously. It took every ounce of the discipline ingrained within her not to cry out. She still dropped to her knees, hands at her ears, as she dropped her forehead to the ground.

"Help me."

"Release me."

Tears spilled from Seere's eyes as she shoved her magic back down to the deepest parts of her. She buried it under that discipline she clung to, desperate to shut out the voices. Desperate to clear her mind of the tormented soul that claimed she was their savior.

When silence finally befell her mind, it was almost deafening. There was no noise in the hall. A pin drop could be heard in such silence.

Seere took a shaky breath, wiped the tears from her eyes, and staggered to her feet carefully. She used the wall as support as she finally rounded the corner, her legs wobbling like a newborn deer. Luckily, she didn't have to walk far before she reached the point in the hallway that few knew existed.

She tapped on the fourth petal on the inside of a rose engraved into the stone. The wall began to vibrate, buzzing with magical energy as it slowly dissolved from the rose into an archway that revealed a spiral staircase. A smirk tugged at her lips as she stepped through, glancing back only to make sure the wall reformed behind her.

When she turned back, her gaze fell to the skeleton in the center of the circular space. A smirk tugged at the corners of her lips. "Hello again, Theodorus," she said coolly. "Long time, no see."

Seere pressed herself close to the wall as she climbed the spiral stairs of the western tower. She regained control of her breath, and her legs no longer wobbled, but with a lack of railing, she needed to be careful. Goose flesh appeared on her skin at the chill of the stairwell, but still she climbed.

She had discovered the secret door by accident during her first year at the assassin's academy. She had been chased through the halls of the school by Theodorus, a fellow student who was far older and much larger than she had ever been. He had sought her death, wanting to end her after she had made him look like a fool in a sparring match because she had slipped poison into his breakfast.

He had managed to catch up to her after a long chase. He had thrown her into the wall, and the wall had given way. She had been quick to recover, quick to race to the top, and even quicker to shove him down the stairwell, sealing his fate. He had been her first kill, and no one had ever confirmed where or how he'd vanished. Seere had scrubbed her body raw back then, desperate to wash away the invis-ible mark of death that she still carried.

The western tower offered the best vantage point, which she discovered when she'd attended many years before. It would allow her to see nearly the full layout of the fortress to uncover what everyone else might have missed.

The stairs opened up to a wide, vacant space when she reached the top. There were no walls, only sturdy pillars supporting the steepled roof and railings to prevent someone from slipping off the edge. A smile tugged at her lips when she realized a handful of the pillows and blankets she'd brought up years before still remained. There was even a book she'd forgotten about, but it was well worn after years of being exposed to the weather.

She sighed softly and crossed to the railing, peering out at the world below. The view was a mix of fortress walls, torch-lit guard posts, and the dense forest that surrounded the stronghold. Seere's sharp eyes scanned the perimeter, noting the guards' movements and timing the intervals.

They were too slow. Too predictable. It was easy to imagine how an assassin might have slipped past. There were too many blind spots, too many places where shadows could hide a lurking figure.

Seere's mind worked rapidly, analyzing potential entry points: the south gate, which was less guarded at night; the storage entrance, where supplies came and went with minimal oversight; and the upper levels of the wall, where gaps in patrol patterns left entire extensions unguarded for minutes at a time.

She wasn't sure what Shax was thinking with the guard placements. Then again, she wasn't sure if it was Orias that she needed to blame.

As she was about to turn away, her eye caught a faint flicker of light in the distance. She leaned over the railing, narrowing her eyes as she focused on the source. It came from a cave, barely visible through the thick line of trees.

Seere descended the tower swiftly but silently, her movements smooth and practiced. When she got to the end, she prayed silently to whatever god might listen that no one stood on the other side of the wall. She had little ability to hide herself, much less a magical archway.

She tapped the rose and waited with bated breath as the archway disappeared once more. She only released her breath when she was certain no one else was around.

Slowly, Seere slipped back into the corridor like a shadow and rushed along the walls to find an exit. As she crept through the halls, she heard the sound of voices from an open doorway just ahead. Carefully, she pressed herself against the wall and peeked inside.

"Why are you so interested in the actions of the assassin queen? You never inquire about a student as often as you do about her," Professor Manfredonia questioned as he seated himself at a table in what looked to be a staff break room.

Orias sipped a mug of some sort of hot drink as he leaned against a counter. "Tell me you aren't just as curious about that one," he said, his voice a low drawl. "Seere attended this school when it was still an assassin's academy and was the youngest to ever graduate. It's intriguing."

"Ah, I was unaware of that," Professor Manfredonia murmured, shifting uncomfortably in his seat. "Well... Her Majesty is doing better than anyone else in my classes. She runs circles around Cotoria. It's also why I think she should be the leader of one of the teams."

"Amusing, is it not, that Cotoria is convinced she will be a general for her sister, and yet she can't outwit Seere in the slightest," Orias muttered, his gaze shifting to the doorway. "I already planned to make her the leader. I think it will be interesting to see how she fairs in battle, mock or not."

Seere froze as his gaze met hers. He smirked, tilting his head in the subtlest hint of acknowledgement. She spun around in the other direction and hurried down the hall. She had just rounded the corner when she heard the sound of footsteps following her, and she knew she had been caught.

"Seere," Orias called softly behind her. "Shouldn't you be in your room?"

Seere sighed and turned to face the Headmaster. "No, I'm a little busy at the moment," she said coolly. "Shouldn't you be translating that note we found?"

A smirk decorated Orias' lips as he crossed over to her. "I'm working on it. Very well, I won't keep you then. Just don't go getting yourself caught by anyone else," he said, his gaze wandering over her curiously.

"I don't intend to," she said coolly, before she turned on her heel and continued down the hall.

Finally, she reached one of the smaller exits near the kitchens and paused, listening intently. The sound of guards' footsteps echoed faintly down the corridor. Seere pressed herself into a dark corner, waiting as the guard passed, oblivious to her presence.

The moment the coast was clear, she eased the door open, slipping into the cool night air. Her gaze wandered over the thick stone walls that surrounded the school, searching for the small exit that was tucked away behind a dorm building.

She was nearly to the door when a chill ran up her spine.

Gooseflesh prickled her skin. She was being watched. Seere spun around, expecting to find Orias. However, she was instead met with the sight of Felix, his hands flying in the air as if in surrender.

Frustration flared within her. "What the hell are you doing out of your dorm room?" she hissed, storming towards him.

"I saw you from my window," he explained, his voice soft but insistent. "You're the only one here with lavender hair, after all. I thought you might be in trouble."

Seere reflexively reached up to her hair, but then dropped her hand and glared at Felix. "I'm not in trouble. But you will be if you keep wandering around at night when there are assassins after you."

Felix crossed his arms, his expression stubborn. "I'm not leaving you out here alone."

Exhaling sharply, Seere's gaze darted between Felix and the wall. With a reluctant sigh, she stormed over and grabbed the prince by the arm, leading him back to the dormitory. "Fine. Let's go."

The walk was quiet, the tension between them palpable. Once they stopped before their doors, Felix turned to her, his brow furrowed. "You should get some rest, too, you know."

Seere rolled her eyes. "Don't lecture me, Felix."

However, as they stood there in the dimly lit hallway, something softened in her expression. With a reluctant sigh, she gestured toward her door. "If you're so worried, you can come in for a while. There are no classes in the morning, so I don't care how late you're up as long as you stay safe," she said, pulling the key to her dorm room out of her pocket.

Felix smiled faintly, following her inside. Whatever

secrets the cave held would have to wait. For now, Seere's focus shifted to the prince in front of her, and the tangled web of truths she kept hidden from him.

Inside her room, the air was warm, faintly perfumed by the rose sachets tucked in the corners of the room. She kept her space modest and neatly organized. Beyond the rose sachets, she had no intention of personalizing a room she wasn't sure she would be in for very long.

"Sit," she instructed, nodding toward the table.

Felix obeyed, sinking into one of the chairs with his usual easy grace. His dark brown hair caught the dim light of the lantern, which cast a golden hue through it. Seere moved to a nearby cabinet, retrieving a small bottle of wine and two glasses.

"You drink?" he asked, raising an eyebrow as she poured.

"I have to if I want to survive this place," she teased, her voice steady. She set one glass in front of him but left hers untouched. "I don't drink often, but you look like you could use it. Running around after me in the dead of night—what were you thinking?"

Felix chuckled lightly, swirling the wine in his glass. "I was thinking I didn't want you to get hurt."

Seere paused, her gaze narrowing slightly as she leaned against the table. "I don't need protecting, Felix."

"That doesn't mean you have to do this alone." His tone was gentle, but there was a firmness beneath it. "You've been on edge since the dinner with Captain Fraser and his family. You barely talk to anyone anymore, not even Enora or Achlys. You think I wouldn't notice?"

Seere looked away, her jaw tightening. "You know, I was brought here to act as your guard, not as a friend. That's what I'm doing."

Felix sighed, setting his glass down with a quiet clink. "Maybe that's true. But I care about you, Seere. And if something's wrong, I want to help."

"You can help me by staying safe," she said softly, her gaze shifting to meet his. "I need you to stay protected. If not with me, then with Foras or the headmaster. I imagine you could even find shelter with Achlys."

Felix sighed heavily. "Fine. I suppose I'm a little sick of losing people, so forgive me if I'm concerned for your safety."

Seere tensed, staring down at her glass of wine. Her reflection stared back at her in the liquid. She could see her pale eyes, her lavender hair, and the mask that covered her mouth and nose.

"I never wanted to get married," he admitted, his voice quiet. "At least, not until I met her."

"Amaris?" Seere asked, though she already knew the answer.

"At first, I resented her. I didn't like the idea of my future being decided for me, so naturally, I blamed her. However, she—she surprised me. She came to visit for the summer. I was fifteen and she was fourteen. She is... was strong, clever, and stubborn. She challenged me in ways no one else ever had. By the time she left, I—"

He stopped, shaking his head as if clearing a thought. "It doesn't matter. She's gone now."

Seere sighed softly, fingering the stem of her glass before she finally set it down on the table. "I met her once," she murmured, offering Felix one half-truth. "In the village that was burned. She had talked about making her way to Noctivagus... She said there was someone there she was going to go see, someone she loved."

Felix wiped a tear from his face, his gaze on the floor. It was that tear that nearly had Seere tearing off her mask. It was that tear that made her want to drop to her knees and beg forgiveness for her lies. She could simply reveal the hidden truth under the leather wrap of the dagger strapped to her thigh, and he would know.

"What was your childhood like?" he asked. She was grateful for the subject change. It distracted her from her temptation of revealing her identity.

Seere thought for a moment, wondering how much and what exactly was safe to tell him. "There isn't much to share. My father sent me to the assassin's academy when I was a child. Said it would make me strong."

"Well, it did," Felix said softly.

"It certainly taught me how to survive," she said. "There were constant tests and lessons in deceit and death. Betrayals were unraveling behind every corner. Many times, there would be students trying to kill me specifically. I had no friends until Shax decided to adopt me as his little sister."

"And how did you manage to build a kingdom at such a young age?" he asked.

"I was fifteen or sixteen when I began that process. I collected a lot of money and recruited former schoolmates whom I viewed as allies. They helped me organize the people who lived on the island already. They helped me promise protection to those who felt unsafe. Then we built up trade with the Eulla blossoms because they grow so abundantly on the island," she explained, a smile tugging at the corners of her lips. "Eventually, people flocked to the island from all over the realm. It was such an honor to be able to care for and protect these people. The fact that they put their trust in me was more than I ever hoped for."

"You truly love your kingdom," Felix said softly.

"I do. I really do," she whispered.

"You've done so much. More than I ever have," he murmured.

"You're a prince," she pointed out.

"And yet, I've never built anything with my own hands," he countered. "Not like you have."

The conversation carried on late into the light, until Felix's eyes began to droop and his words grew slower. Seere finally rose, taking his glass and setting it aside.

"Go to bed, Felix," she said gently.

He smiled sleepily, rising to his feet. "Thank you, Seere. For everything."

He paused at her door. His gaze lingered on Seere's face, and she prayed silently that he wouldn't recognize her eyes there. However, rather than saying anything, he reached up hesitantly and brushed a stray strand of hair behind her ear. Then he smiled and left the room, slipping into his own just across the hall from hers.

As she watched him disappear into his room, her heart felt heavier than ever. Once, that gentle brush of his hand would have made her stomach flutter with excitement. However, it no longer caused a bashful swoop. Rather, she felt only weighed down by everything that had once been between them.

When she finally turned back into her room, she tore off her mask and downed her wine glass.

12

NEWS

ATYSDAY, TWENTY-FOURTH OF THE DRAGON
MOON, YEAR 449 OF THE GODDESS

When the weekend ended and Atysday rolled around, Seere found that the fortress was electric with anticipation. There was a palpable buzz sweeping through the students as whispers of the upcoming Wargames filled every corner.

Seere found herself sitting in the class for courtly protocol, this time at a table with Enora, Rowan, Felix, and an overly enthusiastic noble from Envie who had been monopolizing the conversation for the better part of fifteen minutes. Seere's patience was wearing thin as she stirred her otherwise untouched tea, her eyes darting between the group.

Enora, sensing her friend's quiet frustration, leaned in with a conspiratorial smile. "You look like you'd rather be anywhere else," she whispered.

Seere huffed softly. "You're not wrong. But unfortunately, fleeing the classroom would probably be frowned upon."

"Only slightly," Enora teased. She took a sip of her tea, then set her cup down with a flourish, earning an approving nod from Professor Viné. "Anyway, you should try to enjoy the moment because soon enough, we'll all be thrown into the chaos of the Wargames."

Seere froze, removing her hand from the spoon in her cup. "Wargames?"

Enora's face lit up with excitement. "Oh, yes! It's the highlight of the year's beginning. Everyone gets split into two teams, and we compete in a grand war game. It's not just a free-for-all—there's strategy, objectives, and a whole lot of swordplay involved. It's meant to test what we know at the beginning of the year with little training."

Rowan leaned back in his chair, grinning as he added, "It's like a battlefield simulation, but it's more dangerous than you'd think. People have gotten pretty serious injuries before—nothing fatal, though."

Seere frowned, her fingers tightening around the delicate porcelain handle of her cup. "And when were we going to be told about this?"

Enora giggled. "Oh, Seere, they always spring it on us at the last minute! It keeps things exciting. But don't worry, you'll do great. You're practically a seasoned warrior already."

"Who decides the teams?" Seere asked, her tone sharp.

"It's based on where you're from. Noctivagus versus Envie, naturally. That's how it's always been. They like to stoke the rivalry between the two nations. Though..." He gave Seere a curious look. "I don't know which side you'll be on. You're not technically from either kingdom, are you?"

"I was born in Envie, but I'd rather not be on the side of Cotoria. She'd make my life hell," Seere said, sparing a glance at Felix, who was talking with Foras at another table with Achlys and Alsariph. She needed to ensure that she was there to protect him. Being thrust into the spotlight of Wargames wasn't something she relished, especially not with so many potential dangers at play.

Enora leaned closer, her voice dropping to a whisper. "If I had to guess, Orias will probably assign you to Noctivagus. Considering all the time you have to spend with Felix, after all."

Seere's lips twitched into a faint smirk behind her mask. "I don't think Orias' decisions are ever that straightforward."

Their conversation was interrupted by Professor Viné, who approached their table with a serene smile. "Enora, lovely posture. Seere, perfect as always, if only you'd enjoy your tea. Rowan, hold your teacup a little higher."

The group complied, except for Seere, the atmosphere of their table shifting to one of disciplined silence until the professor moved on to another group.

As soon as she was out of earshot, Rowan rolled his eyes. "She acts like we're all going to tea with a king tomorrow."

"You're having tea with a queen," Enora quipped as she turned back to Seere. Her tone swiftly took on a more serious note again. "You'll see tonight. They always announce the teams during dinner. Just... try not to let it rattle you too much. It's honestly more fun than it sounds."

"Fun," Seere echoed dryly. Her thoughts were already moving ahead to the challenges the Wargames would bring. She wasn't worried about herself—she could handle any opponent. But the thought of Felix stepping onto a battle-field, even a simulated one, made her blood run cold.

Across the table, Rowan and Enora shared a glance, sensing the tension in her silence. It was clear they had no idea what stressed her so badly.

"You're the best fighter I've ever seen, Seere," Enora said

softly, her voice full of reassurance. "You'll be amazing. I'm sure of it."

Seere gave a curt nod, returning to the little spoon in her tea. But her mind was already elsewhere, calculating the steps she'd need to take to ensure Felix's safety—and her anonymity—through whatever chaos lay ahead.

THE DINING HALL buzzed with conversation as students gathered for the evening meal. Seere sat between Felix and Enora. Rowan and Foras sat across from them. Her attention was divided between her untouched plate and the lively chatter around her.

The sound of a spoon clinking against the goblet drew the room to silence. All heads turned to the raised dais at the front, where headmaster Orias stood, his ever-present enigmatic smile firmly in place. Seere had yet to see him stand at the front, acting as headmaster. She was again struck by how young he was for such a position.

"Good evening, students," he began, his voice warm yet commanding enough to carry through the hall. "I hope you've all settled into your routines and are flourishing in your studies. I want to start this off by informing you that the lockdown has been lifted upon finding no further breaches in security. Now that that's out of the way... As you all very well know, this school is not simply about academics. Here, we forge warriors, leaders, and strategists. And so, it is time for one of Malphas University's most anticipated traditions: the Wargames."

A ripple of excitement swept through the hall. Students leaned in, whispering and speculating with their tablemates.

"Indeed," Orias continued, holding up a hand to quiet

the crowd. "For those new to this tradition, allow me to explain. The Wargames are a grand exercise of strategy, combat, and teamwork. The student body will be divided into two teams, representing Noctivagus and Envie. Each team will have a designated leader, chosen for their exceptional skills and leadership potential."

Seere's stomach twisted uneasily.

"This year," Orias went on, his tone light yet deliberate, "we will hold the battle in the abandoned village of Thornmoor, just north of our walls. It will serve as our battlefield."

Seere froze, her gaze snapping to Orias. His own eyes shifted to her, and they seemed to soften in a way she had never seen before. *Thornmoor.* The name rang in her ears, a haunting echo of a place she knew all too well—a village that had burned because she had taken refuge within its wooden walls.

Felix touched her arm lightly, breaking her trance. "You okay?"

"Fine," Seere murmured.

"And now, for the moment you've all been waiting for—the announcement of team leaders," Orias said, smile widening.

If the hall hadn't been silent before, it was then. The anticipation was thick in the air.

"For the team representing Envie, the leader will be..." Orias paused for effect, drawing out the tension. "Achlys Alerie."

Cheers erupted from one side of the room as Achlys, seated with Alsariph and a few other students, stood and offered a modest nod. Cotoria, sitting a few students down from her, clapped politely but wore a tight smile, her eyes narrowing.

Seere's brows lifted in mild surprise. She'd fully expected Cotoria to lead the Envie team.

Once the cheers subsided, Orias raised his hand again. "And now, for the team representing Noctivagus. This year's leader will be... Her Majesty, Queen Seere."

The hall exploded with noise, much to Seere's surprise and chagrin. It was only then that she realized what she'd overheard Professor Manfredonia and Orias discussing only a couple of nights back.

Rowan slapped the table with an exuberant laugh. "You're the leader!" he shouted.

Enora clapped her hands together, grinning brightly. "Oh, we aren't losing this battle!"

Felix's cheer was the loudest, his enthusiasm unrestrained. "I had a feeling it would be you," he said, lowering his voice and touching her hand.

Seere, however, barely heard them. Her mind raced, the weight of the announcement settling heavily on her shoulders. She quietly cursed Professor Manfredonia and Orias for daring to put her in such a visible position. The danger it posed—both to her identity and to the safety of those under her command—was immense.

Across the hall, Cotoria glared daggers at her, so sharp it could have killed. Seere met her eyes briefly, a cool indifference masking her unease, before turning her gaze to Orias, who watched her with a look of mild amusement.

"The battle will take place a week from today on Esladay, the thirty-first day of the month of the Dragon Moon. The objective is to secure key locations and capture the opposing team's flag. No fatal injuries. On the point of injuries, they are expected, but will be treated promptly by healers stationed on-site," Orias said, outlining the rules. "Remember, this is not only a test of your skills but also a chance to forge bonds with your peers and demonstrate values of leadership, strategy, and camaraderie. I look forward to witnessing your brilliance."

As Orias stepped down, the hall erupted into excited chatter once more.

Seere exhaled slowly, her gaze distant. She was startled when she felt Felix squeeze her hand, having forgotten that he'd taken it in his. "You will be amazing, Seere. I'll follow your lead without question."

She met his eyes, her resolve hardening. "Good. I won't tolerate hesitation on the battlefield."

Enora laughed, breaking the tension. "Spoken like a true leader already."

THAT NIGHT, Seere found herself staring out at the stars in the western tower. She sat against one of the pillars and pressed into the railing connected to it. It was quiet, the only sound being the faint whisper of the wind. The cold air bit at her skin, but she barely noticed, too preoccupied with the chaos of her thoughts.

She was supposed to lead a Wargames in a place haunted by her past, and the weight of it pressed heavily on her chest. Her fingers fidgeted idly with her mask that she had long since pulled off, seeking some semblance of calm.

A soft cough broke the silence. Seere's instincts kicked in immediately—she was on her feet, dagger drawn, before she even registered the figure stepping into the room.

"Easy, Seere," came the familiar voice of Orias, his tone calm and unthreatening. She let out a sharp breath, lowering her blade. "Orias," she muttered, her voice edged with annoyance. "Do you make a habit of sneaking up on people?"

He chuckled, holding his hands up in mock surrender. "Not intentionally, I assure you. May I join you?"

Seere hesitated, but nodded. Slowly, she sank back to the floor, one of her old, musty pillows acting as a cushion. Orias took a seat just opposite her, his posture more relaxed than she had ever seen as he gazed out into the night. For several long moments, neither of them spoke.

"Are you angry with me?" Orias asked, looking over at Seere finally.

"Why did you make me the leader of a team?" she asked.

He tilted his head, considering her question. "Because it's the safest option—for you and everyone else."

Seere frowned. "Safest? How do you figure that?"

"You're easily the most skilled tactician in the school," he replied easily. "With you leading, you can control the flow of the battle. That means fewer injuries and fewer surprises. And," he added slowly, "it keeps you in a position where you can protect Felix far easier."

Her lips pressed into a thin line, but she couldn't argue with his logic. "Fine," she muttered. "But why Thornmoor? Of all places, why choose that village?"

Orias leaned back against the cold stone pillar, his expression thoughtful. "Because it's abandoned. There are no civilians to get caught in the crossfire, no unnecessary casualties. It's ideal for our purposes."

Seere huffed, crossing her arms. "A good plan," she admitted begrudgingly. "But I still don't like it."

Orias laughed, the sound warm and light as he nudged Seere's foot with his own playfully. "Isn't that what it means to be a leader? Doing things we hate? You don't have to like it, Seere. You just have to make it work."

She rolled her eyes, but allowed a small smile to tug at the corners of her lips.

After a brief silence, she turned back to Orias. "How did you know about this tower, anyway? I thought I was the only one who came here."

Orias' smile turned enigmatic. "I found it years ago. Back when I attended the assassin's academy."

Seere's eyebrows shot up in surprise. "You attended the academy?"

He nodded. "I did. Graduated long before you took the crown of your little domain."

She leaned forward, studying him more closely. She tried to place his raven-dark hair, his green eyes, and his sharp features. "When did you graduate?"

A faint smirk played on his lips. "It was your first year there. You were what—ten? Eleven?"

Seere blinked, stunned. "I... I don't remember seeing you."

Orias waved a hand dismissively. "I wouldn't expect you to. I was just another face in a sea of students. But *you*," he said, his tone softening, "were impossible to forget. Regardless of how young you'd been, even then, you had a fire in you, a determination that set you apart from anyone else."

She flushed slightly at his compliment, turning her gaze back to the window. "I was a child," she murmured.

"A remarkable child," he corrected. "And now, an even more remarkable queen."

Seere huffed, unsure how to respond. The compliment unsettled her, not because it was untrue, but because it felt oddly personal coming from him. Orias was impossible to read.

"You are quite the puzzle," she whispered. "I can't figure you out at all."

Orias smirked. "Oh, good. That means I am keeping even the Assassin Queen on her toes. Oh, and I had a question for you. Do you know anything about the skeleton that sits at the base of the stairs leading up to this tower?" he asked.

"Theodorus. I don't know if you ever met him... but he tried to kill me during my first year. He was my first kill," she said softly, lowering her gaze.

"I thought your first kill was Malphas himself," Orias said, sounding genuinely shocked.

Seere winced, her skin crawling uncomfortably at the mention of the former headmaster. "No, and I didn't kill either of them intentionally," she whispered, wrapping her arms around herself. "In both cases, it was self-defense."

"What do you mean?" he questioned, the color seeming to drain from his face. "What happened between you and Malphas?"

Seere loosed a breath as she picked at the stone floor absently. "I was only fourteen... He cornered me after my graduation ceremony while my guard was down. He was advancing on me—" She shook her head, wishing she could erase the memory. "It was a choice between jumping off this tower that night and making a spectacle of myself or *his* death. And I wanted nothing more than to live."

"Seere," Orias breathed. "I am so sorry."

"It's in the past now," she said. "It hardly matters anymore."

"No, it matters plenty," he argued. "You shouldn't have had to live through such an ordeal."

Seere shrugged, her gaze lifting to meet his, her brow furrowing slightly. "Why do you care? I was under the impression you still hated me."

Orias was silent for a long moment as he gazed at her. His expression was filled with something new, something she hadn't seen on him before. There was regret and horror behind his dark eyes. "I never told you why Verrine Sallos killed your parents, did I?" he asked softly.

"No."

"It was to avenge his father, Malphas. A man who did not deserve vengeance," he whispered.

"I told you that I really don't care that they're dead," she said. "But things would have been much easier if I hadn't been found standing over their bodies. My sisters wouldn't be monsters, Envie wouldn't be suffering..."

Orias stood and leaned against the railing, his expression unreadable as he stared down at the world below. Seere got to her own feet and stood beside him. She wanted to know what ran through his thoughts. She wanted to know why he seemed so frustrated by her past, as if he felt personally responsible for it.

Finally, he looked at her again, his gaze filled with something entirely impossible to decipher. "I'm sorry, Amaris. You didn't deserve any of it," he said and turned to leave. "Get some rest. Don't fret over the Wargames. You will be safe."

Seere watched him go, her mind still spinning. However, it was no longer caused by the Wargames, but by Orias.

13

PREPARATIONS

IKTUNEDAY, TWENTY-SEVENTH OF THE
DRAGON MOON, YEAR 449 OF THE GODDESS

The days leading up to the Wargames were a blur of preparation and tension. Before Seere knew it, she had less than two days to prepare and figure out a strategy. During her uncle's classes, they went over the layout of the battlefield that would be Thornmoor, which helped to give Seere ideas on where everything was and where to station soldiers. However, none of it was going to be simple.

Each evening, Seere pushed Felix harder in their training sessions, refining his techniques and honing his reflexes. He was improving steadily, but her sharp eyes caught every mistake, and she didn't let him rest until he corrected them.

However, their nightly sessions were rarely private. Cotoria and Malkyn often stationed themselves nearby, their thinly veiled intent clear. Cotoria's gaze was calculating as if trying to dissect Seere's movements and uncover her strategies.

"You're still leaving your left side open," Seere said softly as she crossed over to offer Felix his water canteen. "I can't have you getting hurt during these Wargames."

"It's like you expect to die," Rowan said, panting heavily.

"Perhaps I do," she said, leaning back against the fencing. Her gaze shifted to the sky and the stars that hung bright overhead.

"Quite the leader, aren't you, Seere?" Cotoria called out. "Is this your grand strategy? Babysitting the prince while the rest of us actually prepare for war?"

"This isn't war," Rowan said, frowning at Cotoria.

Malkyn snickered, her arms crossed. "You'd think a queen would have a better grasp on her priorities."

Seere ignored them. Instead, she turned away and started resetting her training equipment. She hoped that, if she paid them no mind, they would eventually grow bored with her.

"Not going to say anything? Did you lose your tongue while you were kissing up to Orias to get this position?" Cotoria jeered.

"Enough," Felix snapped, stepping between Cotoria and Seere. "I think you should focus on your own training rather than wasting our time."

Cotoria raised an eyebrow, her smirk widening. "Touchy, are we?"

Seere looked up as Felix stormed towards her, though when he spoke, his tone was gentle. "Let's go inside."

"Right," she said, looking to Rowan and Foras. "I want to speak with each of you anyway."

Felix led the way after retrieving his sword. His posture was stiff, irritation flashing in his eyes. Rowan fell into step beside Seere, Foras following not far behind them.

"Your Majesty, you better watch your back in the upcoming battle," Cotoria called, flipping her sword in her hand.

"If you kill Her Majesty, there will be a war, Cotoria," Foras growled.

Seere glanced over her shoulder and offered Foras the slightest nod before she placed her hand on Felix's back and ushered him into the dorms. Once inside, she guided them to her room. Foras looked entirely uncomfortable entering, but he followed anyway.

Scattered across Seere's dining table was a pile of papers and books filled with battle strategies. "All right," she said, her voice steady but commanding, "we need to finalize our plan for the battle."

The three boys settled around her small table, waiting expectantly.

"Foras," she began, fixing him with a sharp gaze. "I'm putting you in command."

"What?" Felix exclaimed, sitting up straighter. "That's your role."

"Just listen for a moment," Seere said, pacing the length of the room. "Cotoria will target me. She's predictable, and her ego will demand she take me out personally. If I can draw her and likely the rest of their most powerful players away, it will cripple Achlys' strategy. While they're focused on me, Foras will have free rein to lead our forces and capture their forts and flags."

Felix frowned, his jaw tight. "You're putting yourself in unnecessary danger."

"It's a decent plan, if not half of one. Cotoria is immensely proud. She won't be able to resist going after Seere, especially after their first sparring match. Taking her out early could tip the scales in our favor," Foras said. "Seere, if you can subdue Cotoria and whatever allies she gathers, I know you will have no problem stealthing around to capture flags behind their backs."

"My thoughts precisely," Seere agreed.

"And what if something goes wrong? You said it yourself just a moment ago, if Seere were to die, there would be war," Felix argued, glaring at Foras.

"No, there wouldn't," Seere said softly. "And I have faced far worse problems than Cotoria. Trust me. I can handle them. Foras, I have ideas if you wish to discuss them."

"I would, actually," Foras said.

Seere paused in her pacing and pulled a seat up at the table. Carefully, she rifled through the many papers she'd scribbled on before she found the one she was searching for. "We're playing a game of deception because that's what I do best."

An hour passed swiftly as Seere discussed her strategies until she was certain Foras had them down—though it was Felix's interjections that took up most of the time. It wasn't until Rowan had dozed off that she decided it would be best to call it a night.

"Get some sleep while you can," she said softly, as she stood by the door to see them out. "I imagine most of us aren't sleeping the night of."

As the boys left, Felix lingered at her door. His gaze bore into hers, worry etched across his face. "Are you sure about what you're doing?"

"I am," she said firmly, placing her hand on his shoulder. She gave it a gentle squeeze, hoping it offered some semblance of comfort. "Goodnight, Felix."

· · ·

Seere sat perched on the windowsill of her second-floor dormitory, her silhouette blending into the darkness. She glanced down at the courtyard, ensuring the coast was clear.

With a sharp exhale, she gripped the windowsill and swung herself out, her movements fluid and practiced. Years of training at the assassin's academy and within her kingdom had made her adept at navigating tight spaces and silent descents. She braced herself against the rough stone wall, her boots finding purchase on the uneven surface.

Step by step, she lowered herself, her cloak trailing behind her like a shadow. When she reached the decorative ledge just above the first floor, she crouched, pausing to scan her surroundings. A guard rounded the corner of the courtyard below, his lantern casting long, flickering shadows.

Seere pressed herself flat against the wall, her heart steady as she waited. She counted the guard's steps, timing his pace until he disappeared out of sight. Only then did she drop silently to the ground, her landing cushioned by the soft grass.

The cool night air brushed against her face as she pulled her hood lower, ensuring her lavender hair remained concealed. She wasn't about to have another incident with Felix catching her because of her hair color.

She headed to the hidden exit in the fortress wall, though if guards patrolled this path, they might have already discovered it. She crept along the wall, hiding herself in the shrubbery that grew around it until she found the crevice in the wall.

With an amused huff, she got on her stomach and carefully army-crawled her way through. The squeeze was tighter than she remembered. At eleven, she'd fit through it without a problem. Of course, she wasn't eleven anymore.

When she finally got to the other side, the hills rose steeply, their jagged edges casting deep shadows. The cave she had seen from the tower loomed ahead, dark and undisturbed.

She hurried inside, her footsteps silent on the cave floor as she walked through its long tunnel. She searched the floor for footsteps, frowning when she saw no tracks that indicated a human or even a creature had walked through.

The deeper she went, the more the space opened up into a small chamber. At its center, the ground had been disturbed—scuffed dirt and faint indentations where something heavy might have been dragged or placed.

But there were no footprints. No tools. No signs of life.

Seere's frustration grew as she examined the area. Someone had been there, but they had been meticulous in covering their tracks. She crouched by the disturbed earth, brushing it lightly with her fingers. The patterns reminded her of sigils or runes, though they were faint and incomplete.

Her thoughts raced. She wondered if it had been a meeting place at one point. Part of her suspected the Order. However, another part of her believed such a thing was too far-fetched.

A faint sound from outside the cave snapped her attention back. She extinguished the glow in her palm, wincing as the whispers flooded her mind once more. Still, she unsheathed her dagger and pressed herself against the wall, determined to remain hidden.

The noise passed—a bird taking flight, its wings rustling against the air. Seere let out a slow breath, her grip on the dagger loosening.

The cave held more questions than answers, but she

couldn't risk staying longer. She retraced her steps, her mind a churn of theories and suspicions.

As she slipped back through the crevice of the fortress wall and climbed into her room, she resolved to keep an even closer eye on the people around her. Someone knew more than they were letting on, and she intended to find out who.

14

———

THORNMOOR

ATYSDAY, THIRTY-FIRST OF THE DRAGON
MOON, YEAR 449 OF THE GODDESS

At precisely three in the morning on the day of the Wargames, Seere found herself dressed and waiting at the front of the school to load into one of the many carriages lined up. She was surrounded by groggy students, all of whom were still brimming with anticipation despite the early hour.

Beside her, Rowan stood with his head resting on Foras' shoulder as he attempted to sleep standing up. Enora and Foras looked to be surprisingly alert. Felix, on the other hand, didn't appear to have slept at all.

Seere stepped up to stand beside Felix, shifting her grip on the messenger bag that hung from her shoulder. "You don't have to worry so much," she said gently.

Felix looked up at her and then away again, a frustrated sigh escaping his lips. "I know," he said. "But I can't seem to help it."

A smile graced her lips as she nudged his shoulder with her own. "We will all be perfectly fine," she assured, then pointed towards a carriage. "Get in before someone else claims that one."

Felix nodded and called Foras, Rowan, and Enora over, each of them heading for the carriage. Seere followed suit. She had been about to climb in when she caught the sound of her name being called over the chatter of the students around her.

"Seere," Orias called, his tone calm but firm as he approached.

She turned, hand on the doorframe. "What is it?"

"Ride with me. I need to speak with you."

Her gaze flickered back to Felix, who watched her with curiosity, but she turned away and nodded to Orias. "Of course."

Orias gestured to his carriage at the front of the convoy. She hesitated only briefly before following him. He held the door open, and she slipped inside, settling down across from him as the carriage lurched into motion, leading the procession. She set her bag down on the seat, her gaze shifting to the window.

The carriage rocked gently as it began its descent down the mountain. Inside, the warm glow of a lantern suspended from the ceiling illuminated the finely upholstered seats. Seere sat stiff-postured as Orias watched her. His sharp, calculating gaze lingered on her as though he could see through every layer of secrecy she had painstakingly constructed.

"You've been busy," he said, his tone conversational but edged with something deeper.

Seere tilted her head, feigning casual curiosity. "Have I?"

Orias' lips curved into a faint smile, though his eyes

betrayed nothing. "I've heard about the plan you've devised with Foras. A bold move. Risky."

Seere sighed, leaning back in her seat as the rhythmic clatter of the carriage wheels filled the silence. After a moment's hesitation, she reached up and tugged off her mask, revealing her face to the dim light.

"I know it's a gamble," she admitted, her tone turning soft. "But it's calculated. Cotoria will focus everything they have on me. That's her way—direct, almost to a fault. She won't expect me to use that against her."

Orias frowned slightly. "You're betting everything on Cotoria's predictability."

"I'm betting on myself," Seere countered firmly. Her gaze met his, steady despite the weight of his scrutiny. "I've faced worse odds than this. I'll draw their attention, and the rest of the team will take care of the objectives. It'll work."

Orias studied her for a moment longer before leaning back into his seat. "Rumor has it Cotoria intends to ambush you with her strongest allies."

"I'm counting on it," Seere replied, a small smirk tugging at the corner of her lips. She turned her gaze to the window, watching the valley below as it drew slowly nearer.

For a while, neither of them spoke, the silence punctuated only by the steady rhythm of hooves against the path.

"Tell me," Orias said eventually, breaking the stillness. "Why do you insist on taking these risks? You could lead from the rear, command with the advantage of distance. Yet you choose to place yourself in harm's way."

Seere's expression didn't falter, but her hands tightened in her lap. "Because the front is where I need to be. I've learned that people don't follow orders—they follow strength. If they see me standing firm, unshaken, they'll fight harder. They'll believe we can win."

Orias nodded slowly, as if weighing her words. "So you do all of this to boost morale?" he asked, his gaze flickering to her hands. "What about your own morale?"

"That doesn't matter," she said. "My morale means nothing compared to my soldiers."

"The general's morale means everything in a battle," he argued, leaning closer to Seere. "It prevents them from making fatal mistakes."

She shook her head, crossing her arms over her chest as she settled into the corner of the carriage. "What are you trying to say?" she asked.

He looked at her as though she were a puzzle he couldn't piece together. There was concern in his dark eyes and something else that she couldn't decipher. Finally, he dropped his gaze and leaned away with a frustrated sigh. "Never mind it," he said.

Orias didn't press any further, and neither did she. However, the quiet weight of his last words and the way he had looked at her lingered in the air between them. She didn't understand his cryptic words or his expression, but she didn't dare dig into them. It would only lead to unwanted distractions.

As the conversation shifted to lighter topics—trivial details about the Wargames preparations and logistics—Seere found herself relaxing, if only slightly. Orias had an uncanny way of drawing out truths she didn't want to admit, but he also seemed to understand her in ways few others could.

· · ·

HOURS LATER, as the carriage finally rolled to a stop on the outskirts of Thornmoor, Seere adjusted her mask, securing it back into place. She paused as she stepped out of the carriage, her boots crunching against the frosty grass. She stood still for a moment, her pale green eyes scanning the wreckage before her. It had been years since she last set foot in the village, and the sight of it hit harder than she'd expected. Thornmoor had once been a peaceful settlement, but her actions had reduced it into a desolate wasteland.

The crumbling buildings with caved-in roofs or missing walls had once been homes, bakeries, and general goods stores. The streets, now overgrown, had been a place where children played and merchants hawked their wares. Seere could almost see the ghosts of those that she'd killed indirectly. She could still hear the screams of the condemned rage through her memories. She had suppressed them for so long, but they returned with a vengeance.

Her gloved hands tightened into fists at her sides, the weight of the past pressing against her like a shroud.

A gentle touch on her arm startled her from her thoughts. She turned her head to see Orias, who had remained by her side after disembarking. His face was calm, but his eyes held an unspoken understanding. He squeezed her arm briefly—a surprising, fleeting gesture of comfort—before moving toward the other faculty members who were gathering near the village's entrance.

Seere watched him leave, the lingering warmth of his touch almost foreign to her. It was startling how much such a small action twisted her insides. She shook it off and focused on the task ahead.

She walked toward her team's side of the village, where everyone was already gathering. The banners of Noctivagus fluttered in the breeze, their dark blue and gold hues standing starkly against the gray ruins. Students buzzed with nervous energy, their chatter mixing with the occasional clang of swords being drawn and tested.

Felix spotted her first, breaking away from a group that included Foras, Rowan, Enora, and a few other students she barely knew. "Seere!" he called, waving her over. When she joined them, she noticed Raphael was there, a student she'd seen many times but only met once.

"What do you think? Ready to lead us to victory?" Raphael questioned, grinning broadly.

Seere smirked behind her mask, her gaze meeting his only to fall to Felix a moment later. "Always."

"Are you sure about this?" Enora asked in a low voice. "Putting yourself right into Cotoria's hands? It's really dangerous..."

"I can handle it," Seere said evenly.

Felix frowned, clearly still uneasy about the plan but unwilling to press her further. Foras, on the other hand, was more direct.

"She knows what she's doing," Foras said, crossing his arms. "The other team won't stand a chance."

Seere let the comment hang in the air, unwilling to admit how heavily the weight of the moment pressed on her. Instead, she turned her focus back to the preparations.

She walked the perimeter of her team's side of the village, her sharp eyes taking in every detail—the layout of the village, the terrain, and the positions her team would take. The wind whispered through the ruins, carrying faint voices from the Envie camp on the far side of the battlefield. She could hear the faint ring of steel as their team sparred and prepared.

Her steps brought her to the edge of the forest, where the shadows grew thicker, and the ruins gave way to dense undergrowth. She stopped there, staring in the darkness. It would be her domain during the battle—the place where she would lure Cotoria and her strongest fighters.

The distant sound of a bell chiming brought her attention back to the center of the village, where Orias had climbed onto a raised platform to address the students.

"Gather around!" his voice boomed, commanding attention.

The students on both sides assembled, the excitement in the air reaching a fever pitch. Seere moved back toward her team, standing at the front alongside Felix, Foras, and Rowan.

Orias looked out over the crowd, his gaze sharp. "The rules are simple: your goal is to capture the opposing team's flags while protecting your own. Each team has three forts, and the flags are hidden within them. You'll need strategy, coordination, and skill to succeed. Injuries are to be avoided where possible, but the use of weapons is permitted within reason."

The students murmured amongst themselves, some with excitement, others with apprehension.

Orias continued, his tone growing more serious. "The battlefield is dangerous. This is not a game, though some of you may think of it as one. Be vigilant. Be prepared. And above all, work together."

He let the weight of his words sink in before stepping back. Professor Vidal approached, his booming voice taking over. "Team leaders, step forward!"

Seere stepped forward, her movements calm and deliberate. Across the way, she spotted Achlys doing the same, her black hair gleaming in the morning light. Their eyes locked for a brief moment, and Seere saw the playful challenge written clearly on Achlys' face.

Seere gave a firm nod, then turned back to her team, her voice steady as she said, "Positions. Let's begin."

The students scrambled to their assignments, the energy surging as the battle loomed closer. Seere disappeared into the forest's shadows, where she could become a phantom. A predator waiting for her prey.

15

WAR

ATYSDAY, THIRTY-FIRST OF THE DRAGON
MOON, YEAR 449 OF THE GODDESS

The forest canopy was dense, the soft rays of morning sun barely penetrating the thick branches above. Seere had stationed herself in a tree, her hand resting lightly on the bark as her sharp eyes scanned the undergrowth below. Every sound—the rustle of leaves, the snapping of twigs—set her on edge, though her posture remained as still as the statues back in the fortress.

"She's here somewhere! Spread out, and don't let her escape!"

Seere's lips twitched into a faint smirk beneath her mask. She adjusted her grip on the tree, her gloved fingers steady as her enemies emerged into view.

Cotoria led the group, her white blonde hair shining even in the forest's dim light. At her side, Malkyn stalked forward like a predator, her choppy dark hair clinging to her sweat-dampened face. Six more students trailed behind them, their broad shoulders and heavy weaponry making it clear that Cotoria hadn't chosen them for subtlety.

Seere moved like a shadow as she dropped from her

perch without a sound. Just as she'd hoped, she landed on the largest of the group, her boots slamming into his shoulders with enough force to send him crashing face-first into the dirt. Before the others could react, she rolled forward, springing to her feet with cat-like grace.

"Take her down!" Cotoria snarled, pointing her blade toward Seere.

The others obeyed immediately, fanning out to surround her. Seere didn't wait. She lunged toward the nearest attacker, her dagger poised to strike with the pommel. She struck true—not a killing blow, but enough to knock the boy unconscious. She ducked low, narrowly avoiding the swing of a broadsword, and retaliated with a sweep of her leg that toppled another opponent.

Cotoria's voice rose above the chaos. "Surround her! Don't let her move!"

Two of the larger fighters charged her simultaneously, their weapons raised. Seere sidestepped the first swing and deflected the second with her dagger, the clang of steel ringing out sharply. She used the momentum to spin, driving her elbow into the ribcage of one attacker before flipping him over her shoulder.

The second fighter was faster, slamming into her before she could recover. He locked his arms around her, pinning her arms to her sides.

"I've got her!" he barked.

Seere struggled, her legs kicking as she twisted against his iron grip.

Cotoria approached with a triumphant smirk, her blade gleaming as she reached for Seere's mask. "You've caused enough trouble, Your Majesty," she spat. "Let's see who you really—"

The words died in her throat as Seere kicked Cotoria away and summoned all the power within her that she could muster. In the blink of an eye, her form dissolved into a flurry of black feathers.

A sleek crow burst free from the man's grip, its wings flapping furiously as it darted into the air.

"What the—" Cotoria stumbled back, her eyes wide with shock.

The crow circled once before landing a few feet away. Another shimmer of light, and Seere reappeared, her figure steady despite the throbbing headache. She forced herself to focus. She would not die to her younger sister.

Cotoria's fighters hesitated, glancing between themselves in confusion. Seere took advantage of the opening to strike, her movements a whirlwind of speed and precision. She targeted the largest fighters first, knocking them unconscious before they could recover from the shock of seeing her turn into a crow.

Malkyn lunged at Seere from the side, her short sword aimed for Seere's ribs. Seere parried, their blades locking in a bind with a screech of metal.

"You're clever," Malkyn hissed. "But you're not invincible."

"No," Seere agreed, her voice calm despite the strain caused by her magic-induced headache. "But I'm still better than you."

She broke the bind with a sharp twist, pivoting to slam the pommel of her dagger against Malkyn's temple. She crumpled with a soft groan.

Only Cotoria remained.

The golden-haired princess raised her weapon, her

expression twisted with fury. "You think you're so clever, hiding behind that mask. But I'll—"

"Spare me the monologue," Seere interrupted coldly. She darted forward, feinting to the left before striking Cotoria's wrist. The blade clattered to the ground, and before Cotoria could react, Seere delivered a clean strike to her neck.

Cotoria's eyes widened as she staggered, then collapsed in an ungraceful heap.

Silence fell over the forest, broken only by the distant sounds of battle. Seere stood amidst the unconscious bodies, her chest rising and falling rapidly. She touched her temple, wincing at the pounding headache that pulsed with every heartbeat. She had no time for it.

Straightening, she turned and sprinted toward the battlefield.

THE ABANDONED VILLAGE WAS a chaotic mess of clashing swords, flying arrows, and shouts echoing through the smoke-filled air. Achlys' team had put up a fierce resistance, but Seere's team was holding strong under the strategy she and Foras came up with.

Seere moved through the chaos, her dark cloak blending her into the shadows. She darted from cover to cover until she caught sight of the tattered red flag fluttering atop a crumbling stone tower.

The ground around the tower was swarming with fighters, their weapons glinting in the muted light. Seere crouched behind the ruins of an old cart, formulating a plan. Slowly, she stalked around to the back of the tower, smirking to herself when she realized that Achlys had left the backside defenseless due to the onslaught of the front of the tower.

Seere reached its base with ease and began climbing, her movements swift and well-practiced. The structure was unstable, the stones crumbling beneath her fingers, but she pressed on, her determination outweighing her fear. When she reached the top, she stood for a brief moment, catching her breath as the flag whipped in the wind before her. With a swift motion, she pulled the flag free, the fabric billowing as she raised it high above her head. From her vantage point, she could see that all the flags had been pulled down from the other keeps.

From below, a roar erupted from her team as they spotted her. The cheering echoed across the battlefield, drowning out the sounds of combat as one side celebrated its victory.

Seere descended the tower, clutching the flag like a trophy. The cheers of her team rang in her ears, a victorious roar that reverberated through the ruins of Thornmoor. She dropped to the ground and smiled softly, her gaze immediately falling on Felix, whose face was alight with the brightest excitement. Then her gaze caught on Orias, who approached slowly, applauding lightly with an amused smile.

But the celebration froze in time as a sharp, searing pain struck her abdomen.

Her breath caught, and her grip on the flag faltered. She stumbled forward, the flag slipping from her fingers and falling to the old cobbled road below.

She gasped, clutching her stomach, her fingers growing wet with blood as she pressed against the hilt of a small, cruel knife embedded deep in her flesh. Gritting her teeth, she forced her head up to see where the attack had come from.

Cotoria stood a dozen paces away, her white blonde hair disheveled, her face twisted into a vicious smirk. A second throwing knife was poised in her hand, the blade glinting menacingly in the sunlight.

"Seere!" Felix's voice tore through the moment, raw and panicked.

But it wasn't Felix who reached her first.

Orias appeared at her side, his tall frame blocking the advancing Cotoria from view.

"Get back!" he barked to the surrounding students, his voice carrying the weight of authority. "Someone restrain Cotoria! Now!"

Seere barely registered as Alsariph tackled Cotoria to the ground, wrenching the knife from her grasp. Instead, her focus narrowed to Orias as he caught her by the arm, keeping her upright.

"Seere, stay with me," he hissed, his usually calm tone frayed with urgency.

Healers rushed over, stretcher ready. Seere grimaced, batting their hands away. "No stretcher," she snapped through her gritted teeth. "I can walk."

"Seere—" Orias started, his expression darkening with worry.

"I can walk," she repeated firmly, her voice a growl. She leaned heavily on him as they moved, and each step shot a jolt of pain through her.

Seere's eyes flickered back to Alsariph, who still had Cotoria pinned, his knee pressing into the struggling girl's back. Beyond them, Felix stood frozen, his eyes glued to Seere, his face pale and drawn with fear.

She sighed and did her best to straighten herself, trying hard to walk without aid. The last thing she wanted was to appear weak. She didn't want Felix to think of her as fragile than he already did, and she certainly didn't want Cotoria seeing any of her weakness.

However, once she was out of sight, she dropped the guise. She allowed Orias to hold her up with his arm firmly around her waist. Her arm had snaked around his shoulders to steady herself, her free hand pressed to her wound.

"I don't want the healers," Seere said coolly. "I need to speak with you. Alone."

"But, Your Majesty, that wound is fatal if not properly cared for!" a nurse exclaimed, flabbergasted.

"It's not up for discussion. Leave me," she ordered.

"Headmaster, are you going to stand for this?"

She could feel Orias tense against her, his uncertainty palpable. "Listen to Her Majesty. She does not require your presence."

He waved off the healers, swiftly guiding Seere to the carriage they rode in on. Gingerly, he helped her inside. As he shut the door, Seere dug a cloth out of the messenger bag that she had left inside before the Wargames began. The commotion outside muffled as the door latched, leaving them in solitude as Orias pulled the curtains closed.

"Let me take care of the knife," he began, reaching for her wound.

"Don't bother." Seere's hand shot up, gripping the knife's hilt. Before he could stop her, she yanked it out in one swift motion, a nearly silent cry escaping her lips.

"Seere, what are you—" Orias' voice was filled with alarm, but it trailed off as he watched in stunned silence.

Blood spilled for only a moment before the wound

began to close slowly, the torn flesh knitting itself back together with unnatural speed. In seconds, the injury was no more than a faint scar. It still stung as her insides knit together, but she was able to pull off her corset and wipe up the blood on her skin with the cloth.

Orias stared, his expression unreadable. "How…"

Seere exhaled, the color returning to her cheeks. "I didn't want anyone to see," she muttered, ignoring his question. "And I most definitely didn't want to appear weak. I'm going to pull on a clean top. Look away."

Orias swiftly tore his gaze from her as she pulled her shirt over her head and tossed it onto the floor. Carefully, she found the spare top that she'd stored and a fresh leather corset which she carefully pulled on, glancing over at her companion to make sure he wasn't trying to peek at her.

"You are full of surprises, Your Majesty," Orias said slowly, his gaze firmly on the curtained window beside him. "I've only ever seen healing like that in myself."

"You can look now," she said, intrigued by his words but wary. "And I'm nothing special." She cleaned up her mess of torn clothes and stored them away in her bag. Then she leaned her head back on the carriage wall and closed her eyes. All the energy within her had seeped out of her after healing the wound.

"Hardly nothing," Orias murmured, but he didn't press her further.

After a moment, he leaned out the carriage window and instructed the driver to return to the fortress. It surprised her that he didn't want to step out and address the frightened students.

Seere opened her eyes to watch the forest pass in a blur, the carriage jostling lightly along the overgrown path. The silence inside the carriage felt heavy, broken only by the occasional creak of wood or Seere's tired breathing.

"Cotoria didn't see your face, did she?" Orias asked abruptly, his tone serious. "That's the only reason I can think of for her wanting to kill you."

Seere shook her head. "No, she didn't. She tried, but I didn't give her the chance."

Orias nodded, looking away from her as he processed her words.

The carriage bumped over a root, jolting Seere slightly. She flinched, her hand instinctively flying to the place her wound had been only moments before. It had healed, but the phantom pain still lingered.

"You can take your mask off now," Orias said softly, breaking the silence. "You're safe."

Her eyes widened with surprise as his hand found the back of her ear. He brushed lightly against her skin as he removed the band from around her ear and then the other. His gaze dropped to her lips, which only succeeded in sending a rebellious shiver down her spine.

Immediately, her face was bathed in the warm, dappled light filtering through the curtains. She blinked, startled by his sudden touch and the warmth of the sun. Her pale green eyes met his calm, steady gaze.

For once, he didn't say anything. He simply set the mask aside, his expression softening as he leaned back, giving her space. Seere continued to stare at him for a long moment before her gaze finally shifted from his face.

"Seere, who is your mother?"

"Go to hell."

Orias chuckled, shaking his head in disbelief. "Do you truly believe that a power to heal like ours is common? Do you truly believe that any form of magic is common in mortals?" he asked. "I'm going to guess your mother, whoever she is, is a goddess."

"You're digging in places you don't belong," she hissed, turning a sharp glare on him. "Tread carefully, or I will gut you like a fish."

"Is she Etrix? The Goddess of Penance. Or perhaps it's Vatia, the Goddess of Silence?" he offered, watching her carefully.

"Who is your godly parent?" she countered. "Perhaps Labris, the God of Balance? Or is it on your mother's side as well, and it's Goddess Eulla herself?"

"That is a question you don't want the answer to," Orias breathed, his smirk falling.

"Atysus than? The god of war," she said thoughtfully.

"No, stop guessing."

"Then I think you should stop guessing my parentage, Orias. It's better for both of us that you don't know," she said coolly.

"Eslia," he said, his answer filled with finality.

Seere drew her dagger and was on top of Orias faster than he could react. Her legs straddled his lap, her dagger to his throat. "I will end you, *Headmaster*, if you don't stop," she snarled.

"I have no intention of hurting you, darling," he whispered, his expression infuriatingly relaxed even as she held a blade to his throat. "I don't care if your mother is Eslia or if it's Iktune, our lady of love."

"When every one of your half-siblings is hunted because of your mother, you come to resent the goddess that birthed you," she said coolly. "If you tell another soul, I *will* kill you."

"I won't, but you must tell me, did you use your powers in

front of Cotoria?" Orias asked, gently pushing her blade away from his throat. She saw then that in her panic, she had cut him.

"I did," Seere murmured, remembering finally that Orias had told her once before of Selina's hatred for Eslia. "It was either reveal my powers or reveal my identity."

"That might explain her desire to kill."

A curse escaped Seere as she dropped her dagger, letting it fall to the floor of the carriage. She removed herself from Orias' lap as she fell back into the bench beside him.

"Seere, what exactly did you do that revealed yourself to her?"

"I turned into a crow. The very symbol of Eslia," she whispered, dropping her head back against the wall. "And it wasn't just her that saw."

"I never expected you, of all people, to make such a grave error," Orias breathed.

"I have never claimed to be perfect," she said coolly. "It hardly changes anything. She already wanted me dead just for being the Assassin Queen."

"She will target you more than ever before."

"I can defend myself and Felix," Seere said, turning her gaze to the window.

16

CELEBRATION

ATYSDAY, THIRTY-FIRST OF THE DRAGON
MOON, YEAR 449 OF THE GODDESS

The remainder of the carriage ride back to the school was quiet, the soft creak of the wheels on the gravel path being the only sounds that broke the silence. Seere leaned her head against the wall, her back stiff from the long journey.

As the carriage rolled to a stop before the front entrance of the fortress, Seere straightened and grabbed her bag. She mentally prepared herself to be met with a throng of students, all desperate to know if she was still alive and well. Hesitantly, she reached for the door handle, but not before Orias reached out, his hand gently encircling her wrist.

"Wait," he said, his voice low.

She froze, meeting his gaze. His evergreen eyes were stormy and held a weight she couldn't quite decipher, a mixture of something like concern and hesitation. He opened his mouth as if to speak, but the words didn't come.

Finally, he cleared his throat and said, "There's a letter from your viceroy waiting for you in my office. Come by when you're ready for it. And in case you were unaware, there are no classes tomorrow," he said.

Seere tilted her head slightly, studying him. The line of his jaw was tight, his usual air of unshakable confidence faltering for just a moment. "Understood," she replied simply, her voice carefully neutral as she struggled to read him.

Finally, he released her wrist, and she stepped out of the carriage.

The moment her boots hit the stone path, Seere was surrounded by a swarm of students. Felix was at the fore-front, flanked by Rowan, Enora, and Foras as always. It was Felix who grabbed her by the shoulders, examining her for injuries, the way she had with him when the assassin had tried to kill him.

"Are you all right?" he demanded.

"Do you need us to take you to the infirmary?" Rowan questioned.

Seere sighed heavily, placing her hands on Felix's wrists and gently removing his hands from her. "I'm fine, and no, I don't need the infirmary. The leather of my corset kept the knife from truly harming me," she said. "It's just a scratch."

"It didn't look that way," Foras muttered, eyeing Seere suspiciously.

Seere rolled her eyes. "I'm fine. Truly. It was a surface wound, and I've had far worse," she said, sweeping past them to show that she was fine, more than strong enough to walk on her own. "There's no need to fret."

By the time they reached the dormitory, the air was buzzing with excitement. Students scattered and then returned with various bottles of alcoholic drinks and many instruments. Before long, the common room was alive with laughter, shouting, and recountings of the Wargames. Seere allowed herself to be pulled to the center of it, though she never touched a drink.

"It's a shame you missed it, Your Majesty! My daring maneuvers would have truly impressed you!" Rowan exclaimed, though his gaze flickered around the large group of pretty girls that surrounded him.

"I'm sure you acted heroically," Seere said, shaking her head.

"He was just trying to impress the ladies," Foras muttered beside her, glaring at the girls as if they had personally offended him.

Seere watched Foras and the way he tensed when a particularly pretty young woman set her hand on Rowan's thigh. "Or you," she murmured, barely loud enough for Foras to hear.

Foras glared at her. "I am not delusional, Ris," he hissed and stormed past her towards the coffee table filled with drinks.

Enora took Foras' place then, a sad smile tugging at the corners of her lips. "Careful. Foras has been pining for Rowan for years now, but Rowan is either oblivious or refuses to acknowledge it."

"That's unfortunate," Seere said softly, turning her gaze away. "Foras deserves far better."

"Speaking of relationships, what's going on between you and Headmaster Orias?" Enora questioned. "He seemed more than a little panicked when you were injured earlier."

"Oh, he just doesn't want to lose his head. He knows my kingdom will tear this place down should I fall under his watch," Seere said, shrugging. "There is nothing there. Just a contract."

"Okay, then what about you and Felix? I've noticed that His Highness is very taken with you," Enora said, watching Seere closely.

"Again, Felix is just a close ally," Seere said. She sighed heavily, running a hand through her hair. "Enora, I am the Queen of the Domain of Assassins. I don't take lovers."

"That sounds like a lonely existence," Enora murmured, turning her gaze up to the ceiling. "Have you ever taken a lover?"

"No and, lonely or not, it's safer for those around me," Seere said, giving Enora a hard look. "I have a huge target on my back at all times. I will not put a target on another's back just because I bedded them. It would be monstrous."

Enora was quiet for a long moment. Her gaze bore into Seere as if trying to read into her very soul. "Sounds like you're scared, if you ask me."

"Always," Seere murmured before she turned and walked away, wanting nothing to do with whatever Enora would say next.

As the night wore on, the room grew warmer, the laughter louder. Seere's mask shielded her from the drunken haze that clouded most of the students' faces, but she couldn't deny the lightness she felt in their company. For a moment, the weight of her responsibilities seemed a little easier to bear.

Seere seated herself in a corner, away from the center of the revelry, but near enough that she didn't quite seem like an outcast. She watched as a dance floor formed as the musicians turned to fast-paced dances that required a partner. She watched as Felix got dragged into a dance by Emeline, who blushed brighter than any strawberry Seere had ever seen. Meanwhile, Rowan swapped partners frequently, dancing with each girl who threw herself at his feet.

"Your Majesty, may I have this dance?"

Seere looked to her right as Alsariph crossed over to her. He wore one of those charming smiles she often saw on Rowan.

Seere hesitated for half a moment before she stood and offered her hand to him. "Certainly," she said.

Like a true noble, he led Seere to the dance floor, his back straight, his chin high. The dancers that had already gathered froze as they watched Seere and Alsariph, their eyes wide in disbelief as they cleared the space for them. Seere caught sight of Felix, who seemed to eye her dance companion with suspicion and contempt.

Then the music began to play again. This time it was a dance from Envie. A minuet. A soft curse escaped Seere, which earned an amused chuckle from Alsariph.

"Do you not know this dance, Your Majesty?" he questioned.

Seere shook her head. "On the contrary, I know it very well," she said, allowing her old Envie accent to show through more prominently than ever. She slipped into the dance with the grace only a noble of Envie carried. She'd had this particular dance drilled into her when she was younger. "I was from your Empire once."

"What part?" Alsariph questioned, his curiosity piqued.

"I lived in Soleil," she answered, no longer allowing her accent to slip into her speech.

"Your surname is Cross?" he asked, his brows lightly furrowing.

"Indeed."

He hummed thoughtfully. "An alias, then? I don't recall

ever meeting anyone with the name Cross, and I certainly don't recall ever seeing eyes as pale as yours," he said.

"Perhaps or perhaps not. While I came from an exceedingly wealthy family, I agree that I think I'd remember you had we met before now," she said. "After all, I left long before I made my debut into society."

He nodded thoughtfully. "Interesting. Well, you dance beautifully. It's a shame we never met before, Your Majesty. I imagine we'd have made fast friends."

"Most definitely," she said, hating herself inwardly for the shallowness of the conversation.

Once the dance ended, Seere curtsied low, though she lacked a skirt, and parted ways with Alsariph. As the crowd of dancers finally converged again, Seere took it upon herself to slip away. Her steps were quiet as she made her way to the dormitory, the music fading behind her. She longed for solitude, her mind weary after the long day.

She'd just reached her door when she heard soft footsteps behind her.

"Seere?"

She turned to find Felix standing a few paces away, his expression soft with concern. He had sobered significantly since the party began, though his hair was still slightly disheveled from the evening's excitement.

"I'm fine," she said before he could speak.

"You don't have to lie to me," he said softly as he took a few steps closer. "You've been through an ordeal today."

Seere's gaze softened slightly. "I'm not lying. I just... need some quiet. That's all."

Felix studied her for a moment, then nodded. "Okay. But if you need anything—"

"I'll know where to find you," she finished for him, a small smile tugging at her lips.

He smiled, lingering for a long moment before turning to leave. "Goodnight, Seere."

"Goodnight, Felix."

As his footsteps faded, Seere slipped into her room. She set aside her mask and cloak. Then she removed her corset, eager to examine the spot Cotoria had struck her. Tomorrow, she would visit Orias and retrieve the letter that he had for her, but tonight she wanted to allow herself rest.

Rapid healing and transforming into a crow always took too much energy out of her.

17

THE CAVE

CHAYSDAY, FIRST OF THE SHADOW MOON, YEAR 449 OF THE GODDESS

The morning after the Wargames brought a hush to the academy that Seere was grateful for. With no classes scheduled and Cotoria locked away in the dungeons beneath the school, the students relished the rare chance to rest and catch up on homework. Seere, however, found herself awake before dawn, staring out her window as the snow began to drift lazily from the overcast sky.

The month of the Shadow Moon, the second-to-last month of the year, arrived at midnight, which meant it was rapidly approaching winter and the end of the year. A time she'd always associated with quiet reflection.

When she finally stepped outside, the cold air greeted her like an old friend. She tugged her cloak tighter around her shoulders and smiled faintly as her boots crunched through the thin blanket of fresh snow. Though she wouldn't allow her moment of peace in the snow to delay her.

Seere knocked lightly on Orias' office door. Each time she'd visited before, she'd stormed in; it was a first that she was entering with a light mood. Only the briefest of moments passed before she heard his voice beckon her in.

"Seere," he said warmly, setting down a ledger. "I didn't expect you so early. Please, have a seat. Would you like some tea?"

"Sounds lovely," she said as she accepted the offered chair. The warmth of the teacup was welcome against her chilled hands, and she savored the scent of the sweetened black tea.

Orias slid a sealed envelope across the desk. "Here's the letter, as promised," he said.

Seere broke the seal and skimmed the letter. The contents were mundane: a brief update on her kingdom's affairs, a few minor trade agreements, and a report on the weather patterns over the Domain of Assassins. Nothing demanded immediate action.

"Nothing of note," she murmured, setting the letter aside.

Orias nodded thoughtfully, though his gaze seemed distant. He stood, moving to pace the length of the room, his boots clicking against the polished floor.

"You seem distracted," Seere said, her eyes following him.

Orias paused before one of the large windows, his hands clasped behind his back. He hummed lightly, his usual commanding demeanor softened. "It's nothing," he said after a moment. "Just the weariness of leadership, I'm sure you can understand. There are days when it feels... endless."

Seere rose from her seat and approached him, her curiosity piqued. She stopped beside him, their reflections faint in the frosted glass. "You don't strike me as someone who gets lost in thought so easily."

He glanced at her, his evergreen eyes catching the glow of the winter light. "Even the strongest minds have moments of doubt," he said quietly.

"I didn't think you were capable of doubting yourself," she said softly, her voice almost teasing.

A faint smirk tugged at the corner of his lips, though it didn't reach his eyes. "Perhaps I'm better at hiding it than most."

She studied him for a moment, the firelight that glowed across the room from them catching the faint golden undertone in his skin. Orias turned to face her after a moment, his focus settling on the mask that concealed her mouth. There was a moment of pause before his hand lifted, his fingers brushing the edge of her mask and her skin, causing her to stiffen.

"May I?" he asked softly, his voice barely above a whisper.

For a moment, her instinct was to step back, to deny him. But something in his tone gave her pause. Slowly, she nodded, her heart pounding as his hand gingerly pulled the mask off her ears. The cool air brushed against her skin as he removed it. Orias' eyes lingered on her features with something uncharacteristically open in his expression.

"You don't need to hide in here," he said softly, his voice carrying an unexpected gentleness.

Before she could respond, his hand moved to her hair, his fingers weaving through the lavender strands. Then he leaned down, his movements unhurried, and pressed his lips to hers.

The kiss was warm and deliberate, his hand firm yet gentle as it rested against the back of her neck. For the briefest of moments, Seere stood frozen, her mind racing.

She hadn't anticipated a kiss—not from Orias. But as the initial shock faded, she couldn't resist him as she leaned in, her hands pressing delicately against his chest.

Just as quickly as it happened, it was over as he broke away first. Seere's breaths were shallow, her eyes locked on his as she tried to piece together what had just occurred between them.

"Orias..." she started, her voice uncertain.

He stepped back slightly, his hand falling away as if realizing he'd crossed some unseen line. "I shouldn't have done that," he said quietly, though there was no regret in his tone —only acknowledgement.

Seere didn't reply immediately. Instead, she retrieved her mask from the windowsill with careful movements. "You're a complicated man, Orias," she said finally, her tone neutral, though her heart still raced.

He chuckled faintly, watching her curiously. "And you're a fascinating woman, Queen of Shadows."

She offered an amused smile. "Did you need me for anything else?" she questioned.

Orias' gaze shifted to her lips again before he turned his attention back to the window. The tension between them was palpable. "No, you're free to go," he said, though many unspoken words were left hanging heavy in the air.

Without another word, Seere turned and left the office. Her steps were measured despite the storm of emotions roiling within her. She hated how much she wanted Orias at that moment.

THE WAXING gibbous moon hung low in the sky, casting its silvery light across the snow-covered grounds of Malphas

University. The soft crunch of boots on snow broke the otherwise tranquil silence as Seere and Felix wandered along the top of the curtain wall of the fortress.

"You should be resting," he said, his tone light but edged in concern. "You did get stabbed yesterday, you know."

Seere glanced at him, her lavender hair shimmering faintly in the moonlight. Her mask concealed the smirk tugging at her lips, but it carried in her voice. "You're starting to sound like the headmaster and the nurses. I told you already—I've had worse."

Felix shook his head, a soft laugh escaping him. "That doesn't make it any better, you know. Most people don't measure their well-being against 'worse stabbings.'"

Seere smiled. "Most people aren't me," she said.

They walked in companionable silence for a while, the crisp air biting but not unpleasant. Felix kicked at a patch of snow, sending a flurry of white scattering across the path.

"I envy you sometimes," he admitted suddenly, his tone thoughtful.

Seere turned her head to regard him, one brow lifting. "Envy me? That's not something I hear every day. Why?"

"You seem so... in control," he said, gesturing vaguely. "Like, no matter what happens, you always know what to do. How to adapt. You're never unsure, never scared."

"I'm always scared. I have just learned how to hide it better than anyone I've known," she said, her words a mere whisper as she halted.

"What are you afraid of?" Felix asked, pausing in his steps. His cobalt eyes searched her face.

"Failure," she admitted as she continued walking. "Letting people down. Letting *myself* down. Sometimes it feels like there's so much at stake, and if I falter, even for a moment..." She trailed off, shaking her head. "But you learn to carry it. You have to."

Felix followed after her. "You're still very strong," he said.

She glanced at him, her gaze softening. "And you're braver than you give yourself credit for."

A faint flush colored his cheeks, though it could easily have been blamed on the cold. He let out a breathy laugh, his gaze turning upward to the moonlit sky.

"I'm going to hold you to that," he said, giving her a playful smile. "Do you ever wonder what it would've been like? If we weren't... who we are. If you weren't a queen and I wasn't a prince."

Seere tilted her head, watching him thoughtfully. "I try not to dwell on 'what ifs.' They don't change anything."

Felix nodded slowly, his breath fogging the air. "Still, it's nice to think about sometimes."

Their conversation shifted to lighter topics, Felix recounting stories from his childhood in Noctivagus. "My father used to take me hunting in the royal forests when I was young. He said it was a good way to learn patience and discipline, but mostly, I think he just liked having an excuse to disappear into the forests for a while."

Seere smirked and glanced at him. "And did you learn patience and discipline?"

Felix scoffed. "Hardly. I spent most of the time chasing after shadows, convinced I was about to find some legendary beast. One time, I got lost for hours because I was tracking what I swore was a 'Phantom deer.'"

She blinked. "A phantom deer?"

He nodded solemnly. "A majestic, ghostly creature with silver antlers. Completely real, I assure you."

"And did you ever actually see this magnificent beast?"

Felix sighed dramatically. "Alas, no. But I did manage to find every single mud pit in the forest. When they finally found me, I was covered head to toe, insisting I had been on the verge of a great discovery."

Seere laughed softly at the image. "You? Lost in the woods? I thought princes were supposed to have an impeccable sense of direction."

"I was seven," Felix protested with mock indignation. "And I'm much better now. Probably."

As they rounded a corner, Seere froze mid-step, her eyes narrowing. Ahead, the faint, flickering glow of firelight emanated from the cave she'd noticed before.

Felix followed her gaze, his brow furrowing. "That seems... suspicious. We should inform a guard."

"Yes, it is," Seere murmured, her voice grim. "But I need to see for myself what's going on. This may have something to do with the assassination attempts."

Without another word, she swiftly began descending the curtain wall. Felix hesitated for only a moment before following, his movements clumsy due to a lack of practice scaling walls, though she wouldn't have expected him to be skilled in such things. When Seere was near enough to the bottom, she dropped down the remainder of the way, waiting patiently for Felix.

Once he was beside her, they crept towards the cave, her steps cautious but swift. Felix was close behind her, his hand instinctively resting on the hilt of his sword.

As they walked through the cave, the glow grew brighter until they could make out figures within. Six cloaked individuals stood in a circle, their faces obscured by elaborate silver and gold masks that glinted in the firelight.

"We can't afford another near failure like this," one figure said, their voice sharp and commanding. "Cotoria's reckless actions are jeopardizing everything."

"She nearly killed the queen," another hissed. "If Seere dies, this entire operation collapses. We need her alive, at least for now."

"If it's such a concern, I can slaughter Cotoria and make it appear as though it had been an accident. No one will suspect a thing," one said, his voice low and deadly calm as if he spoke about the weather rather than murder.

"I think not. You will just cause more problems for everyone."

"We will not assassinate the young princess. She still plays a very important role in this game. We must see it through and make sure Seere stays safe."

Felix shifted slightly, his boot scuffing against a rock. The sound, though faint, was enough to draw the attention of the cloaked figures.

"Someone's here," one of them growled, their masked head snapping to attention.

"Get out of here," Seere hissed, grabbing Felix by the arm.

They bolted, the sound of hurried footsteps and shouted commands echoing behind them. Seere led the way, her instincts guiding her through the maze of trees. By the time they reached the safety of the school grounds, Felix was wide-eyed. Breathless.

"We really should tell someone about the cave," he said between gasps.

"I will," Seere agreed, her mind racing. Then she caught Felix's arm and began guiding him back to the dorm building. "First, I need you to get to your dorm. It's long after dark, and the guards will start to get frustrated if we're out any later."

Felix looked at her, his concern evident. "Seere, you're not alone in this. You don't have to do everything on your own all the time," he said.

"I don't do everything on my own," she said, though her tone was firm with finality, as if the last thing she wanted was to speak any further on the matter.

18

CORNERED

EULDAY, FIFTH OF THE SHADOW MOON,
YEAR 449 OF THE GODDESS

Seere followed Felix to the table where Foras, Rowan, Enora, and Achlys were seated for breakfast. However, her sharp eyes caught a glimpse of Orias at one of the smaller side entrances, engaged in conversation with Professor Manfredonia. Her heart quickened with urgency, frustration bubbling to the surface.

Without a second thought, she pivoted on her heel and strode toward the headmaster, ignoring the curious looks of students and staff as she passed. Her footsteps quickened, almost as if she feared he would sense her approach and vanish again.

"Orias!" she called out, her voice firm and just loud enough to cut through the hum of morning chatter.

For a moment, it seemed as though he might finally acknowledge her. His posture stiffened slightly, and his gaze flicked over his shoulder. Their eyes locked for a fraction of a second—a fleeting connection before Orias turned back to Professor Manfredonia, nodding curtly as he made his retreat down the adjacent hallway.

Seere froze mid-step, her hands clenching into fists at her sides. The exasperation that had been simmering inside her for days boiled over as she watched his figure disappear into the crowd.

Days had passed since Seere and Felix had stumbled across the meeting with the Order, each one leaving Seere more exasperated. Every attempt to speak to Orias ended in failure. Whether by sheer coincidence or deliberate effort, the headmaster always seemed to vanish before she could reach him. At first, she attributed it to his busy schedule, but as the days wore on, it began to feel deliberate. As though that kiss he had shared with her ignited a magnet that repelled him from her.

The sound of approaching steps barely registered until a gentle hand rested on her shoulder. Seere tensed, instinctively shifting into a defensive stance, before she recognized the touch. Turning, she found Felix standing there, his expression a mixture of concern and curiosity.

"Still avoiding you?" he asked, his brow furrowed.

Seere's jaw tightened as she inhaled deeply, fighting to rein in her anger. "That makes four days now," she muttered through gritted teeth.

Felix frowned, his blue eyes flicking toward the hallway Orias had disappeared into, then back to Seere. "That's not like him," he mused aloud, as though searching for some explanation. "He usually listens when there's something urgent."

"Maybe he knows what you want to talk about and doesn't want to deal with it," Foras interjected dryly as he approached from the table. His tone was light, but there was an edge of seriousness beneath his words.

"Or maybe he's just busy," Enora added as she joined them, though even her voice held a hint of doubt.

Seere exhaled sharply, her shoulders slumping slightly. "I thought the same at first, but this—" She gestured to the now-empty side entrance. " It feels as though he's avoiding me. He saw me just now, and he still walked away."

Felix exchanged a glance with Foras, the latter crossing his arms as he leaned against the wall. "So, what's the plan now?"

Seere's eyes narrowed in determination, a spark of defiance igniting within them. "If he keeps running, I'll just have to stop him myself. I don't care how busy he claims to be. He can't avoid me forever."

Felix's lips quirked into a small smile, though his concern didn't waver. "I'd pay to see that."

"Be careful," Enora warned, her usual playful tone replaced with rare seriousness. "The man's got a way of slipping out of things—literally and figuratively."

Seere didn't reply, her focus already shifting to her next move. Whatever Orias' reasons for avoiding her, she wouldn't let them deter her. Too much was at stake, and she couldn't afford to waste any more time.

With renewed resolve, she turned on her heel and made her way back to the table, but not before casting one last glance down the hallway.

Seere found the door to Orias' office locked when she tried the handle. However, with her lockpicking skills, it took no time at all before she was allowed in. She closed the door softly behind her as she stepped inside, the weight of her frustration pressing heavily on her chest.

The room was as pristine as ever, its polished wooden furniture and meticulously organized bookshelves betraying none of the chaos Seere felt. The crackling fireplace cast flickering shadows along the walls, and the faint scent of parchment and ink hung in the air.

Her eyes drifted to his desk, an imposing piece of dark oak that dominated the room in a way she had never noticed before. It was the first place she searched, though she didn't know why she decided to snoop around. She slid open drawers and rifled through the carefully stacked papers. Most were mundane—administrative records, faculty schedules, and correspondence with other schools.

"Come on, Orias," she muttered under her breath. "You must have something entertaining in here."

Her hands paused on a locked drawer near the bottom. She grinned faintly, slipping a thin lockpick from her glove. It only took seconds for the lock to yield with a soft click.

Inside, she found a collection of letters bound with a thin cord, the handwriting elegant but unfamiliar. As she skimmed them, her brow furrowed. The letters spoke of political tensions between Noctivagus and Envie, and mentions of alliances and betrayals were scattered throughout. They weren't incriminating, but they confirmed what she already suspected. Orias was privy to information far beyond the scope of a simple headmaster.

Placing the letters back carefully, she closed the drawer and moved on. A cabinet tucked against the wall caught her eye. Inside were neatly arranged scrolls and documents, each labeled in Orias' sharp handwriting. One scroll, marked with a sigil she didn't recognize, drew her attention.

Unfurling it, she found a map of the continent. Several

locations were marked in red ink. Her heartbeat quickened as she glanced over them, swiftly realizing that each one was a place she had been sighted in once before while she'd been on the run. The Domain of Assassins was circled.

She set the map aside and moved toward a door she hadn't noticed before, leading to what she guessed were his private quarters. She hesitated for a moment before opening it, curiosity pushing her forward.

The room beyond was surprisingly modest. A neatly made bed, a wardrobe, and a small table with a lamp made up the bulk of the furnishings. A stack of books sat on the bedside table, their spines worn with age and frequent use. One caught her eye: The Myths of the Queen of Crows.

Seere thumbed through it, noting passages that were highlighted about Eslia's history and anything that spoke of powers she may possess. A bookmark rested near a chapter on Eslia's relations with other gods.

Returning to the office after leaving everything looking untouched, she perched herself behind Orias' desk while she waited for him to return. She propped her feet up on the desk as she stared at the door, determination sharpening her gaze.

When Orias stepped into his office and saw Seere seated in his chair, feet propped on his desk, he froze. His deep green eyes narrowed, the normally calm facade giving way to an edge of irritation.

"What," he began coldly, "are you doing in my chair?"

Seere tilted her head, offering him a saccharine smile. "Waiting for you, of course," she answered. "I've been trying to get your attention for days, but you've been avoiding me, so I decided to wait here until you couldn't."

Orias shut the door behind him, his movements deliberate. "I'm not avoiding you. I've been—"

"Busy?" Seere interrupted, her tone dripping with annoyance. "Running a university? Managing students and professors? What else do you want to add to the list of excuses?" She swung her legs off the desk and stood, closing the distance between them.

Orias bristled. "I don't owe you an explanation, Seere. I think you should see yourself out."

"I will not leave," she snapped, her tone heated now. "Why have you been so determined to avoid me? I overheard something—something important—and I've been trying to tell you, but you just keep slipping away. What are you so afraid of?"

"Don't mistake caution for fear, Your Majesty," he said, his voice dipping low.

Her eyes narrowed at the title. "Don't patronize me. Felix and I stumbled upon a meeting with the Order of the Chimera in a cave just outside the fortress walls. They mentioned needing me alive for a plan and even killing Cotoria to make sure it succeeds. Are you going to do something about it, or should I handle it myself?"

The words hung in the air, heavy with meaning. Orias sighed, running a hand through his dark hair as his shoulders slumped slightly. "Don't be rash, Seere. I don't want to imagine what they might do to you if they get hold of you. It's dangerous."

"I'm constantly in danger, Orias," she countered, stepping closer and tearing her mask from her face. "That's just my reality as the Queen of Assassins and as Amaris."

His jaw tightened, and for a moment, Seere thought he might lash out, but instead, he exhaled slowly, his dark eyes meeting hers. "You should go. I have much to think about. I will send Aamon out to investigate the cave, but for now, you should return to Felix and—"

"Would you stop that?" she snapped. "Stop shoving me away when this is the job *you* signed me up for."

"Do you want to know why I avoid you?" he asked, his voice suddenly quieter, almost vulnerable.

Her brow furrowed. The shift in his demeanor caught her off guard, and her frustration began to waver. "Tell me."

"Because you remind me of everything I've tried to keep at arm's length." His eyes met hers, unguarded for the first time since she'd known him. "You're too clever, too determined. You ask questions I don't want to answer. And you're not the type to let me get away with keeping secrets the way everyone else does."

"Not when those secrets could cost lives."

His lips quirked into a faint smile, tinged with irony. "No, I didn't think so."

Silence fell again, but this time it felt different. Seere searched his face, trying to read the flickers of emotion that crossed it. There was something in the way he looked at her —not just frustration, but something deeper, something she wasn't sure she wanted to name. He looked at her in the way that he had just before the Wargames.

"Why do you do that?" she asked suddenly.

"Do what?" he replied, his brow arching.

"Look at me like that," she said softly, her voice barely above a whisper. "Like I'm some puzzle you're trying to solve."

"Because you *are* a puzzle," he admitted. He reached out, brushing a strand of hair from her face. His touch was so light, it sent a shiver down her spine. "And you're dangerous."

"Dangerous?" She tilted her head, a small smile playing on her lips. "You're the one with the power here, Orias."

"Am I?" His voice was quieter then, almost tender. His hand lingered near her cheek before dropping away, his expression softened in a way that made her chest tighten. "You're far more dangerous than you know, Amaris."

For once, Seere loved the way her true name sounded. "Then why aren't you afraid of me?" she challenged, though her voice lacked its usual sharpness.

"I never said I wasn't," he replied, his gaze dropping briefly to her lips before snapping back to her eyes.

Her breath caught, the tension between them crackling like the fire in the hearth. Before she could think better of it, she closed the gap between them. Her lips brushed his in a kiss that was tentative at first, testing the waters.

Orias froze for the briefest of moments, then leaned into her, one hand finding the curve of her waist while the other cradled her jaw. The kiss deepened, slow and deliberate, like neither of them was willing to rush what had been building over the last couple of weeks.

When they finally pulled apart, their breaths mingling in the space between them, Seere's heart raced. Orias rested his forehead against hers, his voice barely above a whisper.

"This is a terrible idea," he said, though there was no conviction in his tone.

"I know," she whispered, her lips curving into a smile. "But you started it."

His chuckle was low and soft, a sound that sent warmth blooming in her chest. "You're infuriating, you know that?"

"You reap what you sow," she said, her voice laced with playful defiance. "You deserve it."

Orias leaned down again, capturing her lips in another kiss, this one hungrier, filled with everything they couldn't put into words. Each of their touches was careful and deliberate, as though they were both testing the boundaries of something new and fragile.

However, lips soon crashed together harder than before, more desperately, as if they'd finally surrendered to the inevitable. Orias' fingers worked to undo the laces of her corset as he kissed her. He removed her blouse, tossing it aside before it was followed by the remaining items of her clothing. Gently, he guided her to his bed. Seere found herself pulling off his shirt, desperate to feel skin—his skin —against hers.

She was eating her earlier words to Enora. She had claimed that she would never take a lover. However, she found herself unable to resist Orias and the devilish smirk he always gave her. It was a smirk reserved only for her, she'd noticed.

Gently, Orias lifted her off the ground and then laid her out on the bed, removing her leggings and boots until she was bare before him. She had never been so exposed. Her dagger was nowhere within reach, but she found that she didn't want it. Not with the words from Felix written across the hilt under the leather wrap that hid it. The thought struck her sharply, but she shoved it from her mind. She was not bound to anyone, not anymore.

"Your tattoo," Orias murmured, his eyes following the vines that wrapped around her body.

"It hurt like hell," she said, reaching out for him as he

climbed onto the bed. He braced his hands on either side of her head, keeping himself suspended above her.

His fingers grazed over the tattoo where it crossed her stomach, then disappeared around her hip to trail down her left leg. "Where did it hurt the worst?" he asked.

She moved her fingers across her body, from the tattoo on her collarbone to the continuation of it across her stomach, and wherever her fingers touched, Orias kissed. She shivered with pleasure under each press of his lips.

"Has Felix ever seen it?" he asked softly, a hint of frustration and jealousy.

"I've had this tattoo since I was sixteen," she murmured, her fingers tracing the contours of his chest. "No one but you has ever laid their eyes on it or any other part of me."

Orias looked up at her, his gaze stormy with desire. He searched her expression for a moment as a smirk tugged at the corners of his lips. His fingers grazed the curve of her waist, then he dipped two of them inside of her.

"Oh," Seere hissed, her fingernails digging into his shoulders as she arched her back into him.

"I am honored to be the first to worship your body, Your Majesty," he whispered before nipping a sensitive spot under her ear. "You will feel as you have never felt before."

His tongue trailed over her body, his teeth nipping at her unblemished skin and leaving bruises that she knew would fade before the night was over. He whispered praises as he worked his fingers, drawing out moan after moan as if he couldn't get enough.

Seere was lost in the bliss that was Orias. She was lost in the aching blend of pain, pleasure, and desire he gave her. She knew, deep down, that she'd regret their time together in the morning, but for at least one night, she would allow herself to forget her rules, her worry, her position, and even herself. For one night, she would allow herself to belong to someone else.

Soon, his pants were on the floor, and fingers were replaced by his considerable length. Seere cried out as white-hot pain and pleasure lanced through her. His movements were slow, agonizingly so, even as she pressed into him, desperate for more of him. He continued to bite her throat, leaving mark after mark as if to claim her for himself, and she didn't mind.

"Gods," she choked out as he lifted her legs over his shoulders, pinning her in place.

"You're the only goddess allowed in this bed, Your Majesty. Don't invoke any others," he said coolly. "You are mine... at least for tonight."

"I am no goddess," Seere breathed sharply.

Orias gave her an amused smirk before he leaned down and kissed her again.

"But what about you?" she asked, her gaze sharp as it bore into his. "Who do you belong to?"

"Darling, I have belonged to you the moment I set my gaze upon you on your throne," he whispered, slowing his pace once more. "I belong to you and you alone."

Seere cursed as he held her down, forcing her to stay still as he thrust into her with excruciating, delicious slowness. Suddenly, she wasn't sure that she would belong to him for only that night. Part of her wondered if she had truly been his as long as he claimed to have been hers.

She turned her gaze up to the man she gave herself to. Orias cursed as he looked upon her and quickened his pace, unable to hold himself back any longer. Moans tore from

Seere as they convulsed together, bodies pressed tightly against one another.

When they came down from their ecstasy, Orias pulled Seere close as he lay down beside her in silence. The weight of unspoken truths and unacknowledged feelings hung in the air. Each foreign to Seere, yet warm, comfortable, and anxiety-inducing all at once. She loathed the comfort she found in Orias. Still, she allowed herself to belong to him for at least a moment longer.

19

REJECTIONS

CHAYSDAY, FIFTEENTH OF THE SHADOW
MOON, YEAR 449 OF THE GODDESS

It had been a long week since her night with Orias had passed, and though neither Seere nor Orias spoke of it, the memory lingered in every glance, every stolen moment of proximity. It wasn't anger or regret that kept them apart, but the unspoken fear of what might ignite if they let the flames between them burn again.

At breakfast, the dining hall buzzed with the lively chatter of students, a stark contrast to Seere's quiet thoughts. She sat at the long table with her usual companions: Felix, Foras, Rowan, and Enora.

"And then Rowan parried so hard that Vidal's sword went flying and nearly got Raphael's head! I've never seen anyone turn that shade of red," Felix said, recounting a particularly humorous moment from the previous day's class.

Rowan groaned, slumping in his seat. "It wasn't my fault. Professor Vidal said to attack with conviction. I just... over-committed."

Enora smirked, sipping her tea. "That's one way to put it.

You looked like you were trying to knock him through a wall. If you weren't trying so hard to show off for all the other ladies..."

Laughter bubbled around the table, even drawing an amused hum from Seere.

But it was Enora who turned the conversation in a new direction, leaning in conspiratorially. "Seere, I hope you have a gown," she said, her grin devious. "I don't know if you knew, but the Winter Solstice Ball is coming up in about a month."

"They're holding the ball, again?" Foras questioned, sounding as uncomfortable as Seere felt.

"Of course!" Enora exclaimed, glaring at her friend. "It's tradition! The Winter Solstice Ball is a way for the school to celebrate the season and foster connections among the students. Isn't it exciting?"

"More like an excuse for the faculty to spy on us and see who's aligning with whom politically," Foras muttered.

Rowan ignored him, his eyes lighting up. "The music, the food, the dancing..." his gaze flickered toward Seere briefly, but she pretended not to notice.

Seere shifted uncomfortably, her fork still poised over her plate. "A ball," she echoed, more to herself than anyone else. Back in Envie, she hadn't been permitted to attend balls. They weren't traditions in the assassin's academy—and they were much less common in her citadel back in the Domain.

"Oh, come on, Seere," Enora teased, nudging her lightly. "Don't tell me you're not looking forward to it?"

"I wouldn't say that," Seere replied carefully, offering a small smile. "But I wouldn't say I'm thrilled, either. Balls are... a great place for things to go utterly haywire."

"Yes, they are," Foras agreed. "They tend to invite more chaos than they're worth."

"Oh! You know what this means, right? You'll need to find a date. The Queen of Assassins can't attend the ball by herself!" Enora exclaimed. "With the way Seere handled the Wargames, every guy in the school is going to be lining up to dance with her."

Seere massaged her temples, a frustrated sigh escaping her. "Lovely. A sea of politics that I will have to carefully navigate," she muttered.

"Don't worry," Foras said. "You'll just have to turn down, what, thirty suitors?"

"Forty," Rowan corrected with a smirk.

Felix's smile seemed to falter slightly, but he swiftly masked it with enthusiasm. "Well, whatever happens, the night will be wonderful."

"Sure," Seere muttered.

Her gaze shifted to the head of the room, where Orias spoke with Professors Viné and Manfredonia as the table conversation shifted once more. Sensing her gaze, he looked at her, his expression carefully neutral as he searched her face.

THE STONE HALLS of the academy seemed to grow narrower than usual as Seere strode through them, her black cloak trailing behind her like a shadow. She hoped for a quiet day, perhaps a chance to slip unnoticed between classes, but the announcement of the Winter Solstice Ball had shattered that illusion.

The first suitor intercepted her as she exited the dining hall with her companions, a lanky boy with sandy hair and nervous energy. "Uh, Queen Seere?" he stammered, his cheeks flushed. "I was wondering if—well, if you'd consider—"

"No," Seere said flatly, not breaking her stride.

"That was harsh," Enora hissed.

"Yes, well, they should expect it from the Assassin Queen," Seere muttered.

By the time the second suitor stopped her on her way to her first class—a boy who couldn't have been more than eighteen, his voice cracking as he tried to form a coherent sentence—Seere's patience was already wearing thin due to the gazes and whispers that followed her.

"Listen." Her voice was tight with frustration. "I have no intention of taking a partner. Find someone else."

The third came as she was leaving the training grounds after combat training, a charming young man with a rose in hand. "Your Majesty," he began smoothly, stepping in front of her path. "I must say, your performance in the Wargames was nothing short of inspiring. Surely someone as extraordinary as you deserves an equally extraordinary partner for the ball?"

Seere stared at him, unimpressed. "And you think you're that person?"

His smile didn't falter. "I'd like to think so."

"Then think again," she said coolly, stepping around him without hesitation.

The fourth found her in the corridors as she followed Felix to battle strategy, however, this one was slightly more pleasant than the others. Alsariph Farcyne smirked as he stopped her in the hallways, his stance casual and an apple in hand. "Ah, Queen Seere, just the woman I was looking for. Would you grant me the honor of escorting you to—"

"While you are far more tolerable than any of the others that have approached thus far, I must decline," she interrupted.

"Then promise me a dance," he said lightly.

"Certainly."

The encounters left her drained by midday. She was left massaging her temples, trying to get rid of the painful ache that had settled in her head. It was then, in her moment of vulnerability, that she rounded a corner in the main hall and collided with someone.

Strong hands caught her shoulders, steadying her before she could stumble. Her breath hitched when she looked up and found Orias standing over her, his green eyes meeting hers. The touch of his hands burned into her like fire, sending an unbidden thrill through her.

Time seemed to pause as they stood frozen, the air between them crackling with unspoken tension. Her heart pounded against her ribs, traitorous in its longing. His gaze softened, his thumb brushing lightly against her arm. She knew that if they were alone, he would have closed the distance between them—and she wouldn't stop him.

The moment was shattered as Orias' expression shifted to one of wry amusement. He let his hands fall away and stepped back, his usual composure slipping into place.

"Ah, Seere. I imagine you've been quite occupied today," he said, his tone filled with amusement. "Have you had many offers for the ball?"

Seere stiffened. Her voice was sharp when she answered, bitterness lacing her words. "I've had enough to last me a lifetime. Not that it's any concern of yours."

Orias raised an eyebrow, his smirk fading into something more serious. "I was merely curious," he said, his tone measured. She caught the way his gaze softened, the way he reached for her, then stopped as he remembered where they were and that they weren't alone.

"Very well," he said finally, stepping aside to let her pass. "Enjoy the rest of your day, Your Majesty."

She brushed past him without a word, her cloak swirling behind her. But as she walked away, her heart pounded with a mix of frustration and something she couldn't quite name—a lingering ache that wouldn't be silenced.

THE SPARRING GROUNDS were quiet that evening as the snow drifted to the ground. Lanterns strung across the grounds cast a soft glow, their light flickering as Seere tied her hair back. Felix waited patiently, his sword in hand, auburn hair catching the light like a crown.

"Ready?" she asked, retrieving a sword and crossing over to him.

"Always."

They launched into a series of drills, the rhythmic clash of blades echoing in the night. Felix was quick, his strikes deliberate and precise, but Seere's movements were fluid, almost effortless. She danced around him, parrying his attacks with ease, her focus sharper than ever.

"You're holding back," Felix said, his voice strained as he blocked another strike.

"I don't need to go all out to best you," Seere quipped.

Felix chuckled, stepping back to reset his stance. "Cocky, are we? Let's see how you handle this."

He lunged with his blade, aimed for her shoulder, but Seere sidestepped with a graceful pivot, using the momentum to knock his sword aside and press the tip of her own to his chest.

"Point," she said, lowering her weapon.

Felix groaned, rubbing the back of his neck. "I don't know why I even try."

"Because you're stubborn," Seere replied, though her tone was lighter. She stepped back, resting her sword against her shoulder.

For a moment, they stood in silence, the cool air brushing against their skin as their breaths evened out. Felix sheathed his blade and leaned back against the wooden railing, his expression thoughtful.

"You've been distant lately," he said after a moment.

Seere stiffened but didn't respond immediately. She turned her gaze to the horizon, where the faint glow of moonlight could be seen through the clouds. "I've been busy," she said finally.

"With what?" Felix pressed, his tone gentle but insistent. "You don't have to carry everything on your own, you know."

Seere's grip tightened on the hilt of her weapon. She hated how perceptive Felix could be, how easily he saw through the walls she tried to hold up. "It's nothing you need to worry about," she said, her voice carefully neutral.

Felix sighed, running a hand through his hair. "You always say that, but I'm not blind, Seere. I know something's been bothering you. Is it the ball?"

That caught her off guard. She turned to face him, her expression softening slightly. "The ball is the least of my concerns," she admitted.

"Then come with me," Felix said suddenly, his voice earnest.

Seere blinked, startled. "What?"

"To the ball," he clarified, stepping closer. "Let me take your mind off whatever's weighing you down. Even for just one evening."

For a moment, Seere didn't know what to say. She could see the sincerity in his eyes, the unspoken hope that maybe, just maybe, he could make things easier for her.

But she couldn't accept. Not when her duties—and the tangled web of emotions surrounding Orias—loomed so heavily over her.

"I can't," she said softly, her gaze dropping to the ground. "I need to stay focused. However, I will promise you a dance or two."

Felix's face fell, though he quickly masked it with a lopsided smile. "I figured you'd say that," he said, his tone light but tinged with disappointment. "Worth a shot, though."

Seere hesitated, the gnawing guilt a heavy stone in her chest. "Felix..."

"It's fine," he interrupted, waving her off. "Really. Just... don't shut me out, okay? Don't shut any of us out. Whatever's going on, we're here if you need help."

She nodded, though the weight in her chest didn't lift. As they packed up their equipment and headed back toward the dormitories, Seere couldn't help but glance at Felix out of the corner of her eye. He deserved better than the half-truths she gave him. But for now, it was all she could offer.

20

SHOPPING

DHANIRDAY, NINTH OF THE WHISPER
MOON, YEAR 449 OF THE GODDESS

The snow crunched underfoot. With the Whisper Moon in full swing, snow had fallen in heavy heaps all across Malphas University and the rest of Aevrath. The air smelled of pine and smoke from the chimneys, mingling with the soft hum of laughter as Seere and her companions strolled through the winding streets of Cegwin. Every shop and stall seemed to glow with the festive spirit of the winter season, their windows adorned with garlands of holly and twinkling fairy lights.

"This is exactly what I needed," Enora said with a dreamy sigh, tilting her face toward the snowflakes drifting lazily down from the sky. "Doesn't it just feel magical?"

"It feels cold," Foras grumbled, pulling her cloak tighter.

"That's because you're as thin as a broomstick. For being the soldier that you are, you aren't very bulky," Rowan teased, giving him a playful shove that made Foras scowl.

Seere lagged slightly, her gloved hands tucked into her cloak as she surveyed their surroundings. The last time she'd visited Cegwin, it had been in the dark, and she'd been unable to see the charm that it held. If she managed to look past the Envie guards that watched her, she saw the cobbled streets that wove around brightly painted buildings, their rooftops frosted with snow.

The buzz of life was surprising to her. Cegwin, it seemed, was one of the few towns that didn't allow Empress Selina's cruelty to mar it. The thought brought some semblance of peace to Seere.

Felix appeared at her side, his auburn hair gleaming in the afternoon light. "You've been quiet," he said, his voice warm with concern.

"I'm always quiet," she replied, giving him an amused look. "But I suppose this is a bit overwhelming. So many people."

Felix chuckled. "Stick with us. Enora's enthusiasm will drown out everything else."

Up ahead, Enora darted between stalls, her sharp eyes scanning the wares. She stopped abruptly at a stand selling silver hairpins shaped like snowflakes.

"Oh, Seere!" Enora waved her over, her grin practically splitting her face. "These would look amazing in your hair. Come try one!"

"I don't need a hairpin," Seere replied, though she let herself be dragged to the stall.

"It's not a matter of whether you need it or not," Enora said, holding up a pin and tilting her head as if imagining it in Seere's hair. "It's about looking like the mysterious, ethereal goddess you are."

Foras groaned loudly. "Here we go. Enora's on a mission."

Rowan laughed. "You might as well surrender, Seere. It's faster."

The hairpins were quickly forgotten as Enora spotted a

boutique with elegant dresses displayed in the forested windows. She gasped dramatically and grabbed Seere's hand, dragging her toward the door.

"Enora—" Seere began, but the protest died on her lips as they entered.

The boutique was warm and inviting, the air perfumed with lavender and cedarwood. Dresses of every style and color hung on racks and mannequins, their fabrics shimmering in the soft candlelight. Enora clapped her hands in delight.

"This is it," she declared. "We're finding you the perfect dress for the ball."

"I don't need a dress," Seere argued, crossing her arms. In truth, Seere had a couple, none of which were the fanciest, but they would suffice.

"You're going to the ball, aren't you?" Enora countered, already rifling through the racks. "You can't just show up in your typical leathers."

"I have a dress."

Enora turned to her with a look of incredulity. "I'm fairly certain you're just saying that."

"Come on, Seere. Enora has a point. You need to look like the untouchable, ethereal Assassin Queen that you are," Rowan said, joining Enora in the hunt for dresses. "You should look the part of royalty."

Seere sighed, defeated. "Fine. But just one dress."

Enora lit up like a child on the morning of the first frost. "You won't regret it!"

She began pulling dresses from the racks, piling them into Seere's reluctant arms. Foras and Felix lounged in a corner, more or less uninterested in the fashion spectacle, while Felix offered occasional input that only seemed to egg Enora on.

The fitting room was a snug little alcove tucked away at the back of the boutique, separated by a heavy velvet curtain. Seere stood inside, staring at the assortment of dresses draped over a small bench. Each one seemed more elaborate than the last: deep burgundy velvet, shimmering silver satin, and a black gown whose intricate details were hard to make out.

"Enora, this is ridiculous," she called through the curtain, frowning as she held up a gown that looked far too ornate for her taste.

"It's fun, is what it is!" Enora chirped from the other side. "Just try them on! You'll look stunning in anything, but we need to find *the* dress."

Seere sighed, shaking her head as she began to remove her cloak and boots. The first dress she tried was the burgundy velvet, its heavy fabric hot against her skin. The bodice hugged her figure tightly, with long sleeves that flared at the wrists, giving it a regal, almost severe appearance.

When she stepped out of the fitting room, Rowan gaped at her. Felix gave a low whistle, his lips quirked upward in amusement. Seere shifted uncomfortably, watching Enora for her verdict.

"You look like you're about to sentence someone to an execution," Felix commented.

"Probably your execution," Enora said, shooting a glare over her shoulder at Foras. "But... he's not inherently wrong..."

"Go try another one," Felix said.

Enora waved Seere back toward the fitting room with a dramatic flourish. "Next!"

The silver gown came next. It was sleeveless, with a high collar and a flowing skirt that shimmered like moonlight when she moved. Seere studied herself in the mirror, turning this way and that. She had to admit it was beautiful, but it felt... too delicate. Too unlike her with all her rough edges. It would put her under a spotlight, and she was meant to always be a shadow.

When she stepped out, Enora clasped her hands together, stars in her eyes. "You look gorgeous. Like an assassin who's decided to murder people at a masquerade ball in style!"

Rowan snorted. "Enora, that's not a compliment."

Seere arched a brow. "And yet, it somehow fits."

Foras, who had been trying to nap in a chair near the corner, opened one eye. "You look like a ghost," he muttered. "Next one."

With a roll of her eyes, Seere turned to the fitting room, slipping into the black gown. It was simpler than the others, a sleek gown that hugged her figure with a halter neckline. It moved like water with each step, and she decided that this would be the one she took back if only to get Enora to stop hounding her.

When she finally emerged, her four companions fell silent. Felix, who had been leaning casually against the wall, stood up straighter, his cobalt eyes locking on her. Rowan let out a soft "Wow," while Enora clutched at her chest as if she might faint.

"Now *this*," Enora breathed, "is very elegant."

Felix nodded slowly. "You look... lovely."

Seere crossed her arms, suddenly feeling exposed under their gazes. "It's good enough?" she asked, trying to mask her discomfort.

"It's definitely suitable," Rowan said thoughtfully.

Enora was already making plans. "I think a smoky eye and a sharp wing will suit it well. Light blush, but sharp contour. In your hair, we can add a mourning veil just for the extra bit of flair and mystery."

Seere rolled her eyes, though she couldn't help the small smile that tugged at her lips. "Fine. I'll take this one," she said and disappeared back inside the changing room to return to her ordinary clothes.

The sky was tinged with soft pinks and oranges as Seere and her friends stepped out of the boutique. The cold air was a welcome contrast to the stifling warmth of the boutique, and Seere let out a long breath. She carried her new dress and a few accessories that Enora had forced her to purchase, but she didn't mind too terribly.

Enora twirled a pale blue scarf around her neck. "I'm starving. Let's find a place to eat before Rowan and Foras collapse," she said.

"I'm fine," Rowan protested, though his empty stomach betrayed his words with an audible grumble.

Felix clapped him on the back, smirking. "To the pub, then. A warm fire and some food will do us all some good."

The group made their way down the cobblestone streets dusted with fresh snow. Lanterns flickered to life against the creeping dusk, their golden light blurring across frost-slick windows. Enora recounted every gown Seere had tried on in painstaking detail, much to her amusement and Seere's mild irritation.

"I'm just saying," Enora smirked, nudging Rowan, "that silver gown made her look like an actual queen."

"She is a queen. Pretty sure that doesn't depend on the gown," Foras said.

Rowan, walking at the back of the group, grinned. If that's the case, she should've bought the burgundy one. It would have screamed 'bow before me, peasants.'"

Seere rolled her eyes. "You're all lucky I didn't leave you in the boutique."

When they arrived at the pub, a wave of warmth and the scent of spiced cider greeted them. The wooden interior was dimly lit but inviting, with patrons scattered across worn tables. A crackling fire burned in the hearth, casting a golden glow over the room.

They claimed a corner booth, settling in as a waitress approached to take their orders. Felix immediately asked for one of the delicious, smelling ciders, which Enora hurriedly copied. Seere stuck to water, knowing she wasn't consuming anything while she wore her mask.

As they waited for their drinks, Rowan leaned across the table, a mischievous grin on his face. "So, Seere, how does it feel to have every eligible man at school begging you for a dance?"

Enora cackled. "Oh, they're not just bachelors. I heard even Professor Bael, the alchemy instructor, asked her, too."

Seere groaned, resting her head in her hand. "Can we not talk about this?"

But the teasing didn't stop. Rowan and Enora launched into exaggerated reenactments of her supposed suitors, complete with dramatic sighs and declarations of love. Even Foras cracked a rare smile at their antics.

Their laughter was interrupted by the arrival of a familiar figure. Shax, with his usual warm atmosphere, stepped into the pub. He scanned the room before his gaze landed on Seere, who watched him.

"Your Majesty," he said brightly as he approached. "I didn't expect to see you here."

"Join us!" Rowan called, sliding over to make room.

Shax slid into the booth beside Rowan.

"I was dragged out to go shopping," Seere said, sparing a glance at Enora, who grinned triumphantly.

Their drinks arrived, and the group quickly fell into easy conversation. Shax melded in seamlessly, offering his more than amusing "Dad jokes" that earned bursts of laughter from the table.

"Are you going to the ball, Shax?" Enora asked, swirling her cider.

"I'll be there," he confirmed, his sharp gaze meeting Seere's briefly. "But only to ensure everything goes smoothly."

Enora sighed dramatically. "You two are so serious. Can't you enjoy yourselves for once?"

"I find plenty of joy in my life. I have a wife and children that I cherish," Shax said, amusement decorating his lips.

Seere found herself smiling despite the chaos. For a moment, the weight of her responsibilities lifted, replaced by the warmth of good company. As the evening wore on, the conversations turned to topics of childhood memories, misadventures in combat training, and hopes for the winter ball.

When it was finally time to leave, all but Seere, who hadn't had anything to drink, stumbled out into the chill of the night, their laughter echoing through the snow-covered streets. Shax parted ways with them at the gates where their carriage waited, offering a nod of farewell before disappearing back into the town.

As they returned to their dorms, Seere found herself

feeling more at ease than she had in weeks. It was a rare, precious reprieve—one she knew wouldn't last, but one she treasured nonetheless.

However, when she opened the door to her dorm and stepped into her bedroom, she froze.

On her bed lay a gown—a masterpiece of black silk, its fabric adorned with silver flowers that mirrored the delicate Eulla blossoms from the Domain. Beside it rested a matching half-mask, black with intricate silver lace. The craftsmanship was exquisite, far beyond anything she had ever seen.

A small note rested atop the gown.

You'll need something special for the ball.

There was no signature.

Seere's heart raced as she picked up the dress, the cool silk slipping through her fingers. She tried on the gown, the fabric molding perfectly to her form. The silver flowers caught the dim light of her room, glinting like stars against the night sky.

She had a feeling that she knew exactly who'd sent it to her. Only he would give her something so extravagant for no apparent reason. Only he would find something that suited her so well, perhaps too well.

21

WINTER SOLSTICE

LABRISDAY, TWENTY-FIRST OF THE WHISPER MOON, YEAR 449 OF THE GODDESS

The Winter Solstice Ball was the kind of grand, opulent event that Seere usually avoided. Crowded halls, fluttering gowns, and forced pleasantries weren't her style. But tonight she had little choice in the matter.

Enora burst into her room hours before the event, armed with brushes, pins, and a near-overwhelming amount of energy. Seere had barely settled into a chair before her friend began tugging at her hair.

"Enora, I can do my hair," Seere murmured, wincing as a comb snagged a knot.

"You will do no such thing, Your Majesty. Consider me your humble servant for the evening," Enora said, deftly twisting strands into an intricate style. "You might not care, but this is the Winter Solstice Ball. It's tradition here. Everyone is going to look their best, and I'll be damned if I let you show up looking like you just rolled out of bed."

Seere gave her a dry look, but said nothing. She knew better than to argue with Enora when she was in this state.

The process felt endless. Enora chattered without pause as she worked, detailing everything from the decorations in the great hall to the rumored rivalries brewing over who was taking whom to the ball. She tuned most of it out, her mind drifting to the gown waiting for her in the closet.

When Enora finally stepped back, a triumphant gleam in her eye, Seere glanced at her reflection. Her hair was swept into an elegant updo, stands of silver pins woven through it to give a subtle sparkle.

"You already look stunning," Enora said, hands on her hips as she admired her handiwork. "Now, go get dressed. I'll see you at the ball!"

She left in a whirl of excitement, leaving Seere alone with her thoughts.

Once the door closed, Seere rose and crossed the room, opening the closet where she had hidden her gown. The black silk shimmered faintly in the dim light, the silver flowers catching the glow like frost on a winter morning.

She ran her fingers over the fabric, marveling at its soft weight. The matching mask sat neatly atop the gown, its silver lace woven into delicate patterns.

As she slipped into the dress, she couldn't help but admire the craftsmanship. The gown fit her perfectly, hugging her figure while allowing ease of movement. The slit along her left leg revealed the tattoo spiraling down her thigh, a subtle but striking detail that balanced elegance with danger.

She strapped her dagger into the hidden sheath beneath the skirt, appreciating the practicality of the design. The designer of the gown understood her perfectly, which only helped to solidify her guess as to who it had been.

When she slipped the mask over her face, she took a

moment to examine herself in the mirror. The transformation was startling. The girl staring back at her looked like a phantom of the winter night, cloaked in mystery and power.

Seere smiled faintly, her fingers brushing against the mask's edges. She didn't know for certain who had sent the dress, but they had given her a weapon in its own way—an armor of silk and steel to wear into the battlefield of the ballroom.

With a deep breath, she stepped out of her room, the soft rustle of silk following her.

The journey to the great hall was more nerve-wracking than Seere had anticipated. The faint echoes of music drifted through the stone corridors of the academy, growing louder with each step she took. Her dress flowed like liquid shadow around her, the silver flowers catching the light of torches and casting fleeting glimmers on the walls.

She paused just outside the massive double doors of the hall, taking a steadying breath to calm her nerves. Voices buzzed from within, laughter and conversation mixing with the melody of a waltz.

The heavy doors creaked as a pair of guards pushed them open for her. The moment she stepped inside, she heard the herald announce her. "Her Majesty, Seere Cross, of the Domain of Assassins!"

The hall fell silent.

All eyes turned toward her as she stepped into the room, her heels clicking softly with each measured step. The great hall was resplendent, draped in white and silver decorations that shimmered like frost under moonlight. Chandeliers hung low, their crystals scattering light across the gathered students and faculty.

Seere kept her head high, her expression serene and

carefully neutral. The gown she wore felt like a second skin, its tailored perfection exuding confidence and grace. The crowd parted as she entered the hall, her every movement commanding attention.

Felix was the first to approach, his face awash with awe. He was dressed in a crisp, burgundy suit that complemented his princely demeanor, but even he seemed diminished in her presence.

"You look... incredible," he said, offering his hand.

"Thank you," Seere replied, placing her gloved fingers in his.

He guided her to the dance floor, where others instinctively stepped aside to make room for them. The music shifted seamlessly into a waltz as Felix led her into the first steps. His movements were precise, his hand steady at her waist, but Seere's attention was elsewhere.

Her gaze shifted beyond Felix to Orias, who stood like a statue amidst the crowd. His suit was inky black with subtle silver embroidery that mirrored the blossoms on her gown. His sharp, piercing eyes were locked onto her, a flicker of frustration and something deeper swirling within them as he watched Felix claim her first dance.

The weight of his gaze sent a thrill down her spine, though she refused to let it show.

"I noticed this isn't the dress you purchased at the store. Why didn't you say you already had one?" Felix questioned, drawing Seere's attention to him.

"If memory serves, I did say that I had dresses already," she said, narrowing her gaze on the prince. "Neither you nor anyone else listened. And this one was a gift. It felt rude not to wear it."

"A gift? From who?" he questioned.

"The note didn't say."

Felix hummed, pulling her close before he guided her into a spin out onto the floor. It was then that a strong hand caught her mid-motion, pulling her away with undeniable authority.

"It's rude to steal another's date, Your Highness," Orias said coolly as Seere found herself pressed against his chest, his voice sending a ripple of gasps and murmurs into the crowd. Then his eyes locked onto Seere's, the faintest smirk ghosting across his mouth.

Orias swept her away from Felix, his hand firm at her waist as he led her into a slower, more intimate dance than the one before. The music seemed to fade into the background, the space around them clearing as if the crowd had been pushed back by an unseen force.

"You look stunning," Orias murmured, his voice low enough for only her to hear.

"So I've been told," Seere replied, her tone carefully neutral.

Orias chuckled softly, spinning her with a deftness that left her momentarily breathless. When he pulled her back, his hand lingered at the small of her back, holding her closer than was proper.

"The dress suits you," he continued, his tone light but his gaze intense. "I knew it would."

Seere smirked, her hand shifting from his shoulder to the silver trim on one of his lapels. "So you admit to it," she noted.

His smirk widened. "Of course. I wouldn't style myself to match you if I hadn't wanted you to know," he said. "As much as I try to keep my distance from you, *Amaris*, I am a moth and you are the pyre that I will burn on."

"I thought it was the other way around," she whispered. "I thought you were the pyre."

"I told you, darling, you're the dangerous one here. I am drowning in you. All I want *is* you," he breathed.

The tension between them was electric, their movements fluid yet charged with unspoken words. Around them, the crowd watched in awe, but Seere, caught in Orias' orbit, barely noticed.

For a moment, it felt as though they were the only two people in the room. Even as she saw Alsariph dance with Achlys and Enora twirling around the room with a young man Seere didn't recognize. But then, her gaze flickered past Orias' shoulder and deeper into the crowd, catching sight of Felix standing at the edge of the floor, his expression dark with frustration and hurt.

The spell broke. Seere's steps faltered for a fraction of a second, but Orias steadied her effortlessly, his smirk fading into something softer.

"While I have you here," Orias began, his tone low. "I wanted to let you know that I am being forced to release Cotoria."

Seere sighed softly and nodded. "When?"

"Tomorrow."

"Very well," she whispered. "I appreciate the warning."

His gaze shifted from her eyes to where her lips were beneath her mask, then back up. "I wish I could have given you a better warning."

"Don't worry about it."

As the music ended, Orias spun her into one final flourish, his grip lingering as the applause echoed through the hall. He leaned in, his breath warm against her ear.

"Stay by my side tonight," he said softly, his words more command than request.

"As you told Felix, I'm your date this evening," she said, an amused smile tugging at the corners of her lips.

The crowd had begun to shift as the dancing gave way to conversation, laughter, and the clinking of glasses. Orias offered Seere his arm with an air of casual command, a faint smirk playing on his lips. Seere hesitated for only a moment before slipping her hand into the crook of his arm, the silk of his suit warm beneath her touch.

The subtle murmur of whispers followed them as they moved through the hall, their presence magnetic and commanding. Orias led her with ease, his steps measured and confident, while Seere maintained an air of regal poise.

"Smile, darling," Orias murmured under his breath, leaning slightly toward her. "It's important they see you enjoying yourself."

Seere tilted her head, the faintest curve of amusement touching her lips beneath the mask. "Enjoyment is a relative term. Besides, they can't see my smile."

Orias chuckled, his eyes glinting with mischief. "Touché, but I would still like to make you smile."

Orias led her to a cluster of ambassadors, their richly adorned attire a clear indication of their status. Seere stiffened slightly as she recognized the crests of Noctivagus and Envie among them, her pulse quickening at the realization.

"Orias, these people—"

"Ambassadors," Orias greeted warmly, inclining his head. "I trust you're enjoying the evening?"

The Noctivagian ambassador, a tall man with salt-and-pepper hair and piercing brown eyes, stepped forward. "The festivities are exquisite, Headmaster. And this must be Her

Majesty, Seere Cross." His gaze swept over her with interest. "I was asked on behalf of King Hubert to thank you for all you have done to aid the kingdom."

Seere met his gaze steadily, though surprise flickered within her. "Of course, Ambassador. I do my best."

The man chuckled, clearly amused by her words. "Indeed. Though I must admit, I hadn't expected the Queen of Assassins to be so... young."

"And yet here I am," Seere replied smoothly.

The ambassador from Envie, a severe-looking woman whom Seere once knew to be Edith Carman, stepped forward next. "It is a rare pleasure to meet someone with your... particular skill set, Your Majesty. Tell me, how does one with such a background find themselves at an academy like this?"

Orias interjected before Seere could respond, his voice smooth as silk. "A fascinating story, no doubt, but one best saved for another time. For now, I'd prefer we focus on the future rather than the past."

The ambassadors exchanged glances but didn't press further. Seere, however, felt the weight of their scrutiny, as though they were dissecting every move she made, every word she spoke.

As they continued to circulate, Orias introduced her to nobles, dignitaries, and faculty alike, each interaction leaving Seere more aware of how he was presenting her. He didn't simply accompany her—he showcased her, holding her in the spotlight with a confidence that bordered on possessiveness. It was as though he wanted the entire hall to know that she belonged at his side. The thought amused her.

It was during one such introduction that Seere caught

sight of Professor Vidal standing at the edge of the room. His dark eyes were fixed on Orias with a strange intensity, his expression unreadable but unmistakably tense.

"Something wrong?" Orias asked softly, his voice pulling her attention back to him.

Seere tilted her head slightly, keeping her voice low. "Vidal is watching you."

Orias' expression didn't falter, but a flicker of something unreadable passed through his eyes. "He always does. Pay it no mind."

However, Seere couldn't shake the feeling that there was more to Vidal's scrutiny than mere curiosity. The professor's gaze lingered too long, his posture too rigid.

Orias seemed unbothered; however, he tightened his hold on her ever so slightly. He continued to guide her through the room, his demeanor unshaken but his focus sharper. Seere followed his lead, her mind racing with questions she dared not voice.

As the evening progressed, the ball became a whirl of music, laughter, and opulence. The crowd around them grew thicker, but for Seere, Orias' presence made everything else blur into insignificance.

Each dance they shared was an intricate game, a push and pull of power and tension. Orias led her with practiced ease, but she wasn't content to simply follow. With every step, she challenged him, her movements sharp and deliberate, earning amused glances and subtle smiles from her enigmatic partner.

When the orchestra began a slower piece, Orias leaned closer, his breath brushing against her ear.

"Step outside with me," he murmured, his voice low enough that only she could hear.

"What about Felix?" Seere asked, her gaze darting around the crowd before she found the prince talking with both Foras and Shax.

"He's safe," Orias assured her, his hand finding her waist. "I have Shax tailing him."

"Fine."

Orias didn't waste time. He took her hand and wove through the throng of dancers, his grip firm but gentle. Seere felt the weight of curious eyes following them as they slipped out of the great hall and into the dimly lit corridors of the university.

The sound of the ball faded behind them, replaced by the soft echo of their footsteps against the stone floor.

"Where are you taking me?" she asked, a hint of amusement in her voice. "I hope you are aware of all the rumors that are going to spark now."

Orias whirled to face her, then pushed her back into a wall. A gasp of shock escaped her as he pulled her mask below her chin and kissed her. The world seemed to fall away around them. His kiss was both demanding and reverent, as though he was trying to convey everything he couldn't say aloud. Seere's hands found their way to his chest, clutching the fabric of his suit as she deepened the kiss.

When they finally broke apart, their breaths mingling together, Orias rested his forehead against hers.

"Let them talk," he breathed. "I don't care what they think anymore."

"This is reckless," she murmured.

A chuckle escaped him before he kissed her again. "You have no idea, Your Majesty. But you are addicting. The very forbidden nature of this is delicious, don't you think?"

"Who said this was forbidden?" she asked, amusement lacing her tone. "I thought you said you didn't care."

"Amaris, my darling, your very identity makes this forbidden," he whispered, his thumb caressing her cheek.

Seere rolled her eyes as she replaced her mask over her mouth and nose. "Then I suppose we should find somewhere a little more private if this is so forbidden," she teased, glancing around the hallway to verify that they were completely alone.

"To bed then, shall we?" he asked, his smirk returning. "That is... if you wish to join me."

Seere lifted a brow. "I'm going to need a change of clothes."

Orias let out a low groan, his lips finding the sensitive spot below her ear. "Borrow my clothes," he hissed, nipping her skin.

Seere moaned quietly, melting into him. "Fine."

He wasted no time in grabbing her arm and leading her in the direction of his office. As they walked, Seere pulled out the pins that held her hair together until the lavender strands fell around her shoulders in soft waves.

The moment they walked into the office, Orias' hands were on her. He pushed her back into his desk, unlacing the corset of her dress with the desperation of a man who was starving. A man who was starving for her.

Orias kissed her as the gown slid from her body. His hands roamed wildly, touching every part of her that he could. Her skin burned under his fingertips, leaving her aching for more. She wanted him. She wanted the pleasure he offered.

She unbuttoned his suit, letting each layer fall to the ground as he lifted her onto the desk. Then he was sliding his length into her, drawing out moans of pleasure and desire. Her legs wrapped around his waist as he moved agonizingly slow in and out of her.

Seere's back arched as a wave of intoxicating pleasure shot through her with each rock of his hips. Orias let out a low growl as each deliberate movement he made had her body quivering.

"Goddess," Orias murmured, his head dropping to the crook of her neck where he bit and sucked.

"I am still no goddess," she bit back, her nails digging into his shoulders.

Orias huffed, his mouth trailing up to her ear slowly. "Oh, but you are," he breathed. "And I will worship you as such, darling. I will worship your body until you ascend into godhood."

A soft cry escaped her as he lifted her off the desk and carefully carried her back to his bed. She felt his muscles tense under her fingers, her body clenching around him until he dropped her onto the plush mattress. She cried out as he trapped her legs over his shoulders and thrust into her desperately.

Seere's fingers dug into the sheets before he captured her wrists and held them above her head with one hand, the other roaming her body until it rested on her waist. His gaze raked over her, unable to get enough of the vision that she was.

He rasped out a word she couldn't make out, hanging his head as if merely looking at her would do him in. Seere squirmed underneath him, her head falling back as pleasurable whimpers and moans escaped her mouth.

"Please," she whispered, spasming around his length. "Orias, please."

He swore and dropped her legs, pulling her close as they both released their building ecstasy. Pressed together, their bodies were sticky with sweat, their breathing coming out in heavy pants. Then Orias slid from her and fell onto the bed beside her, his fingers tracing the curve in her waist as he gazed over her body.

"I should leave," she murmured.

A low growl escaped him, pulling her impossibly closer. "No, you shouldn't."

"Yes, I should," she argued, meeting his gaze. She ran a hand through his hair. "I can't spend the night with you. Everyone will be suspicious enough."

"I don't give a damn what they think. You are mine."

22

RUMORS

IKTUNEDAY, TWENTY-SECOND OF THE
WHISPER MOON, YEAR 449 OF THE GODDESS

Seere sat on the edge of her bed as the first pale light of dawn slipped through her curtains, casting a faint glow over her room. The coolness of the winter night seeped through the air, a stark contrast to the warmth of the ball she'd danced in with Orias only hours ago.

She remained in her place for a long while, her gaze on the skirts of the dress she'd slipped back into just to sneak back into her dorm. The echo of the dance still lingered in her mind—the music, the swirling colors of gowns, Orias' touch...

With a sigh, she finally slipped from the gown, her movements slow and deliberate as she replayed the night over and over in her mind. The way Orias had stolen her away from Felix, the way he paraded her around the ball for all to see, the way he claimed her in his bed once again as if she were something he truly cared for.

She shook herself out of her haze as she pulled on her blouse and leggings, followed by her leather corset and sheath. She slipped her mask on and relaxed slightly, grateful for the secrecy it provided her now more than ever.

As Seere opened the door to step out of her bedroom, she immediately froze, startled by the sight of Foras standing just outside. His hand was raised to knock against the door, his sharp eyes narrowed with an intensity that made it clear he wasn't there for a casual chat. The tension radiating off of him was palpable, his jaw clenched as if he were barely holding back a tide of frustration.

"Foras," she greeted warily, her voice low and controlled. "Is there something you need?"

He didn't answer immediately. Instead, he stepped into her room without invitation, the weight of his presence making the small space feel even smaller. Seere stepped back, shutting the door so that no one could overhear whatever was about to be said.

"You're playing a dangerous game," he said finally, his voice taut with anger.

She tilted her head, her eyes narrowing. "What exactly is that supposed to mean?"

"You know exactly what I mean." His gaze burned into her. "Half the school is buzzing with rumors about you and Orias. Do you have any idea what you've done?"

Her expression darkened. "What I've done?" She dropped her hands to her sides so that they were close to her dagger. "What the hell are you referring to?"

Foras took a step closer, his glare level with hers. "You're betrothed to Felix, Amaris. Or have you conveniently forgotten that little detail?"

The words struck a nerve, but Seere didn't flinch. Instead, she met his glare with a calm intensity. "I'm not betrothed to anyone," she replied evenly. "That arrangement ended the moment I was framed for my parents' murders. Noctivagus cut all ties with Amaris, Foras. If they truly wanted me to marry Felix, they could have offered their protection."

Foras' expression hardened, but Seere pressed on, her voice growing sharper. "My only connection to Noctivagus now is my mission. As you know, I was hired to uncover the Order of the Chimera's plans and to protect Felix from them. That's it. Beyond that, who I spend my time with is none of your concern."

Foras' fists clenched at his sides. "None of my concern?" he repeated, his voice rising. "You're making a mockery of everything Felix has worked for—everything I have worked for. You're letting your emotions cloud your judgment. Don't let him manipulate you."

"You think I don't know my own mind? Orias hasn't manipulated me, Foras. If anything, he's one of the few people who's treated me as an equal, not just as some pawn to be used and discarded."

Foras winced, her words hitting their mark. "This isn't about equality or feelings, Seere. This is about duty. And right now, you're putting everything we've worked for at risk."

Seere sighed heavily, massaging her temples. "Leave me out of whatever scheme you have planned. I am not the same girl that you met all those years ago. I am not the girl that Felix fell in love with back then!" she snapped. "That girl is dead."

The silence that followed was heavy, the air between them charged with unresolved tension. Foras stepped back, his expression a mixture of anger and disappointment. "Do whatever you want," he said curtly, turning toward the door. "But don't say I didn't warn you when it all falls apart."

As he left, the door clicking shut behind him, Seere stood in the middle of her room, her heart pounding with a mix of anger and frustration. She clenched her fists at her sides, willing herself to calm down.

Shaking her head, she adjusted her cloak and left the room, determined to face whatever awaited her.

THERE WERE no classes that day, which left the fortress halls busy and filled to the brim with students. Seere's senses were razor-sharp, catching snippets of gossip as they passed.

"Is it true? The headmaster and *her*?"

"She's nothing more than a glorified killer. What could he possibly see in her?"

"A queen sharing a bed with her headmaster? How scandalous."

"No wonder she's at the top of all the classes."

Her steps faltered only slightly, her mask concealing the tightening of her jaw. The words were like knives, sharp and meant to wound, but she forced herself to keep walking, her back straight and her head high. Still, the whispers clung to her like a second skin, and she could feel her companions bristling around her.

Foras cast her a sidelong glance, his expression dark and unreadable, but she could feel the reprimand simmering just beneath his composed exterior.

Seere shot him a sharp glare, daring him to say anything to her as they walked. The gossip was nothing. She'd dealt with hatred and disdain her entire life; she was raised by it and overcame it. "Let it go," she said softly, her voice low enough for only him to hear.

Foras' lips pressed into a thin line, but he said nothing.

Just as she thought they might make it through the hall without further incident, a familiar, haughty laugh cut through the air like a whip.

"Well, if it isn't the Queen of Assassins," came Malkyn's mocking voice. "Or should I say the Queen of Scandal?"

Seere stopped in her tracks, turning to face the source of the voice. Malkyn was leaning against the wall, her arms crossed and a wicked smirk on her face. But it wasn't Malkyn who caught Seere's attention—it was the girl standing beside her.

Cotoria.

The princess of Envie's lips curled into a sneer. "I have to say, it's impressive how quickly your reputation has plummeted. Then again, what can one expect from someone like you?"

Seere tilted her head, forcing her voice to remain calm even as her mind whirled with questions. "Princess Cotoria," she said evenly. "It's lovely to see you again. How did you manage to get out of the dungeons and remain here in the school?"

Cotoria's smirk widened, her gaze dripping with venom. "It was well within the law to kill you while we were on the soil of Envie, considering what you are," she said coolly. "I also have a sister and many allies in high places. Unlike some people."

Malkyn laughed, clearly enjoying the show. "You should take notes, Your Majesty. Maybe then you wouldn't have to rely on sleeping your way to the top."

Seere took a slow step forward, her posture poised and

commanding. "I am already at the top," she said, her tone icy and precise. "I would watch your words very carefully."

Cotoria's smirk faltered for a fraction of a second, but Malkyn quickly stepped in, her laugh louder and more forced now. "Careful, Queen Seere," she said mockingly. "You wouldn't want to upset the wrong people."

With that, they turned and sauntered away, though not without one last glance over their shoulders, as if to ensure their words had landed.

The hall was silent for a long moment after that. Seere noticed Alsariph leaning against a wall, his gaze icy as he observed her. He nodded slightly to her, then pushed off the wall and walked in the opposite direction.

They finally reached the library, which was as grand and silent as ever, its towering shelves filled with ancient tomes and whispered secrets. The group stepped inside, the soft click of their boots against the polished floor the only sound that followed them. The tension, however, was palpable.

Seere led the way to their usual table near the corner, where the faint glow of lanterns offered a warm respite from the chaos outside. As they settled into their seats, the silence between them stretched unbearably.

Enora sat closest to Seere, her hands moving restlessly as she pulled out parchment and ink. However, she refused to look at Seere. There was a furrow in her brow, one that deepened whenever her focus strayed from her work.

Foras positioned himself at the far end of the table, deliberately putting as much distance as he could between himself and Seere. He dropped his bag onto the table with an audible thud before pulling out a stack of books, all of which were on dragons, their current topic in history. His jaw remained tight as he opened one of them with more force than necessary, the sound of pages flipping too sharp in the quiet.

Felix was uncharacteristically subdued, sitting across from Seere but refusing to look up. He kept his head down, feigning interest in his notes, though his pen barely moved across the paper. His usual warmth was gone, replaced by a quiet brooding.

Rowan, perhaps the most unnerving of them all, remained silent and still. He leaned back in his chair, his arms crossed, his eyes fixed on a spot far away. His usually lighthearted demeanor was nowhere to be seen, and the look on his face was one of quiet contemplation, as though he were trying to piece together a puzzle that didn't quite fit.

Seere stood silently and wandered the shelves until she found a book interesting enough to read before returning to her seat. She tried to ignore the heavy atmosphere around her. But every scratch of a quill and turn of a page only reminded her of the unspoken frustrations that lingered between them.

They were angry with her. Disappointed because she had chosen to give her affection to someone other than the person they had wanted. Though they didn't say it outright, she could feel it in every glance they avoided and every word they chose not to speak.

The silence became a living thing, oppressive and suffocating, pressing on Seere until she couldn't focus on the text in front of her. She shifted uncomfortably in her seat, glancing at each of her companions in turn, but none of them acknowledged her.

The door to the library creaked open, breaking the tension like a blade slicing through taut rope. Seere looked up to see Orias stepping inside, his presence commanding even in the hushed atmosphere of the library. He moved with an air of calm authority, his dark coat trailing behind him as he strode toward their table.

The others noticed him immediately. Enora stiffened, her quill halting mid-word. Foras' grip on his leather-bound book tightened as if he wanted to beat Orias with it. Felix's eyes flicked up briefly before darting away, his jaw tightening. Only Rowan remained impassive, though his gaze followed Orias' every move.

Orias stopped at the head of the table, his sharp eyes sweeping over the group. "Seere," he said, his voice low but firm. "May I speak with you in private?"

Foras made a noise of protest, but Orias didn't so much as glance his way. The weight of his gaze fell solely on Seere, expectant but not unkind.

She hesitated before she pushed her chair back and stood, the scrape of wood on wood loud in the oppressive silence. "Of course," she said, her voice steady despite the turmoil roiling in her chest.

She followed him out of the library, her steps echoing in the quiet. As the door closed behind them, she glanced back at her companions one last time, finding them still immersed in their silent frustrations. The distance between them felt wider than ever, and for the first time in a long while, Seere felt truly alone.

The hallway outside the library was quiet, its tall windows letting in streams of pale winter light that painted the stone walls in shades of silver. Seere followed Orias down the corridor, the soft echo of their steps the only sound. He didn't speak, his usual composure giving nothing away.

They turned into a smaller, rarely-used study room

tucked away from the busier parts of the school. The heavy oak door creaked as Orias opened it, gesturing for Seere to step inside. The room smelled faintly of parchment and old wood, a faint glow emanating from a lantern that held a strange purple crystal within it, sitting on a desk at the front of the room.

As the door clicked shut behind them, Seere finally spoke. "What do you need from me now?" she asked, leaning back against an old desk.

He walked up to her, his gaze searching hers. "Are you okay?"

Seere shrugged, her gaze falling to the floor. "It doesn't matter whether I'm 'Okay' or not," she said bitterly. "What do you want?"

"I want to make sure you're okay," he whispered, reaching a hand up to her face. "Believe it or not, I have grown to care for you. You're under a lot of pressure because of my actions, and for that I am sorry. I never expected this level of backlash."

"I am the Assassin Queen," she said softly, shaking her head. "I expected this sort of thing. It follows me everywhere I go. In truth, I expected you to avoid me, too."

"I'm too far into this grave that I've dug to hide from you now, darling," he said, offering a faint smirk. "Unfortunately, I have come to warn you that I am leaving."

The words hit her like a blow, her breath catching in her throat. "Leaving?" she echoed, her voice barely above a whisper.

He nodded, his expression unreadable. "I've been summoned to Noctivagus. There are matters there that require my attention. I'll be gone for at least a month, possibly longer."

Her mind raced. "But... what about the Order? What about—"

"Amaris," he interrupted, his tone firm but not harsh. "You'll continue to do what you've been doing. Watching, listening, protecting. I trust you to handle things in my absence."

A foreign part of her wanted to argue, to demand that he stay, but words wouldn't come. Instead, she looked up at him, searching his face for some hint of reassurance.

"You'll be fine," he murmured, his voice filled with a tenderness she hadn't expected.

As if sensing her turmoil, Orias reached up, gently lowering her mask just enough to expose her lips. He leaned in, brushing a soft, lingering kiss against them.

The gesture left her breathless, her heart pounding in her chest. For a moment, the weight of the rumors, the tension with Felix and his friends, and the looming threat of the Order all seemed to fade away.

When he pulled back, his expression was calm but resolute. "I'll return as soon as I can, Amaris. Until then, stay vigilant. And trust no one completely."

She nodded, swallowing the lump that had formed in her throat. "Just stay safe, or I will bring you back from the dead and kill you again," she said coolly.

Orias chuckled, shaking his head as if in disbelief. "You can't kill me very easily," he said, pressing another kiss to her lips.

When he left the room, closing the door behind him, Seere stood alone, the reality of his departure sinking in. The weight of everything pressed down on her once more. It had been a long time since she'd felt the world press down so painfully.

23

DISCONTENT

Seere moved through the quiet halls of the school, which were painted in shades of gold as the sun dipped before the horizon outside the windows. Her footsteps were soft, practiced, and the gait of someone accustomed to staying unnoticed. Despite her efforts, she felt the weight of invisible eyes—the whispers, the rumors, all clinging to her like a second skin.

The cold stone walls loomed around her. Her thoughts swirled chaotically, circling back to Orias. It had been three weeks, and already his absence gnawed at her. She clenched her fists tightly, willing herself to focus. She couldn't allow a man to distract her.

She turned a corner and gasped as she collided with a solid chest. Strong hands grabbed her shoulders to steady her as she stumbled.

"Easy there, Seere!" Shax said, his face breaking into a smile. "Sneaking around again, are we?"

Seere's brow arched as she took several steps back. "I

could ask you the same thing, Captain. Don't you have recruits to scold or a fortress to patrol?"

He chuckled, crossing her arms over his chest. "I am patrolling. And here I thought I was keeping the shadows safe from assassins, only to find one walking among them."

A small smile tugged at her lips. "If I were here for you, you wouldn't have seen me coming."

Shax laughed, a warm sound that echoed softly in the empty corridor. "Fair point." He gestured for her to walk with him. "Come on. I need a second pair of eyes anyway."

Seere hesitated for a moment, then fell into step beside him. The rhythmic click of his boots against the stone floor contrasted with her silent tread, a sound that somehow felt grounding.

"I've noticed that you've kept the prince and his companions at a distance all week," he said.

Seere shrugged nonchalantly, though she felt anything but nonchalance. "He doesn't need me at his side all the time."

Shax nodded knowingly. "It's the rumors, isn't it?"

She didn't answer, but the flicker in her eyes told him enough.

"You look like you're carrying the weight of the world on your shoulders," he said. "Just know, people always talk, but they will get bored quickly, and the rumors will fade. Just give it time."

"The judgment directed towards me will never fade, Shax. You know who I am... exactly who I am..."

"I do." Shax tilted his head, his sharp gaze studying her. "That's also why I know that the rumors are eating at you, and you're worried about Orias while he's away, which confuses you. On top of that, the friends of the man you were once betrothed to are giving you grief because they wanted you to belong to Felix."

Her head snapped toward him, her eyes narrowing. "How exactly do you know all of that?"

"Like you said, I know you. Better than most, I like to think. Beyond that, I was trained to be an assassin right alongside you. I can pick up on things—whispers, tensions in the air, the way people carry themselves. And you? You've been walking around like a storm cloud ready to strike."

Seere crossed her arms defensively. "So you're saying I'm obvious?"

"No," Shax said gently. "Your storm cloud is very subtle. For what it's worth, I think it's good that you've found Orias."

Her steps faltered, and she glanced at him sharply. "Everyone else seems to think it's quite the mistake. Perhaps they're right. Perhaps I don't deserve—"

"Stop." Shax's voice was firm, cutting through her sentence before she could finish it. "Don't do that."

"Don't do what?" she asked, her tone sharper than she intended.

"Doubt yourself. Let other people's opinions twist your thoughts. You've survived more than most people here could even imagine, and you've done it on your terms. Why start letting their judgment matter now?"

Seere's jaw tightened. "You know it's not that simple, Shax. You don't know what it's like to constantly be seen as —" She faltered, her voice dropping. "As a monster."

Shax stepped closer, his gaze steady and unflinching. "You are not a monster, Seere. Not even close. And anyone who says otherwise doesn't deserve to stand in the same room as you."

She blinked, surprised by the conviction in his tone. "You're awfully confident about that."

"Because it's true," Shax said without hesitation. "I know Orias agrees."

"You can't possibly know that."

Shax smiled. "I've seen the way he looks at you when you're sitting across the great hall with Felix. I've seen him watching you as you train in the courtyard in the evenings. And the things he's asked me to do..."

Her brows furrowed. "What things?"

"Small things, mostly. Extra guards near your quarters, constant updates on any threats to you. And once, he even asked me to make sure the kitchens kept your favorite blend of rose tea stocked."

Seere blinked, startled. "He... did that?"

Shax chuckled. "Don't tell him I told you. He'd deny it outright, but it's true. Look, Orias sees you for who you are, not who people think you are."

They stood in silence for a moment, the halls swiftly turning dark as night fell around them. Seere glanced up as torches lit magically throughout the hall.

"Orias, for all his secrets and the way he keeps people at a distance, when he lets someone in, it's real. That man would move mountains for you if you asked."

She exhaled a shaky breath and looked away. "I didn't ask for that."

"No," Shax said, his voice gentler now. "But you deserve it. Just as you deserve someone who won't try to tame you the way Felix would."

The sincerity in his words left her momentarily speechless. She looked away, trying to mask the emotions threatening to surface. "Thank you, Shax. I... needed that."

He gave her a crooked grin. "Anytime. Just don't tell Orias I said all that. He'd skin me alive."

Despite herself, she laughed softly. "I would never allow that."

"I know," Shax said with a wink. "But I'll take the risk. Now go get some rest. You've got a long road ahead, and you'll need your strength."

As he turned to leave, Seere called after him. "Shax."

He paused, glancing back over his shoulder.

"Thank you," she said, her voice quiet but earnest.

He smiled, tipping an imaginary hat. "Anytime, Your Majesty."

And with that, he strode down the hall.

She lingered in the hallway, Shax's words echoing in her mind. For the first time in what felt like days, the weight on her chest lightened, if only slightly. Still, the dread of returning to the dorms, her original destination, remained.

As she slipped through the fortress halls like a phantom walking through walls, she felt that dread grow. The last thing she wanted was to listen to the ridicule of those around her, especially not from Foras.

She had to brace herself as she approached the heavy oak doors, pushing them open and stepping inside. The common room was bustling with students, the low hum of chatter filling the air. The warmth of the hearth contrasted sharply with the icy glares she immediately felt upon entering.

Her shoulders tensed as she caught sight of Felix, Foras, Rowan, and Enora seated together near the large window overlooking the snow-covered courtyard. Their gazes flickered to her, and though no words were exchanged, the coldness in their stares was enough to make her feel unwelcome.

Seere scanned the room, searching for a quiet corner, somewhere to disappear. Still, the whispers followed her like a shadow:

"There she is—how brazen to show her face here still."

"She should return to the crooked shadows that she came from."

"Right? She doesn't belong here. She never has."

The venom in their voices was like a dagger to her already fragile composure. She clenched her fists, her nails digging into her palms as she fought to keep herself impassive. It was the same mask she wore in her kingdom—stoic, adamant—but inside, the words cut deep.

As she made her way to the farthest corner of the room, she passed a pair of girls who didn't bother to lower their voices.

"You know, I think Cotoria was right. She's sleeping her way to the top."

"I bet that's how she became queen of her little domain."

Seere's stride faltered for only a moment, but she didn't look their way. She wouldn't give them the satisfaction of a reaction. Instead, she reached the shadows of the room, the dim light from the fire barely reaching her chosen seat. She slid into the chair, pulling her hood up and leaning back, her eyes scanning the room for any threats—a habit she couldn't break, even in her supposed refuge.

It wasn't long before the crowd began to thin. Groups of students filed out, all heading for bed. Eventually, only Felix and his companions remained in the room. Silence fell. An uncomfortable, suffocating silence.

Enora was the first to break that horrible silence. "You have some nerve, you know that?"

Seere stiffened but didn't respond, her gaze fixed on the

flames flickering in the hearth. Enora's words hung in the air, sharp and accusatory, but Seere forced herself to remain still. She wasn't about to let Enora's indignation rattle her—at least not outwardly.

"What, nothing to say?" Enora pressed, stepping closer, her arms crossed tightly over her chest. "No defense? No explanation? You're just going to sit there and act like you've done nothing wrong?"

Rowan shifted uncomfortably. "Enora, maybe we shouldn't..."

"No!" Enora snapped. "She owes us an explanation! Achlys avoids me now because of this drama!"

Seere exhaled slowly as she stood, her pale gaze meeting Enora's furious expression. "I don't have to explain anything to you," she said, her voice calm but firm. "I don't owe you anything."

Enora scoffed, her voice rising. "You don't *owe* me? Seere, you're making a fool of yourself—and all of us! Do you even understand what people are saying about you? About how it looks?"

"How does it look?" Seere's eyes narrowed, her voice dropping into a dangerously soft tone. "What exactly are you implying, Enora? That I'm tarnishing your precious reputation by associating because I chose to accept someone's love?"

"You know that's not what I mean," Enora snapped, but her voice faltered slightly. "It's just... he's Orias. The *headmaster*, Seere. There are boundaries—rules! You've crossed every one of them."

Seere crossed into the light, tossing her hood back. "Do you truly believe I'm a student?"

"Because you are. You go to all of our classes."

Seere took a deliberate step closer. Her voice, though quiet, carried a weight that silenced everyone else in the room. "I was fourteen when I graduated from Malphas as an assassin. Fourteen, when I killed the school's namesake," she said coolly. "I am here as a bodyguard to Felix. That is why I attend every one of your classes. Not because I'm a student, but because I am making sure your prince doesn't get himself killed. I forgot you weren't clued into that meeting, though I thought Felix would have told you by now."

Enora looked hurt by Seere's comment, but the emotion was swiftly replaced by anger. "Well, then you're supposed to be protecting Felix! You're supposed to be focused on the mission—not... whatever this is."

Foras, who had been sitting silently by the window, finally spoke up. "I agree with Enora. Your duty should come first. This... relationship with Orias—it's reckless. Dangerous. And it's making us all vulnerable."

"Vulnerable? My duty?" Seere turned on him, her voice rising for the first time. "My duty is to *my* kingdom, not you, and yet here I am. The only thing I have left vulnerable is my people. I was blackmailed to protect Felix, to uncover the Order of the Chimera's schemes, and I've been doing exactly that since my arrival here. But if you think for one second that means that I am not allowed to *live*—to make choices for myself—then you're no better than the people who've used me as a pawn—the Order, the original headmaster, my very own father."

Foras lowered his gaze away, his jaw clenching tight, but he said nothing further. He knew he was at fault for the blackmail. For pulling her away from those that she was truly meant to protect.

"You act like my friends, but the moment I step outside

the lines you've drawn, you treat me as if I've betrayed you—as if I'm nothing more than a tool in your grand plans."

"Seere, that's not—"

Seere cut Enora off. "Do you know why I chose Orias? It's because he treats me like a person. Because he doesn't see me as a monster or a tool to be used. Because for once in my life, someone sees me and not my reputation, not my title, not my scars."

Enora faltered, her anger momentarily replaced by surprise. "That doesn't—"

"I don't owe you, or Felix, or anyone here an explanation," Seere continued, her voice rising slightly. "For years, I've done nothing but serve others. Protect others. Sacrificing everything for others. And yet, here I stand, ridiculed for daring to do something for myself."

The room fell silent, the weight of her words hanging heavy in the air. Foras looked away, his jaw clenched. Felix's expression unreadable, his eyes fixed on the floor. Rowan shifted uncomfortably but said nothing.

Seere turned away, wiping a rebellious tear from her face. "I've had enough of this," she muttered. "If you can't accept my choices like the rest of the realm, then stay out of my way."

Without another word, she turned and walked toward the door. As she pushed it open, the cold air of winter swept in, but it felt like a relief compared to the suffocating tension inside. She didn't look back.

24

FLOWERS

LABRISDAY, TWELFTH OF THE FROST MOON,
YEAR 450 OF THE GODDESS

The sparring grounds were alive with the rhythmic clash of practice swords and the murmur of students paired off for training. Sunlight reflected off the snow that blanketed the ground, blinding the students. Seere adjusted her bracers with a practiced ease, her sharp eyes scanning the open space. She wasn't surprised when Enora approached her, sword in hand and an unreadable expression on her face.

"Partner up?" Enora asked, her voice calm but edged with hesitation.

Seere regarded her for a moment, her face betraying none of her thoughts. "Fine," she replied, stepping into the circle marked for their duel.

The two circled one another like predators, the air between them thick with tension. Enora made the first move, lunging with surprising speed. Seere parried effortlessly, her sword moving like an extension of her arm.

"You've been avoiding me," Enora said between strikes, her voice strained but steady.

"I've been giving you space," Seere countered, her movements measured and unyielding.

Enora pressed forward, her strikes gaining force. "I shouldn't have said what I did. It wasn't my place to question your choices."

Seere didn't respond immediately. Instead, she allowed the rhythm of their sparring to speak for her. Her sword met Enora's over and over with careful precision.

"You're right," Seere said finally, deflecting another strike. "It certainly was not your place."

Enora faltered slightly at the coldness in Seere's tone, but she recovered quickly, launching a more aggressive assault. Seere's movements became sharper, faster, forcing Enora to retreat again.

"I just..." Enora ducked under a swing, hesitating. "I wanted you to help Felix move on from Amaris finally."

Seere's expression remained stoic as she deflected another blow and countered with a sweeping strike that disarmed Enora, sending her sword flying into the snow. Before Enora could recover, Seere's foot swept her legs out from under her, and she landed hard on her back.

Breathless, Enora looked up at Seere, who stood over her with the tip of her sword pointed at her chest.

"I'm well aware of the plan you had for me. It was a very similar plan to the one Foras had. However, as a queen, I have the right to choose whomever I wish to give my heart to. I am not going to allow anyone to dictate that for me anymore," she said coolly.

Enora nodded, a flush of embarrassment creeping up her cheeks. "You're right," she admitted. "I'm sorry, Seere."

Seere lowered her sword and extended a hand. For a

moment, Enora hesitated, but then she grasped Seere's hand and let herself be pulled to her feet.

As they stood face to face, a flicker of understanding passed between them.

"I accept your apology," Seere said, her tone neutral but with a hint of warmth.

Enora gave a small, sheepish smile. "Thank you," she murmured. "Your Majesty."

Seere smirked faintly. "Right."

THE DINING HALL buzzed with the familiar noise of students chatting and clattering utensils. Seere sat with Felix and his companions at their usual spot, though the atmosphere was far from relaxed. Seere tapped her fingers anxiously on the long table as she listened to the whispers and noticed the glances cast her way from nearby tables. She could hear the faint murmur of her name, her keen ears catching snippets of rumors that snaked through the room like venomous tendrils.

Enora noticed the tension in Seere's jaw and leaned closer. "Ignore them," she said softly, placing a hand on Seere's arm.

"I'm trying," Seere muttered, her voice low but laced with steel.

Rowan, ever the peacekeeper, tried to shift the conversation. "History class is getting tough, don't you think? These tests on the dragons of old are not very easy. Especially when the dragons aren't so common anymore—"

A loud clatter interrupted him as Felix's goblet tipped over, spilling water across the table. He swayed in his seat, his complexion turning ashen.

"Felix?" Enora's voice was sharp with alarm as she reached for him, but before she could do anything, Felix's body convulsed, eyes rolling back.

The hall fell into stunned silence as students turned to watch.

Seere was on her feet in an instant, her sharp instincts taking over. She was at Felix's side before anyone else could move, supporting his weight as he slid from the bench. Her keen eyes scanned his pale face, his trembling hands.

"Enora, get a healer," Seere commanded, her tone brooking no argument.

"What's happening to him?" Rowan asked, panic edging his voice as he knelt beside Seere to help.

"Hold Felix," she said, rotating the prince so he rested against Rowan's chest.

Seere turned her attention to Felix's food, which had consisted of roasted chicken, potatoes, and fresh bread. She skewered a strip of chicken on a fork and brought it to her nose. After glancing around to ensure no one was watching too closely, she slipped the fork under her mask to taste it. The sweet flavor hit her tongue like a warning bell—belladonna.

"He's been poisoned," she said grimly, her mind racing.

Gasps erupted around the hall, and students began to murmur.

"Poisoned? Here?"

"Who would do such a thing?"

Seere didn't wait for the whispers to subside. She pulled a hidden pouch of Eulla blossoms out of her sheath and dumped it into her untouched cup of water. Then she forced it between Felix's lips.

"Swallow, Felix." Seere tipped his head back with Rowan's help. "You *have* to swallow."

Felix coughed weakly, but the potion went down. Seere held her breath as moments crawled by, her hand on his pulse, counting the seconds between each beat. Slowly, his convulsions subsided, his breathing stabilizing to a shallow but steady rhythm.

Enora returned moments later with two healers, who gently lifted Felix onto a stretcher. Seere followed them as they carried him from the hall, her movements purposeful and unwavering.

Foras walked at her side, his expression dark with guilt. "Seere, I'm sorry. I shouldn't have accused you of—"

Seere glared at him. "No, you shouldn't have," she interrupted, her tone sharp but without malice.

He winced but said nothing more.

The air in the infirmary was thick with the scent of herbs and the soft murmur of healers tending to patients. As they entered, Seere stayed close to Felix's side. Searching the open space for any sign that someone was waiting to finish the job of ending his life. Felix was carefully relocated to a bed, fast asleep. She watched as they worked to heal him, forcing him to consume more Eulla blossoms.

"How the hell did this happen?" Foras demanded when he stopped at Seere's side. His fists were clenched at his sides.

"I'll find out," she promised. "But you need to stay here and watch over Felix. He'll need someone he trusts when he wakes."

Foras hesitated, then nodded. "Fine. But be careful. I think... Orias would have my head if you came to harm."

"If I'm hurt, it's because of my shortcomings," she

replied, though she couldn't help the amused smile that tugged at her lips.

Felix's shallow breathing lingered in Seere's ears even as she stepped out of the ward, her cloak swirling behind her as she moved with purposeful strides. Her jaw was set, her eyes cold and calculating.

The hallways were full as students left the dining hall to attend their next classes. She found herself dodging more than one person asking for news on the prince's well-being. It wasn't until Cotoria jumped in her way that she was forced to stop.

"Running from the scene of the crime, are we?" the princess questioned, flanked by Malkyn and one of the brutes that had attacked Seere in the forest during the Wargames. "My new theory is that Orias brought you here to kill Felix."

"Then you will be sorely disappointed to learn that it's false," Seere said, her fingers twitching at her side to reach for her dagger. "Now move or I won't hesitate to end you."

Seere jumped as a hand rested on her shoulder. Her dagger flashed into her hand, pressing against the underside of Alsariph's chin before her mind could catch up. "Don't touch me."

"Forgive me, Your Majesty. Cotoria, please give the Queen some space. This corridor does not need to be drenched red today," Alsariph said, giving Cotoria a meaningful look.

Cotoria scowled, then nodded at her goon and Malkyn to move over. Seere spared a glance at Alsariph before she continued her way through the hall. Her mind raced, replaying every detail of the incident. She'd tasted belladonna in Felix's food, but she didn't understand how it had gotten there. The kitchens should have been heavily monitored, and poisoning a meal required precision and stealth.

She slipped through the heavy wooden door leading to the kitchens, her steps silent as a shadow. The room was vast, with high ceilings and rows of long counters cluttered with pots, knives, and bowls. Large ovens radiated heat, their fires reduced to embers until dinner preparations began. The smell of flour, spices, and cooked meat lingered faintly in the air.

Seere's eyes scanned the room, her assassin's training kicking in as she searched for anything out of place. Her movements were methodical, starting with the counter where Felix's plate would have been prepared. She ran her fingers lightly over the surface, her sharp gaze picking out the smallest crumbs, the faintest stains.

Nothing.

Her search expanded. She examined the knives hung neatly on the wall, checked the pantry shelves for unusual substances, and even sifted through the spice jars. Everything was as it should be. Whoever had done this had been meticulous.

Seere moved to the washbasins, her hands dipping into the water that still lingered in the sinks. She rubbed her fingers together, testing for any trace of residue that might suggest tampering. The water was clean, cold.

Her frustration began to mount. There was no trace of foul play, no indication that anything had been out of the ordinary. She closed her eyes, taking a deep breath to steady herself.

She turned her attention to the serving area where the meals were plated before being taken to the dining hall.

Again, she searched, her fingers brushing over the edges of the trays and inspecting the ladles and serving spoons. Not even a whisper of poison was left behind.

Her sharp ears picked up the faint creak of floorboards behind her. She whirled, her dagger already in hand, but it was only one of the kitchen stewards, a young man clutching a bucket of water. His eyes widened when he saw her, and he froze.

"My—my lady," he stammered, bowing awkwardly. "I didn't mean to startle you."

"You didn't," she replied curtly, sliding her dagger back into its sheath. "Were you on duty during lunch today?"

The steward nodded, his hands trembling slightly. "Yes, Your Majesty. I was assigned to the vegetables and sauces. Is —" He hesitated, glancing around nervously. "Is something wrong?"

"Did you see anyone acting suspiciously? Anyone who lingered in the serving area or near the food meant for Prince Felix?"

The steward shook his head quickly. "No, my lady. Everything was normal. The meals were prepared as usual, and the dishes were served promptly. No one touched the prince's plate except the server who delivered it to the dining hall."

Seere's frown deepened. "Who was the server?"

"A freshman student, Misha," the steward said, biting his lip. "But she's still so new and timid—barely knows her way around the kitchens. She wouldn't..."

"I'll decide what she would or wouldn't do," Seere interrupted, her tone sharp. "Where is she now?"

"She's probably in her arithmetic class," the steward replied, wringing his hands.

Seere nodded curtly and left the kitchens, her thoughts swirling. Whoever had poisoned Felix had been careful—so careful that even the utensils and counters bore no trace of tampering. If the server, Misha, had been involved, it was unlikely she had acted alone.

But if she was innocent, that left far more troubling possibilities: the poisoner was either someone skilled enough to cover their tracks completely or someone she trusted.

Seere found Misha's dormitory easily and broke into it with even greater ease. She slipped inside, locking it behind her. She was startled to find that the entire room was decorated in pastel pink. It looked like a little girl's dream with silk curtains, stuffed animals, childhood dolls, and many more things that Seere found utterly pointless.

She searched through cabinets, drawers, and anything that might hold a secret stash of belladonna, but she found nothing. With a frustrated sigh, she sat herself at the dining table and waited for Misha to walk in.

Hours passed before the door creaked open, revealing a sleepy young girl with untamed brown hair. The girl screamed and stumbled back when she looked up and finally noticed Seere.

"M-milady?" the girl stammered.

"Misha, correct?" Seere asked, her tone calm but firm.

The girl nodded, clutching a pendant that hung from a thin chain around her neck.

"I need to speak with you," Seere continued, remaining in her seat in the hopes of looking slightly less menacing. "This is important."

Misha hesitated, looking nervously back at the hallway she had just entered from. Finally, she nodded, closing the door softly.

"You were the one who served Prince Felix's meal today," Seere said, her voice even. It wasn't a question.

Misha blinked rapidly, her face going pale. "Y-yes, Milady. I—I was assigned to that table."

"Did you notice anything unusual about his food—the plate, the utensils, anything at all?" Seere asked, her tone sharp but not unkind.

Misha shook her head quickly, her hands trembling as she fidgeted with the hem of her uniform jacket. "No, Milady. The plate was brought out from the kitchens like all the others. I only carried it to his table and placed it before him. I swear, I didn't do anything to it."

Seere's piercing gaze didn't waver. "Did anyone approach you while you were carrying it? Did you leave it unattended, even for a moment?"

"No, Milady," Misha said, her voice trembling. "I carried it straight from the serving counter to the dining hall. I didn't stop or talk to anyone. I didn't even look at anyone!"

"Were you the one to select the plate, or was it handed to you directly?"

"It was handed to me by Cook Marlot," Misha replied, her brows furrowing as she tried to recall the details. "She said it was ready, and I took it right away."

Seere's gaze softened slightly. The girl's fear was palpable, but her answers were precise and consistent. Misha's nervousness didn't seem to stem from guilt but rather from being dragged into something far beyond her understanding.

"Do you remember who was working in the kitchen

when the plates were being prepared?" Seere asked, shifting her approach.

Misha hesitated, biting her lip hard so it turned white as she struggled to think. "Cook Marlot was there, and... um, some of the senior kitchen staff. I'm still new, so I don't know all their names. But there were a few others, just like always."

Seere sighed softly and pushed herself to her feet. "Very well," she murmured. "I will leave you in peace then. I have places I must be."

She slipped past Misha and back out into the hallway. Several freshmen students stopped and gaped as Seere walked by, none of them expecting to ever find her in their dorm building.

As she walked back towards the hospital wing, Seere had the horrible feeling that someone had tampered with the food once it was at the table—someone sitting within Felix's vicinity.

25

DAGGER

EULDAY, FOURTEENTH OF THE FROST MOON, YEAR 450 OF THE GODDESS

The sterile quiet of the hospital wing weighed heavily on Seere as she leaned against the wall, flipping her dagger in her hand. Felix rested against the pillows, his expression weary but curious as he listened to Seere's rant. Foras, stationed near the door, kept a watchful eye on both of them, his arms crossed defensively.

"I've been replaying everything over and over in my mind," Seere said, her voice filled with frustration but steady. "And I keep circling back to the conclusion that someone close to you, someone who has access to your meals, must have poisoned you."

Felix frowned, his brow furrowing. "You mean one of my allies?"

"Yes." Seere's gaze flickered toward Foras. "Right now, the two most likely suspects are Enora or Rowan."

At the mention of Rowan, Foras stiffened, his arms dropping to his sides. "That's absurd," he snapped, stepping closer. "Rowan would never harm Felix."

Seere raised an eyebrow at his vehemence. "How can you be so sure?"

Foras' jaw tightened, his amber eyes narrowing as if daring her to press further. "Because I trust him," he said, his voice low but firm. "Rowan has been at Felix's side for years. He is loyal to the crown, to Noctivagus. You're chasing ghosts if you think he'd betray that."

Seere sighed softly, dropping her head back against the wall. "Loyalty can be a fragile thing. People betray for all sorts of reasons—fear, ambition, desperation." She paused, her gaze sharp. "Or love."

Foras' face turned red, his composure cracking for a split second. "What are you implying?"

Seere tilted her head, studying him. "I'm not implying anything. I'm observing. You defend Rowan with a conviction I haven't seen from you before."

Felix, who had been silent up to this point, interjected weakly. "Rowan wouldn't poison me. He's my friend."

"I'm not saying that he's guilty," Seere clarified, softening her tone as she glanced at Felix. "But we can't rule anyone out just because of personal feelings." She turned back to Foras, her expression serious. "You, of all people, should know that."

Foras glared at her, but he said nothing more.

Silence passed for a long moment. Seere turned her dagger over in her hands. Its blade caught the light, casting fleeting glimmers on the walls. She hesitated, her grip faltering for just a moment before she caught it again. Somehow, the weapon felt heavier than it ever had before.

Felix noticed. "What's on your mind?" he asked, his voice still weak but laced with curiosity.

Seere straightened, her lips pressed into a thin line as

she stepped closer to his bed. Foras watched her like a hawk, suspicion creeping into his gaze.

Without a word, she turned and crossed to Felix's bedside. She turned the dagger so that the hilt was extended towards him as she held it out for him, her expression unreadable.

"This belongs to you," she said softly.

Felix blinked, confused. He hesitated before reaching out, his fingers brushing the leather-bound hilt. He didn't take it right away, his eyes searching her face.

"I don't understand. How does it belong to me?" he asked as he hesitantly took it.

"I've had it for years," she admitted, her tone measured. "I should have returned it sooner."

Felix stared at the weapon for a long moment before finally accepting it, his fingers slowly unwrapping the leather binding that had protected—or hid—the hilt. As the material fell away, the engraved words shimmered faintly in the light that filtered through the chiffon curtains: *For my betrothed. May we carve out our futures together.*

His breath hitched, his fingers trembling as he traced the words. He clutched the dagger to his chest, the weight of realization hollowing his eyes. "This... this belonged to Amaris," he whispered, his voice thick with emotion.

Foras stiffened, his gaze snapping to Seere, but she didn't look at him. Her attention remained on Felix, whose eyes filled with unshed tears.

"She gave it to me," Seere lied smoothly, her voice soft but steady. "After I became queen, she came to my kingdom. She told me to keep it safe, that one day I might have the chance to return it to you."

Felix's grip on the dagger tightened as a single tear slid

down his cheek. "So it's true, then?" he murmured, his voice breaking. "Amaris is gone?"

Seere faltered, the weight of the lie heavy on her chest. She swallowed hard, nodding. "Yes," she said quietly. "I gave her a proper burial in the cemetery of my citadel. She... she wanted me to tell you that she's sorry."

The words felt like a knife twisting in her own heart, but Felix needed to hear them. His face crumpled as a sob escaped his lips, and he clutched the dagger to his chest like a lifeline.

Foras glared at Seere from across the room, his eyes blazing with silent fury. He knew the truth, yet he said nothing. He wasn't going to reveal her identity.

Felix's grief filled the room, his shoulders shaking as he wept. Seere stood stiffly, unsure of what more she could do, until he suddenly reached out and pulled her into an embrace.

"Thank you," he whispered, his voice raw.

Seere stiffened at first, her hands hovering awkwardly in the air, but then she let herself relax. Her arms wrapped loosely around his shoulders.

When he finally released her, Felix wiped his eyes and smiled faintly, though the pain still lingered in his gaze. He looked down at the dagger again, turning it over in his hands. "I don't deserve this," he murmured.

"Yes, you do," Seere said firmly. "More than anyone."

The silence of the room stretched uncomfortably as Felix continued to cradle the dagger, his eyes fixed on the familiar inscription. The tears on his face dried, but his grip on the weapon betrayed the emotions still roiling within him. Seere could feel Foras' glare drilling into her, an unspoken condemnation for the lies she had just told.

"What would Enora have to gain," Seere began softly, breaking the tense quiet, "by killing you, Felix?"

"Absolutely nothing," Foras said, his voice sharp. "She is betrothed to my brother, Gabriel. Do you honestly think she'd jeopardize that by getting involved in Felix's assassination?"

"I don't know what to think," Seere admitted.

"Gabriel is a knight of Noctivagus and the heir to the Andromal name. Enora has more than secured her future with that match. She most certainly doesn't need Felix dead."

Seere sighed, massaging her temples. "Then I don't know. I don't understand how anyone could have poisoned him while the food was at the table and surrounded by us."

"Your Majesty," a guard called as he entered the room, drawing Seere's attention from Foras and Felix. "Headmaster Orias has returned."

Seere's heart leapt at the news. Orias had returned a week earlier than she'd expected. Foras sighed heavily, his glare only darkening. It was clear he still didn't forgive her for choosing Orias over Felix.

Seere gave Felix a nod before she hurried out of the infirmary. She wanted to know what news Orias might bring. She also, above all, wanted to know that he was unharmed at least.

26

SAFE

EULDAY, FOURTEENTH OF THE FROST MOON,
YEAR 450 OF THE GODDESS

Seere paced restlessly at the edge of the school's snow-dusted front step, her boots crunching on the thin layer beneath her feet, though the chill of the mountain air nipped at her cheeks and crept into her fingers, she hardly noticed. Her focus was entirely on the path that led up to the school.

Every so often, her hand drifted to her thigh, her gloved fingers searching for the dagger that was no longer there. She felt naked without it, utterly exposed and vulnerable.

It had been so long since Orias left, and though she told herself that he was more than capable of handling himself, a nagging worry had taken root in her chest. She hated the waiting. The stillness. It gave her too much space for her mind to wander—to imagine everything that could have gone wrong.

"Where are you?" she murmured under her breath, her gaze locked on the path ahead. The guard had said he'd returned, yet his carriage was nowhere in sight. The snow had begun to fall harder, flurries dancing around her in the bitter wind.

A faint rumble in the distance made her stop in her tracks. Her heart leaped as she strained her ears, hope sparking in her chest. Moments later, the dark silhouette of a carriage appeared through the swirling snow, its lanterns glowing faintly in the dim winter light.

As the carriage drew nearer, her pulse quickened. She stepped forward instinctively, her boots slipping slightly on the ice. When the horses finally came to a halt, the carriage door creaked open, and there he was.

Orias stepped out slowly, his movements deliberate, but Seere's sharp eyes immediately picked up the weariness in his stance. Her breath caught as her gaze zeroed in on the bandaged cut that slashed across the left side of his face. Bruises had bloomed around the wound, a harsh contrast against his pale skin.

Her stomach twisted.

"Orias," she breathed, rushing forward before she could stop herself.

He turned at the sound of her voice—or footsteps; she wasn't sure, his lips curving into a familiar smile despite the injury. "Seere," he greeted warmly, his voice carrying over the cold air as if they were the only two people in the world.

The sight of him smiling—injured yet still composed— only made her worry deepen. She reached him just as he stepped onto the snow-covered path, her eyes scanning his face as if confirming for herself that he was truly there.

"What happened?" she demanded, her tone sharp with concern. Her gloved fingers hovered near the bandage on his cheek, but didn't touch it. "Why hasn't this healed?"

Before she could press further, Orias pulled her into his

arms, his hands firm but gentle as he embraced her. She froze for half a second, startled by the sudden gesture, but then relaxed into him, the familiar warmth of his presence easing some of the tension in her chest.

He lowered her mask just enough to press his lips to her, ignoring the snowflakes that landed in his hair or the glances of a few students lingering near the entrance. The kiss was soft, unhurried, a silent reassurance that he was still there, still hers.

When he pulled back, his gaze softened, his thumb brushing over her jawline. "Are you alright?" he asked, his tone gentle yet tinged with concern.

Seere froze as she reached up to slip her mask back on, her brows drawing together. "*Me*?" she asked incredulously. "You're asking about *me* when you look like—" She gestured to his injured face, her voice trailing off.

He chuckled, the sound low and warm despite the cold. Of course, I'm asking about you," he said, fixing her mask for her.

Her exasperation only grew as she gestured again, her hands animated as she spoke. "Orias, this is serious! That wound—it hasn't healed. Why not?"

"There are weapons in this world, My Queen, that even we are not immune to," he explained, his tone light as if he were discussing something mundane. "It slows the healing, that's all. I've had worse."

"You sound like me," she muttered.

"What happened while I was away?" he asked, shifting the topic.

Her brows furrowed, but she relented. "Felix was poisoned," she said grimly, crossing her arms as the memory of that moment resurfaced. "With belladonna. If I didn't carry Eulla blossoms with me everywhere, he might have died."

Orias' jaw tightened, the warmth in his expression giving way to something colder—anger, perhaps, or concern. "I see," he said, his voice low.

They fell into step together as they entered the school, the warmth of the halls a stark contrast to the biting cold outside. Though students and staff whispered and stared, Seere ignored them, her focus entirely on Orias.

"I'll need you to explain everything," he said as they reached the infirmary.

"While I take care of that wound," she countered firmly.

INSIDE, Foras sat in a chair by Felix's bedside, his posture tense and his arms crossed as if he were guarding the prince with his very presence. Felix lay propped up against a stack of pillows still, his face pale but his eyes clear. He glanced up as the door opened, his expression shifting from mild curiosity to something sharper the moment he saw Orias.

Foras' glare followed soon after.

"What happened to you?" Foras questioned, his gaze fixed on the bandage across Orias' face. His tone carried more suspicion than concern, not that Seere couldn't blame him. Foras had lacked trust in Orias before, and that distrust seemed more pronounced than ever.

"I've had worse," Orias replied evenly, shrugging off the question as he removed his cloak and draped it over the back of a nearby chair. "It's a scratch, nothing more."

"It doesn't *look* like a scratch," Seere muttered as she guided Orias to sit on a stool near one of the sterile tables laden with medicines and bandages.

"What exactly caused it?" Foras demanded.

Orias sighed as Seere carefully peeled the bandage away and began to clean the wound. "A minor skirmish. However, that hardly matters now. What precisely is going on here?"

"Felix's meal was poisoned with belladonna, and Her Majesty is convinced that it was either Rowan or Enora."

"I think we have to consider every possibility," Seere replied evenly, her tone giving nothing away.

Foras scoffed, a sharp shake of his head betraying his disbelief. "You're wasting your time."

"That's enough," Orias said, his voice quiet but commanding. "Seere is doing her job, and she's doing it well. If you can't contribute something useful, I suggest you step aside."

Foras opened his mouth to speak, then shut it, falling silent with irritation. A faint smile tugged at the corner of Seere's lips behind her mask. Orias, as if sensing it, gave her thigh a subtle squeeze, one that was affectionate and filled with warmth.

"It was the Order," Foras said suddenly, breaking the silence. His arms still crossed, but there was something sharper in his expression now.

Orias gave him a sidelong glance. "They're persistent, I'll give them that."

Foras shoved back his chair with a scrape and stood abruptly. "And yet you're sitting here like it's no big deal. Do you have any idea what kind of threat they pose? How close they've come to—"

"I am more than aware," Orias cut in, his tone firm but still calm. "And I handled it."

"Handled it?" Foras repeated, his voice rising slightly.

"You've been gone for weeks, and while you were off 'handling' things, Felix was nearly *killed!*"

"Foras," Seere said sharply, her tone brooking no argument. She didn't even look up from her work, her hands steady while she applied a layer of salve to Orias' wound. "That's enough."

Foras glared at her but said nothing, though his frustration was palpable. Felix, who had been silent throughout the exchange, finally spoke.

"Seere," he said quietly, drawing her attention. "Do you think this was the Order's doing? The poison, I mean."

Seere straightened, her hand resting lightly on Orias' shoulder. She glanced at him briefly before turning her attention fully to Felix. "It's highly possible," she admitted, her voice calm and measured. "But nothing adds up to me. Of course, they are incredibly crafty—far better at commanding the shadows than even my assassins and spies."

"Seere, we should talk," Orias said quietly. "In my office."

She nodded and glanced at Foras and Felix. Orias allowed her to place a clean bandage over the wound before he stood and followed her out of the infirmary.

In the hallway, he matched his pace to Seere's, his hand brushing hers briefly before falling to his side. "You're worried," he said simply, breaking the silence.

"I'm always worried," she replied without looking at him. "But now... It's worse."

His lips quirked into a faint smile, though there was a flicker of something deeper in his eyes—guilt, perhaps, or regret. "Let's talk," he said, his tone soft. "There's much to discuss."

And there was. But first, Seere would get her answers.

The halls were quiet as Seere and Orias made their way toward his office. Her mind swirled with unanswered questions, suspicions, and the faint sting of Foras' continued accusatory glares as if everything was her fault. She walked beside Orias, her gaze fixed ahead, though she was acutely aware of his every step beside her—the subtle limp he tried to mask, the tension in his shoulders.

As they reached his office, Orias pulled a key from his pocket. The metal glinted faintly as he turned it in the lock, the sound of the tumblers clicking open louder than usual in the stillness around them. He pushed the door open and stepped aside, gesturing for her to enter first.

Seere hesitated for a fraction of a second before stepping inside. The office was just as she remembered it—warm and inviting, at least to her.

"Sit," Orias said softly, nodding toward one of the chairs near the hearth. His voice held none of the authority it usually carried—it was softer now, almost tentative.

She didn't respond immediately. Her gaze lingered on the snow that fell outside the windows and the mountain peaks beyond. After a moment, she turned and took the offered seat, resting her gloved hands on the armrests as she watched him close the door behind them.

Orias crossed the room with a slow, deliberate grace, his movements measured despite the fatigue he carried. He didn't sit at his desk or take the chair opposite her. Instead, he leaned against the edge of his desk, his arms crossed loosely over his chest as he regarded her.

"You have questions," he said simply, breaking the silence.

"That's putting it lightly," Seere replied, her voice steady despite the emotions churning within her. "What is happening out there, Orias? And don't give me some half-truth about 'handling it.' I need to know. I deserve to know."

Orias' lips twitched into a faint, humorless smile. "Straight to the point, as always."

Seere didn't reply, her gaze unwavering as she waited for his response.

He sighed, running a hand through his dark hair. "The Order is displeased," he said bluntly. "They... intercepted me on the road, a small group of them. I recognized one of their leaders—a woman named Solenn. She was... formidable."

"Formidable enough to wound you," Seere said quietly, her gaze shifting to the bandage that hid the gash left behind.

Orias inclined his head. "She's skilled. And she's armed with a weapon imbued with power gifted by Aldros. It's why the wound hasn't fully healed."

"Aldros? As in the god of hatred?" Seere asked, staring in disbelief as she leaned forward. "What did she want from you?"

"She wanted me out of the way," he said simply. "Or dead, preferably. They don't take kindly to interference, especially when it comes to you and Felix."

Seere frowned, her fingers digging into the seat cushion. "What do you mean, 'especially when it comes to Felix and me'? What are they planning?"

Orias hesitated, his gaze flickering away for a brief moment as if weighing his words carefully. "They see you as... critical to their plans," he said finally. "Your connection to Felix makes you a valuable pawn in their game. Marrying him, aligning yourself with him—it's what they wanted all along. Their assassination attempts were likely a way to draw you closer, to force you into a position where they could manipulate you."

The weight of his words settled over her like a heavy cloak, and for a moment, she couldn't speak. Her mind raced with questions, doubts, and a gnawing frustration that she hadn't seen this sooner. She stood and began pacing across the room, unable to sit still.

"And you," she said finally, her voice barely above a whisper. "They targeted you because you're standing in their way."

Orias nodded, his expression softening as he met her gaze. "Because I love you," he said simply, the words so quiet they almost didn't reach her ears.

Seere froze and her breath hitched, her carefully constructed walls faltering for the briefest of moments. The confession hung between them, filling the space with an almost tangible warmth. For a moment, the weight of everything—the whispers, the accusations, the lies—seemed to lift. She looked at him, really looked at him, and saw not just the headmaster, not just the mysterious figure who entered her life and upended everything, but the man who had stood by her side, who had seen her for who she truly was.

She opened her mouth to speak, but no words came.

Orias stepped closer, his hand reaching out to gently tilt her chin upward so she would meet his eyes. "I won't let them take you from me," he murmured, his voice low and steady.

Her heart ached at the sincerity in his voice, the weight of his devotion. "And I won't let them take you," she said finally, her voice firm despite the emotions threatening to overwhelm her.

Orias, just as he had done many times before, pulled her

mask from her face and set it aside. His hand cupped her cheek, his thumb tracing the sharp line of her jaw. When his lips met hers, it was slow and deliberate, a kiss that spoke of longing and reassurance. Her hands found his shoulders, her fingers curling into the fabric of his shirt as she pulled him closer. The firelight flickered, casting their shadows against the walls as the kiss deepened.

He broke away just enough to rest his forehead against hers, his breath warm against her skin. "I love you," he whispered, the words soft but unwavering.

Her heart skipped a beat. She opened her eyes, meeting his gaze. She wasn't sure how to say those three little words or if she was even ready to. She'd never uttered them before. Not to her parents, her sister, or a pet. They were utterly foreign and completely terrifying.

So she didn't say anything. She kissed him again, this time the kiss was hungrier, more desperate, as if they were both trying to drown out the world beyond the walls of his office. He lifted her easily, her legs wrapping around his waist as he carried her toward his bed chamber.

Seere clung to him, her lips trailing down to a sensitive spot beneath his ear. He was hers, and she knew that her body, her heart, perhaps even her very soul, belonged to him and him alone. He set her down on his bed, his fingers slow and deliberate as he peeled away each layer of her clothing. Between each removal, his mouth found a new patch of skin to worship—her collarbone, the hollow of her throat, the sensitive dip of her hipbone. Each kiss made her tremble, made her burn.

His hands slid down her thighs, parting them with a reverence that made her breath catch. He kissed the inside of one knee, then the other, slowly working his way upward until she was trembling, until she was silently begging. Only then did he lower his mouth to the tender, aching place between her legs. He groaned into her, sucking and biting until she was a moaning disaster. Her fingers laced through his hair, trying to pull him closer as she squirmed against him.

"I have never heard more beautiful noises, Your Majesty," he hissed into her, his tongue unrelenting as he swirled and licked. "Give me more."

She whimpered, her hand moving to her mouth to muffle the sounds she made. Orias, however, was faster. He snatched her wrists, trapping them against the bed. A low growl escaped him, and she let out a moan as pleasure raced up her spine. He would be the death of her, and she was going to let him.

"Gods, you're the most exquisite thing to ever grace this realm," he whispered, earning a soft cry in protest for having taken his mouth from her. He chuckled as he returned his tongue to her, only for her to gasp and spasm against him as he brought her to her climax.

He finally stepped away from her after a moment, pulling his shirt over his head. Seere pushed herself upright, watching him carefully, noting the way he still needed attention. Wordlessly, she slid from the bed and carefully began removing his pants.

"Seere, you don't have to—"

"I know," she said, and turned him around only to shove him back onto the bed.

Carefully, almost hesitantly, she straddled his hips. She took his length inside her with a soft gasp, his head fell back with a groan that sounded like it had been torn from his soul.

"Amaris," he rasped, voice thick with emotion. "You're mine. Always."

His hands gripped her hips, urging her to move. She rode him, her movements desperate, savoring the stretch and heat between them. But Orias, ever impatient, flipped her beneath him with a growl. He kissed her like a starving man, swallowing every gasp and whimper.

Their bodies moved in a frantic rhythm, hands clawing, mouths bruising with kisses that tasted like devotion and desperation. When Seere came again, nearly sobbing his name, Orias followed with a broken groan, spilling himself inside her as he clutched her close, as if letting go would kill him.

27

DEATH

ESLADAY, FIFTEENTH OF THE FROST MOON,
YEAR 450 OF THE GODDESS

Seere stirred awake to the gentle warmth of Orias' body pressed against hers, his arm draped protectively over her waist. The soft light of dawn filtered through the curtains, casting golden streaks across the room. For a fleeting moment, the world outside ceased to exist—no battle to fight, no secrets to guard, no past haunting her steps.

She tilted her head slightly to look at Orias, his expression soft and unguarded in sleep. The bruises from his encounter with the Order of the Chimera had darkened, and yet, even injured, he looked serene.

She shifted carefully, hoping to untangle herself without waking him, but the moment she moved, his arm tightened around her waist.

"Where do you think you're going?" he murmured, his voice rough with sleep. He pressed his face into the crook of her neck, his breath grazing her skin and sending a shiver down her spine.

"I thought I might get up and face the day," she replied, her voice soft but teasing.

"Not yet," he murmured, pulling her closer. "Just a little longer."

She sighed, torn between exasperation and contentment. She wasn't used to moments like this—quiet, intimate, and free of the weight she always carried. The feeling of being cherished was almost foreign, but she allowed herself to indulge for a moment longer, resting her hand over his where it sat on her waist.

"You don't get enough sleep," Orias said, his voice still muffled against her neck. "Let me take care of you for once."

She laughed quietly, though the sound was more bitter than amused—like the echo of a wound that never quite healed. "I think you've mistaken me for someone who can afford to relax."

"Amaris," he said, shifting so that he could look at her. His deep green eyes met her lighter ones; the intensity in them stole the breath from her lungs. "You're allowed to rest. You don't have to carry everything alone."

His words struck a nerve, and she turned her gaze away, the figurative mask she wore even in vulnerability slipping back into place. "If I don't carry it, who will?"

"I will," Orias said without hesitation, his hand lifting to brush a strand of lavender hair from her face. "You've done enough."

She swallowed hard, her throat tight as she tried to dismiss the raw emotions his words stirred. "You don't even know the half of it."

"Then tell me," he said, his voice gentle but firm. "Tell me everything. Let me share the weight."

For a moment, Seere considered what such a thing might be like. Part of her wondered if she could truly allow herself to share her burdens with someone—if she could share her crown with Orias. But before she could respond, a sharp knock at the door shattered the moment, jolting both of them out of their quiet intimacy. Orias groaned in frustration, burying his face further into her neck for a second before sitting up.

"I'll deal with it," he muttered, running a hand through his tousled hair.

She quickly slipped out of bed, searching for her clothes and mask. The warmth of the moment had evaporated, leaving her feeling exposed as reality crept back in. But the warmth of Orias' words lingered in her mind—a fragile reminder that she wasn't as alone as she always believed.

By the time Orias was dressed and reached the door, she had already pulled on her attire from the day before.

Orias swung the door open, irritation radiating from every inch of his posture. His evergreen eyes, still heavy with the remnants of sleep, locked onto the guard standing in the hallway.

"What is it?" Orias snapped, his tone sharp.

The guard stiffened, his gloved hands gripping his helmet nervously. "Apologies, sir, but this couldn't wait. There's been an incident."

Orias arched a brow, his irritation replaced by a growing concern. "What kind of incident?"

"It's Captain Fraser, sir. He's dead. Empress Selina executed him. She has accused him of treason."

Seere's world tilted. Her body felt weightless, as though she had stepped off a cliff with nothing to catch her. The words pounded through her mind like thunder. Something fragile within her snapped, and she stumbled, her hip catching on a silver tray on a nearby table. The tea set crashed to the floor in a discordant, shattering symphony.

Orias was there before she hit the ground, but she barely registered his presence. Cold seeped into her bones, a hollow, gut-wrenching chill that no amount of warmth could chase away.

Shax.

He was gone.

Seere dropped to her knees amidst the shards, her breath coming in sharp, shallow bursts. The edges of the world blurred, sounds muffled and distant as if she were sinking underwater.

"You're dismissed," Orias barked at the guard without even glancing back.

Her fingers curled into fists, nails biting into her palms hard enough to draw blood. She had tried. Gods, she had tried. But what did it matter? What did any of it matter when her oldest friend was nothing but a memory now?

She had killed him.

"This is my fault," she whispered, the words barely audible, her body breaking. "If I had just—if I had let Selina kill me—Shax would still be alive. His family... He has a wife and daughters—"

"Don't," Orias said, his voice a low, soothing rumble. He held her tighter, his chin resting on the crown of her head. "Don't blame yourself for this. None of it is your fault."

She shook her head violently, her tears soaking into his shirt. "He was my oldest friend, Orias. He protected me— he gave everything for me. And now he's gone because of me."

Orias swayed gently, his hand running up and down her back in slow, comforting strokes as he held her. "Shax made his choice. He was loyal to you, not to Selina. That's not on you, Seere. That's on her."

His words didn't soothe her; they couldn't. The grief was too raw, the guilt too heavy. Her sobs turned into quiet gasps as her strength seemed to leave her entirely, and all she could do was cling to Orias like he was the only thing anchoring her to the world.

"I should've protected him," she whispered after what felt like hours.

"You can't protect everyone," Orias replied, his voice soft but firm. "No one can."

"But I'm supposed to. It's the entire reason I built my kingdom."

"I know," he whispered, kissing the top of her head. "I will have his family relocated. I know King Hubert will be more than happy to house them within his kingdom and offer them aid."

"Thank you."

They stayed entwined on the cold floor of his office until Seere's sobs faded into silence. The weight in her chest didn't lift, but the solid presence of Orias' arms around her kept her grounded.

Finally, she pulled back, her hands trembling as she adjusted her mask. Orias didn't stop her but watched her carefully, his eyes full of worry.

"We need to go," she said, her voice hollow.

"Are you sure you're ready?" he asked.

"No," she admitted, standing on unsteady legs. "But I can't stay here. Not when Felix is still unwell and there are so many things that need to be done."

Orias stood with her, steadying her with a hand on her shoulder. "You don't have to face any of it alone."

"I've always faced it alone," she murmured, her gaze fixed on the floor.

"Not anymore."

As Seere and Orias moved through the halls of the academy, the atmosphere was heavy, the somberness palpable. Snow continued to fall outside, visible through the tall arched windows, its serene beauty a stark contrast to the weight pressing down on Seere's chest. Students and staff stepped aside as they passed, their gazes a mixture of pity and fear.

Whispers trailed behind them, growing louder as word of Captain Shax's death spread. Some students murmured about what had happened, others about Seere's unusual stiffness and the exhaustion in her eyes. Orias' presence kept most from approaching, his protective hand resting firmly on her back, a silent reassurance that he wouldn't let her fight alone.

Seere kept her eyes fixed ahead, her mask hiding little of the grief etched into her face. Her mind was a storm, replaying the guards' words over and over. Shax was dead. It didn't feel real. It couldn't be real. Yet the ache in her chest told her otherwise.

By the time they reached the infirmary, her legs felt like they were made of lead. Orias opened the door, and the room fell silent as all eyes turned toward them.

Felix swiftly pulled a shirt over his head, where he stood in the center of the room, freshly dressed and looking far better than he had when she'd seen him only the day before. Foras hovered protectively at his side, his brow furrowed with tension. Rowan and Enora stood nearby, their expressions a mix of worry and confusion.

"Seere!" Enora stepped forward, her voice tentative. "Are you—"

"I'm fine," Seere interrupted, her tone clipped and hollow. She didn't meet Enora's gaze, didn't look at any of them.

Rowan exchanged a glance with Enora, their concern only deepening. Foras, meanwhile, narrowed his eyes at Orias, clearly not pleased with the way he kept so close to Seere. Felix, however, was silent. His usually composed expression was clouded with something unreadable, his hands clenched at his sides. The tension in the room thickened as the group exchanged glances, each unsure of what to say or do. Finally, Enora broke the silence.

"Cotoria," she said hesitantly, "was bragging earlier. She said that she was the one who... who sent the guards after Shax."

Seere's head snapped up, and for the first time since entering the room, fire lit in her eyes.

"She *what*?"

"She was with Malkyn and the group that acts as her bodyguards," Rowan added quickly. "They were talking in the main hall. We overheard them."

Seere's hands curled into fists, her nails biting into her palms. Fury surged through her, momentarily drowning out the grief. Without another word, she turned on her heel and strode toward the door.

"Seere, wait!" Orias called, his voice firm but tinged with worry.

She ignored him, her steps quick and purposeful as she stormed down the hall.

The walk to the main hall felt like a blur. Seere's focus was singular, her anger a sharp blade cutting through the haze of her emotions. She barely noticed the students who scrambled out of the way, the gasps and whispers that followed in her wake.

When she reached the main hall, her eyes locked onto Cotoria and Malkyn immediately. The two were standing near one of the grand windows, Cotoria laughing as she gestured animatedly. Malkyn smirked, entertained by whatever story she was telling. Seere snatched a knife from a passing student's sheath as she stormed over.

"Cotoria!" Seere's voice rang out, sharp and commanding.

The princess turned, her smile widening when she saw Seere.

"Well, well," Cotoria said, her tone dripping with mockery. "If it isn't the grieving queen. Come to thank me for ridding you of that disobedient dog?"

The words were a match to Seere's already smoldering rage. With a swift, practiced motion, she shoved Cotoria against the wall, her stolen blade pressed against her throat. "Give me one reason," she hissed, her voice low and dangerous, "not to end your wretched life right here."

Cotoria's grin didn't falter. If anything, it widened, a glint of amusement in her eyes. "Because," she said, her tone mocking, "I'm your little sister."

The words hit Seere like a blow. Her grip faltered, her mind reeling as she stared at Cotoria. "He told you, and you still killed him?" she snarled.

Cotoria leaned in, her grin wicked. "Obviously. We couldn't have him warning you. Come now, *Amaris*. I know you aren't a fool. You've managed to survive this long and even became queen of your own pathetic country."

Before Seere could react, strong hands grabbed her and

yanked her back, twisting her arms painfully behind her. Malkyn darted forward and tore the mask from Seere's face, and gasps echoed through the hall as her true identity was revealed.

For a moment, there was stunned silence. Then, someone whispered her name.

"Amaris..."

The sound of her real name sent a shiver down Seere's spine. She glanced toward the doorway, her heart sinking as she saw Felix standing there, his face pale as though he had seen a ghost—and, as far as Seere was concerned, he had.

"Amaris," he repeated, his voice shaky.

The hall erupted into chaos, students whispering and shouting, but Seere didn't hear any of it. Her focus was on Felix, the hurt in his eyes cutting deeper than any blade.

Cotoria smirked, wiping a thin line of blood from her neck as she reached for her sword. "Well, this just got interesting," she said, her tone gleeful.

She raised her sword and then swung. Seere had closed her eyes, resigning herself to death, waiting for the blow. However, it never came.

Seere staggered as a powerful blast of magic swept through the hall. Cotoria was sent crashing to the floor with a surprised scream. Her sword clattered well out of reach.

"Enough!" Orias roared, his voice echoing through the hall.

He turned to Seere, freeing her from the brutish grip and pulling her close. His grip was tight and shaky as though fearful.

"Are you alright?" he asked, his evergreen eyes scanning her face.

Seere nodded numbly, her body trembling.

Orias' expression hardened as he turned towards Cotoria. "You've caused enough damage for one day. Leave. Now."

Cotoria glared at him, but she didn't argue. Instead, she pushed herself to her feet, spat a curse under her breath, and stalked out of the hall. Malkyn followed close behind, along with the three large men who had pulled Seere back.

Orias wrapped an arm around Seere, guiding her out of the hall as the crowd continued to buzz with murmurs. Felix and the others followed silently, their faces etched with a mix of shock and concern.

Once the door to Orias' office clicked shut, the room filled with a heavy silence. Seere sat stiffly in one of the chairs by the fireplace, her mask back in place, her hands clasped tightly in her lap. Orias stood behind her, his hand resting protectively on her shoulder. Felix, Foras, Rowan, and Enora stood in a loose semi-circle, their expressions ranging from shock to anger to deep concern.

Felix was the first to break the silence, his voice soft but trembling with emotion. "You lied to me," he said, his gaze locked on Seere. "You told me that Amaris—that you were dead. I trusted you."

Seere flinched at his words, but she did not look up. "I thought it was better that way," she replied, her voice hollow.

"Better for *who*?" Felix's voice rose, frustration seeping into his tone. "Do you have any idea what it was like? Mourning you? Thinking I had lost you forever?"

Seere looked up at him, her pale green eyes filled with guilt and bitterness. "Do you know what it's like to be hunted for a crime you didn't commit? Do you know what it was like for me when I traveled to Noctivagus for shelter, only to hear your father announce that they would join the hunt for my head? That our betrothal was off and that the one place I felt myself in had turned against me entirely? I saw you there, that day, standing firm at his side, just as angry as the rest of them," she said coolly. "It was hell."

"I wasn't angry at you, Amaris! I was angry at my father for ignoring my pleas to harbor you! I loved you! I still love you!" Felix shouted, unable to rein in his anger any longer.

"Felix, stop, I think Seere has suffered enough," Rowan said softly, putting his hands up in a placating gesture.

However, Felix didn't listen. His hurt and anger were too explosive to keep at bay. "Do you have any idea what it felt like to discover that the woman I loved had murdered her parents—just weeks after she left from visiting you? Or what it was like to learn that my father planned to join Empress Selina in hunting her down?" His words were sharp, cutting into her like claws. "Do you know what it felt like to find out—months later—that she was innocent the entire time, only to be told by the Queen of Assassins that she was dead?" His voice cracked, raw with emotion. "I fell for Seere, tormented myself for weeks with guilt because she wasn't Amaris—only to have her stolen from me too. And now I learn that Seere was Amaris the entire time."

His words sliced through her armor, each accusation reopening wounds she had long since tried to stitch closed.

"Enough." Orias' voice cut through the tension, calm but commanding. He moved to stand between Seere and Felix, his eyes sharp as they fixed on the prince. "She does not owe you an explanation for the choices she made to survive."

Felix's jaw tightened, his hands balling into fists. "And you?" he asked sharply. "What role have you played in all of this? Are you protecting her? Hiding her? Or is there more you're not telling us?"

Orias' lips curled into a faint, humorless smile. "I've done what I must. Nothing more, nothing less."

Foras, who had been silent to let Felix speak, stepped forward, his voice cold. "You mean you've been keeping her for yourself, haven't you?"

Orias' expression darkened, and the air in the room seemed to shift, charged with tension. "Watch your words, Foras."

"Why?" Foras snapped. "You think I don't see what's going on here? The way you look at her? The way you cling to her as if she's yours?" He turned to Seere, his tone softening slightly. "Amaris, don't let him manipulate you like this. You're not a fool! You're meant to be with Felix."

Seere's head snapped up, her eyes narrowing. "Don't call me that," she said sharply. "I am not Amaris."

"Did you ignore her earlier words when she said that the Noctivagus King broke the arrangement seven years ago?" Orias interjected, his voice low but firm. "It's Seere's choice who she gives her love to."

"That doesn't change what's right," Foras retorted.

"What's right," Orias countered, stepping closer to the other men, "is what she decided. Not you. Not Felix. Not anyone else. She is the queen of her own country. And a prince that seeks to tame her and separate her from her people should not be allowed to have a say in what she chooses to do."

"I would never try to tame her," Felix growled.

"We all know that's not true," Orias hissed.

The tension between the two men was palpable, and it felt as though the room might ignite from the sheer force of their opposing wills. Seere stood suddenly, drawing their attention. Her voice was calm but carried an edge of steel.

"Enough. All of you." She looked between the three men, her gaze steady. "This isn't about alliances or promises made years ago. This is about survival. Shax is dead because of me. Cotoria and Malkyn are circling like vultures. The Order is likely going to be livid and work harder than ever to get me back under their control. I do not have time to listen to you shouting at me about who I should love."

Her words hung in the air, a stark reminder of the stakes they were all facing. Foras averted his gaze, his jaw tight. Felix looked down, his frustration ebbing into a quiet sadness. Even Orias seemed to relax, his stance softening as he stepped back to stand at Seere's side. He was the only one who chose to stand at her side.

"Seere's right," Enora said gently, breaking the silence as she so often did. "We need to focus on what's important. If the Order is making moves, we need a plan."

"And that plan starts with keeping Seere safe," Orias said, his tone final. He turned to Seere, his expression softening. "I'll have your belongings moved up here. It's the safest place for you right now."

Seere's eyes narrowed on him. She could see what he was doing, carefully maneuvering himself further between her and Felix. "I don't need to be coddled. What about Felix? I am meant to protect him."

"It's not about coddling," Orias said, his voice gentle but firm. "It's about strategy. They'll come for you again, Seere. I am the most capable of keeping you safe. As for Felix, I will see to it that he is also kept safe. Seere, I will not lose you."

Rowan stepped forward, his brow furrowed. "And what about Cotoria and Malkyn? Are we just going to let them roam the school after trying to kill Her Majesty twice?"

Orias shook his head. "They will be sent back to Envie

for breaking the rule of neutrality at this school. I will ensure there are guards to escort them."

Felix spoke up then, his voice quiet but resolute. "We should also consider how to address the students. The hall was full when—" He paused, struggling for words. "When her true identity was revealed. People are going to ask questions."

"I'll handle it," Seere said, her voice firm. "I will just have to face whatever comes next."

Orias frowned, clearly wanting to argue, but he nodded. "If that's what you want."

Foras, though still visibly displeased, sighed and folded his arms tightly. "Then we need to act quickly. The longer we wait, the more dangerous this becomes."

The group exchanged tense but determined glances, a silent agreement forming between them. Despite their differences, they all knew what was at stake. For now, survival took precedence over everything.

28

PEACE

ESLADAY, FIFTEENTH OF THE FROST MOON,
YEAR 450 OF THE GODDESS

Late morning light filtered through the small window of Seere's room, painting everything in a washed-out gold that felt mocking in its brightness. Seere knelt beside her trunk, her hands running over the fabric of each garment before folding it carefully and tucking it away. The familiar motions felt oddly mechanical, a way to busy her hands while her mind wrestled with the whirlwind of recent events.

Nearby, Orias leaned against the doorframe that separated the bedroom from the small dining room, his arms crossed over his chest. His evergreen eyes followed her every movement, a mixture of affection and amusement softening his sharp features.

"Do you really need to fold every single thing so neatly?" he teased, his voice breaking the silence. "I now understand why you took so long while I was trying to take you from the Domain."

Seere paused and looked back at him. She allowed a faint smile to touch the corners of her lips, the first since she'd heard of Shax's death. "Old habits die hard, I suppose... A messy trunk makes it harder to find things later."

Orias chuckled, stepping further into the room and stopping beside her. He reached for one of her tunics, folding it haphazardly before setting it into the trunk. "There. Efficient."

Seere raised an eyebrow only to pick up the shirt he'd just tossed in and throw it back at him. He still caught it with ease. "Efficiently chaotic, maybe."

She knew he was trying to make her feel better. She could see his sorrow behind his evergreen eyes. The teasing was a coping mechanism, a way to ease their grief.

Orias shrugged, folding it properly. "You'd be surprised how effective chaos can be."

She shook her head. Her hands moved to another item— the dark cloak she'd been gifted by a little girl of her kingdom. Her fingers lingered on the fabric, memories flooding her mind. Her throat constricted, her vision blurring. She remembered the little girl's smile, her desire to be just like Seere, and Seere's joy when she realized that she had finally done something right by building her kingdom. It all felt like a lifetime ago, even though it wasn't so far back.

"Are you alright?" Orias' voice was softer, his teasing replaced with genuine concern.

Seere nodded, though her grip on the cloak tightened briefly before she placed it in the trunk. "It's just strange, I suppose. Packing feels like... closing a chapter. Leaving behind the person I was once again," she said softly. "I suppose I am, though... or the two people I once acted as have finally combined."

Orias reached out, his fingers brushing against hers.

"You're not leaving anything behind. You're just making room for what's next."

His words hung in the air, and for a moment, they simply looked at each other. Then Seere reached for one of her spare masks resting on the bed beside her and placed it gently on top of her belongings.

"The masks were supposed to make me invisible," she murmured. "Now, it feels like everyone sees me more clearly than ever."

Orias' hand closed over hers, giving it a reassuring squeeze. "Let them see. You're too beautiful to hide away."

Her gaze softened, but before she could respond, he glanced at the trunk and smirked. "Though if you keep packing at this pace, we'll be here until next week."

Seere scoffed, the sound light and fleeting. "Fine, then. Make yourself useful."

He raised an eyebrow in mock offense. "I thought I already was."

She rolled her eyes and handed him a stack of books. "Start with these."

As they worked side by side, Seere found herself relaxing slightly, though the weight of Shax's death was still agonizing. Orias occasionally made a quip or exaggerated the difficulty of lifting her heavier belongings if only to make her laugh when he noticed her shoulders fall. He even pulled out a set of daggers she had stashed in a hidden compartment, holding them up with mock alarm.

"Planning to stab me in my sleep?" he teased, twirling one of the blades deftly.

"Only if you keep folding things wrong," she shot back, snatching a dagger from his hand.

By the time they finished, the trunk was neatly packed, with only a few personal items left to carry by hand. Seere sat back on her heels, letting out a small sigh of relief.

Orias leaned against the trunk, his expression thoughtful. "You know," he began, "when we first met, I thought you were insufferable. Arrogant, stubborn, too clever for your own good."

Seere raised an eyebrow. "Thank you for the glowing review. Though I can't say I thought much better of you at the time."

He chuckled, shaking his head. "What I'm saying is... I never expected this. Us." His voice softened, the amusement giving way to sincerity. "If you'd told me then that I'd one day be helping you pack up to move into my quarters... That I'd fall in love with you..." He trailed off, shaking his head with a hint of self-deprecation.

Her breath caught, and for a moment, she didn't know what to say. Then, she reached up, her fingers brushing against his jaw. "I didn't expect it either," she admitted. "But I wouldn't change it."

Orias stepped closer, his fingers hooking under her mask as he slid it down to reveal her face. Their lips met, soft and warm, and for an instant, the weight of the world lifted. The kiss was unhurried, a quiet exchange of emotions that they rarely spoke aloud. Seere melted into it, her hand sliding down to rest against the strong line of his jaw while his fingers traced a path along her arm, leaving goose flesh in their wake.

Orias pulled her closer, his other hand coming to rest at the small of her back. The warmth of his touch grounded her, steadying the whirlwind of thoughts and emotions that had plagued her for days. It silenced the guilt that waged a war within her. She felt herself exhale into the kiss, surrendering to the fleeting solace he offered.

The door to her room slammed open, the sound ricocheting off the walls like a thunderclap.

"Foras and Felix are impossible!"

Enora's voice was loud as she barreled into the room. She froze mid-step, her wide eyes darting between Seere and Orias, who had instinctively pulled back but still held Seere protectively close as if expecting an enemy and not Enora.

"Enora!" Seere snapped, frustration spiking out of nowhere.

"Oh! Oh no!" Enora's face flushed crimson, her hands flying up to cover her mouth. "I am so sorry!"

For a second, silence hung thick in the air. Seere swiftly turned away as she pulled her mask up with a practiced, exasperated motion. The mask settled into place, but it did little to hide the heat rising to her cheeks.

Orias, for his part, looked far less flustered. He leaned back slightly, one arm still draped around Seere's waist as he regarded Enora with a raised eyebrow. "You know, Enora, knocking is a very useful skill. You should try it sometime."

"I—I didn't realize—" Enora stammered, taking a step back. "I mean, I just—"

Rowan walked into the room and froze. He took one look at the scene and burst into laughter, his shoulders shaking as he leaned against the doorframe.

"Enora, you *really* need to work on your timing," he said, his grin widening with every second.

"I know!" Enora wailed, her hands flailing as she turned to shove Rowan lightly. "Why didn't you tell me to knock?"

"Because this was infinitely more entertaining," Rowan replied, ducking away from her half-hearted shove. His gaze flicked to Seere and Orias, a teasing spark in his eyes. "Though, to be fair, I didn't expect this."

Seere sighed, shaking her head as she pushed away from Orias slightly. "Could you both *not* make this any more awkward than it already is?"

Rowan held up his hands in mock surrender. "Hey, I'm just glad to see Orias finally admitting what the rest of us already knew."

Orias smirked, the corner of his mouth quirking up as he leaned casually against the edge of the bed. "And what exactly did you know, Rowan?"

"Oh, you know." Rowan waved a hand vaguely. "That you were hopelessly in love with Her Majesty and utterly terrible at hiding it."

Enora groaned, covering her face with her hands again. "Rowan, stop talking!"

"At least someone isn't angry about any of this," Seere murmured.

She glanced up at Orias, her irritation melting into something softer. He caught her eye and gave her a small, knowing smile—a silent promise that their moment wasn't lost, just postponed.

"Right," Seere said, cutting through the chaos. "If you two are done making fools of yourselves, I would like to finish packing."

Enora and Rowan exchanged sheepish looks before stepping outside, though not without Rowan throwing one last mischievous grin over his shoulder.

As the door closed behind them, Orias let out a soft

laugh, his hand brushing against hers. "So... where were we?"

Seere rolled her eyes but couldn't suppress the faint smile that tugged at her lips. "We were packing," she said, though her tone was far less stern than she had intended.

Orias grinned. "If you say so."

THE GUARDS MOVED EFFICIENTLY, lifting Seere's trunk and smaller cases as though they weighed nothing. Enora, ever eager to help, grabbed the dress Orias had given Seere for the Winter Solstice Ball and cradled it in her arms like a precious artifact. Her excitement buzzed in the air, a stark contrast to Seere's nervous energy.

Seere adjusted the mask on her face, an instinctive gesture of comfort that did little to shield her from the weight of the stares they encountered as they walked through the halls. Every step seemed to draw murmurs from the students gathered nearby, their whispers swirling around her like an oppressive fog.

"Amaris."

"It's really her."

"I can't believe she was here the whole time."

Seere's heart clenched at the sound of her true name—but it wasn't just her heart. Something deeper twisted inside her, a grief so raw it made her stomach roil. She kept her head high, her posture straight, though her fingers twitched against the hem of her sleeve.

Orias was a steady presence by her side, his hand resting lightly on the small of her back. He leaned in slightly, his voice low and soothing as he murmured, "They'll get over it. Focus on me, darling."

She gave a faint nod, though her body remained tense. His touch anchored her, a lifeline amidst the chaos.

Enora's bright chatter barely reached Seere through the thrum of her tension. "This is such a gorgeous piece! Honestly, Orias, you've got good taste."

Orias chuckled softly. "It's easy when you have the right inspiration."

Seere shot him a sidelong glance, her cheeks warming beneath the mask. She said nothing, but her steps quickened slightly, the need for sanctuary sharpening her movements.

Rowan, trailing behind the group, grinned at the display. "You two are disgusting, you know that?"

"Disgusting?" Orias raised an eyebrow, his tone light. "Coming from you, that's rich. Who is it that has a different date each weekend?"

"Hey, I'm just saying. The way you two look at one another, it's like a bad romance novel come to life." Rowan smirked, dodging a playful swat from Enora.

She smiles, but it doesn't quite reach her eyes. The hollowness in her chest was too all-consuming.

As they ascended the staircase to Orias' office, the murmurs began to fade, replaced by the quiet thuds of steps on stone and the occasional clink of metal as the guards adjusted their grip on Seere's belongings.

When they finally reached the office, Orias opened the door and gestured for the guards to set everything down near the bedchamber. Seere stepped inside, exhaling softly as the familiar scent of parchment and cedar wrapped around her like a protective cloak.

"Home sweet home," Orias said warmly.

As the guards filed out, Enora carefully laid the dress

across a chair, smoothing out any wrinkles with meticulous care. She beamed at Seere. "There. Perfect."

Rowan leaned against the doorframe, his arms crossed. "So, what now? You're going to hole up in here like some kind of recluse?"

"Maybe," Seere replied with a slight shrug. "Recluses don't have to deal with people like you."

Rowan laughed, his easy demeanor lightening the mood. "Fair enough. But don't think we're going to let you disappear entirely. You've got a lot of explaining to do."

"Not now," Orias interjected, his tone firm but not unkind. He stepped closer to Seere, his hand brushing against hers. "She needs time."

Enora nodded, her expression softening. "He's right. You've been through a lot, and we'll be here when you're ready."

"Thank you," Seere murmured, her voice barely audible.

The soft click of the door as it closed behind Rowan and Enora left the office in peaceful stillness. Seere let out a slow breath, her shoulders dropping as the weight of the day began to lift. She glanced at Orias, who leaned casually against the desk, watching her with a mix of affection and concern.

She moved to her trunk and carefully opened it, pulling out a small bundle of neatly folded clothes. "Thank you," she murmured, not looking up as she placed the clothes into a nearby drawer that Orias had emptied for her earlier.

"For what?" Orias asked, stepping closer.

"For... this," she said, gesturing vaguely around the room. "For giving me space. For letting me be here. For... you."

A small smile played on Orias' lips. "You don't have to

thank me for any of that, Seere. It's the least I can do after dragging you away from your kingdom with blackmail."

She paused for a moment, her fingers resting on the edge of the trunk. Then, almost imperceptibly, she nodded. Orias moved behind her. His arms encircled her waist, pulling her gently against him. Seere stiffened at first, her hands faltering over the items in the trunk. But then she exhaled, leaning back slightly into his warmth.

"Are you alright?" he asked, his voice low and steady, his breath caressing her ear.

"Yes," she murmured. "I just... I'm not used to this."

"Being cared for? Wanted?" he teased lightly, his tone laced with affection.

"Something like that," she replied with a faint smile.

Her fingers trembled as she lifted them to her mask. It felt heavier, like it had fused to her very skin. Slowly, almost reverently, she lifted it away and tossed it onto the bed—banishing it with a sharp, aching motion.

Orias said nothing, his arms tightening around her slightly.

"I've been thinking," she began quietly, her voice tinged with uncertainty. "About what might come next."

He remained silent, waiting patiently for her to continue.

"I was wondering..." She hesitated, biting her lip before forging ahead. "Would you ever consider coming back with me to the Domain of Assassins? Not now, but in the near future."

"The Domain?"

She nodded, her gaze lowered to the trunk. "It's my home. Or at least, it used to be. If I am ever welcomed back there, I'd like to do it differently. I will take my throne back as Amaris, and I will need another advisor who is loyal to Amaris before they are loyal to Seere."

Orias tilted his head slightly, studying her. "What are you saying?"

She swallowed, her fingers twisting the edge of her sleeve. "I want you to come with me to the Domain. I want to court you publicly," she said softly. "You have shown me what it feels like to be cared for, and I don't want to give that up... ever"

Her words hung in the air for a moment, heavy with implication.

Orias turned her around to face him, his expression unreadable. For a brief, heart-stopping moment, she feared she had overstepped. But then his face softened, a slow smile spreading across his lips.

"You truly mean that? The Assassin Queen is willing to show vulnerability and love me openly?" he asked teasingly, and she knew it was to ease the tension in her shoulders.

"Well, if you put it like that," she said with a roll of her eyes. "But yes, I wouldn't say these things if I didn't mean them."

He cupped her face gently, his thumbs grazing her cheeks. "Then yes," he whispered. "If that's what you want, I'll be at your side, loyal to both Amaris and Seere, and I would be honored to court you publicly."

She opened her mouth to thank him again, but the words snagged in her throat, splintered by the tears she refused to let fall. Finally, she nodded. Orias, seeming to sense her struggle, smirked before he leaned in, pressing a soft kiss to her lips, one that was filled with quiet promise and unwavering devotion.

When they parted, she rested her forehead against his, her hands clutching his shirt. "You're sure?"

"Seere—Amaris," he said, his tone firm but gentle. "There's no place I'd rather be than with you. Wherever that takes us."

For the first time in what felt like an eternity, a genuine smile curved her lips. "Thank you," she whispered once more, though this time it carried a deeper meaning.

And for a little while, they simply stood there, holding onto each other, the rest of the world fading away.

29

———

DARKNESS

DHANIRDAY, TWENTIETH OF THE FROST
MOON, YEAR 450 OF THE GODDESS

Seere stood beside the large window behind Orias' desk, watching the sun disappear behind one of the mountain peaks at the same height as the window. The golden light of the lanterns and fireplace cast long shadows across the room. She was holding a book, long forgotten, in her hands when his voice broke through the silence.

"I have a staff meeting tonight," he began, his tone measured. "You're welcome to join me if you'd like."

Seere blinked, her gaze lifting from the window to catch sight of Orias' reflection as he adjusted the cuffs of his suit. Then she turned around to face him. "You're inviting me to a staff meeting?"

He crossed over to her, pressing a kiss to her lips. "Yes. You're a queen—and everyone knows you're no student," he said, gently taking the book from her and setting it aside on his desk. "And I think you have every right to be at a meeting that is about you."

"Of course it's about me," she muttered, turning her gaze back to the window. "Sure. I will join you."

Orias held his hand out to her, drawing her attention back to him. There was a warmth in his gaze that was reassuring. "Let's go then."

The staff room was an imposing chamber, its high ceilings adorned with intricate carvings and shelves lined with books and scrolls. Seere felt a flicker of unease as she entered, acutely aware of the weight of many gazes falling upon her.

She took a seat beside Orias, her back straight and hands folded neatly in her lap. To her left sat Professor Vidal, his expression as stern and unreadable as ever. Across the table, other professors murmured amongst themselves, casting glances her way.

Before the meeting began, Professor Manfredonia approached her, his sharp eyes taking her in as if seeing her for the first time again. Seere's eyes burned with tears she wouldn't shed as realization struck her sharply. For years, he had likely believed that she was dead. Seere rose swiftly, blinking as she properly took in the features of the man who had treated her as though she were his daughter and not just his niece.

"I had hoped that you could be Amaris," Professor Manfredonia whispered with a familiar warmth he had reserved only for her. His eyes clouded with tears, though they did not fall, just as her own refused. "I didn't want to give myself hope. My dearest niece, it's good to see you again after so many long years. You have done well for yourself, better than I could have hoped."

Seere offered a small smile and rested her hands on his shoulders. "It's good to see you again, uncle," she said softly.

"I am sorry I did not write to you, and I am more sorry that I did not tell you who I was earlier when I saw that you'd come here."

Her uncle's smile only deepened, the lines around his eyes crinkling. "Don't think anything of it. I understand why you couldn't. I'm just relieved to see that you are still alive. I'm proud to see how far you've come, Your Majesty."

Seere allowed him to pull her into an embrace for a moment before he stepped away from her. The exchange had brought a rare sense of ease to her—though she knew it would be short-lived. As the other professors settled in, the atmosphere grew tense.

"Why is Amaris here?" Professor Dubois demanded, her tone sharp.

"This meeting is about her, not for her," Professor Viné added.

Orias' expression darkened. He remained seated, but the weight of his authority was palpable as he spoke. "She is here because, as you all know, she is not a student. She is a queen, and as such, she has the right to be wherever she chooses. And I invited her."

"Her presence is a danger to the school," the alchemy professor, a wiry man called Professor Cortland, argued, his voice sharp and edged with frustration. "The Domain of Assassins has always been a source of controversy. If words spread that their queen is Princess Amaris of Envie, we risk drawing Empress Selina right to our doorstep."

Professor Maribelle Alden, the arithmetic instructor, was the next to chime in, her tone clipped. "Have you forgotten the blood-soaked reputation of Princess Amaris? How can we justify allowing her to walk these halls? *Especially* now that we know Amaris and Seere are one person and have been since the beginning!"

Professor Dubois raised her hand to speak. "Let's not ignore the broader implications. The students are aware of her true identity now. Whispers have already spread through the corridors. We're supposed to foster education and peace, not embroil ourselves in the political power plays of the Domain and Envie."

Seere sat tall, her mask of calm firmly in place. She met each comment with quiet dignity, but her hands clenched tightly in her lap. She was accustomed to the setting of a meeting as they reminded her of the many councils she held in the Domain.

Orias' expression darkened, though he remained silent, letting the professors speak their minds.

"She's a queen, yes," Professor Maribelle continued, her voice tinged with disdain. "But a queen of *assassins*. She should never have had a place in an institution dedicated to enlightenment."

"The academy has always prided itself on neutrality. Allowing a figure like Amaris, an enemy of Envie, risks undermining that completely," Professor Viné said.

At this, Professor Manfredonia slammed a hand on the table, his voice cutting through the growing din. "Neutrality? Spare me the sanctimony, Viné. You didn't raise these concerns when we welcomed students from disagreeing nations or royal families embroiled in scandal. Amaris is no different. She has as much right to be here as anyone else— perhaps more, considering her position."

The room erupted into a cacophony of voices, some supporting Professor Manfredonia's stance, others arguing vehemently against it.

Professor Vidal, who had remained silent so far, finally spoke, his deep baritone silencing the room. "Enough," he growled, his piercing gaze sweeping over the table. "You're all missing the point. This isn't about neutrality or optics. It's about responsibility. Amaris—or Seere, if you prefer—is under this school's protection. To cast her out now would be a betrayal of that responsibility."

"That's easy for you to say," Professor Cortland shot back, his voice rising. "You don't have to worry about alchemical reagents being stolen or poisons being brewed in your classroom—"

"Enough."

This time, it was Orias who spoke, his voice low and commanding. The room fell silent, all eyes turning to him.

"I have allowed this discussion to continue because I value your input," he said, his tone icy and precise. "But make no mistake—this is not a debate. King Hubert and Queen Frieda of Noctivagus invited Seere to remain here. That decision is final. It is not up for negotiation."

"But—" Maribelle began, only to be cut off by Orias' sharp glare.

"No buts," he snapped. "Amaris is not a threat to this academy. If anything, your paranoia and baseless accusations are the real disruption. She is a queen, and she will be treated with the respect she deserves. Is that clear?"

The professors exchanged uneasy glances, but no one dared to argue further.

Professor Manfredonia, who had remained quiet during Orias' speech, finally spoke again. "For what it's worth," he said, his voice steady, "I think keeping Amaris here is the right decision. She's proven her loyalty and capability time and time again. This school could stand to learn a thing or two from someone with her experience."

"You're only saying this because you are her uncle," Professor Dubois muttered.

"To me, Professor Dubois, she *is* my daughter," Professor Manfredonia said sharply.

Seere couldn't help the small smile that decorated her lips at his words. She startled when she felt a hand slide into hers. Her gaze darted to Orias, who offered her an assuring look. He didn't smile, but his eyes were filled with a warmth meant only for her.

The heavy oak doors to the staff room burst open. The sudden noise silenced the room instantly, heads turning in unison toward the source of the interruption.

A young messenger stood in the doorway, his face pale and his breath coming in sharp gasps. The insignia of the Noctivagus royal court glinted on the brooch fastened to his cloak.

"Headmaster," the messenger said, his voice taut with urgency as he addressed Orias. "A message—urgent news from Hesperus."

The room fell into a tense, expectant silence. Orias rose from his seat, his imposing presence commanding the room without effort. He strode toward the messenger, his boots echoing on the stone floor.

The young man extended a sealed letter, his hands trembling slightly. "From the palace," he added, his voice barely above a whisper.

Orias broke the wax seal with a flick of his fingers, unfolding the letter and scanning the contents. Seere watched his expression carefully, noting the way his jaw tightened and his grip on the parchment turned white at the knuckles. He crossed back to his place at the head of the table, but he did not sit.

"What does it say?" she asked softly as she stood.

Orias didn't answer immediately. He finished reading, his gaze lingering on the final lines of the letter before he folded it and pressed it against the table. When he finally looked up, his face was a mask of controlled fury.

"King Hubert and Queen Frieda of Noctivagus," he said, his voice low and deliberate, "have been assassinated."

The weight of his words hit the room like a thunderclap. Gasps and murmurs broke out among the professors, their earlier arguments forgotten in an instant.

Seere's breath caught in her chest. Though it had been years since she'd seen the king and queen, the news struck her deeply. Her eyes darted to Orias, who stood rigid, his gaze fixed somewhere distant.

"There's more," Orias continued, his voice cutting through the growing murmurs. "Prince Felix must return to Hesperus immediately to take the mantle of king. I will escort him there personally."

The room erupted into questions and concerns, but Orias silenced them with a raised hand. "Until my return, Professor Manfredonia will oversee the academy."

A ripple of surprise went through the room at this announcement. All eyes turned to Professor Manfredonia, who straightened in his seat but remained silent.

"What about Professor Vidal?" one of the professors ventured hesitantly.

Orias turned a sharp gaze on the speaker. "My decision is final."

He looked to Seere then, his voice softening. "You'll need

to pack your things again. You're coming with me—I am not about to leave you here unprotected."

Seere nodded faintly, her mind racing. "Of course," she murmured.

Without another word, Orias turned on his heel and strode out of the room, the messenger trailing after him. Seere followed moments later, her heart heavy with a mixture of shock, grief, and unease.

When Seere caught up, she placed a hand on his shoulder. "Are you okay?" she asked.

"Frustrated," he answered, then he removed her hand so that he could lace his fingers through hers. "Things aren't going the way they are meant to."

Seere nodded. "No, I don't believe they are..."

Orias sighed softly, glancing at her. "At least... you're mine," he whispered. "Now, let's go find Felix."

THE COMMON ROOM was alive with chatter and the faint crackle of a fire in the hearth when Seere and Orias stepped into the doorway. Felix's voice rose above the others, sharp and defensive, cutting through the warm ambiance like a blade.

"You don't understand!" Felix snapped, glaring at Enora, who sat across from him. Her arms were crossed, her expression a mix of exasperation and determination.

"I do understand," Enora countered, leaning forward. "But you can't keep holding on to something that was never going to happen, Felix. She's happy with Orias. Can't you see that?"

Felix's face flushed with anger, his fists clenching on the table between them. "She was supposed to marry me! It was arranged. It was expected. Why aren't you angry about this anymore? Wasn't it just the other day that you were shouting at her?"

"That was before I understood what she was going through," Enora said. "She doesn't deserve your anger."

Foras was leaning back in his chair with his boots propped on the edge of the table. "Amaris has always had a bit of a gift when it comes to disappointing people."

Enora shot Foras a withering glare. "That's enough, Foras."

"Is it?" he asked lazily, tilting his head. "I'm beginning to think Empress Selina—"

"Finish that sentence, Sir Andromal, and it will be the last sentence you ever utter," Orias said coolly, his voice loud and commanding in the charged room.

Every head turned toward the doorway, the tension crackling like a storm on the verge of breaking. Felix's gaze hardened when he saw Orias, his expression shifting from anger to defiance. He pushed back his chair, his chin lifting as if ready to challenge whatever Orias had come to say.

Orias, however, didn't spare him even the faintest flicker of emotion. His voice was cool, almost detached, as he addressed Felix directly. "Prince Felix," he began, the formal title cutting sharply through the informal atmosphere, "your parents have been assassinated."

The room fell into a stunned silence. The fire popped in the hearth, but no one moved, no one spoke. Felix's face drained of color, his defiance crumbling into shock and disbelief.

"What... what did you say?" he whispered, his voice barely audible.

Orias stepped further into the room, his gaze steady.

"King Hubert and Queen Frieda were murdered in the palace of Hesperus. You are the rightful heir, and as such, you must return to Noctivagus immediately to take the throne."

Felix staggered slightly, gripping the back of his chair for support. "No... that can't be..." His voice cracked, and for a moment, he looked much younger, his grief raw and unguarded.

Seere's heart twisted at the sight of his pain, but she stayed where she was, unwilling to cross the invisible line that now separated them.

Enora's eyes widened, and she covered her mouth with her hand. "Felix... I'm so sorry," she murmured, but he didn't seem to hear her.

Foras, for once, had no clever remark. He stared at the table, his expression falling blank.

"You'll need to be ready to leave by midnight," Orias continued, his voice unyielding. "The journey to Hesperus will take a week, and there's no time to waste."

Felix's head snapped up, his grief momentarily replaced by anger. "And you—what gives you the right to decide this?"

Orias met his gaze unflinchingly. "I am tasked with ensuring the safety of this academy and its students. Right now, that includes you. You are not in a position to argue, Your Highness."

Felix's jaw clenched, but he said nothing, his fists trembling at his sides.

Orias turned to address the others. "Foras, Enora, Rowan —you will accompany him. Pack what you need for the journey. We leave at midnight."

Rowan nodded solemnly, rising from his chair without a word. Foras hesitated but eventually followed suit, his usual bravado replaced by something quieter. Enora stayed by Felix's side, her hand hovering uncertainly, as if she longed to comfort him but couldn't find the way.

As Orias turned to leave, Seere followed him, glancing back only once. Felix remained motionless in the center of the room, his grief and anger warring behind his eyes. Seere's heart ached, but she forced herself to look away. Felix would have to carry this burden alone—just as she had carried hers.

THE NIGHT AIR WAS CRISP, scented with pine and alive with the distant murmur of nocturnal creatures. The moon hung high above the fortress, casting pale light over the scene as Seere and Orias stood near the carriages. The soft clatter of hooves on stone echoed through the courtyard, mingling with the muted voices of guards issuing last-minute instructions.

Felix and his companions moved with slow, deliberate motions, their exhaustion visible even in the dim light. Rowan hefted a satchel onto the second carriage with ease, while Enora fussed over the placement of their belongings, muttering about keeping the heavier items balanced. Foras leaned against the side of the carriage, arms crossed, his usual smirk nowhere to be found. Felix, however, moved as if in a daze, his shoulders hunched as he loaded the last of his luggage without a word.

Orias' voice broke the quiet tension. "The arrangements are simple," he said, his tone commanding. "Seere and I will take the leading carriage. The four of you will ride in the second. Guards will flank us on horseback, both ahead and behind. We must maintain a steady pace; there will be no unnecessary stops."

Enora nodded, her expression determined, while Rowan gave a small grunt of acknowledgement. Foras' lips pressed into a thin line with displeasure. Felix remained silent, his gaze fixed on the ground.

Orias turned to Seere and held out his hand. "Come, Seere," he said softly, his voice losing its edge as he addressed her.

She hesitated for a moment, her eyes flicking to the group by the second carriage. Enora glanced at her with something like concern, but Seere quickly looked away, slipping her hand into Orias'. He guided her to their carriage, his movements as smooth as ever. Holding the door open, he gave her a small nod of encouragement. She climbed inside and settled herself on the cushioned seats.

A moment later, Orias joined her, the door clicking shut behind him. The interior of the carriage was dim, illuminated only by the faint moonlight filtering through the small windows. Seere adjusted her cloak, her fingers tugging at the fabric, restless tension as she leaned back into her seat.

Outside, a guard called for the drivers to get moving, his voice sharp in the stillness of the night. The carriage jolted as the horses leapt into action, their hooves scraping against the cobblestones.

The fortress walls slowly receded into the distance, replaced by the shadowy outline of trees as they entered the darkened forest. Seere stared out of the window for a moment, watching as the world outside passed by in muted grays and blacks.

Breaking the silence, she turned to Orias. "Are you certain about bringing me along?" she asked quietly, her voice barely audible over the steady rumble of the carriage. "You know as well as I do that Selina won't let this go—she will come after me."

Orias scoffed, leaning back into his seat with a calm that seemed almost out of place given the circumstances. "Selina," he said, his tone laced with derision, "can try whatever she pleases. She will never get her hands on you, Amaris. Not while I live."

The way he said those words sent a shiver down her spine. It was not out of fear or confidence—it was determination. He swore a promise, one she knew he intended to keep. It was startling to think that he would fight an entire kingdom to keep her safe.

Her lips curved into the faintest of smiles, and she shifted slightly closer to him on the cushioned seat. "I'll hold you to that," she said softly, her voice carrying the barest hint of warmth.

Orias reached for her hand, his fingers curling around hers in a firm but gentle grip. "You won't need to," he replied simply, his gaze meeting hers with unwavering resolve.

The carriage swayed slightly as it moved over uneven ground, the forest growing denser around them. The world outside felt distant, as if they were traveling through a realm all their own. For now, it was just the two of them, the weight of the night held at bay by the quiet promise shared between them.

30

SNOW

DHANIRDAY, TWENTY-FIRST OF THE FROST MOON, YEAR 450 OF THE GODDESS

As the carriages rolled into Anderida, the first rays of dawn cast a golden glow over the rooftops of the town, just beginning to stir. Its cobblestone roads were blanketed with fresh snow. Chimneys puffed out gentle wisps of smoke into the cold morning air in a beautifully picturesque way.

The town was sizable, its buildings tall and ornate, with signs hanging from wrought iron brackets announcing bakeries, apothecaries, and clothiers.

The streets were eerily quiet, save for the rhythmic clatter of hooves and the crunch of carriage wheels against the frosty road. Their procession drew curious eyes from the few townsfolk who were already up, their faces peeking out from windows or around doorways as they wrapped shawls or cloaks tightly against the cold.

The inn Orias had chosen stood at the edge of the town square, a grand building with carved wooden beams and frosted glass windows that gleamed in the early light. It was the kind of place that spoke of warmth and comfort, with glowing lanterns lining the entryway and the faint scent of cinnamon wafting from within.

The carriages came to a halt just outside the inn's wide double doors, the horses stamping and huffing in the cold. Orias stepped out first, his sharp gaze scanning their surroundings as a precaution before he turned and offered a hand to Seere.

She hesitated only for a moment, her fingers brushing his as she stepped out into the crisp morning air. The sudden cold nipped at her face, and she pulled her cloak tighter around herself, her breath visible in soft puffs.

"Wait here," Orias said, his voice low and steady. "I'll arrange the rooms."

Seere nodded, watching as he disappeared into the inn. Around her, guards dismounted from their horses, shaking the frost from their cloaks as they began unloading luggage from the carriages. Felix and his companions emerged one by one, their expressions heavy with exhaustion and grief.

The group waited in silence, the weight of the journey and the news of the assassinations settling over them like a thick fog. Foras leaned against the side of the carriage, arms crossed, while Rowan muttered something to Enora, who only nodded absently. Felix stood apart from them, his arms crossed as his cobalt eyes fixed on the snow-covered square, lost in thought.

When Orias returned, his authoritative presence snapped them out of their reverie. "I've secured three rooms," he announced, his voice carrying a note of finality. "Rowan will stay with me. Felix and Foras, you'll share a room. Seere and Enora will have the third."

Seere blinked, surprised by the arrangements but unwilling to argue. She was already accustomed to Orias keeping her close even after such a short time of them being more than just bedmates, but his tone made it clear that his decision was final.

"Guards will patrol the perimeter," Orias continued, his gaze sweeping over them. "Stay alert, all of you."

With that, everyone gathered their belongings and followed him into the inn. The warmth inside was a stark contrast to the icy streets, the air filled with the inviting scents of woodsmoke and freshly baked bread. A crackling fire roared in the hearth, casting a golden glow over the polished wooden floors and high-beamed ceilings.

Despite the comfort of the inn, the group's spirits remained subdued. Orias handed keys to each pair, his expression unreadable as he gave them instructions to rest and prepare for the next leg of their journey.

Seere followed Enora up the wide staircase to their room, her boots echoing faintly against the steps. She couldn't shake the unease that lingered in the back of her mind, though whether it was from the journey, the looming threat of her sister, or the news of the assassinations, she couldn't tell.

The room was cozy, with a large bed nestled against one wall, thick quilts piled high to ward off the winter chill. A small writing desk sat beneath the frost-laced window, and a single armchair was positioned by the fireplace, where embers glowed faintly, promising warmth.

As the guards dropped off the ladies' trunks and left, Enora tossed her travel bag onto one of the beds with a sigh, brushing a stray lock of hair from her face. Seere's gaze trailed over to Enora from where she remained by the door, her gloved hands resting lightly on the edges of her hood. The tension in her posture was unmistakable.

"You can relax now," Enora said softly, offering a reassuring smile.

Seere nodded slightly. She took a moment to inspect the room. She checked the window to make sure it was locked and checked behind the furniture to be sure there were no secret access points. Finally, removed her hood and pulled off her mask. Enora knew who she was. There was little point in keeping her mask up anymore.

"In many ways, you're the same person that I met all those years ago," Enora said, her gaze sweeping over Seere's features even as Seere rifled through her belongings for fresh clothes. "I feel silly for not having recognized you. Your eyes should have given you away. But in every other way, you are an entirely different person from Amaris. For one, Amaris enjoyed dressing up."

Seere sighed and shook her head. "For seven years, I tried to convince the world and myself that Amaris was dead. That Amaris was someone else I never knew. It's surprisingly exhausting carrying the weight of a ghost."

Enora nodded slowly, her gaze softening as she leaned forward. "You're not a ghost, Amaris. You're here. You're alive. And I'm grateful for that." She hesitated, then added, "Even with the ridiculous bounty on your head."

Seere smiled, her gaze flickering to Enora before she shut the lid of her trunk with fresh leggings and a blouse. "I'm shocked that you're not terrified of me, or of what having me in your company means. My sisters will try to wage war to get their hands on me, and I have no intention of going down willingly."

Enora scoffed, crossing her arms. "Afraid? Please. I'd like to see anyone try to come after you. I think Felix and Orias both would tear apart anyone who so much as raises a hand to you." Her lips quirked into a teasing grin before she sobered. "But seriously, Seere... or Amaris, I've always believed in you. You're stronger than anyone I've ever met. I'm just glad you're still here, with us, despite everything."

Seere looked away, her throat tightening with an unfamiliar emotion. "Thank you," she murmured.

Enora stood and crossed the room, placing a hand gently on Seere's shoulder. "Don't thank me. Mask or no mask, we're in this together. Always. Even if Orias is around."

She released a quiet breath. For the first time in what felt like ages, a small, fragile flicker of hope stirred within her—hope that she wasn't as alone as she felt.

SEERE SLIPPED from her room long after night had fallen, unable to find any ounce of tiredness within her body. Rather than lie awake and stare up at the ceiling, she wandered.

The lounge of the inn was quiet, dimly lit by the faint amber glow of wall sconces and the flicker of a low-burning hearth. The air carried a hint of roasted coffee beans and aged wood, mingling with the faint chill of winter that seeped through the walls. Seere crossed the room, her cloak swaying with each step and her hood casting shadows across her face. She paused near the doorway, her gaze catching on the lone figure by the window.

Felix sat with a steaming cup in hand, his silhouette sharp against the frost-dusted panes. His posture was rigid, the line of his shoulders taut as though he carried an invisible weight. The steam from his drink curled lazily upward, but his eyes remained fixed on the darkness beyond the glass.

Seere hesitated. Part of her wanted to retreat, to leave him alone with his thoughts. But something in his expression—a fragile mix of determination and despair—drew her in.

Carefully, she approached, her footsteps soft on the thick rug. Felix's gaze flickered towards her as she slid into the armchair opposite him, but he quickly turned back to the window, his features unreadable.

"Couldn't sleep?" she asked, her voice barely above a whisper.

He nodded once, his fingers tightening around the cup. "No," he admitted after a moment, his tone low and raw.

The silence between them stretched, broken only by the occasional crackle of the fire. Seere's fingers laced together in her lap as silence thickened between them.

"You're a queen," he said abruptly. His words were filled with something like strange disbelief that she wasn't sure how to decipher. It was as if he couldn't believe Amaris had built a kingdom, but he had believed her when she was Seere. His eyes stayed on the window, but there was a tension in his voice, as if he were reminding himself of a fact he couldn't quite accept. "How do you... do it? Knowing that so many people depend on you to make the right choices? To lead them? I don't even know where to begin." He gestured vaguely toward the window, his hand trembling slightly. "All of that... It's *mine* now. And I don't even know how to handle it."

Seere followed his gaze, her eyes tracing the delicate patterns of snowflakes falling softly under the streetlamps. She took a deep breath before responding, her tone quiet and reflective.

"I won't lie to you, Felix. It's overwhelming." Her fingers

toyed with the hem of her cloak as she spoke. "There were nights I thought I'd never be able to bear the weight of it. When I built my kingdom, I was only seventeen. I had no guide, no precedent. Just desperation and determination." She paused, her voice softening. "You're already more prepared than I was when I began."

Felix shook his head with a dry, bitter laugh. "I doubt that. You make it look effortless. You built an entire kingdom on your own. When I was seventeen, I was going on hunts with the noblemen and wondering where in the realm you had gone."

Seere's lips curved into a faint smile, though it didn't reach her eyes. "It's not. It has never been effortless." She leaned forward, her voice steady. "But you don't have to do it alone. I didn't. I had a court that I trusted. You have allies, Felix—people who care about you and want you to succeed. I will always be one of them. If you ever need help, advice, or simply someone to share the burden with, I'll be there."

Her words hung in the air, a promise that seemed to ease some of the tension in Felix's posture. He turned to look at her then, his cobalt gaze sharp and searching. For a moment, he seemed on the verge of saying something, but instead, he ran a hand through his messy auburn hair, exhaling slowly.

He hesitated, then asked, "Will you... take off your mask?"

Seere stiffened, her hand unconsciously rising toward the mask before falling away. "I'd rather not," she said softly.

Felix frowned. "Why not?"

"It's not about you," she murmured, her gaze dropping to the floor. "Even I look at myself and see little more than a ghost."

Felix watched her for a long moment, his expression

unreadable. Then, to her surprise, he nodded. "I suppose I can understand that," he said quietly.

Seere finally settled back into her chair. She brought her legs up to her chest, her gaze shifting to the window. "You should get some rest."

"Yeah," Felix breathed, looking down at his mug. He set it aside and got to his feet. "Goodnight... Seere."

"Goodnight."

31

FUNERAL

DHANIRDAY, TWENTY-SEVENTH OF THE
FROST MOON, YEAR 450 OF THE GODDESS

The city of Hesperus stretched before Seere, a labyrinth of cobblestone streets and towering stone buildings. It was bustling despite the somber occasion, the usual vibrancy of the capital muted by an air of mourning. Black banners bearing the royal crest—two crescent moons overlapping to form an eclipse—fluttered in the cold wind, and citizens paused to bow their heads as the carriage passed.

Seere peered out the window while she tried to keep herself hidden behind the fluttering curtains. Though she had been to Noctivagus before, the sight of the city now was different. Its usual warmth and hospitality had been replaced by a chilling sense of loss.

The gleaming spires of the palace emerged from the haze like ivory spears piercing the heavens, their surfaces glinting with golden accents that caught the midday light.

The palace gates stood open, an honor guard lining the wide, cobbled courtyard. Their armor shone brilliantly, polished to perfection for the solemn occasion. They held their halberds upright, their faces stern as the carriages came to a stop in the circular drive before the palace's grand entrance.

Seere glanced back at Orias. He leaned over and pressed a sweet kiss to her lips. "Everything will be alright," he promised.

She nodded, slipping her mask on before he opened the door.

Orias stepped out first, his figure composed and authoritative. He turned to offer a hand to Seere, who hesitated only for a moment before accepting. Her black leathers contrasted sharply with the alabaster stones of the palace, and even with her face obscured by her mask, she radiated an air of regal command.

Behind her, Felix and his companions emerged from their carriage, their expressions varying from solemn to apprehensive. A murmur swept through the assembled servants and council members as they caught sight of the group, their focus flitting between Felix, Seere, and the towering presence of Orias.

The council members approached immediately, their finely tailored robes swishing as they bowed low to Felix. "Your Highness," one of them began, his voice reverent but firm, "we must begin preparations for the funeral immediately. There is no time to waste."

Servants moved forward, bowing deeply as they ushered each of the travelers toward their assigned rooms. Seere stood apart for a moment, her gaze fixed on the palace. Memories of her youth here swirled in her mind, fleeting but vivid—the laughter in the corridors, the warmth of the late Queen Frieda's smile, and the stern yet kind words of King Hubert.

A young maid stepped forward, her expression a mixture of awe and shyness. The girl appeared no older than eighteen, her dark hair neatly tucked under a white cap. Her hands were clasped tightly in front of her, as though she feared they might betray her nerves. She bowed deeply, her voice soft but clear. "Your Majesty, if you would please follow me to your chambers."

Seere inclined her head gracefully, but as she turned to follow, Orias caught her hand. His evergreen eyes, usually so calculating, held a flicker of worry. "Will you be alright?" he asked quietly, his voice meant for her alone.

She nodded, a faint smile touching her lips behind the mask. "I'll be fine," she said, her voice steady. "I am still the Assassin Queen." She gently pulled her hand free and followed the maid toward the familiar halls of the White Palace.

As they entered, the interior took her breath away anew. Gleaming white marble columns lined the main atrium, their surfaces carved with intricate depictions of the moon phases and constellations sacred to Noctivagus. The ceilings soared high above, adorned with murals of the night skies painted in exquisite detail. Stained glass windows flickered the daylight into soft hues of blue and silver, casting an ethereal glow over the polished floors.

Her room, when they reached it, was well appointed, though it carried an air of quiet restraint befitting the occasion. The delicate scent of lavender lingered in the air. The room itself was lavish yet tasteful, with its high ceilings, soft silken drapes, and a massive canopy bed adorned with velvet and brocade. But the youthful memories of this space felt foreign to her, like echoes of someone else's life.

Two burly servants set her trunk down against a wall and

then left swiftly. The maid bowed again, then slipped out behind the servants, leaving Seere to her privacy so she could prepare herself for the day ahead.

Taking a deep breath, she moved toward the gilded wardrobe that stood against the far wall. Much to her surprise, there was an array of garments hung neatly, all in the traditional shades of mourning: deep blacks, muted greys, and dark violets. Seere's fingers brushed over the smooth fabrics, pausing on a gown of black silk. It was understated yet elegant, its bodice fitted with delicate embroidery resembling intertwining vines and crescent moons.

She pulled it from the wardrobe and laid it across the bed before turning her attention to the adjoining chamber. A servant had already prepared a bath, the warm steam curling into the air and beckoning her tired body.

In the privacy of the bathing room, Seere shed her travel-worn attire and lowered herself into the hot water. The heat seeped into her muscles, easing the tension that had built up over the week-long journey. She scrubbed her skin clean of the grime of travel, using fragrant oils and soaps that smelled faintly of rose and sandalwood. Her mind, however, was anything but calm.

Memories of King Hubert and Queen Frieda surfaced unbidden, mingling with the present reality. She recalled the warmth of Queen Frieda's embrace and the quiet strength of King Hubert's words when they had spoken of alliances and the future. The weight of their loss settled heavily on her chest, though she kept her emotions tightly reined.

Once she was cleaned and dried, Seere returned to the bedroom, her steps purposeful but unhurried. She donned the black silk gown, the fabric cool and smooth against her skin. The bodice fit snugly, accenting her regal bearing, while the skirts flowed around her like a shadow. She fastened the small clasps along the back before turning to the vanity.

Her lavender hair was still damp even as she blotted it with a towel. Eventually, she gave up and worked it into an intricate updo, pinning it securely beneath a black mourning veil to hide the fact that it was still damp. The veil cascaded over her shoulders, its fine lace partially obscuring her face and adding an air of somber mystery.

Next, she reached her mask—the one Orias had gifted her for the ball. She knew there was no point in wearing it; she was certain almost everyone knew her true identity by now. Still, it had become more than a disguise—it was her armor, the face she chose to show to the world.

She glanced at her reflection and sighed softly. The woman staring back at her looked like Seere as she set her diadem upon her head, her signet ring gleaming on her finger. However, it was Amaris' eyes that stared back at her, pale green and haunted. She hated how the illusion frayed— that she wasn't the fearless Seere, but still frightened little Amaris beneath it all.

As she rose from the vanity, she caught her full reflection in the floor-length mirror. The image was striking. Draped in mourning attire, her figure was regal yet spectral, as if she were a ghost risen to claim her rightful place.

She took a steadying breath, her hands brushing down the skirt of her gown. A knock at the door broke the silence, and the young maid's voice called softly from the other side.

"Your Majesty, the time has come. I am here to guide you to the royal cemetery."

Seere's gaze lingered on her reflection for a moment

longer before she turned away. "I'm ready," she replied, her voice calm and steady despite the weight of the moment.

The maid opened the door, bowing deeply as Seere stepped out. As she walked through the familiar halls of the white palace, her heels clicking softly against the marble floors, she felt the eyes of servants and guards on her. Whispers rippled through the air in her wake, soft and low as a tide.

When she reached the palace's grand entrance, Orias was waiting for her. His evergreen eyes swept over her, his expression unreadable, but his presence reassuring. He extended an arm to her without a word, and she took it, allowing him to escort her to the awaiting carriage bound for the cemetery.

As they stepped into the bright light of the afternoon, the chill in the air was a stark reminder of the somber occasion. Yet Seere held her head high, her grief a quiet storm buried beneath the regal composure she had perfected.

The journey to the royal cemetery was slow and solemn, the clatter of wheels against the cobblestone the only sound to pierce the silence. Seere sat beside Orias, hands folded neatly in her lap, her mourning veil casting shadows across her face. Outside the carriage window, the streets of the capital were lined with citizens dressed in muted tones of mourning, their faces etched with sorrow and respect.

Finally, the cemetery gates came into view. The sprawling grounds, enclosed by wrought iron fencing and tall, ancient trees, exuded an air of reverence. Beyond the gates, a marble pathway led to the centerpiece of the cemetery: a towering, intricately carved mausoleum flanked by rows of statues of Noctivagus' past monarchs. The white stone gleamed in the midday sun, its radiance tempered by the solemn occasion.

As the carriage came to a stop, footmen hurried to open the doors. Orias stepped out first, turning to offer Seere his hand. She accepted, her movements graceful yet deliberate as she stepped down. The gathered nobles and dignitaries immediately took notice of her, whispers rippling through the crowd.

The procession moved toward the cemetery's heart, where an open-air platform had been erected before the mausoleum. The caskets of King Hubert and Queen Frieda lay atop it, each draped in royal blue and gold banners of Noctivagus. A sea of chairs was arranged for the attendees, with the most prominent seats closest to the platform.

Seere was guided to the front row on the left side of the aisle, placing her in full view of the mourners. Beside her was Orias. Council members who passed her to take their seats on the front row nodded their greeting to her, but kept their distance. Across the aisle to the right, Felix stood with Foras and several council members. His face was pale, his jaw tight with suppressed emotion.

The atmosphere was heavy with grief and respect. Nobles, foreign dignitaries, and commoners alike had gathered, united in mourning for the beloved king and queen. A gentle breeze rustled the leaves of the nearby trees, carrying the faint scent of roses and myrrh from the funeral wreaths that adorned the platform.

As the attendees settled, the Archbishop of Eulla stepped forward. Clad in white and gold robes, the archbishop lifted his arms, calling the gathering to stillness. The gathering fell still, the rustling of fabric and the occasional sniffle the only sounds that remained.

The archbishop began with a prayer to Eulla, the goddess of light and life, asking for guidance and solace for the kingdom in its time of loss. Seere's hands clenched subtly in her lap at the mention of Eulla, her unease with the goddess and her clergy simmering beneath her composed exterior.

The speeches followed, each one heartfelt and heavy with emotion. Members of the royal council spoke first, recounting King Hubert's wisdom and Queen Frieda's kindness. Lords and ladies from neighboring kingdoms shared their condolences, their words formal yet sincere.

When Felix rose to speak, the atmosphere shifted. The weight of his grief was palpable as he stepped onto the platform, his shoulders squared but his expression raw.

"My parents were not just rulers," Felix began, his voice steady despite the sorrow that threatened to choke him. "They were the heart of Noctivagus. Their love for this kingdom was boundless, and their guidance unwavering. They believed in unity, in strength through compassion, and in leaving the world better than they found it. I can only hope to honor their legacy."

A hushed murmur of agreement rippled through the crowd as Felix stepped down. Seere's gaze followed him, her heart aching for the young prince who had been thrust into a role he was not yet prepared for.

The final rites were performed by the archbishop, who blessed the caskets with holy water and recited sacred passages. The procession then moved toward the mausoleum, where the caskets were tucked away inside the marble structure. The sound of earth being placed over the caskets was a solemn reminder of the finality of death.

As the graves were sealed, white doves were released into

the sky, symbols of the spirits of the departed ascending to Eulla's embrace. The gathered attendees bowed their heads, a collective moment of silence marking the conclusion of the ceremony.

As the crowd began to disperse, Seere remained seated, her gaze fixed on the mausoleum. Her expression was unreadable beneath her mask and veil, but her hands were clasped tightly in her lap, betraying the tension she felt.

Orias leaned closer, his voice a murmur. "Are you alright?"

She nodded faintly but didn't look at him. "I've never liked Eulla... for obvious reasons. It feels sacrilegious of me to be here while the priests pray to her. It should be Eslia, the true death goddess..."

Orias placed a comforting hand over hers, his warmth grounding her amidst the chill of the cemetery.

When they finally rose to leave, Seere moved like a shadowed queen, measured steps, posture unshaken, grief cloaked in dignity. As she walked back to her carriage, she made a silent prayer to Eslia to bless the departure of the king and queen.

THE GRAND HALL of the Noctivagus palace had been transformed into a somber yet elegant setting for the funeral feast. Heavy black and gold drapes adorned the walls, and the long banquet tables were set with gleaming silverware and plates rimmed in intricate patterns of royal blue. The flickering light of countless candles bathed the room in a warm, muted glow, their flames reflected in the polished surfaces of crystal goblets and ornate chandeliers.

At the far end of the room, a raised dais held the high

table where Felix was seated. The atmosphere was thick with subdued conversations and the clinking of cutlery against porcelain. Despite the occasion, the aroma of rich dishes filled the air, a testament to the palace's renowned chefs. Platters of roasted meats, fragrant soups, and an array of delicately crafted pastries were carried in by silent servants.

Seere sat directly to Felix's right at the high table, her presence both commanding and enigmatic. She still wore her mourning veil and mask, the signet ring of the Domain catching the candlelight in sharp glints. Though food lay before her, she did not eat—her veil and mask serving as both a barrier and a declaration. Orias sat to her right, his demeanor calm though vigilant, his sharp eyes scanning the room periodically as if for threats.

Felix looked every bit the grieving prince, his face pale and his expression distant. To his left sat Foras, and next to him, council members who whispered among themselves, their eyes occasionally drifting toward Seere.

The conversations around the table swirled between mourning, political maneuvering, and lighthearted distraction. A lord Seere didn't know spoke to Orias about Malphas University, expressing condolences while subtly inquiring about the academy's role in the future of Noctivagus. Orias responded politely but kept his answers brief, his attention partially focused on Seere.

Council members and high-ranking officials spoke with Felix, their words too low for Seere to hear. However, she noticed the glances Felix cast her way, a mixture of lingering bitterness and something she couldn't quite decipher.

"Is it true that you sit beside Princess Amaris of Envie?" the lord, talking to Orias, questioned.

Orias spared a glance at Seere, and she offered him the slightest shrug of her shoulders. With an amused smile, Orias turned his attention back to the man. "You disrespect Her Majesty. She is Queen Seere of the Domain of Assassins."

"Of course, forgive me, Your Majesty."

As the feast continued, Felix stood and tapped his knife against his crystal goblet, and a chime rang out, silencing the room. All eyes turned to him as he stood, his expression unreadable but his gaze sharp as it swept over the assembled guests.

"I would like to make acknowledgements to our guests of honor," he began, his voice steady despite the grief that lingered beneath the surface. "We are joined tonight by Queen Amaris of the Domain of Assassins and the esteemed Headmaster Orias Roderick of Malphas University."

The room fell into a tense silence. Whispers stirred, the weight of Felix's words sinking in like stones. His use of Seere's real name, Amaris, carried an edge that did not go unnoticed.

Felix's gaze lingered on her. "Queen Amaris has long been a figure of intrigue and controversy, but let it not be forgotten that she was once my betrothed, and that her innocence was long ago proven as the true killer of Emperor Montague and Empress Berenice resides in our dungeons."

Orias shifted in his seat, his displeasure evident in the way his jaw tightened. Seere, however, remained perfectly still, her regal composure unshaken.

Felix continued, the chill in his voice deepening with each word. "Let us hope that her presence here will serve as a reminder of the alliances that tie our kingdoms together, even in the face of tragedy."

The tension in the room was palpable as Felix sat down, his announcement leaving an uncomfortable silence in its wake. Orias leaned closer to Seere, his voice barely audible. "Petty as ever," he muttered.

Seere huffed a soft laugh, shaking her head. "Perhaps a little."

32

STITCHES

EULDAY, TWENTY-EIGHTH OF THE FROST
MOON, YEAR 450 OF THE GODDESS

The sun had long since risen, bathing the room in warm, golden light, when a tentative knock echoed from Seere's door. She glanced up from *Seere and His Bride*—the book she had found Orias reading—and called out, "Come in."

The door creaked open, revealing the young maid standing stiffly on the threshold. "Y-Your Majesty," the maid stammered, bowing deeply. "The royal seamstress has requested your presence. She wishes to prepare your gown for the coronation."

Seere set the book aside and stood, her movements causing the maid to flinch slightly. "Thank you for informing me. Lead the way."

The maid stepped back into the hallway, and Seere followed, her sharp heels clicking softly against the marble floor. As they exited the room, two guards standing at attention near her door immediately fell into step behind her.

She turned to glance at them, her brow furrowing. Both

were clad in the armor of Malphas University's guards, their expressions stoic and watchful. "Why are you following me?"

The shorter of the two guards, a stern woman with sharp features and piercing gray eyes, stepped forward. "Captain Zuriel Parish, Your Majesty. Headmaster Orias has ordered that you be protected at all times during your stay in Noctivagus.

"Protected?" Seere's lips pressed into a thin line, mildly annoyed that Orias had set up guards without informing her first. "From what, exactly?"

"Anyone foolish enough to underestimate the strength of a queen," Zuriel replied smoothly, her tone respectful but firm.

She studied the woman for a moment. "Sounds like Orias is underestimating the strength of a queen," she muttered. However, after a long moment, she nodded. "Very well. I imagine I can't send you away. Do as you're instructed."

Zuriel inclined her head, and the group resumed their journey down the hall.

After a few moments of silence, Seere spoke again, directing her question to the maid walking ahead of her. "What's your name?"

The maid hesitated, her pace faltering. She fidgeted with the hem of her sleeve anxiously. "Avra, Your Majesty."

Seere arched a brow at the girl's timid demeanor. "Well, Avra, thank you for guiding me. Have you worked in the palace long?"

"N-no, Your Majesty," Avra answered quickly, her voice barely above a whisper. "I was hired only a few months ago."

Seere hummed thoughtfully, her sharp eyes observing the girl's tense shoulder and quick breaths. Avra feared her;

that much was obvious. Seere didn't blame her. The rumors surrounding her were always less than savory.

"Relax," Seere said softly. "I don't bite."

Avra glanced over her shoulder, startled, and quickly looked away. "Y-yes, Your Majesty."

Though Seere said nothing more, she made a mental note to build trust with the young woman. A maid like Avra, unassuming and unnoticed, could make for a valuable ally in the days to come.

The group finally reached the seamstress's sewing room, its double doors standing slightly ajar. From inside, Seere could hear the bustling of fabric and the occasional sharp instruction.

"Evangelia," Seere murmured under her breath, her mind already recalling the fiery old woman from her youth.

Avra stepped forward and knocked timidly on the door. A loud, cheerful voice called out, "Come in!"

The maid pushed the door open, and Seere stepped inside, followed closely by her guards.

"Well, if it isn't the little shadow queen herself!" Evangelia's voice boomed as she turned. The seamstress's eyes sparkled with recognition and pride. "Amaris, darling, it's been far too long."

Seere couldn't help the faint smile that tugged at her lips. "Indeed, it has, Evangelia."

The seamstress clapped her hands together, her grin widening. "Come, come! We've got work to do!"

The seamstress's sewing room was a whirlwind of movement and color, even though most of the fabrics were muted shades of black and lavender. Bolts of silk and lace were draped over chairs, with half-finished gowns hanging from racks along the walls. A large wooden table in the center of the room was piled high with sewing supplies—spools of thread, pins, scissors, and small, intricate embellishments.

Evangelia bustled about the room with the energy of someone half her age, her silver hair tied back into a loose bun as she rifled through her collection of garments.

"Now, where is it..." she muttered, half to herself, as she rummaged through a wardrobe far taller than she was. "Ah-ha!"

With a dramatic flourish, she pulled out a gown draped in protective cloth and laid it gently over a nearby mannequin. She peeled back the covering to reveal the dress, and Seere couldn't help the soft gasp that escaped her lips.

The gown was breathtaking. The black silk base shimmered faintly in the light, like the surface of a moonlit lake. Delicate lavender lace adorned the bodice, forming intricate floral patterns that cascaded down the skirt. The overskirt featured a dramatic window of lace down the center, creating an illusion of shadow and light that seemed almost otherworldly. Tiny silver accents had been sewn into the lace, catching the light with every movement.

"You've outdone yourself," Seere murmured, stepping closer to the dress.

Evangelia beamed, waving a hand dismissively. "Oh, hush. Ever since Orias sent the request for your Winter Solstice gown, I've been dreaming up more fitting things for you. Originally, this was based on a wedding dress I'd designed for you, only with a white base and maroon lace."

"I should have known it was your handiwork that designed my Winter Solstice gown. How is it that you got my measurements so perfectly?" Seere questioned, crossing her arms.

"I am blessed by Iktune, Goddess of Beauty, I always say!" Evangelia chimed, placing her hands on her hips. "But seriously, I made you a gown when you were fourteen. You've always been a reed, and I suspected that never changed."

"Then you've known my identity this entire time?" A flicker of unease passed through her. The thought of her identity having been known by more than just Orias and Foras made her pulse quicken.

"Orias let it slip when he requested a dress," the old woman said, waving a dismissive hand through the air. "Now, stop gawking and put it on!"

Seere huffed out a laugh and allowed herself to be ushered behind a folding screen where she changed out of her leathers and into the corseted masterpiece. Evangelia immediately descended upon her when she stepped out, lacing up the back with practiced ease.

Seere stepped out from behind the screen and stopped before a tall mirror as Evangelia circled her like a hawk, tugging at the fabric here and there, pinning sections that needed adjustment.

"Lift your arms. Turn. Walk a few steps." Evangelia commanded, her sharp eyes catching every detail.

The gown fit surprisingly well, though Seere could feel the occasional tightness around her shoulders and the slight drag of the hem. The seamstress tsked under her breath as she knelt to pin the excess fabric at the bottom.

"You haven't grown at all—what are you, five feet tall?" Evangelia questioned.

"I'm five feet and five inches," Seere corrected indignantly.

"You've also been skipping meals, haven't you?" Evangelia gave her a pointed look.

Seere blinked, momentarily caught off guard. "I'm an Assassin Queen who wears a mask wherever she goes. I can't eat in public."

"That is no excuse for looking like a ghost, darling," Evangelia chided, rising to her feet. "You're a queen and a brilliant one at that. You'll need to look the part—and not like someone who's just crawled out of her grave."

Seere laughed softly. "I will request my assigned maid to bring my meals to my room. Is that better?"

"Marginally," Evangelia muttered, returning to her work.

As the hours stretched on, the fitting turned into something more casual, almost nostalgic. Evangelia chatted animatedly, regaling Seere with stories of the palace staff and reminiscing about the summer she had spent designing a gown for fourteen-year-old Amaris.

"I remember how stubborn you were back then," Evangelia said with a grin. "You didn't want lace, didn't want ruffles, didn't want anything that sparkled. You wanted to look 'serious.'"

"I was fresh out of the assassin's academy back then," Seere admitted with a glance at the floor. "I didn't want to seem frivolous. I was trying to fit into a world that didn't feel like my own."

"Well, look at you now," Evangelia said, stepping back to admire her work. "You're the picture of elegance and authority—though I must say, this hair of yours..."

"What about it?" Seere asked, raising a brow.

"It's unnatural, isn't it? Magic?"

Seere hesitated before nodding. "A spell changed the color permanently."

Evangelia hummed thoughtfully. "I'll admit, it's striking. Suits you in a way I wouldn't have expected."

Seere turned back to the mirror, studying her reflection. The gown now fit perfectly, accentuating her slim figure while exuding regal authority. With her lavender hair swept up into a loose bun, her mask concealing the lower half of her face, and the diadem resting atop her head, she looked every bit the queen.

"Perfect," Evangelia declared, clapping her hands. "You'll turn every head at the coronation."

Seere gave the seamstress a small, genuine smile. "Thank you, Evangelia. It's beautiful."

The older woman waved her off. "It's my pleasure, darling. Now change out of the dress so you don't ruin it before the coronation."

Seere laughed softly and swiftly disappeared behind the folding screen. She changed back into her leathers and returned the dress to Evangelia. Finally, she turned to leave, her guards falling into step behind her.

The hall of the Noctivagus palace stretched before her. She finally allowed herself a moment to truly admire their high ceiling adorned with intricate carvings of constellations. Heavy velvet curtains hung from arched windows, allowing just enough light to spill onto the gleaming marble floors. Every step echoed faintly, a quiet reminder of the stillness that had settled over the palace since the funeral only the day before.

Zuriel Parish strode confidently at her side, her sharp eyes scanning their surroundings. A second guard trailed just behind, his gloved hand resting lightly on the hilt of his sword. Seere felt their watchfulness but didn't acknowledge it.

They walked in silence for several minutes, the halls growing quieter with each turn. Seere found herself glancing out the tall windows at the sprawling gardens that had long since fallen asleep with the arrival of winter. She remembered running through those gardens as a young girl with Felix—sneaking out of the castle at night and, for a brief moment, feeling truly free. That had also been the moment they shared their first and only kiss.

The thought made her chest tighten, a pang of nostalgia mixing with something more complicated.

It was as she turned a corner that she nearly collided with someone coming the other way. She stepped back quickly, Zuriel's hand instinctively darting to her sword.

"Careful!" a familiar voice snapped.

Seere froze. Standing before her was Felix, looking just as startled as she felt. His black mourning attire was impeccable, but his usually warm eyes were shadowed with exhaustion.

"Felix," she said softly, her tone neutral, though her heart raced.

Felix blinked, his surprise quickly melting into something more guarded. "Seere." His voice held a sharp edge, the bitterness in her false name unmistakable. His gaze swept over her, lingering briefly on the guards before landing back on her face. "I wasn't expecting to see you wandering the halls alone."

"I'm not alone," she replied evenly.

He ignored her comment, his expression tightening. "Where's Orias?"

"I don't know," she answered truthfully. "I imagine he has his own affairs to attend to."

Felix's jaw tightened, and for a moment, she thought he

would leave without another word. Instead, he sighed heavily and ran a hand through his auburn hair. "I was on my way to the gardens. Walk with me."

It wasn't a request, and Seere hesitated, glancing at Zuriel. The captain's eyes narrowed, but she didn't object. Seere gave a small nod and motioned for her guards to follow at a distance.

Felix led her through the palace with a quiet familiarity, his steps purposeful but unhurried. When they reached the gardens, he paused at the edge of a stone path, his gaze fixed on the fountain in the center of the courtyard.

"This place hasn't changed," he murmured, almost to himself.

"No," Seere agreed. "It hasn't."

They walked in silence for a while, the sound of their footsteps blending with the subtle sounds of winter. Finally, Felix stopped and turned to her, his expression conflicted.

"Why do you despise me?" he asked abruptly, the rawness in his voice cutting through the air like a blade.

Seere's breath caught. She hadn't expected him to jump on her so quickly, and for a long moment, she was lost for words. She could feel his gaze on her, searching her face for an answer.

"I... I don't despise you, Felix." She looked away, rubbing her hands together to alleviate the chill. "It's not about love or hate, Felix. It's about control. Marrying you—being with you—would play right into the hands of the Order. And my kingdom... they need me as much as I need them."

Felix frowned, his brow furrowing deeply. "I wouldn't force you to give up the kingdom you've built, Amaris. But the Order?"

"The Order of the Chimera has always tried to control

the continent. Once, they had intended for me to marry you only to kill you immediately after so they could have control over both Envie and Noctivagus," she whispered, glancing over to see the shock and pain written across his face. "I refuse to let them hurt you."

His frown deepened. He took a step closer, his voice lowering, but it wasn't harsh. "And who told you this? Orias?"

"My father was a member before the Order killed him," she murmured. "And... yes, Orias informed me of the rest of it."

Felix scoffed, his eyes flashing with frustration. "Of course he did. Have you ever considered that Orias might have his own agenda? You don't think that he might want you to stay away from me for his own reasons?"

Her stomach twisted at the implication, but she kept her voice calm. "Of course I have, Felix, but—"

"He's a master manipulator, Ris. He always has been. Perhaps he is using you to become more powerful than he already is and making the Order seem like a greater threat than it is so that you stay by his side instead of mine."

The use of his old nickname for her brought a sharp pain to her heart that nearly knocked the wind from her lungs. "I don't want to be used as a pawn in someone else's game anymore, Felix—not the Order's, not yours, and not his."

Felix's expression faltered, the fight draining from his cobalt eyes. He looked away, his shoulders slumping slightly.

"You were never a pawn to me," he said quietly. "You were everything."

"You will find someone else, Felix. Someone who loves you more than I ever could," she whispered.

He smiled faintly, but it didn't reach his eyes. "I've tried. I've tried to love others, but it's no use. You bewitched me a long time ago. Heart and soul."

She swallowed hard, the guilt swirling in her chest. "I'm sorry," she whispered.

He nodded, the motion stiff and reluctant. "I know you are."

Without another word, Seere turned and walked away, her guards following close behind her. She didn't look back—even though every step felt heavier than the last.

33

THE CORONATION

ATYSDAY, THIRTIETH OF THE FROST MOON,
YEAR 450 OF THE GODDESS

The morning of the coronation began before dawn, the first rays of light barely cresting the horizon when Avra knocked softly on Seere's chamber door. The maid entered with quiet precision, bowing low before bustling about the room to prepare the Queen's attire for the day. Seere, still seated by the window, gazed out over the palace grounds, her mind heavy with thoughts of the coming event.

"Your Majesty," Avra murmured, hesitant yet insistent. "It's time to begin preparations."

Seere turned, her expression calm despite the restless undercurrent in her chest. Rising, she allowed Avra and the other maids to take over. They moved like a well-rehearsed orchestra, their hands deft and practiced as they began the hours-long ritual of readying her for the most important event she'd attended since her exile.

The first step was her bath. Warm water scented with rose petals filled the tub, steam curling into the air. She sank into the bath, letting the tension melt from her shoulders as the maids carefully washed her hair with fragrant oils. She remained silent throughout, her thoughts wandering to Felix, to Orias, and the tragedies that seemed to follow her like a phantom.

After the bath, Seere was ushered to her vanity. Avra and two other maids began the painstaking process of styling her hair. Her long, lavender locks were dried and brushed until they shone like a spun twilight sky. The maids gently curled her hair with hot tongs and left her hair to hang free around her face and down her back. Her crown was carefully placed atop her head, its intricate design a reminder of her title and the weight it carried.

"Beautiful," Avra whispered, stepping back to admire their work.

After some light makeup, came the gown. Seere stood still as the maids assisted her into the masterpiece Evangelia had created. The black silk flowed like liquid shadow, the lavender lace overlay adding an ethereal softness. The fitted bodice accentuated her frame, while the full skirt gave her the imposing presence of a queen. Tiny gemstones stitched into the lace caught the light, making her seem as if she were adorned with the stars themselves.

As Avra smoothed out the final wrinkles, Seere's gaze lingered on her reflection in the mirror. She appeared every bit like the queen she should have been while standing beside Felix.

A knock at the door pulled her from her thoughts. "Enter," she called, her voice steady.

The door opened to reveal Orias. He stepped inside, his piercing gaze sweeping over her before his lips curled into a smirk. "Gorgeous," he said simply, his voice carrying a note of admiration that made her heart flutter despite herself.

He crossed the room in long strides, stopping before her. Cupping her face, he leaned down to press a kiss to her lips. When he pulled away, his smirk deepened at the faint smile that tugged her lips.

"Where have you been hiding these past two days?" she asked, slipping her mask on as she regarded him with a curious tilt of her head.

"I've been stuck running odd errands for the court," Orias replied bitterly. "Believe it or not, I was one of the late king's most trusted advisers—it keeps me busy."

Seere sighed and nodded her understanding. "I suppose that's fair," she said softly. "But I've missed you."

"I know," he breathed, pressing another kiss against her lips, this one tender and filled with all of the comfort he had been unable to offer the last couple of days. "I've missed you, too. That's why I'm not leaving your side today."

She smiled softly, then looked down as he offered his arm to her. She took it hesitantly, allowing him to guide her out of the room.

The procession of carriages waited in the grand court-yard, flanked by soldiers in ceremonial armor. Horses snorted impatiently, their hooves striking against the stone in a rhythmic clatter.

Seere and Orias descended the marble steps, their move-ments perfectly in sync, drawing the attention of nobles and servants alike. Seere's gown shimmered in the morning light, her lavender lace catching faint hints of sunlight as the hem brushed the ground. Orias, dressed in a dark suit adorned with gold accents, carried himself with an air of quiet authority, his dragon-like presence undeniable.

He glanced down at her as they reached the carriage, his evergreen eyes studying her face even with the mask she wore. "Did I tell you that you look every inch a queen?" he murmured, his voice low enough that only she could hear.

"And you look like a shadow ready to devour a kingdom," she replied.

His smirk widened as he helped her into the carriage, his touch lingering for a moment longer than necessary. The door clicked shut behind him as he joined her, and soon the carriage jolted forward, the rhythmic sound of wheels against cobblestones filling the air.

The journey to the Cathedral of Eulla felt strangely solemn. Streets once bustling with the vibrancy of Noctivagus' citizens were lined with silent spectators. People bowed their heads as the royal procession passed, their faces a mix of grief for their late monarchs and anticipation for the new king. Seere gazed out the window, her expression calm, though her mind was anything but.

"You're quiet," Orias noted, breaking the silence between them.

"There's much to think about," she admitted, her voice barely audible above the sounds of the procession.

"Such as?"

"Felix. The nobles. The Order." She hesitated. "And you."

Orias raised an eyebrow, leaning back against the plush seat. "I hope you're not doubting me, Amaris."

She glanced at him, the use of her real name stirring something fragile within her. "I don't doubt you," she replied softly. "I just... wonder what game we're all playing and who set the pieces on the board."

His lips quirked into a small, knowing smile. "I assure you that I never play a game unless I intend to win."

Somehow, his words didn't reassure her in the slightest. Somehow, it only made her feel more anxious.

When they arrived at the cathedral, the air was thick with reverence and anticipation. The grand structure loomed before them, its towering spires piercing the sky like gilded arrows. Sunlight streamed through intricate stained-glass windows, casting vibrant patterns across the stone facade.

Seere stepped out of the carriage first that time, her gown billowing around her like a tide of midnight silk. Orias followed closely, his hand lightly resting on her lower back as they ascended the cathedral steps. The crowd gathered around the courtyard fell silent, their collective gaze fixed on the enigmatic queen and the imposing headmaster.

Inside, the cathedral was a masterpiece of divine architecture. Marble pillars reached skyward, their surfaces carved with depictions of Eulla's blessings. The high, vaulted ceilings seemed to stretch into infinity, their intricate frescoes illuminated by the golden glow of hundreds of candles and torches.

Seere and Orias were led to the front of the nave, their seats situated near the altar. In front of her stood Felix, clad in ceremonial robes of deep blue and gold, his expression solemn yet tinged with unease. Beside him were his closest companions, Foras and a man Seere recognized as Foras' elder brother, Gabriel, as well as several other councilmen.

The ceremony began with the Archbishop of Eulla stepping forward, his resplendent white robes trailing behind him. His voice, rich and commanding, echoed through the cathedral as he spoke of the sacred duty of kingship and the divine right bestowed upon Felix by the gods.

Felix approached the altar, where he knelt before the

archbishop. The ceremonial objects were presented one by one: the sword symbolizing his duty to protect, the scepter as a mark of authority, and the orb representing the unity of the kingdom.

When the crown was lifted high for all to see, a hush fell over the room. The golden circlet, encrusted with sapphires and diamonds, seemed to shimmer with an almost other-worldly light.

"Felix of Noctivagus," the archbishop intoned, "do you swear to rule with wisdom and justice, to uphold the laws of this kingdom, and to serve your people with humility and strength?"

"I swear it," Felix replied, his voice steady despite the weight of the moment.

The crown was placed upon his head, and the gathered nobles and clergy rose to their feet in unison, their applause echoing through the vast space.

Seere stood as well, her hands folded neatly before her as she observed Felix. Their eyes met briefly, and she saw the flicker of longing and regret in his gaze. She inclined her head slightly—a silent acknowledgment of the path he was now bound to walk.

After the coronation, each noble and guest approached Felix to pay homage. When it was Seere's turn, she stepped forward with the grace of a goddess, her gown whispering against the marble floor.

"Congratulations, Your Majesty," she said softly, her voice carrying a note of sincerity.

"Thank you," Felix replied, his tone formal. "You look radiant."

Seere offered him a faint smile that barely reached her eyes. "I wish you strength and wisdom for the trials ahead," she said, offering a shallow bow before retreating to Orias' side.

Orias met her gaze, his expression unreadable as he offered his arm once more. Together, they exited the cathedral and joined the processional back to the palace, the day's weight already pressing on them both.

34

FEATHER

ATYSDAY, THIRTIETH OF THE FROST MOON,
YEAR 450 OF THE GODDESS

As the festivities roared, laughter and the sound of a lively orchestra spilling through the grand corridors, Seere slipped away unnoticed. The grand ballroom, dazzling with light and color, held no appeal for her. While nobles celebrated Felix's coronation, Seere had her mind set on something more pressing.

She moved swiftly but deliberately, her footsteps muffled by the plush carpets as she reached her chambers. Closing the door behind her, she leaned against it briefly, exhaling. The gown she wore—the black and lavender masterpiece felt suffocating now.

Peeling it away, she slipped into her leathers. She cinched the buckles of her boots and adjusted the holster at her thigh, where a slim dagger rested—though it was no longer the heavy one. She drew her hood up, its shadow concealing her face, and glanced at her reflection one last time.

The woman in the mirror was no longer the illusioned,

elegant queen that Noctivagus had made her into. Rather, she was Seere, the hardened Queen of Assassins and Shadows.

Slipping out of her room, Seere stayed close to the walls, her movements as fluid as water. The palace, now steeped in celebration, was both more vulnerable and more dangerous. Servants bustled through the corridors, carrying trays of wine and platters of food to the revelers. Guards stood at attention near the ballroom, distracted by the occasional laugh or drunken toast.

She took care to avoid them all. Every step she took was calculated, every corner approached with the precision of someone trained in the art of concealment. She pressed herself into alcoves when footsteps grew near, waiting for the telltale fade of sound before she moved again.

The palace at night was an entirely different place. Gone was the warmth of daylit marble and sunlight streaming through tall windows. The hallways were bathed in silvery moonlight and shadows, the flickering glow of wall sconces doing little to pierce the gloom. It was every bit the palace of Noctivagus. A kingdom of moonlight and Eulla.

She navigated the twisting halls with uncanny familiarity, her mind piecing together memories of her fourteen-year-old self wandering the palace the very same way she was at that moment. She passed doors she remembered from her childhood, a faint pang of nostalgia hitting her as she recalled playing games of hide-and-seek with Felix, Rowan, and Enora. Foras had thought too highly of himself and his position to join in on the mischief. Those days felt like they belonged to another life.

Her path finally brought her to the private wing of the

late king and queen. This part of the palace was eerily quiet, its grandeur dulled by the lingering sorrow of the tragedy that had taken place here. The double doors to the royal bedchamber loomed ahead, framed by intricate carvings of ivy and flowers.

Seere hesitated for a moment, her hand hovering over the door's handle. She knew this room would have been cleaned and sealed after their deaths, yet something compelled her to enter. Taking a breath, she pushed the door open silently and stepped inside.

The bedroom was a haunting reflection of the king and queen's presence. The massive four-poster bed was neatly made, its velvet drapes pulled back as if waiting for occupants who would never return. The air smelled faintly of lemon, a scent likely left by the cleaning staff.

She moved cautiously, her eyes scanning every detail. A gilded mirror above the vanity reflected her dark form as she passed. The dresser drawers were empty, the surfaces dusted and polished to perfection, yet she couldn't shake the feeling that something was out of place.

Then she saw it.

A single black feather lay on the plush carpet near the edge of the bed. Seere froze, her breath catching in her throat. She bent down and picked it up with trembling fingers, turning it over in the dim light. The feather was sleek and dark as midnight, a crow's feather. An unmistakable calling card. It had belonged to one of her assassins— an operative from her kingdom.

Seere's mind raced as she made her way back to her room. The corridors that had once felt like a maze now seemed simple to navigate, her singular focus leading her back with a steady resolve. Her heart pounded in her chest, the feather in her pocket feeling heavier with every step.

Upon reaching her chambers, she slipped inside, locking the door behind her. The room, with its lavish decor and soft lighting, felt stifling—a prison of expectations and pretense. She let out a sharp breath, leaning against the door for a moment to collect herself before moving swiftly to her desk.

Pulling out a piece of parchment, she sat down and dipped a quill into its inkwell, her hand hesitating briefly before she began to write.

Orias,

I have found something troubling, something I cannot ignore. I know you will be furious when you discover I am gone, but I must return to the Domain to uncover the truth. Please do not follow me. It will likely be too dangerous. Trust me when I say I will return when I have answers.

Seere.

She stared at the words for a moment, her chest tight. She wanted to write more, to explain the storm of emotions swirling inside her, but she knew Orias wouldn't need the details to understand, and she didn't trust that someone else wouldn't find the letter before he did. Folding the letter carefully, she placed it on the desk, anchoring it with a small, large inkwell so that there was no chance of it being lost.

Turning to her wardrobe, she grabbed a simple leather satchel and began packing. She moved with efficiency, selecting only the bare necessities: extra clothes, her extra weapons, a heavy pouch of coins, and a flask of water.

With the bag packed, she slung it over her shoulder and moved to the window. She pushed it open, letting the cool night air wash over her. The sounds of the ball drifted faintly from the great hall—laughter, music, the clinking of glasses. For a moment, she lingered, her gaze falling on the distant silhouette of the mountains.

Finally, she climbed out of her window, using the vine-laden trellis to descend to the courtyard below. The shadows embraced her as she darted from cover to cover, her movements silent and swift. She avoided the main paths, sticking to the periphery where the guards' patrols were less frequent.

The smell of hay and horses greeted her as she slipped inside the stables. She couldn't help but scrunch her nose at the smell. Most of the horses were asleep or lazily shifting in their stalls. She moved quietly, scanning the rows until she found a sturdy chestnut mare.

The horse regarded her curiously as she approached, but she placed a calming hand on its neck, murmuring soft reassurances. She quickly saddled the mare, her fingers deftly fastening the straps. Finally, she pulled her hood over her head and led the mare out of the stable.

She paused at the edge of the courtyard, scanning the area for any sign of movement. Satisfied that she was alone, she mounted the horse, the saddle creaking faintly beneath her.

With a soft nudge of her heels, the mare started forward, her hooves muffled against the dirt path. Seere kept her movements deliberate and slow until she reached the edge of the palace grounds. The gates were open for the party, though she knew the guards would be roused with suspicion as she slipped out like a shadow. It would cause them to panic, but they would not catch her.

Carefully, she spurred the horse into a gallop, the wind whipping through her hair as she raced through the gates and into the streets of the city of Hesperus. Shouting rose from behind her, but she ignored it. She spurred the mare faster, weaving through the busy streets.

Eventually, the glow of the city lights faded behind her as she pressed onward. Her destination was clear: the port town of Basilia, which was northwest of Hesperus. From there, she would find passage to the Domain of Assassins and uncover the truth behind the feather that now burned like a brand in her mind.

DAWN WAS BREAKING by the time Seere reached Basilia, her body aching from the relentless pace, but her resolve unshaken. She left the horse at a stable near the docks, tossing a few coins to the stable hand before making her way toward the harbor. The comforting salty air of the ocean stung her nose as she approached a line of ships, their sails furled against the morning breeze.

A grizzled captain with a salt-and-pepper beard and a hard, weathered face eyed her warily as she approached his vessel.

"I need passage to the Domain of Assassins," she said firmly, her voice leaving no room for negotiation.

The captain hesitated, his gaze flicking to the signet ring she wore over her glove. Recognition dawned in his eyes, and he stepped aside with a curt nod.

"Board quickly," he muttered. "We leave within the hour."

"Good."

Seere climbed aboard, her eyes scanning the horizon. As the ship began to pull away from the dock, she leaned against the railing, her thoughts already racing ahead. She knew her absence would be discovered soon. Orias would be more than angry with her, Felix would panic, and both of them would come after her regardless of her request.

35

POWERLESS

CHAYSDAY, FOURTEENTH OF THE REBIRTH
MOON, YEAR 450 OF THE GODDESS

The rocking of the ship had grown gentler as they neared the harbor, a welcome reprieve from the waves that had tossed them about for the past two weeks. Seere stood at the bow, her cloak pulled tight against the biting breeze. The silhouette of her kingdom loomed on the horizon.

She gripped the wooden railing tightly, her knuckles white. The salty wind tugged at her hair, but she barely noticed. Her thoughts were a storm of apprehension and determination. It had been months since she'd set foot in the Domain of Assassins. Her memories of home were a comfort, and yet there was a fear that lingered. She was scared to discover why one of her assassins had dared to kill the previous rulers of Noctivagus.

As the ship drew closer to the docks of Ilatin—a port town on the north side of the island—its modest silhouette became clearer. It was just large enough for most ships from Noctivagus to dock there. Its harbor was lined with wooden piers, squat warehouses, and stone buildings topped with red clay roofs.

"Land in sight!" the ship's lookout shouted from the crow's nest, breaking the silence. The crew erupted into activity, their voices calling orders and ropes snapping taut as sails were adjusted. The ship shifted, angling toward the port, and Seere let the wind carry away the lingering remnants of exhaustion that clung to her shoulders.

"You've a look of someone who's seen enough sea for a lifetime," a gruff voice said behind her. The ship's captain approached.

"Perhaps I've grown weary of being at sea, but I could never grow tired of the waters," she replied evenly, keeping her gaze on the shore.

The captain grunted in agreement, folding his arms as he joined her at the railing. "What made you flee Noctivagus so swiftly, Your Majesty?" he asked.

"It seems that my kingdom has betrayed me," she said softly, twirling the crow feather between her fingers. "I intend to find out why."

"Fair enough." He hesitated for a moment, as if contemplating something. "I know it's not my business, milady, but I'll say this: whatever it is you're rushing into... you'd best be ready. The air's got a strange feel to it this morn'."

"I always am," she replied coolly, though his words lingered longer than she would have liked.

The ship glided into the harbor. Sailors shouted as they secured lines and dropped the gangplank. The harbor itself was alive with the quiet bustle of early morning—fishermen repairing their nets, dockworkers unloading crates, and merchants setting up stalls with sleepy movements. The scent of freshly caught fish mingled with the earthy smell of the damp stone streets.

Seere inhaled sharply, centering herself.

Her boots clacked softly against the gangplank as she descended, the sea wind tugging at her black cloak. She stepped onto solid ground for the first time in what felt like an eternity—steady, though her body still swayed, as if the sea refused to let her go.

The dockworkers and passersby turned to glance at her. The moment they saw her, however, they dropped to their knees in reverence. Immediately, her cloak and mask were recognized, the signet ring on her finger glinting menacingly. She also carried herself with the unmistakable authority of the Assassin Queen, her posture regal.

She ignored the stares, moving with purpose to the streets where a carriage was already approaching. It had been called by her guards, the ones who hid in the shadows and wore leather instead of metal plate mail.

"Where may I take you, Your Majesty?" the driver questioned as he opened the door for her.

"My citadel," she answered sharply and climbed into the carriage.

It felt unusually empty without Orias.

She watched as Ilatin faded into a forest which swiftly turned into Acron, her looming capital city. Her gaze then lifted to the citadel, its sharp spires and dark stone walls piercing the gray sky. The rising sun gilded it in gold, softening the sharp angles of the palace she called home.

The carriage slowed as they approached the gates surrounding her citadel. Massive, wrought-iron doors loomed before her, adorned with metal crows and the emblem of her kingdom.

Two guards flanked the gate, their faces obscured by dark helmets and black cloaks. For a long moment, neither moved. Seere felt their wary gazes settle on the carriage as it stopped before them. She opened her carriage door and stepped out, her hand raised to show off the signet ring that glinted on her hand.

"Open the gates," she commanded, her voice cold and unwavering.

The guards shifted uneasily, exchanging a glance as if uncertain whether they should obey. Seere's patience snapped like a taut wire.

"Did you not hear me? I am your queen. Open the gates, or I'll see your heads on pikes before the sun sets."

That seemed to have lit a fire under them. The two guards stiffened to attention, one turning and pounding the hilt of his spear against the iron gate three times. A heavy groan shuddered through the air as the gates slowly began to creak open, the grinding of gears and chains reverberating off the castle walls.

Seere climbed back into the carriage and shut the door.

The courtyard looked just as it had been when she left it; only the plants had long since hibernated with winter having set in.

Finally, she stormed through the main entrance into the heart of the citadel. Servants and guards stopped to gape at her as she swept through the halls. She hadn't warned them of her impending return, but the way they ducked out of sight from her only proved to infuriate her. She wasn't sure if it was the way she charged her own citadel or if it was because they were all in on the assassination of the late king and queen of Noctivagus and feared the wrath of the Queen returned.

Seere entered the throne room, her gaze falling upon the man who was lounging in her place. A man she had once trusted. A smirk curved his lips as though he had been expecting her, his body draped lazily across the throne, his chin propped on his knuckles as he regarded her with dark amusement. The raw power radiating from him was almost palpable, swirling through the air like smoke.

Belial rose slowly, like a predator savoring the moment before striking. He no longer shrank before her the way he had done only months prior. Rather, he had cleaned up and draped himself in the royal regalia of a king. A golden crown sat atop his black hair, making his dark skin glow almost with ethereal light. His amber eyes glittered with amusement, but there was something soulless about them—something wrong.

"Welcome home, *Amaris*," he drawled, his voice like silk wrapped around a blade. "What a surprise to see you back so soon. I thought you would be too wrapped up in your romance with Sallos to visit me."

Confusion rippled through Seere, but she kept her expression clear. "And what, exactly, do you think you're doing?"

Belial tilted his head, the dark smile widening. "I am sitting in my rightful place. For this—" He gestured to the throne. "—is no longer yours."

Rage flared like a storm inside her chest, hot and unforgiving. "You dare sit in *my* seat, traitor?"

Belial chuckled darkly. "*Your* seat? Oh, no, little princess. You were merely keeping it warm for me."

Seere's patience was shattered. In one swift motion, she drew her dagger and hurled it at him. The blade spun through the air, aimed for his throat. But Belial merely smirked with the slight flourish of two fingers, the dagger veered sharply mid-flight, striking a stone pillar and sparking on impact before clattering to the ground.

Seere drew more blades, but before she could throw any more of them, guards emerged from the shadows. Their hands were iron, their grip unrelenting as they seized her arms and forced her to her knees. She thrashed against them, even tried to turn into a crow, but they were too strong and she couldn't focus. It was only then that she saw it—the faint mark of a lion tattooed behind their ears.

"The Order," she hissed under her breath, the realization crashing over her.

Belial descended the dais, his steps slow and deliberate as he loomed over her.

"You see, little princess," he said softly, almost tenderly, "you've gone too far astray from the carefully plotted plan I had come up with, and now I need you to step back."

"Get your soldiers off of me," she snarled, but the guards only tightened their grip, and the blades she held clattered to the ground.

Belial smiled. "Lock her in the dungeons. I will decide her fate later."

Seere's world blurred as she was dragged through the hall, the grand throne room growing smaller behind her. But her fury burned bright and merciless.

The guards' iron grips bruised her arms as they dragged her down one stone staircase after another, deeper and deeper into the bowels of the citadel. Torches lined the narrow corridors, casting jagged shadows on the rough walls as Seere's boots scraped against the uneven floor.

She fought the entire way, twisting and snarling in their grasp, but the guards remained unfazed as if inhuman.

There was no humanity in them—only cruel strength and cold purpose.

She couldn't understand how they were so strong, but she guessed that her answer lay in the faint lion tattoos she had glimpsed behind their ears. She wondered what sort of powers one received as a member of the Order. The same Order that had been an ever-present shadow in her life, manipulating kingdoms and kings, had taken hold of *her* throne—and of her innocent people.

At last, the stairs ended, and they reached the dungeon. The air was damp and stale, heavy with the stench of mildew and iron. Water dripped somewhere in the darkness, the sound slow and mocking, like the cruel tick of a clock counting down to her end.

A gate groaned open ahead of them—a massive iron door reinforced with black runes that seemed to hum faintly with magic. Seere's instincts flared in warning, but before she could react, the guards shoved her forward. She stumbled into the cell, the uneven stone catching her off guard, and she hit the ground hard, catching herself on her hands and knees.

The door slammed shut behind her with a finality that made her chest tighten. She shot up to her feet, whirling around and throwing another hidden blade. However, it bounced harmlessly back as it struck the space between the bars. Cold dread settled within her as she reached a hand out and found the strange, invisible barrier that prevented her from reaching a hand through. She had never witnessed anything like it before, which only meant that the man she had once trusted to be her viceroy had reinforced it just for her. The guards stood just beyond the cell, indifferent to her fury as they turned and disappeared back up the corridor.

Then silence fell.

Seere banged her fist against the barrier, but only pain shot through her. Slowly, the realization crept in: she was alone. She was trapped. Her kingdom was no longer hers.

Her chest heaved as she stepped back, turning to take in the cell that confined her. It was no larger than a storage closet, its walls carved from cold, damp stone. A narrow cot sat in one corner, its thin blanket threadbare and stained. A bucket sat in another, its purpose obvious and humiliating. The single torch outside the cell offered only the faintest light, leaving shadows to crawl across the floor like living things.

Seere cursed. She reached for her powers. She could feel the threads of Eslia's magic coiling within her, familiar and sharp. It rose like a tidal wave in her chest, building and building—

—and then nothing.

The magic didn't flow through her. It didn't even flicker.

Nothing. The power that had always hummed within her —the magic she had always condemned yet had wielded as a weapon—was *gone*.

Seere stumbled back a step, her heart pounding with panic. She tried again, summoning the magic that had always obeyed her command. She could almost hear it, whispering from the corners of her mind, but it refused to move. Refused to answer her call.

"No," she breathed, eyes wide. "No, no, no."

Her hands trembled as she tried spell after spell, calling upon every ounce of magic she had ever wielded, but the result was the same.

Silence.

Emptiness.

It felt like a limb had been severed. Like something essential had been ripped away from her without her even realizing it.

She staggered to the wall, bracing her hands against the cold stone as her chest rose and fell with ragged breaths. The truth was undeniable now—this cell had been *crafted* to strip her of her power. The black runes etched into the iron gate hummed softly, almost mockingly, confirming her suspicion.

Her hair caught her attention then, its pale strands falling into her face. Seere froze, her breath catching as she pulled a lock of hair forward.

It was no longer lavender.

The once vibrant color that had marked her as *Seere* was gone, replaced by the icy platinum blonde she had fought to hide for years—the same color shared by her sisters, Empress Selina and Cotoria. She imagined she looked identical to her sisters, if not for Eslia's pale eyes that marked her as the bastard princess no one had wanted.

Her stomach turned as she dropped the hair back to her side. It was as though the cell hadn't just taken her magic—it had stripped away the *mask* she had built over the years.

Powerless. Exposed. Alone.

36

GAMES

UNKNOWN, UNKNOWN OF THE UNKNOWN MOON, YEAR 450 OF THE GODDESS

Seere jolted awake, the remnants of her nightmare clawing at her chest. Her breath came in shallow gasps as the phantom sensation of cold iron shackles still lingered against her wrists. The damp, suffocating air of her dream had felt real—too real. It pulled her back to a memory she had tried desperately to bury, a time when she was a scared girl locked away by people she had once trusted.

She sat up slowly, the chill of the cell biting into her skin. Darkness pressed against her from all sides, thick and impenetrable. It was impossible to tell how much time had passed since her capture. Days, perhaps even weeks, blurred together in a monotonous haze of silence and shadow, each day indistinguishable from the last.

Her stomach growled faintly, a weak protest against the meager scraps of food she was occasionally given. Her body felt heavy, worn down by exhaustion and the weight of uncertainty.

The sharp sound of metal boots echoed down the stone corridor, breaking the suffocating stillness.

Seere tensed, her heart hammering in her chest. She pushed herself to her feet, retreating into the furthest corner of her cell and drawing one of the many weapons she'd been allowed to keep, though only because they were so ineffective. Her eyes focused instinctively on the direction of the noise.

The heavy steps grew louder, closer, until the guards finally came into view, their torches casting flickering light onto the damp walls. They were the same kind of guards that had dragged her down there in the first place.

One of them produced a ring of keys, the metallic jingle sending a shiver down her spine. The lock clicked open a second later, the iron door creaking as it swung outward.

Seere eyed them carefully, feeling like a frightened animal about to be sent to its extermination. She'd felt this way only once before.

Two guards stepped into the cell, their movements swift and mechanical. Before she could react, their gloved hands seized her arms in an unrelenting grip. She wanted to demand answers, but she knew it was pointless.

Her boots scraped against the stone floor as they dragged her out of the cell and into the dimly lit corridor. She stumbled first, her legs unsteady from disuse, but she quickly found her footing.

The guards remained silent, their grip unyielding as they marched her down the twisting passageways. The light of their torches barely illuminated the path ahead, leaving the corners and branching corridors shrouded in darkness.

They ascended the staircase that led out of the dungeons. The light of day that filtered through windows into the halls was blinding, but she did not flinch. She would not show weakness.

She was guided through the halls and up a flight of stairs before they came to a stop before a familiar set of doors.

Her former suite.

The sight of the intricately carved wood sent a wave of conflicting emotions through her. This was the room where she had spent countless hours pacing as she figured out how to best ease her people's fears—or their dissent. It was the room where she had most distinctly felt the weight of her responsibilities as queen. Now it was another reminder of how far she had fallen in such a short period of time.

Without ceremony, the guards shoved her inside and slammed the doors shut behind her.

For a moment, Seere stood in silence. She took careful note of the way it hadn't changed much since leaving it all behind with Orias. Then her eyes fell to the fresh clothes and weapons laid out for her on the bed, just as she noticed that the bathroom light was on and the smell of vanilla and lavender oils was wafting out into the room. They expected her to bathe and dress.

The sight filled her with unease. It felt like a trap, a twisted game orchestrated by Belial to toy with her.

But she wasn't one to waste an opportunity.

Taking a steadying breath, Seere stepped further into the room, her mind already working through her next move. If Belial wanted to play games, he would find she was no mere pawn.

Seere moved to the bathroom and stared transfixed at her reflection. She looked like a frightened animal—a wild creature, both terrified and crazed. Her icy blonde hair was matted and wild, her pale green eyes full of frantic rage. She was covered in grime. She truly had fallen to rock bottom.

She stripped off the clothes she'd been wearing since her capture, tossing the fabric haphazardly to the tile floor. The cold air bit at her skin, but it was the sight of the steaming bath before her that promised relief. She stepped into the water gingerly, hissing as the heat met her chilled flesh, and then sank into its depths.

The warmth enveloped her, soothing muscles that had long since ached from confinement in the cold dungeon. For the first time since her capture, she felt the tension in her body begin to ease, but her mind remained a storm of unresolved thoughts and emotions.

She leaned back against the edge of the tub, staring at the ripples in the water as her fingers traced the tattoo on her arm. The silence pressed against her, and memories rushed to fill the void.

She thought of Malphas University, of the strange twists of fate that had brought her there. A bitter laugh escaped her lips as she remembered another bath—months ago, but it felt like a lifetime—when she'd been haunted by nightmares. Back then, Orias had barged into her throne room without warning. He had hated her. She still remembered the cruel look in those evergreen eyes. That was the day her world had started to shift, pulling her away from the solitary path she had always walked.

Orias.

Her heart clenched as she thought of him. She had no doubt he was searching for her now, furious at her reckless disappearance, but she also knew he'd understand why she had to leave. He always understood. A faint smile flickered across her face, but it faded as quickly as it came.

Her thoughts turned darker, drawn to the faces of those she had failed to protect.

Shax.

She closed her eyes, and the image of his face burned into her mind. She had failed him—failed to shield him from the wrath of her sister, Empress Selina. His laughter, his loyalty, his life had been snuffed out because of her inability to protect him.

Then there was King Hubert and Queen Frieda, their lives also tangled in the chaos that seemed to follow her. The guilt weighed heavily on her chest. She shook her head. But apologies meant nothing to the dead. They couldn't bring back laughter, love, or peace.

The bathwater began to cool, pulling her back to the present. She scrubbed her body and her hair, detangling it as she went. Then she stood and stepped out. She dried herself off with methodical care, giving her mind one final moment of quiet before reality crashed back in.

Her gaze drifted to the clothes laid out for her: a blouse and leggings of fine craftsmanship, practical yet fitted for ease of movement. The leather corset gleamed faintly in the dim light, its design both elegant and functional. There was even a black mask set neatly on the bed. She dressed swiftly, adjusting the straps and fastening the weapons Belial had so thoughtfully provided into their sheaths.

She caught her reflection in the polished metal of a dagger. Her icy blonde hair framed her face, loose and unbound, a stark contrast to the tightly controlled image she had once presented to the world. She thought of the masks she had worn—literally and figuratively—throughout her life. Today, she would wear none.

Turning toward the door, she straightened her posture

and lifted her chin. Determination burned in her eyes, and her expression was one of calm defiance.

She was no longer the frightened girl of her nightmares, nor was she the queen desperately seeking to hold her kingdom together. She would become something new— something stronger. Something that could end Belial.

37

VERRINE SALLOS

UNKNOWN, UNKNOWN OF THE UNKNOWN MOON, YEAR 450 OF THE GODDESS

The heavy doors of the throne room groaned open, revealing the vast chamber within. Shadows clung to the high ceilings, the flickering torches doing little to banish the oppressive atmosphere. Seere walked forward, her boots echoing against the polished stone floor. The guards at her sides flanked her like predators, their weapons glinting menacingly in the dim light.

She held her head high, refusing to let the chill of the room—or the situation—touch her composure. Her sharp eyes swept over the room, landing immediately on the figure lounging arrogantly on *her* throne. Belial.

He exuded power, the kind that suffocated and bent wills. His topaz eyes met hers, and a smirk curved his lips. But her attention didn't linger solely on him. On either side of the so-called viceroy stood robed figures, their faces hidden behind ornate masks. All except one.

Her breath hitched.

Orias.

He stood tall, his posture stiff and his expression unreadable—unfamiliar. It was as if looking into the hollowed-out shell of someone she loved. Her Orias was gone, and in his place stood a stranger wearing his face. He didn't so much as flinch when their gazes met. If recognition flickered in his dark eyes, it was buried too deeply for her to see. There was no love in his gaze, but she saw no hatred either. Only a blank expression that she wasn't sure how she was meant to decipher.

The moment stretched until one of the guards shoved her forward.

She stumbled, blonde hair spilling into her face as she steadied herself. Brushing it back with a sharp motion, she straightened and resumed walking, her expression blank, save for the steely glint in her eyes. Her steps carried her closer to the throne and the man who dared occupy it.

When she finally stopped, she stood tall, her back straight, exuding all the dignity of a queen despite the guards at her back.

"Why have you summoned me into *my* throne room?" she demanded, her voice cutting through the stillness like the edge of a blade.

Belial chuckled, a low, rumbling sound that grated on her nerves. He lounged on the throne, the picture of ease and arrogance. His cold, dark gaze swept over her slowly, as though weighing her soul.

"You're as sharp as they said you'd be," he commented at last, rising leisurely. His presence was overwhelming, a force that pressed down on the room like a storm cloud. "I've called you here to offer you a choice. An ultimatum, if you will."

She said nothing, her jaw tightening as she watched him step forward, his robes trailing behind him like shadows.

"Verrine Sallos," Belial gestured to Orias without glancing at him, "has convinced me that you are too valuable to discard outright. He believes you'd make a formidable ally. So here is my bargain."

Her silence spoke volumes, her narrowed eyes urging him to continue.

"If you join me," Belial said, a cruel smile curling his lips, "I will return your throne to you. Your kingdom will remain untouched. Your people unharmed. In return, you will lend your power to the Order of the Chimera. Specifically, to the Serpent faction." He paused, his smirk widening. "As Verrine's right hand."

The words landed like a blow, but Seere's mask didn't crack. Her gaze slid briefly to Orias, whose face remained inscrutable. Not even a flicker of emotion betrayed his thoughts.

"And if I refuse?" she asked coolly, her voice a dagger in its own right.

"Then I will see to it that you never sit on this throne again," Belial said with a casual chill, as if discussing the weather. "I doubt your people would appreciate your stubbornness."

Her lips twisted into a scowl. "You seem to think I trust any bargain you offer."

A flash of movement caught her eye. Her gaze darted to a shadowed corner of the room, where a familiar figure lingered. Ingram. His sharp amber eyes gleamed as he shook his head subtly and offered her a small wink. Relief flooded her chest, though she didn't dare show it.

Her eyes flicked back to Belial. "And why, exactly, do you need my help?"

"It's simple," Belial said, his tone condescending. "I have

been searching for Rosyn, the Goddess of Angels, for a very long time. That search led me here to this desolate realm, where I discovered Rosyn had split herself into two halves. Now, I need both Eulla and Eslia, and you happen to hold the latter's very soul within you."

A quiet laugh escaped her lips. The sound was full of both mocking and disbelief, causing Belial's eyes to narrow. She was certain he had to be messing with her, but his expression was so severe. Seere's gaze shifted briefly towards Orias. She finally saw pain flicker in his eyes. There was heartbreak there, which gave her some semblance of hope.

"Six years ago, I found Eslia. Unfortunately, someone had given her word that I was hunting both her and her twin. Rather than work with me, she slit her own throat. While her physical form died, her soul lived on and found a host in your body. Haven't you ever wondered why you can hear a voice every time you use your powers?" Belial questioned, his words filled with quiet amusement.

Seere recalled a time when she had felt a shadow enter her. She recalled when the voice began whispering to her. When her power had grown stronger, fiercer, she had to fight harder to hide it.

"Of course," she whispered, the weight of it crashing over her like a wave. "That would explain a lot."

Seere stretched her arms wide. A dark pulse of energy rippled through the air, and massive black wings erupted from her back, their feathers shimmering like obsidian. The torches flickered wildly, as though her power had stolen the air from the room.

The guards moved to attack, but they weren't fast enough. Seere launched herself into the air, her wings propelling her toward them with supernatural speed. She slammed into the nearest guard, her dagger flashing as she incapacitated him with one clean strike.

The room descended into chaos. Guards charged her, but she danced around them, her movements a blur of deadly precision. Energy crackled around her, each pulse of her magic throwing attackers off balance.

In the fray, she caught sight of a cluster of out-of-place guards moving in unison toward her. Recognition dawned. Felix, Foras, Rowan, and Enora.

Her allies.

Confidence surged through her. With her allies at her back and divine power thrumming through her veins, they would not win. Her grin widened as she turned her gaze back to Belial, who stood casually at the throne.

The throne room became a battleground, the clash of steel and the roar of magic reverberating off the walls. Seere's wings beat powerfully as she soared above the chaos, her fingers crackling with divine energy. She unleashed another pulse, a wave of dark power rippling outward. Guards were thrown from their feet, their armor sparking as they collided with walls and pillars.

Felix and Foras tore through the fray like a storm. Felix's blade was a blur of motion, every strike precise, while Foras moved with raw, brutal strength, each swing of his axe toppling multiple opponents. The Order fought as if they shared a single mind, their coordination honed to perfection.

Ingram was a ghost in the chaos. His silver hair shimmered in the dim light as he darted between combatants, striking with lethal precision before vanishing into the shadows once more. His amber eyes hardly left Seere, ensuring her path remained clear.

At the heart of it all, Seere's gaze locked on Belial, her fury burning hotter with every second. The voice that she now knew to be her mother's echoed in her mind, its tone insistent and vengeful.

End him.

Avenge what he has stolen.

Avenge what he has done.

Her power surged, and the air around her shimmered with an oppressive heat. She dove toward Belial, her wings slicing through the air like blades, but just as she was about to strike, Orias stepped into her path.

"Orias," she snarled, her voice heavy with disbelief and rage. Her blades slashed toward him, forcing him to raise his weapon defensively. "Out of my way!"

"I can't do that," he replied, his tone calm but resolute. He deflected her blows with expert precision, his movements measured and careful. He wasn't attacking—he was holding her back.

Her strikes came faster, wilder, the fury in her veins overtaking precision. But Orias blocked them all, his dark eyes meeting hers with an intensity that sent a shiver down her spine. There was something there—something deeper than the stoic mask he wore. Regret? Pain?

"Why?" she demanded, her voice cracking as fury bled into heartbreak. "Why are you doing this? I trusted you! Was that nothing to you?"

"I won't fight you," he said, his voice soft, barely audible over the clamor around them. "I can't."

She stared at him, breath heaving, disbelief clawing at her throat. This man—the one who once traced the curve of her jaw with reverence, who worshipped her like she was his goddess—now stood between her and vengeance.

"Then move!" she shouted, her wings flaring as she launched another attack. Her blade swung toward him, but he sidestepped with a grace that only angered her further.

Before she could press him again, a glint of silver caught her eye. Time seemed to slow as she turned, her gaze locking on the dagger flying through the air. Belial had thrown it, its blade gleaming with a cruel light as it streaked toward Felix, who was too focused on the guard before him to see it coming.

"No!" Seere's voice rang out like a crack of thunder.

Without hesitation, she hurtled herself into the dagger's path, her wings beating once to propel her forward. In the same motion, her hand snapped forward, her dagger slicing through the air with unerring accuracy.

Her blade struck true, sinking deep into Belial's shoulder. Her so-called viceroy let out a snarl of pain, staggering back, but the dagger he had thrown found its mark as well.

The cold steel bit into her side, tearing through flesh and sending a wave of searing pain through her body. Her breath hitched, and for a moment, the world blurred.

"Ris!" Felix's voice was a roar, filled with panic and fury.

As she faltered, her wings vanishing, a blast of dark energy erupted from her, rippling outward in a shockwave that struck every enemy in the room. Guards crumpled where they stood, their weapons clattering to the ground.

Seere's eyes found Orias, who still stood. Somehow, she hadn't managed to blast him off his feet. His face was pale, haunted. His eyes were wide with something between fear and heartbreak. The love he'd hidden before filled his expression once more as he watched her fall to her knees. His lips parted as if to call her name, but Felix's voice cut through the haze.

"Ingram," Felix barked, his voice taut with urgency as he dropped at Seere's side, "rally everyone. We need to move—now. Back to the ship."

Seere's vision blurred further as pain and exhaustion overtook her. The last thing she heard was Ingram's voice barking orders and the sensation of Felix cradling her against his chest. She vaguely registered Orias rushing over, his tender fingers caressing her face before the darkness claimed her.

38

EMBRACE

ATYSDAY, TWENTY-SEVENTH OF THE
REBIRTH MOON, YEAR 450 OF THE GODDESS

The first thing Seere became aware of was the gentle sway beneath her, a rhythmic motion that hinted at a ship slicing through waves. Then came the sound of waves lapping against the hull. Her eyes fluttered open to a dimly lit, unfamiliar room.

Across from her, Felix stood like a statue, his broad shoulders slightly hunched as he stared at the floor, lost in thought. His cobalt blue eyes, usually so sharp and alert, were vacant, filled with an emotion she couldn't quite place.

She shifted, trying to sit up, and winced as her muscles protested. The faint creak of the bed caught Felix's attention, and his gaze snapped to hers.

"You're awake," he said, his voice soft but strained. His eyes widened with a mix of relief and worry as he crossed the room in long strides, kneeling beside her bed.

"How are you feeling?" he asked, his hand hovering near her arm as if afraid to touch her, afraid she might shatter under his care.

Seere managed a faint smile, brushing her blonde hair

back from her face. "I'm fine," she murmured. "There's no pain."

Felix let out a breath. But his relief was tinged with apprehension, his gaze searching her face as though trying to confirm her words.

"You were... You almost died," he said, his voice barely above a whisper. His expression was guarded, but there was a tremor in his tone.

"How did you manage to escape?"

Felix grimaced. A war seemed to wage behind his cobalt eyes. "Ingram," he said finally, his tone cool. "He got us out."

Seere nodded thoughtfully then glanced around her room as if expecting to find another there. "And Orias," she whispered, her heart clenching painfully. Her throat constricted as she struggled to get the next words out, not wanting the answer that she knew would come. "Where is he?"

Felix stared at her for a long moment before he turned away. "He remained with your viceroy."

Seere stared at her hands in her lap, her composure fraying under the weight of everything she had been through. Her vision blurred with tears that she tried to brush away, but they only kept falling. Before she could think better of it, she leaned over and wrapped her arms around Felix. She hid her face in the crook of his neck, clinging to him as the emotions she'd kept bottled up for so long came rushing out.

Felix froze for a heartbeat before his arms slid around her, pulling her closer. He held her tightly, as if afraid she might dissolve into mist and slip away. She listened to his heart thud against her ear, grounding her even as her own heart threatened to break.

Tears slipped down her cheeks, quiet sobs wracking her shoulders. Felix didn't speak. He didn't try to calm her or hush her. He simply held her, his hand gently brushing over her hair, letting her release the storm she'd been holding inside.

When the sobs finally subsided, she pulled back slightly, though she couldn't quite meet his eyes. Felix's hands remained on her shoulders, steadying her, as he asked the question that she had dreaded answering most.

"Back in the throne room," he began, his voice tentative, "That man on the throne said you were Eslia. What... what did he mean?"

Seere's gaze dropped to the blanket over her lap. "As you likely know very well by now, my father, Emperor Montague, had an affair with the goddess Eslia," she said, the words tasting bitter as they left her tongue. "I was the result. A bastard, a shameful secret kept hidden by the Envie Court. When I was about fifteen or sixteen and in the middle of building the Domain, Eslia's body was destroyed, and her soul... it had nowhere to go but to me. I remember that day, but I hadn't understood what had truly happened before now."

Felix's brows furrowed, his jaw tightening. Yet he stayed silent, allowing her to continue. He wanted to hear this truth after all the lies she had fed him.

"She chose me as her vessel," Seere said, her voice shaking slightly. "Her power, her soul—it's been merging with mine ever since, and I had no idea. I don't know if I will stay as myself or if Eslia... will take over completely. I don't know how long I have left to exist. Everything is just a big mess at the moment..."

Felix turned his gaze from her, his eyes locked on the

floor. Then he shook his head slowly, his voice tinged with disbelief. "So one day, you might just... cease to be?"

"My soul might. One day, you may blink and it isn't me who sits before you, but Eslia in my body," she murmured, her voice cracked.

The silence that followed was heavy, oppressive. Felix pushed himself to his feet, pacing to the other side of the room. His hand raked through his hair, his movements tense as he processed her words.

Finally, he turned back to her, his expression unreadable. "You should rest," he said, his voice calm but distant. "Or join us on deck when you're ready. We'll figure this out. I won't allow Eslia to take you from me—from us."

Seere nodded, her smile faint and sad. "Thank you," she whispered.

He lingered for a moment as if he wanted to say more, then turned and left the cabin.

Seere sat on the edge of her bed, staring at the faintly swaying lantern on the wall. The soft creak of the ship and the rhythmic crashing of waves were constant reminders of her location, but her mind was far away. The events of the throne room replayed in her head like a haunting melody she couldn't escape.

Belial's dark smirk, the cold glint in Orias' eyes, and the blinding pain of the dagger that had struck her—each memory tugged at her, threatening to unravel her composure. But it was Orias that lingered. The man who had once guided her through the twisted halls of Malphas, who'd placed a steadying hand on her back—he'd looked at her like a stranger in the throne room. No... worse. The pawn he promised she would never be.

She'd trusted Orias, had let herself believe he was different, only to find herself betrayed. The sting of that wound, emotional rather than physical, cut deeper than she cared to admit. She wondered who was playing the role of Verrine Sallos in the dungeons of Noctivagus.

And then there was Eslia. The goddess whose soul coiled with her own, an ancient force she barely understood, and a truth she hadn't wanted to acknowledge. How much of Seere was still Seere? How much of her future belonged to her? How much would be claimed by the goddess whose voice whispered in the corners of her mind?

The distant sound of music broke through her thoughts. It started softly—a lilting tune carried by the night air—but it grew louder, vibrant, filled with life. Laughter and the clatter of boots on wood followed, a stark contrast to the heaviness she felt.

For a moment, she considered staying in the solitude of her cabin, but the pull of the lively atmosphere above was too tempting. Rising slowly, she crossed to the wardrobe where a set of fresh clothes waited, neatly folded. Someone, likely Ingram, had thought ahead to retrieve them for her.

She dressed quickly, slipping into a fitted tunic and leggings that allowed for movement but still carried an air of regality. The familiarity of her clothing steadied her, grounding her as she made her way out of the cabin.

The deck was alive with energy. Lanterns strung across the masts cast a golden glow over the scene, illuminating the faces of her companions. Rowan was the first to spot her, his dark hair glinting in the light as he waved her over with a grin.

"Seere!" he called, weaving through the crowd of sailors to reach her. "Finally! I was starting to think you'd sulk all night."

"I'm here," she said, unable to keep a small smile from tugging at the corners of her lips with his infectious enthusiasm.

"Good."

Rowan grabbed her hand, dragging her into the heart of the revelry. He spun her into a dance, his movements exaggerated and playful.

The mood was infectious. Even Seere, who rarely allowed herself moments of levity, found herself smiling more freely as the celebration unfolded. It was as if the weight of the past few weeks—the betrayal, the imprisonment, the near-death experience—had been temporarily lifted.

When Rowan passed her off to Ingram, she let herself relax further.

Ingram's steps were precise and smooth, his sharp amber eyes crinkling with rare amusement. "I didn't think I'd see you up here," he said as they moved in tandem. "Since when have you been one for parties, my Queen?"

"I have nothing to lose anymore," she said, her smile fading slightly. Then, very softly, she whispered, "I'm glad you're here, Ingram. It's good to have one familiar face."

Ingram led her into a graceful spin and pulled her close again. "I am loyal to you until the end, Your Majesty. We will get the Domain back, mark my words."

She smirked, glancing around the deck and catching sight of Enora dancing excitedly with one of the younger sailors. "Of course, we'll get it back. The Order needs me alive if they want to get to Eslia," she said.

"Why did you hide that your mother is Eslia for so long?"

Seere shrugged. "It was a closely kept secret of mine. When your half-siblings are slaughtered for their parentage, it really turns you off from telling anyone about it. However, I'm not hiding myself anymore. The world plays my game now."

Ingram grinned deviously. "Allow me to help you set the board," he whispered. "I want a front-row seat to watch the game master work her magic. And maybe light the board on fire when it's over."

"You will have it."

Finally, Seere slipped away from the dancing and stood off to the side. Someone had produced a barrel of spiced rum, and the crew cheered as the first mugs were passed around. Felix, who had been quietly observing from the sidelines, took a swig of the potent drink and immediately coughed, his cheeks turning crimson as laughter erupted around him.

"Not your usual poison, I take it?" Seere teased, raising an eyebrow at him as she approached.

He offered a sheepish grin and set the mug down. "Not exactly," he admitted, wiping his mouth with the back of his hand. "But I'm willing to adapt."

As the night wore on, the music grew louder and more spirited. Sailors and companions alike began to dance, their movements uninhibited by the rolling of the ship or the limitations of the small deck.

Seere found herself pulled into the fray once more by Rowan as he grabbed her hand and spun her around. She stumbled at first, laughing as she tried to keep up with his steps that had only grown more exuberant with the rum. The two of them made a chaotic pair, their movements more clumsy than coordinated, but their laughter drowned out any complaints.

When the song ended, Seere found herself catching her

breath beside Enora, who was swiftly dragged into the next dance by a particularly enthusiastic sailor.

"You look like you're having fun," Felix said, appearing at her side with a fresh mug of rum for her.

She accepted it gratefully, raising it in a mock toast. "Don't get used to it," she said with a smirk. "I'm not exactly the dancing type."

"I don't know," he replied, his eyes twinkling. "You seemed to be enjoying yourself with Rowan."

She rolled her eyes but couldn't suppress her grin. "He's impossible to say no to."

Felix chuckled, and for a moment, they stood in companionable silence, watching the revelry around them.

Then, as another lively tune began, Felix set his mug down and extended a hand toward her. "One more dance?" he asked, his tone light but hopeful.

Seere hesitated for only a moment before placing her hand in his. "Fine," she said, feigning reluctance. "But don't expect me to be any good."

The two of them joined the dancers, their movements tentative at first but gradually growing more confident as they found a rhythm. Felix had a boyish charm to him as he spun her around, his laughter mingled with hers as they stumbled and recovered. Seere found that the other dancers had scattered to the sidelines to watch and cheer them on.

As the dance came to an abrupt end, Seere and Felix found themselves standing chest to chest in the center of the deck, their breaths coming in short bursts from the exertion of dancing. Cheers echoed loudly around them.

"That wasn't so bad, was it?" Felix asked, his voice low and warm.

Seere shook her head, a small smile playing at her lips. "Not bad at all," she admitted.

For a moment, they simply stood there, the distance between them narrowing as the sounds of the sea and the gentle sway of the ship surrounded them. When Seere finally realized that Felix was leaning in to kiss her, she pushed him away in a playful manner and rushed back to her mug of rum. She was not about to allow herself such a lapse in judgment.

The rest of the night passed in a haze of laughter and camaraderie. Seere remained close to Ingram, whose steady presence was a comfort amidst the chaos. Her spymaster, seeming to understand her dilemma, kept an arm casually draped over his shoulder like a protective friend.

For the first time in what felt like ages, she allowed herself to simply exist, leaving the burdens of betrayal, power, and destiny behind—if only for a little while. But beneath her smile, the question remained: how long could this peace last before the storm returned?

39

COUNCIL

CHAYSDAY, FOURTEENTH OF THE LONE
MOON, YEAR 450 OF THE GODDESS

Seere's boots echoed softly as she wandered through the palace halls of Noctivagus. Her thoughts were as tangled as the labyrinth of corridors. The weight of the past few months pressed heavily upon her.

Returning to Hesperus had been an unspoken agreement—a temporary refuge until they could decide what to do next. But the familiarity of the palace did little to comfort her. Instead, it only reminded her of the life she'd been forced to leave behind and the burdens she had yet to face.

Seere found her gaze drawn to the windows. Outside, the gardens sprawled in meticulous arrangements. Though all the plants slumbered for the winter, the scene was still beautiful. She paused, letting her fingers brush the cold stone of the window ledge, and gazed out at the sunlit paths below.

The palace exuded a sense of timelessness, but to Seere, it felt like a gilded cage. Here, she was a guest, a figure to be tolerated, not truly welcomed. The courtiers who glanced at her as she passed either lowered their eyes or whispered behind her back.

"Amaris," they would murmur. *"The assassin queen."*
"The daughter of Eslia."

Their words didn't hurt as much as they once would have, but they still gnawed at her resolve.

She sighed, her fingers idly tracing the engraved patterns on the stones of the window ledge. She'd admired them once when she was so much younger. She remembered the vibrant celebrations, the dances, and the stolen moments when Felix had whispered promises of a shared future.

All of it felt like a lifetime ago.

Her reflection caught her attention in the window. She paused, studying the woman who stared back at her. Her blonde hair was loose, falling in soft waves around her shoulders. Her pale face was no longer gaunt from the days she spent imprisoned by Belial. Her pale eyes held a sharpness that hadn't been there before—a weight that spoke of betrayal, loss, and survival. She hardly recognized herself anymore.

The sound of footsteps brought her back to the present. Turning, she saw a servant bowing hesitantly at a safe distance. "Your Majesty," the woman said softly, her tone betraying a mixture of respect and fear, "is there anything I can assist you with?"

Seere shook her head, offering the servant a faint smile. "No, thank you. I'm just... walking."

The servant nodded and retreated, leaving Seere alone once more.

Seere turned and continued in the opposite direction of the servant, not wanting to cross the woman's path again. She noticed a familiar corridor, one that led to the royal wing. She had stormed down the hall not long before to investigate the former king and queen's chamber, but hadn't stopped to allow herself to truly appreciate it. She hadn't allowed herself to find proper closure.

Her steps faltered as memories surged forward. She could still recall the night she and Felix had planned their future together in these halls, her laughter echoing alongside his. But that was before Selina's machinations, before Eslia's influence began to seep into her soul, before everything had crumbled.

She stopped before a pair of grand wooden doors, the entrance to what had once been her quarters. Her hand hovered over the brass handle, but she didn't open it. The room would be exactly as it had been left—untouched but eerily empty, like a mausoleum of a life she no longer lived.

With a heavy sigh, she turned away.

It was then that she heard his voice, deep and familiar. "You shouldn't linger in this part of the palace, Amaris."

She turned to find Gabriel Andromal a few feet away, his tall figure framed by the dim light of the corridor. His eyes studied her carefully, and his expression was a mixture of concern and curiosity.

"I was just... reminiscing," she admitted, her voice quiet.

Gabriel stepped closer, his polished boots clicking against the marble. "This place holds memories, I'm sure. But it also holds expectations. Not all of them are kind."

Seere met his gaze, her lips curving into a faint, rueful smile. "Trust me, Gabriel. I am used to unkind expectations," she replied, eyeing him carefully. "I was once a queen, too."

Gabriel tilted his head, his expression softening. "This is true. But you're not alone here, you know. You have allies— true ones."

Seere gave Gabriel a once-over. Unlike Foras, his younger brother, he was kind and warm. Yet he was just as impossible to read—and she hated it. "Perhaps, but none of them are among the court here," she finally said, turning in the direction she had come from and walking away from the royal wing.

Gabriel joined her, his pace matching hers. "Trust me, Amaris. Felix would die for you if it came down to it. His loyalty to you assures the loyalty of the rest of the kingdom."

As Seere and Gabriel walked side by side, their conversation tense, weaving reflections on the challenges ahead, the sound of light but hurried footsteps echoed down the corridor. Both turned toward the source, their conversation pausing as the figure of Ingram emerged from the shadows.

The spymaster moved with purpose, his silver hair catching the light from the chandeliers overhead, his amber eyes sharp and assessing. His presence, though familiar to Seere, always carried an air of unease; a man whose every step was calculated, every word measured. Yet for her, Ingram was more than a shadow in the background—he was a trusted ally, one of the few she could truly rely on.

"Your Majesty," Ingram addressed Seere first, his tone respectful as always. His gaze flicked briefly to Gabriel, then back to Seere. "I've been looking for you."

Seere arched her eyebrow, her arms crossing loosely over her chest. "You've found me. What's so urgent you had to go racing through the palace halls?"

Ingram's lips quirked upward, though the smile didn't reach his eyes. "You've been summoned by His Majesty." He nodded toward Gabriel, his tone gaining a hint of dry humor. "And I see you've recruited a knightly escort."

Gabriel chuckled softly, unbothered by the subtle jab. "I was merely ensuring her safety. You can never be too careful in a palace full of political intrigue."

"Indeed." Ingram's eyes narrowed slightly, his words laced with a veiled edge. "But I assure you, Her Majesty's safety has always been my responsibility."

The tension between the two men was subtle but palpable. Seere sighed, sensing the brewing undercurrent. "Enough posturing," she said, waving a hand dismissively. "What does Felix want?"

Ingram stepped closer, lowering his voice. "The council is convening again, and it seems that a letter from your sister has stirred quite the storm." His expression darkened, the faintest flicker of worry crossing his face. "Felix has requested that you join him in the throne room. As for you, Sir Andromal, you have also been requested. It seems you're deemed necessary."

Gabriel smirked, the faintest hint of amusement in his expression. "I'll take that as a compliment, coming from you."

Seere rolled her eyes. "If you two are done sparring, let's get on with it. Felix is waiting, and I'd rather not leave him to deal with those vipers alone."

Ingram inclined his head, a gesture of agreement, but his sharp gaze lingered on Gabriel for a fraction longer. The spymaster's expression softened ever so slightly when he turned back to Seere. "Stay close," he said quietly, his voice stripped of its usual formality. "I don't trust everyone in that room."

"I don't either," Seere replied, her tone grim but resolute. "But when have I ever let that stop me?"

With that, the three of them set off toward the throne room, the weight of impending conflict pressing heavily on their shoulders. Seere could feel the stares of passing servants, their whispered conversations stopping as soon as she came into view.

The throne room's grand doors loomed ahead, a testament to Noctivagus' might and legacy. As Seere approached, flanked by Gabriel and Ingram, she could already hear the low hum of heated discussion seeping through the thick wood. The tension in the air was palpable, and the faint echoes of raised voices promised discord within.

The guards standing at attention gave a synchronized bow, then stepped aside to push the heavy doors open. The creak of the hinges reverberated through the chamber as Seere, Gabriel, and Ingram stepped inside. The room sprawled with marble and gold, high arched ceilings and tall stained-glass windows casting fragmented light across the polished floors. Council members, nobles, and advisors clustered near the base of the dais, their faces a mixture of anxiety, anger, and determination.

At the center of it all stood Felix. He cut a regal figure even amidst the chaos, his cobalt-blue eyes scanning the room with a mixture of frustration and command. His posture was upright and immovable as he addressed the assembled crowd, his tone sharp enough to silence a few of the more vocal nobles. In his hand, he held the letter from Empress Selina—its broken seal visible even from a distance.

As the trio entered, heads turned, and the murmur of conversation briefly died down. Seere felt the weight of every gaze upon her, a mix of judgment, curiosity, and thinly veiled hostility. She met their eyes without flinching, her icy composure a shield against their scrutiny.

"Ah, Queen Seere," a sharp voice rang out. It belonged to Lord Caldre, one of the more vocal members of the council.

He was a portly man with a slicked-back hairstyle and a penchant for dramatics. "How fortuitous of you to join us. Perhaps now we can move this discussion forward."

Felix's eyes flicked to Seere. His expression was unreadable, but his shoulders relaxed slightly at her arrival. "Amaris," he said, stepping down from the dais and offering her the letter. "You should see this for yourself."

Seere took the parchment, her fingers brushing briefly against Felix's as she did. She scanned the letter, her frown deepening with every line. The ultimatum was surgical in its cruelty, dripping with Selina's trademark venom.

"I see my sister hasn't lost her flair for dramatics," Seere said dryly, handing the letter back to Felix. "But her intentions are clear enough. She wants war—or me, preferably both."

"That's precisely the issue," another councilman interjected, his voice quivering with indignation. "Why should we sacrifice our kingdom for her? Surely one life is worth less than an entire nation."

The statement drew murmurs of agreement from several nobles, their voices low but fervent.

She passed the letter over to Ingram, who read it with a deepening scowl.

"We can't give in to this," he said firmly, stepping forward to place himself protectively beside Seere. "She's innocent."

"Why don't we just turn in the Sallos then. We have him in custody, wouldn't that suffice for Empress Selina?" a councilwoman asked.

"The man in the dungeons is not Verrine Sallos," Foras said coolly. "The real Sallos walks free, having framed another."

"Innocent or not," one of the councilmen countered,

stepping out from the crowd. "It's better to lose one life than an entire kingdom."

The murmurs of agreement that rippled through the room made Seere's blood boil. Before she could speak, Ingram stepped toward the council, the casual side of him that Seere had only begun to discover was swiftly replaced by the calculated seriousness she was used to.

"You might want to think very carefully about what you're saying," he said, his voice low and menacing. "Because the next time you suggest handing her over, I won't miss when I throw my knife."

The councilman paled but didn't back down. "She's no queen of ours. She is *the* Assassin Queen—a demon."

Seere smirked coldly, stepping forward to meet his gaze. "You're right about one thing," she said, her voice cold. "I am no queen—not while Belial sits on my throne. But let me be clear: whether I reclaim it as Seere Cross or as Amaris, the Daughter of Eslia, I *will* take it back. And anyone who stands in my way will regret it."

The room fell silent, her words cutting through the tension like a knife.

Felix stepped forward then, his voice ringing dangerously. "Enough." His voice carried a quiet authority that cut through the noise. "This council will not debate the worth of Seere's life. She is under my protection, and that is final."

Gabriel's words were calm, but carried the promise of violence: "And if anyone even thinks about turning on her, they will have to go through me first."

The council exchanged uneasy glances, their murmurs hushed. Seere could see the fear in their eyes, and though it didn't ease her anger, it gave her a small sense of satisfaction.

"I think we should have a more thorough discussion in

my study," Felix said, his gaze shifting to Gabriel and Ingram briefly. "I will gather Enora and Rowan. Meet me there."

Seere met Ingram's gaze, gave a curt nod, and turned toward the king's study.

THE STUDY WAS a stark contrast to the tension of the throne room—smaller, quieter, and far more intimate. The walls were lined with towering shelves filled with ancient tomes and scrolls, their spines glinting faintly in the light of the flickering hearth. A large oak table dominated the center of the room, maps and scattered papers spread across its surface. Felix stood at its head, his hands resting on the table's edge.

Rowan and Foras leaned casually against the far wall, their postures deceptively relaxed despite the weight of the situation. Enora stood near the hearth, her expression pensive, though she kept glancing at her betrothed. Gabriel remained near the door, his arms crossed—a silent sentinel. Ingram moved to Seere's side, ever her shadow, his silver hair gleaming in the firelight.

"Thank you all for coming. We need to determine our next steps. Seere," he said, turning to her, "I believe you're the greatest tactician I have ever met. What do you propose?"

Seere stepped forward, her fingers trailing lightly over the edge of the map on the table. "My sister may have the advantage in numbers, but I have something she doesn't: loyalty. My spies are scattered throughout Envie and beyond —many of them are in key positions of influence. If I can reach them, we can gather intelligence, sabotage Selina's plans, and even rally forces to our side."

Rowan frowned, pushing off the wall. "That sounds risky.

You'd have to cross into enemy territory just to contact them. If you're caught..." He trailed off, but the implication was clear.

"Risk is a given," Seere replied, her tone unwavering. "But it's necessary. My spies aren't just tools—they're people I trust, and they've been waiting for me to return. If Belial hasn't corrupted them, they'll stand with us. I also know someone at Malphas whom I want on our side. I am convinced he will join us as well."

"What makes you so certain of their support?" Gabriel asked, his deep voice steady.

"Of my uncle? Completely," she said. "The university has long been a neutral ground, but if we can take charge there, we would have a great advantage. If I approach them correctly, they could provide not only manpower but also resources and information."

Felix crossed his arms, his expression skeptical. "And the Order of the Chimera? You said you planned to recruit them. How do you intend to do that when they're aligned with Belial?"

A wry smile tugged at Seere's lips, though it didn't reach her eyes. "The Order needs me alive as the host of Eslia's spirit. That gives us leverage to win their favor-until the war against Envie is won, at least."

The room fell into a tense silence as everyone processed her words.

"Foras," Felix said, breaking the quiet. "What's your assessment?"

Foras shrugged, his expression uncharacteristically serious. "It's a bold plan. Dangerous, but bold. If Seere's allies are as loyal as she says, they could be a game-changer. But we'd need a fallback strategy in case things go south."

Rowan chimed in, his voice soft but firm. "We're outnumbered as it is. If we don't do something unconventional, we're doomed. This might be our best shot."

Enora, who had been silent until now, finally spoke. "I agree with Rowan. We can't win this war through brute strength alone. We need to outmaneuver Selina—and Seere's plan gives us a way to do that."

Felix exhaled slowly, his gaze shifting back to Seere. "You've clearly thought this through. But if we're going to proceed, we need to coordinate every step carefully. No unnecessary risks, no improvisation. Agreed?"

Seere nodded, though a flicker of defiance sparked in her eyes. "I'll do what needs to be done, Felix. But don't mistake caution for inaction. If an opportunity presents itself, I won't hesitate."

Felix's lips pressed into a thin line, but he didn't argue. Instead, he turned to the others. "We'll need to divide our focus. Foras, Gabriel—I want you to oversee the preparation of our troops. Ensure they're ready for whatever Selina throws at us."

The two men nodded, their expressions grim.

"Rowan, Enora," Felix continued, "you'll assist me with the political side of things. We need to secure alliances with the other houses and ensure the council doesn't fracture under the pressure."

Enora inclined her head. "Understood."

"And Seere—"

"It's Amaris," Seere corrected, her voice firm but not unkind. She offered Felix an apologetic smile. "I've spent far too long hiding behind an alias, and since it no longer has any meaning, I see no use in keeping it."

"*Amaris*," Felix said, his gaze softening slightly. "You'll focus on gathering your allies. But promise me you won't take unnecessary risks."

Amaris smirked faintly. "I'll try to stay alive, if that's what you're worried about."

Ingram, who had been silent throughout the conversation, finally spoke. "She won't be alone. Wherever she goes, I'll be there. You have my word."

Felix gave him a curt nod, his shoulders relaxing slightly. "Good."

Amaris stayed behind as everyone filed out. Ingram remained at her side, but when she offered him a curt nod, he understood and slipped from the study. Felix watched her as Enora shut the door quietly behind them. His expression was unreadable, but not unkind.

"Did you need something?" he asked softly.

Amaris' gaze shifted towards the hearth. "Only to warn you that I will be leaving tonight. I don't want to delay."

Felix sighed softly and nodded. He took a few steps toward her, then paused. "Be safe," he said softly.

He looked as though he wanted to reach for her. To pull her close and never let go. A terrible part of Seere wanted to let him, but she turned away and headed for the door.

"When am I not?" she asked, playfully.

"Do you want me to answer that?" Felix questioned, his tone light.

"Not at all," she said and waved to him as she opened the door.

"Amaris."

She glanced back.

He crossed the room in two strides and held something out to her—her old dagger, the one she had returned to him. The leather wrap had long since been removed.

"Slit Orias' throat with this for me, will you?" he said, voice almost playful but his eyes devastatingly serious.

Amaris laughed dryly. She leaned against the doorframe, studying him. "You're just trying to stake your claim again, aren't you?" she asked, trying for levity.

He shrugged, still holding the weapon out for her. "It's yours."

For a heartbeat, she simply stared at the dagger—then at him.

Her hand tightened on the doorframe. "No," she whispered. "I don't deserve it."

Without taking the dagger, she turned away, each step away from him heavier than the last.

Ingram met her at the end of the hall. She spared him only a glance, brushing a trembling hand over her sleeve.

"When are we departing?" he asked.

"Pack your things. Meet me in the entrance hall in fifteen minutes," she said, her voice mercifully steady. "We leave tonight."

Ingram nodded, already walking. "Of course, Your Majesty."

GLOSSARY

Months

Frost Moon
Rebirth Moon
Lone Moon
Flower Moon
Medicine Moon
Golden Moon
Phoenix Moon
Death Moon
Reaping Moon
Dragon Moon
Shadow Moon
Whisper Moon

Days of the Week

Eulday - First Day of the week. A day of Worship.

Esladay - Second day of the week, the first day of the workweek.

Atysday

Chaysday

Labrisday

Iktuneday

Dhanirday - Final day of the week.

Gods

Eulla - The Goddess of Light, Life, and Doves

Eslia - Goddess of Death, War, and Crows

Chaysus - God of Medicine

Vaemis - God of Illness

Dhanir - God of Music

Vatia - Goddess of Silence

Etrix - Goddess of Penance and Scribes

Dases - God of Grudges

Iktune - Goddess of Love and Sexuality

Aldros - God of Discord and Storms

Labris - God of Order

Atysus - God of War

Anir - God of Peace

ACKNOWLEDGMENTS

Writing this book was a wild, emotional, magical journey—equal parts caffeine, chaos, and quiet determination. It wouldn't exist without the people and the forces that carried me through, lit a fire within me, or reminded me exactly what I'm capable of. So here we are: a book born of late nights, loud music, deep love, and just a touch of spite.

To my husband—you've seen every version of me—exhausted, exhilarated, terrified, obsessed—and loved them all. Thank you for your steady belief, your unshakable patience, and the way you always held space for this dream of mine. For feeding me when I forgot to eat, for giving me space when I needed to spiral, and for being my first reader, last reader, and every chapter in between—I love you more than words (especially these ones) could ever describe.

To Sleep Token—to the Vessel and the music that cracked something open in me. Thank you. Your songs were the soundtrack to every word written, every plot twist, every emotional spiral. You gave this story a heartbeat and helped me find my own rhythm when the world was too loud or too quiet. This book wouldn't exist without the ache and beauty you create.

To the doubters—to those who didn't quite see the vision —thank you. Your Skepticism, whether intentional or not, helped me dig deeper, work harder, and believe in myself more fiercely. Sometimes, a little doubt is the push we need to prove to ourselves that we were always capable.

ABOUT THE AUTHOR

Layla King is a small-business owner and lifelong storyteller who sets out to write D&D campaigns—but somehow always ends up with novels instead. Raised with a heart full of magic and imagination, she never quite outgrew the belief that the world is full of wonder. These days, she lives in Idaho with her husband and their two cats. When she's not lost in book ideas, she's probably blasting Sleep Token loud enough for the neighbors to wonder what kind of wizard lives next door.

9 798999 571213